HARD
NIGHT

Books by Jackie Ashenden

The 11th Hour Series

Raw Power

Total Control

Hard Night

The Motor City Royals Series

Dirty for Me

Wrong for Me

Sin for Me

Published by Kensington Publishing Corporation

To Darth Vader,

If you want to know where I get my love

of dark heroes from, look no further.

PROLOGUE

"She's had a traumatic brain injury, Mr. Night," the doctor said. "I'm not sure what else to tell you. Her memory may come back or it might not. It's very unpredictable."

It was not the news Jacob wanted.

He kept himself very still, his gaze flicking over to the small, emaciated-looking woman in the hospital bed. Her eyes were closed and there were dark circles staining the delicate skin beneath them, purple as bruises. Her cheeks were sunken, her body beneath the sheets all angles. A bandage wrapped her head, black hair peeking out from underneath it.

Fuck.

He'd hoped this woman would be the final piece of the puzzle. The last link in a chain he'd been following for years while trying to find his brother.

Tracking her down had been risky and now he'd found her. And she remembered nothing.

"What kind of memory loss is it?" he asked.

The doctor pursed her lips. "It's confined to her identity. Her global memories appear to be intact—her knowledge of the world, etcetera. But her episodic memory is the one primarily affected. We think it's either a consequence of her brain injury or something called a dissociative fugue. People in a fugue state can forget their identities after suffering trauma, either mental or physical. It can be a way of protecting themselves."

"I see." Jacob glanced away from the woman in the bed and back at the doctor. "But those memories will return, won't they?"

"Usually. Though it can take weeks. Or even months."

Shit. Shit. *Shit.*

The doctor was consulting her tablet. "So, you're her cousin, I believe?"

"Yes. That's correct." It wasn't. But the doctor didn't need to know that.

"And you understand that she can't be alone after she gets out of the hospital? Memory loss is frightening even without her physical injuries so I recommend that she has someone keeping an eye on her at all times. If she's living alone, it's a good idea if she has someone who can stay with her for a week or so, or until her memories return."

"That's fine." He'd already decided what he was going to do. She'd been hurt and whoever had hurt her would return and finish the job, if what he'd suspected was true. And he couldn't allow that to happen. "She'll be living with me."

"Good." The doctor's fingers moved over the tablet screen. "Oh, one more thing. We can't keep calling her Jane. What's her actual name?"

"Her name is Faith," Jacob said. "Faith . . . Beasley."

It wasn't her name. He didn't know what her real name was. But faith was all he had left.

CHAPTER 1

Faith Beasley was a mystery inside an enigma, wrapped in a tight black pencil skirt that did very good things to her delicious ass.

Jacob Night watched her from the privacy of his town car as she made her way up the stairs to the bar at the top of them and disappeared through the doorway.

Christ, that ass had been taunting him for the past five months at least and he wasn't a man who denied himself anything. Yet he was also a man who never let himself be at the mercy of his baser desires, either, and there were too many reasons why going there with the exquisite Faith was a bad idea.

Not the least being that even after six months she still had no memory of who she was.

Then there was what he'd learned very recently from Phillip Blake, Kellan Blake's father. Many fascinating little facts and tidbits that went into the jigsaw that made up Faith Beasley.

Such as her real name. Parts of her background. A man she'd been involved with before Jacob had brought her home from the hospital and into the 11th Hour team—a paramilitary organization that did special "jobs" for people. He'd set it up six months earlier, and since then Faith had operated as his go-between. She didn't need her memory for that, turning out to be one of his team's best assets. Cool, calm, and totally professional.

He'd been in possession of these facts for a couple of weeks now and as soon as he'd learned about them, he'd wanted to tell her, especially since they could be the key to unlocking her memory.

Unfortunately, though, Ms. Faith Beasley had not wanted to hear about them. In fact, she'd flat-out told him that she wasn't ready to know.

That had been a surprise since she was a very strong woman and hadn't struck him as being a coward. But although he might have small pieces of the puzzle, he didn't yet have the whole picture, and upsetting her needlessly would only make her recovery longer. So he'd kept up the fiction that he was her cousin—even though he was pretty sure she knew by now that he wasn't—and that he was taking care of her until she was better, keeping his real motivation secret.

He hadn't pushed.

But he wasn't going to put it off forever.

Deep in her memories somewhere was the knowledge of where his brother was, the brother he'd been searching five years for, and he wanted it.

And after six months of waiting, he wanted it sooner rather than later.

"Is it okay if I take a break for a smoke, Mr. Night?"

Jacob flicked a glance at his driver. "Keep it short."

"Yes, sir." The man gave him a brisk nod before getting out, digging around in his uniform pocket for his cigarettes as he did so.

Jacob checked the street again, an automatic reflex so ingrained that he could no more stop doing it than he could stop breathing.

The San Diego street was quiet, traffic at a minimum, which was odd considering it was in the middle of the day. The sun was out, summer just a few months away, and there were a few people sitting in the café next to the bar that Faith had vanished into, enjoying the sunshine.

They didn't look like threats so Jacob ignored them.

After a couple of minutes, Faith reappeared out of the bar. The expression on her lovely face was neutral, giving nothing away.

As she came down the stairs toward the car, her straight, ink-black hair gleamed in the sun, glossy as crow feathers.

She was a small woman, and when she'd first come home from the hospital with him, she'd been far too thin, her muscles wasted. But the program of good food and lengthy gym sessions he'd put her on had helped to build those muscles up and round her out. She would never be very big or muscular, but now she was toned and athletic. Her hair was no longer lank and dull, and her cheeks had lost that sunken look.

Physically, she was healed.

Now all he needed was for her mind to do the same thing.

Faith came down the steps, moving gracefully on her high heels. There were many things she'd had to relearn and moving in heels was one of them—her choice. All of the clothing she wore had been her choice. He'd thought her little pencil skirts and blouses were more suited to a legal office than a paramilitary organization, but fundamentally he had no issues with it. He was a control freak, yes, but she'd been adamant about her clothing choices and he hadn't seen the point of arguing.

She pulled open the door and slid onto the seat next to him, arranging herself in a series of small, precise movements. "I think it went well," she said, folding her hands in her lap. "He seemed interested."

Faith had gone to the bar on a recruitment mission, following up on a former Green Beret with a reputation for being a stellar marksman. Jacob needed a sniper to add to his collection of specialists.

"Good." Jacob made another reflexive check of the street outside. "We'll give him a week to think about it and then do another follow-up."

"We might not even need a week. When I left him my card he pocketed it immediately."

"What about the psych report?"

All new recruits were thoroughly vetted by both Faith and himself, psychologically and physically. Loose cannons who wouldn't do what they were told were not welcome, no matter how attractive their skills were.

"It's clear." Faith pulled a tablet out of her briefcase, delicate fingers moving over the glass surface. "The physical was clear too. He'd be an asset, I think."

Jacob went over the team as it stood: Jack King, their former marine and all around badass. Kellan Blake, helicopter pilot and former Navy SEAL. Isiah Graham, team leader and ex-Army Ranger. All proven members of the field team with solid skill sets. Then there were their nonmilitary members: Sabrina Leighton, their tech expert and what she couldn't do with computers wasn't worth talking about. And Callie Hawthorne, who hadn't been actively recruited but had joined by dint of being Jack's fiancée. She had no military background to speak of, but she came from a rich, political family and her knowledge of that world and her contacts had proved useful on more than one occasion.

The potential recruit's success or failure would lie with how well he fit into the team as it stood. All current members were essential and had developed a good rapport with one another, and it was always tricky adding a new recruit since they changed the team dynamic.

Maybe, given the delicacy of the mission he was about to send them on, it would be a mistake adding someone new. Isiah had some sniper skills, so it wasn't as if they had no marksman at all.

"I'll take that under advisement," he said, dismissing the issue of the recruit as he noted Faith's pale cheeks and the dark circles under her eyes. "You look tired. How are you sleeping?"

Her normally full lips thinned. She didn't like his questions about her health, but he made no apology for them. Since the day he'd taken her from the hospital she'd become his responsibility and it was a job he took very seriously indeed. Especially since her continued good health was vital to her regaining her memory.

"Fine." Her voice was crisp and clear, her gaze sliding away from his. "Thank you."

She wouldn't often look him in the eye. Sometimes she did, but it was rare and not for very long. Most of the time she gave him sidelong glances, or brief, fleeting looks. Or would focus on a point directly behind him. She didn't get too close to him either, as if he was a strange dog and she was wary of his temperament.

He knew why that was. He'd felt it as soon as she'd started to regain her health. They had an undeniable physical chemistry, which clearly made her both suspicious and uncomfortable. As if she didn't know what it was or how to handle it.

He could have given her a few ideas, but that wasn't and wouldn't ever be in the cards. Not with her. Too many reasons not to and all of them ironclad.

For the last five years he'd been consumed with finding his brother and now that he was getting close, or at least closer than he'd ever been, the last thing he needed was to get distracted.

Not that he'd allow himself to anyway.

Especially not with his brother's lover.

"Bullshit," he said. "I know you're waking up in the middle of the night and have been for the past week. What is it? Nightmares?"

She was sitting close, filling the car with the delicate scent of the lavender bath gel she used. When she'd first come to live with him, he'd asked her what kind of toiletries she wanted and she'd told him she had no idea. So he'd gotten everything a woman might potentially need and in a variety of scents so she could choose which one she liked.

Lavender bubble bath was apparently her favorite.

"No nightmares." She shifted minutely, putting a subtle distance between them, which amused him since he hadn't moved once since she'd gotten into the car. "I'm not sure why I'm waking up. But broken sleep is all part of it so I'm assuming it'll resolve itself." Her attention returned to her tablet. "Now, as I was saying about the new recruit—"

"You think I don't know?" Jacob watched her face carefully. "I can hear your breathing change. I know what fear sounds like."

Faith looked up and this time she met his gaze head-on, a blaze of dark blue flame. "If you're spending time listening to my breathing at night on those monitors, then you might need to find yourself a hobby."

No one else talked to him the way she did. Everyone was too afraid. But not Faith. For all her wariness and distance, she didn't seem to have any problems with giving him a tongue-lashing if she thought he deserved it.

He enjoyed that about her, got off on the little challenges she threw at him, which was probably a bad thing. Especially when she got off on them too, though he thought she probably wasn't aware of that herself. But he knew. Her pupils would dilate and her delicate cheekbones would flush, and on more than one occasion, he'd seen her nipples push against the fabric of her blouse, the hard tips giving her away.

On another day he might have teased her, messed with her a little since it had been a while since he'd allowed himself time to play with a beautiful woman.

But not today. Not given how close he was to the end of his mission. And definitely not when all that was standing between him and finally finding Joshua was this woman's fears.

So he ignored her dig and instead said, "Nothing at all to do with the fact that I know who you really are?"

She gave him a look. "Aren't I supposed to be your cousin?"

So he'd been right. She knew he'd been lying.

"And when did you realize I wasn't?" he asked.

"When you insisted on calling me 'Ms. Beasley.'" She made another flicking motion on the screen of her tablet. "By the way, if you're looking for hobby suggestions, you could start by playing hide and go fuck yourself in the parking lot."

That startled a laugh out of him despite himself. "You've been spending too much time with Mr. King. Marines are assholes."

"So are . . ." She gestured to him. "Whatever it is you are."

No one knew his background. He'd made sure of it. But it wasn't difficult to figure out that he, too, was ex-military.

Not that it was relevant. At all.

"Thank you for the suggestion, but I'll pass. There's another question I'm far more interested in." This time he allowed a hint of steel to bleed through into his voice, so she knew. So she was aware of exactly whom she was playing with. "If you know I'm not your cousin, then don't you want to know who you really are?"

Faith looked down at the tablet in her hands, trying to ignore his intense, black stare.

Being in a car with Jacob Night was like being in a very small box with a very large lion.

A very large, *hungry* lion.

She didn't like it. She didn't like the question he'd asked her either. Because the answer was no. She didn't want to know who she really was. She even felt cold at the thought.

What she did know was that she'd spent the last six months building up an identity for the person she was *now*. A familiar identity that she was only just starting to be comfortable with and the thought of finding out that she was someone completely different . . . scared her.

So yes, she *was* scared about it.

She'd already lost one identity. She didn't want to lose another.

"Can we have this discussion later?" She brushed her finger over the screen of the tablet to get rid of the document she was looking at, pleased that it didn't shake. Pleased too that her voice was steady. "I have a few important e-mails to send."

The driver's door opened, their driver starting to get in.

"We're not ready." Jacob's deep, rough voice was curt. "Go have another smoke."

The driver obeyed instantly, shutting the car door once more.

Faith focused hard on the tablet screen as the tension in the car climbed, trying not to be aware of it or the man sitting bare inches from her.

He was very long, very muscular, and very, *very* powerful. So much bigger than she was, so much stronger in just about every way.

She didn't know why she found that exciting or why he scared her, a combination of feelings that should be mutually exclusive but weren't. There was also a familiarity to him that she'd sensed the moment she'd woken up that morning in the hospital to find him bending over her, which was why she'd never questioned being told he was her cousin.

Except, as the days had gone by, she gradually realized that he couldn't be her cousin. He never talked about their supposed family, plus cousins generally didn't call each other by their surnames. Of course, that left her with no explanation for that sense of familiarity, though it did suggest she'd known him or met him before she'd lost her memory. Whatever, it was . . . disturbing.

Basically, everything about him disturbed her.

In the six months since she'd been living with him, he'd been nothing but kind. Nothing but generous. Taking care of her and making sure she had everything she needed. Yet, that threat sense went off whenever he was around and so she made sure there was always distance between them, both physical and emotional.

She checked her physical distance now, surreptitiously from beneath her lashes. His powerful thigh, wrapped in black wool, was near hers, but not too near. Not touching. Even so, she could feel his heat. He radiated it like a furnace.

Her breath caught and she glanced up at him, again through the protective veil of her lashes, unable to help herself.

He wasn't at all pretty, not like Kellan, one of the other 11th Hour team. No, his features were too strong, like a boxer's or a warrior's. Hard jaw, a blade of a nose that looked like it had been broken not once but twice. Scars on his cheeks and deeply set eyes that were the blackest she'd ever seen. An undeniably compelling face, if not strictly handsome.

He was watching the way he always did. Intense. Sharp. Like an X-ray searching the contents of her soul.

Well, if he could see it, then good luck to him. Maybe he could tell her what was in it because she hadn't a clue.

He can tell you, remember?

A rush of cold iced her veins.

She tore her gaze away, looking back down at the tablet and trying for calm. Getting emotional was a mistake. It brought back those horrible days after she'd first gotten out of the hospital, when she hadn't known who she was and there was nothing but a black hole where her memory was.

It had taken her months to overcome her terror of finding nothing familiar and everything strange, but overcome it she had. Taking comfort in a new identity and a new life, finding familiarity in a new routine.

She didn't want anything to put that at risk.

Like finding out her real name, for instance.

Jacob said nothing. Waiting.

Faith gritted her teeth.

There was an exercise that the psychologist she'd seen in the first month after leaving the hospital had recommended to her, where she paid attention to her body, focusing on her muscles and the way she was sitting, the movement of air across her skin. It was a grounding exercise, designed to make her feel more present in her body and in the moment, and she liked it because it calmed her.

She practiced it now, letting herself become aware of the stiff fabric of her blouse and how it felt against her skin, the tightness of her skirt around her thighs, reminders of the armor she wore every day, the shell of her identity.

Faith Beasley. Who worked with the 11th Hour team. Whose boss was Jacob Night. Who liked lavender bath gel, Cinnamon Toast Crunch cereal, and good Earl Grey tea.

Who was very, very conscious yet again of her boss's thigh near hers, and his heat. And of the strange, compelling, magnetic quality to his presence that she tried daily to ignore and failed to most of the time.

"As I said," she murmured into the silence, calmly swiping over the screen, "we can have this discussion later."

"No." Jacob was just as calm. "We can't."

Damn.

"Fine." She risked a fleeting glance directly at him, felt the impact of his dark gaze deep inside her. It was always unsettling, which was why she seldom looked him in the eye. "I've only just gotten comfortable with being Faith. I'm not in any rush to be someone else."

HARD NIGHT / 13

"But you wouldn't be someone else," he pointed out. "You'd be yourself."

"I'm myself already, thank you very much." She looked down at her tablet once more, conscious of how fast her heart was beating. "Why do you want to tell me so badly anyway? Getting sick of the invalid already?"

He was silent.

She wasn't going to risk another glance at him, so she busied herself with calling up the mail app and checking her e-mail.

"No," Jacob said eventually. "You know that's not the case."

"Well then." She typed in a couple of words, not paying attention to what she was writing. "I'll tell you when I'm ready to know. But I'm not ready now."

And quite honestly, she didn't know when she would be.

She'd lied when she'd told him that her sleep was fine and that she wasn't having nightmares. They'd begun a few weeks ago, completely out of the blue. Nightmares about fire and running down a dusty street, her feet bleeding. About knowing someone was behind her, chasing her, and a terrible, awful fear tightening every muscle . . .

They were so real, so vivid, and every time they woke her up she wondered if they meant her memories were returning. Because if so, she didn't want them to.

Right now she lived moment to moment and although she may not be exactly happy, she wasn't actively unhappy. She was comfortable with how her life was going. She liked her job and the people she worked with. She had a home she was familiar with, a routine that helped her stay on track when she forgot things, as she did from time to time, and an identity that made her feel grounded, like part of the world again.

She didn't want anything to change.

The silence lengthened, deepened.

Jacob shifted, leaning forward, his hands clasped loosely between his knees, and she tried to keep herself still, resisting the urge to pull away from him and his heat.

"Here's the problem, Ms. Beasley." He never called her Faith. "I need you to remember who you are."

A cold rush of shock hit her.

Things are going to change whether you like it or not.

Very carefully she typed another word in her e-mail, though she had no idea what it was, using the time it took her to think past the shock clouding her brain.

He hadn't talked directly about her memory before, not beyond the usual physical health questions. He'd always been very calm, very patient. Allowing her distance and never pushing.

But she didn't make the mistake of thinking he was doing this out of the kindness of his heart.

He wanted something from her. And she couldn't shake the sense that she was like a lamb in a cage and he was the hungry lion prowling around outside it. Waiting for the cage to open.

And now he has the key?

She fought to keep her breathing steady. "I see. And why do you need me to do that?"

"Because there are things in your head that I want." He sounded so reasonable. "Things that only you know."

The rush of shock became a river, threatening the stable little life she'd built over the past six months. A life built on foundations that she'd always known were made of sand, that were now being washed away.

Oh, come on. Did you really think he was one of the good guys? A man like him doesn't take care of a stranger with no memory for six months for no reason at all.

It was true. So why was she so very shocked? If she'd learned anything about Jacob Night, it was that he never did anything without a reason. Those reasons might be oblique, but he always had them, and even subconsciously she'd been aware of that. Why else would she have kept her distance from him all this time? Despite the fact that he fascinated her in a way she didn't want to think too deeply about.

"Here I was thinking you were my Good Samaritan," she said, pleased that her voice was quite level. "You never do anything for free, do you?"

"Oh, come now, you didn't really think I was your Good Samaritan, did you? I'm a mercenary. You know that."

Yes, it was true and essentially that's what the 11th Hour was: guns for hire. But she'd never thought of them like that. The missions Jacob accepted usually entailed protecting people who needed it, or taking down people who deserved it, so it seemed simplistic to label them as basic mercenaries.

"So." She typed another word into her e-mail. "You lied to the doctors by telling them I was your cousin, and you took me out of the hospital, gave me a job, took care of me for six months, purely because you want something I have no memory of."

He didn't reply.

She was suddenly angry, though that may have been her shock and, deeper, the fear that ran underneath everything like an underground stream, acid and bitter, undermining her strength. The fear that had never gone away. The fear she didn't want him to know about.

The fear of who she really was.

Her fingers dug into the sides of the tablet. The doctors had told her emotional extremes would happen after a TBI and she'd had a fair few of them in the first month or so. But not since.

Shit, she didn't want one now.

But he'd casually destroyed the fragile bubble of normality she'd built for herself with one simple sentence.

You knew. Deep down, you knew he was the lion outside the cage.

"You know what I am," he said eventually, lifting the thought directly from her head, a dark current running through his already dark voice. "You knew the day I took you home."

Her throat was dry. She tried to swallow, conscious more than ever of just who she was sharing the car with.

Despite that lingering sense of familiarity, he'd always been a stranger to her. The mysterious man who'd pulled her from her hospital bed and taken her back to his huge home on the clifftops above the ocean in San Diego. He hadn't told her anything about himself and even though she was living in his home, she hardly ever saw him. He kept to himself and any discussions they had were limited only to his inquiries about her health and management of the 11th Hour team.

The only thing she knew about him was that he was dangerous and he was right, she'd known that the day he'd taken her out of the hospital. But she'd accepted everything he'd given her without thinking too hard about it because she'd had no other choice.

She'd let him become the only familiar thing in a world where nothing else was, because he was the only person she knew.

A lion is just a big cat. Until you come face to face with his teeth.

Long, blunt fingers wrapped suddenly around her tablet and before she had a chance to protest, it was pulled from her hands.

Her head snapped up, his gaze clashing with hers.

There was no anger in his expression, only an intensity of purpose that made panic claw up inside her.

"After all," he went on, perfectly calm as he laid the tablet down on the car seat beside him. "There's a reason you keep me at such a distance. Isn't there, Ms. Beasley?"

Faith opened her mouth, but nothing came out.

"I'm normally a patient man," Jacob Night said. "But my patience is not limitless, especially not after six months. I want your memories, Ms. Beasley. And I will do everything necessary to help you remember."

He was going to tell her, wasn't he? Right here, right now, he was going to tell her who she was and there was nothing—*nothing*—she could do to stop him.

Faith put her hand on the door handle, a reflexive movement she was hardly aware of making.

But before she could pull it open, she heard a strange sound, like a muffled impact. Then something whined in her ear.

She only had time to wonder if a bee had somehow gotten trapped in the car before the window next to Jacob suddenly exploded in a shower of glass.

And he lunged for her.

CHAPTER 2

She had no time to scream or make any kind of sound. One minute she was upright and ready to bolt—though she still didn't know why her automatic reaction had been to run away—the next she was lying on the floor of the car, pressed right down onto it, with over a hundred pounds of hard male muscle piled on top of her.

She couldn't see anything, could barely hear anything. He covered her almost completely, the astonishing heat of him soaking through her clothing and imprinting itself on her skin. He smelled of burning wood and smoke, and for a second she couldn't do anything but lie there, too stunned by the feel of his body curled protectively over hers.

Or was it protectively?

Her brain began to work again, replaying the sound that she'd heard before Jacob had pushed her down onto the floor. A bee.

But no, it wasn't a bee.

She felt his warm breath on the side of her neck, giving her a shiver that raced the entire length of her body.

"Bullets," he said roughly. "Stay down."

For some reason she wasn't surprised. Of course the bee was a bullet and how she'd thought otherwise she had no idea.

More sounds came. An impact above her somewhere and the crack of glass shattering.

Jacob cursed, low and harsh.

By rights, she should have been scared—she might work for a paramilitary operation but she never went out into the field because she wasn't trained for it—and she *was* scared.

But that's not all she was.

Beneath Jacob's sheltering heat, her muscles had tightened in a kind of . . . readiness. As if her body was waiting for a signal. Like a runner listening for the starting gun, she felt like she was all set to explode into motion.

But . . . bullets. Why the hell were there bullets?

"What's happening?" she asked, her voice more breathless than she wanted it to be.

He didn't answer. Instead the weight on top of her shifted and he moved again, agile as a cat for such a large man, angling himself, then sliding into the driver's seat, keeping his head low.

"Stay where you are," he ordered in a tone that brooked no argument. "And keep your head fucking down."

Faith didn't protest, not when there came another whine and a hole was punched through the driver's side window, a bullet burying itself into the leather of the seat right where she'd been sitting.

Her heart was beating fast, fear gathering in the pit of her stomach. And yet that readiness was still there in her muscles, waiting for that signal. As if part of her wanted to grab a gun from somewhere and start shooting back. How strange. Jacob had asked her if she wanted some weapons training but she'd politely declined, some part of her instinctively recoiling at the thought of handling a gun. Again, she had no idea why.

Not that it was the time to be thinking about those things now.

The car abruptly started, Jacob gunning the engine.

"The driver?" Faith asked, remembering.

"Dead," Jacob replied brusquely.

She went cold, but then he must have jammed his foot hard down on the accelerator because the car took off, the air full of burning rubber and the squeal of tires on asphalt.

Faith was propelled back against the foot of the seat behind her and as the car picked up even more speed, taking corners way too sharp for safety, she had to brace herself with her arms against the seat in front to stop from being tumbled around on the floor like a ball in a pinball machine.

She had no idea what was happening and even less of an idea where she was going, but again, although she was scared and upset about the driver, she wasn't beside herself with fear.

Puzzling. Then again, maybe that had to do with being part of the 11th Hour and bullets were somehow . . . expected?

"Jacob," she managed to force out, bracing herself harder as the car screeched around a corner. "What the hell is going on?"

"We're being shot at." His voice was hard and cold. "So I'm getting us out of here."

"Where are we going?"

"Shut up and stay down. I can't concentrate on driving this motherfucking car and answering questions as well."

The car screeched again, making Faith slide toward the other side of the car, and she had the weird urge to tell him of course he couldn't do both because men couldn't multitask.

Why on earth are you wanting to make a joke? Now?

She had absolutely no idea.

The car made yet another turn and then straightened out, picking up even more speed. Were they on the . . . freeway maybe? There were no more corners but the car made a subtle motion every now and then as if it was weaving between other cars.

Yes, they were definitely on the freeway though she couldn't see which direction they were traveling in. Obviously, they weren't heading toward the 11th Hour HQ in San Diego's Gaslamp District because the bar she'd visited just before wasn't that far away—certainly not enough to warrant a freeway trip. And anyway, Jacob wouldn't want to lead whoever it was who was shooting at them back to their HQ, which definitely ruled out going back to his place on the cliffs as well.

They were heading somewhere else, somewhere she didn't know, leaving behind what was familiar . . .

The fear in her gut clenched tighter and she had to fight not to panic.

"Jacob, please." She hated the shaky note in her voice, but she couldn't mask it. "I need to know where we're going."

And maybe he heard it because he said shortly, "The airport."

That was something. She knew the airport. She'd been there before many times. The 11th Hour had a company jet in a hangar and she'd gone to send team members off and to greet them when they came back, and to supervise equipment being loaded on and off.

The panic receded somewhat, though it wasn't helped by the car giving a sudden lurch to the left, making her have to push hard against the door with her leg.

"Why the airport?"

"Didn't I tell you to stop talking?" He sounded irritated.

Faith gritted her teeth. "If you want me to stay calm like a good girl and not freak out like a woman with no memory who really, really likes her routine, then I need to know where the hell we're going."

He grunted, cursed, and the car rocked. "Deal with it, Ms. Beasley."

His voice was even rougher now and alarm echoed through her. The bullets that had smashed the driver's window would have come awfully close to him. Had he been . . . shot?

That thought made her feel even colder than she already was. He was the only person in the entire world who knew what had happened to her, the only person who even knew who she was, and the thought of him dying from a gunshot wound was—

No. It wasn't happening. It couldn't.

"Are you hurt?" Fear made her tone sharp. "Have you been shot?"

"Jesus, I told you to shut up and yet you're still asking fucking questions."

The car lurched again, but this time Faith was fully braced and didn't move. "Deal with it, Mr. Night," she snapped.

There was a silence and then he gave a rough-sounding laugh. "In the leg. It's not a problem."

So he *had* been shot. "You idiot. You should have let me drive."

"*Can* you drive, Ms. Beasley?"

Faith blinked at the back of the seat directly in front of her face. Good point. She had no idea. The past six months she'd gotten around in his limo and since she stuck to places she was familiar with, she hadn't felt any great urge to simply get into a car and drive.

"Not sure," she admitted, feeling the familiar frustration that came with any admission that she didn't know what she could and couldn't do. "Are you bleeding?"

"I don't know. It's not as if I've had time to fucking check."

"Jacob—"

"Be quiet." The two words were grated out. "And let me drive the goddamn car."

She dearly wanted to protest, but considering the only thing standing between her and fiery death in a flaming wreck was his driving skills, that would be a stupid thing to do. Especially considering he'd been shot into the bargain.

Clamping down on both her questions and her panic, she lay on the floor of the vehicle, trying to ignore the lurches and vibrations, and wondering why she wasn't hearing any sirens considering he was driving like a bat out of hell.

Then, after some time had passed—maybe ten minutes, she wasn't sure—the car came to a screeching halt.

"Stay there until I tell you to move," Jacob ordered brusquely as he dug his phone out of his pocket, hitting a few buttons to make a call.

It made sense, it really did. But she was sick of lying on the floor, not knowing what the hell was going on. She twisted around, looking through the shattered windows and seeing blue sky.

They must be at the airport because she could smell jet fuel and hear the roar of a plane taking off. Unfortunately, the roar also drowned out Jacob's voice so she had no idea what he was saying or who he was talking to.

Luckily, she didn't have to wait long. A minute or two later one of the back doors was pulled open, Jacob standing in front of it.

His expression was set, his dark eyes glittering, clearly in no mood to be screwed with. "Get out quickly and follow me. We don't have much time."

She did as she was told, cautiously getting out of the car and looking around. Jacob had parked the car directly outside the hangar where the 11th Hour jet was kept. Except the jet wasn't in the hangar, it was on the runway and a man in a pilot uniform was getting out of it and hurrying to meet them.

Jacob walked up to him with no discernible limp and said something briefly. The pilot gave a sharp nod.

Jacob turned and before Faith could say anything, he'd wrapped his long fingers around her upper arm and was pulling her along with him in the direction of the jet.

Faith couldn't help but notice that the pilot wasn't following.

"You're really going to have to explain what's happening," she said as they approached the stairs. "Why don't we have a pilot?"

"We have a pilot." Jacob pushed her in front of him to go up the stairs first. "Me."

Faith stopped, half turning around. "What? You can fly a jet?"

"I can fly anything." He jerked his chin toward the jet's entrance. "Get inside. The quicker you're in there, the quicker we can get off the ground and away."

Her heart had begun beating fast again, her legs feeling a little shaky. "We're leaving?" she demanded, ignoring him. "We're leaving San Diego?"

"Yes." Jacob's gaze gave nothing away. "Get into the plane, Ms. Beasley. If you don't, I'll pick you up and put you in there myself."

There was a roaring sound in her ears and it wasn't a jet engine this time. It was fear and encroaching shock.

A deep, animal instinct wanted her to shove him out of the way and make a run for it back to the car, to familiarity and safety. But she knew how well that would work. As in it wouldn't.

He *would* pick her up and carry her into the plane if she protested or tried to make a run for it.

He told you to deal with it so deal with it.

Taking a breath, she made an attempt to steady herself before turning around and climbing the rest of the way up the stairs, stepping into the luxurious interior of the 11th Hour's private jet.

There was no flight attendant to welcome them, Jacob shutting the door and arming it himself. Then he turned to her and gestured toward one of the seats. "Sit down."

"But I—"

"Sit. Down."

Faith gave him a cool look, but she went and sat down—albeit slowly—because she knew that tone of his. It was the one he got when he was in charge and things weren't going to his liking. It promised violence, with extreme prejudice to anyone who got in his way.

Not that he'd hurt her—at least she didn't think he would. He wasn't the kind of man who hurt people who didn't deserve it. But she suspected he wouldn't be above sitting her down forcibly if she decided not to obey him.

The moment she sat, he bent over her, reaching for the seat belt and clicking it shut, and she caught that hot fiery scent of his, along with something else. Something metallic.

Instantly her annoyance with him and the fear she was trying hard to ignore fled. She reached out and caught his arm as he began to move away. "You're bleeding. I can smell it."

He gave her an oddly intense look from beneath his straight dark brows, then his gaze dipped to her hand where it rested on his forearm.

And all of a sudden she became conscious that she was touching him.

She *never* touched him.

Her fingertips abruptly felt as if they were burning and she snatched her hand away before she was even conscious of doing so.

The look in his eyes sharpened for a second, a black arrow piercing her straight through, making her cheeks heat for some inexplicable reason.

"It's nothing," he said flatly. "I'll deal with it later."

Then without another word, he turned and strode toward the cockpit, pulling open the door and disappearing inside.

Leaving her alone.

Jacob didn't think. He was in military mode; dealing with the immediate threat was the only thing that concerned him.

He'd been stupid, complacent. Sitting in his fucking town car and checking out Faith's ass when he should have been checking for danger.

Sure, he'd given the street a couple of sweeps and he thought he'd been paying attention. But clearly, he hadn't. And those fuckers had taken advantage and now his driver was dead and Faith was in danger. Christ, there was another reason he'd taken her to live with him and it wasn't solely about his wanting her memories. He'd done it for her own protection. There were people out there who wanted her dead, and he should have been on top of figuring out who they were. But his sources had been slow with their intel and as yet they didn't have a firm fix on who was after her or why.

Jacob sat down in the pilot's chair and ran through the pre-flight check as quickly as he could. The jet had been all set for a flight in a couple of hours to Chicago, so it was fueled and ready to go, and the phone call from the car had rushed through a new flight plan.

Just as well.

Faith couldn't stay in San Diego, not now that those bastards had tracked her down. He couldn't take her back to his place either because if they'd followed her to the bar, they'd be able to follow her there, too. It was best to leave the city completely and ASAP, before they were found.

He had a safe house in Washington State he kept well supplied and ready in case of any unexpected circumstances, so he'd take her there, where she'd be safe. And then he'd figure out whose heads were going to roll for failing to keep him informed.

Jacob flicked some switches, then radioed Control. Been a while since he'd piloted a jet but the skills were still there. You didn't forget.

His leg hurt like fuck but he'd been shot before and was able to tune it out.

Not so much the feel of Faith's hand on his forearm. Her fingers had been cool against his skin, yet the touch had hit him like an electric shock.

She'd never touched him before, not spontaneously like that, and he could have sworn he'd caught something like concern in the deep blue of her eyes.

Neither of those two things should have been a problem and maybe it had something to do with the adrenaline pouring through his system and the gunshot wound in his leg, but he couldn't get them out of his head. Not what he should be thinking about when he had a plane to fly.

Clenching his jaw, Jacob shoved Faith from his head. Blood was oozing down his leg, but he ignored that, too, busying himself with readying the jet for takeoff.

Air traffic control was efficient and ten minutes later they were in the air and he was leveling the jet off at cruising altitude.

Hitting the autopilot, he sat there for a moment staring out at the brilliant blue of the sky unrolling ahead of him. Now that the immediate threat had been dealt with, it was time to think about all the rest of the shit he'd pushed to the side while they'd been escaping. Though probably the first thing he needed to deal with was his goddamn leg.

Shoving himself out of the pilot's chair, he opened the cockpit door and stepped out into the main cabin.

Faith was still sitting there all buckled up, her hands clutching her seat belt. Her face was white, the dark shadows beneath her eyes even more pronounced. She looked scared, which he couldn't blame her for.

She had lots to be scared about.

"You can take off your seat belt now," he said curtly, moving over to the storage locker where the extensive first aid kit was kept. Should be everything he needed in there. Hopefully, he wouldn't have to dig a bullet out, but again, it wouldn't be the first time he'd had to do that; he did have some basic first aid training. He knew what he was doing.

As he dragged the kit out of the locker, he heard the click of Faith's belt and a couple of seconds later, her crisp, clear voice. "Let me help."

He turned.

She was standing behind him, a very direct do-not-mess-with-me expression on her face. If he hadn't spent six months making himself an expert on her every expression, he would have thought she wasn't afraid.

But she was. He could see the darkness lingering in her eyes.

First rule of leadership was to see to the health of the people under his command and sometimes that simply meant giving a person something to do as a distraction.

He couldn't afford a freak-out, not up here. Not now. And even though Faith's mental state was a lot healthier than it had been six months ago, he suspected it was still fragile. It didn't need to be put under any sort of pressure just yet.

Shoving the first aid kit into her hands without a word, he brushed past her, moving over to one of the seats and sitting down. Pain shot through him, bright and sharp, making him have to grit his teeth against it.

Faith followed, then knelt on the floor in front of him, starting to pull supplies from the kit, her movements quick and precise. "You need some painkillers," she murmured, grabbing a bottle of pills.

"Just Tylenol. I need to be still able to fly this fucking jet."

She gave him one of those fleeting glances, a crease between her brows, but she didn't say anything, only nodded.

His leg ached like a motherfucker now that he was sitting down and the adrenaline was fading. Enough that he couldn't even notice the soft warmth of her body leaning over him as she peered at his left thigh. The fabric of his pants was torn and bloody, and sticking to his skin.

She picked up a pair of scissors and efficiently cut the fabric, then pulled it wide to reveal the wound. Which wasn't as bad as it could have been, though it was going to require stitches. Nothing he couldn't handle.

"Looks like the bullet went straight through." He frowned at the blood. "Pass me some of those antiseptic swabs."

"Let me clean it up for you."

"No." His tone was brusque but he didn't give a shit. He didn't like other people taking care of him and if he needed fixing he'd do it himself. "I'll do it."

"Idiot." Faith made no move to put the swabs in his hand. "You've been shot, Jacob."

"Believe it or not, I am aware of that."

She made an annoyed sound, frowning at the wound. "Which means taking ten minutes to rest isn't a totally stupid idea. No painkillers, fine, but at least let me stitch you up."

Fuck, he did not want to have this argument, not right now, but he could feel the tide of adrenaline going out, leaving him with the pain and a growing feeling of cold. If he wasn't careful he was going to go into shock.

"*Can* you stitch me up?" he asked roughly. "I didn't see you at the first aid courses the others took."

He knew how she hated being reminded of all the things she couldn't do, but he didn't have any energy to spare for her feelings. Christ, if he hadn't spared her feelings a couple of months ago and told her what he knew about her real identity, then maybe they wouldn't be in this mess now.

But hindsight was always 20/20 and the simple fact was that he hadn't told her. She'd been scared after she'd gotten out of the hospital and he'd wanted her trust. So he'd made the decision not to push her and even though she knew that he knew her real identity, she hadn't asked him to tell her. And so here they were.

An expression of irritation passed across her face, though she didn't look at him. "Okay, fine. I can't. But at least let me clean you up." The swab was already in her hand and she didn't wait for him to respond, leaning forward to clean the wound.

Fucking woman. Everyone else was afraid of him, racing to do what he told them to without argument. Not Faith. She was fearful about a good many things, but not, apparently, him. She seemed to have no problem arguing with him. In fact, she even seemed to relish it, which was as irritating as it was exciting.

Another maddening consequence of the chemistry between them.

And speaking of . . . he was aware of it now, the warmth of her body pressed against his legs as she bent over his lap, dabbing at the blood around the wound. She seemed oblivious, a frown of concentration creasing her forehead. A lock of glossy black hair slipped over her shoulder to lie across his uninjured leg and he had the oddest urge to take it between his fingers and stroke it, see if it was as smooth and silky as it looked.

The pain was annoying him as was his own stupidity back in San Diego, and here she was, calm as ever, arguing and cleaning his wound as if nothing was wrong. Grabbing his arm as if putting her hands on him wasn't dangerous.

It aggravated him for no good reason, which was in itself an annoyance, so just to be a prick he reached out and took the end of that lock of hair between his fingers, brushing his thumb along it. And yes, it *was* as smooth and silky as he'd expected.

Faith didn't seem to be aware that he was touching her hair

at first, too busy swapping one dirty swab with a fresh one. Then suddenly she froze and looked up at him sharply.

He didn't let go, relishing the flicker in her eyes. She so rarely met his gaze that some part of him felt vaguely triumphant that he'd caught her attention.

"You really don't like doing what you're told, do you?" He rubbed the silky strands between his thumb and forefinger lazily. "What's up with that, Ms. Beasley?"

Color stained her high cheekbones, but she made no move to pull away. "I don't have a great deal of control over my life, Mr. Night. Part of the having no memory thing, you understand. The only control I do have is over my actions and my own choices. And so I like to exercise that choice whenever I can." She arched one delicate dark brow. "That explain things for you?"

It did. In fact, he understood all too well. When it came to the day-to-day process of living, control over your own actions was all you had. Fuck, he'd learned that lesson well enough in his own goddamn life.

"Yes." He ran his thumb along that lock of hair, feeling the softness of it. "Makes perfect sense. In which case avoiding learning about certain things is also a choice, wouldn't you say?"

Her jaw tightened. "If you're wanting me to—"

"You haven't asked me why you were shot at. You haven't asked me where we're going now. You haven't asked me anything at all." He tilted his head, studying the finely drawn lines of her face. "Is that another choice, Ms. Beasley?"

"I—"

"Because if it is, it's not a choice that gives you any control at all. Knowledge is power. You do understand that, don't you?"

Her mouth closed and she looked down at the wound in his leg. Her movements were firmer and they hurt, and he didn't make the mistake of thinking she wasn't doing it deliberately.

She didn't like having that pointed out to her, clearly. Too bad, though. Things had changed now.

"We're going to a place I have in Washington State," he continued. "It's a safe house no one knows about and where you'll be protected. And you want to know why, Ms. Beasley? It's because those shots were meant for you."

CHAPTER 3

Faith stared down at the wound on Jacob's leg, focusing her entire being on that and not the soft, deep rumble of his voice. A voice that kept on going, rolling right over the top of her like a steamroller.

"Some very bad people are after you," he continued, "and to be honest, I thought we'd have more time before they tracked you down, but apparently not. Which means there are some things you have to know and know now."

Panic curled like a small animal in her chest. No, *not* now. Not here, not after she'd been taken without ceremony from one place she'd only just gotten familiar with and transported somewhere else she didn't know.

Knowledge is power.

It might be for him, but maybe for her it wouldn't be. Maybe for her it would mean yet another plunge into chaos. Into that terrible place she'd discovered when she'd woken up in the hospital, when she'd realized, with a terrible, sickening lurch, that not only could she not remember how she'd gotten there, she couldn't remember her own name, either. Groping for something familiar and finding nothing.

Nothing but a black hole where her memory should have been.

The fear she'd known in that moment had been like a lead blanket, weighing her down, suffocating her. Making her wish that whatever had put her in the hospital had been bad enough to kill her.

It felt like that blanket was wrapping around her now, twice as heavy and twice as thick.

Washington State. Bad people. Shooting at her.

"You'll need a needle and thread." She shifted away from him, turning back to the first aid kit, feeling the slight pull as her hair came free of his hold.

There had been something oddly calming about the way his thumb had been rubbing at her strand of hair, as if his touch was familiar, an anchor in the sea of chaos that threatened to overwhelm her.

And now that calming touch was gone . . .

She couldn't breathe, having to force air into her lungs and out again as she reached for the surgical thread and needle.

"Your name isn't Faith," Jacob went on relentlessly. "That's the name I gave you in the hospital. Your surname isn't Beasley, either, it was one I chose at random from the list of nurses who were caring for you."

She picked up the needle and thread. Her hands were shaking. "Perhaps you shouldn't do this until you've had the Tylenol. It's going to hurt."

"Your real name is Joanna Lynn and you were a—"

"*Stop.*" Something went off in her head like a lightbulb exploding and she found she was on her feet, the needle and thread dropped onto the floor.

Jacob sat back in the chair, his long body stretched out like he was about to watch a football game instead of preparing to sew up a gunshot wound in his own leg.

His battered, scarred face was nothing but hard lines, his mouth uncompromising, his eyes glittering and cold as jet.

He was like rock, like stone. There was no softness in him, no sympathy. And absolutely no mercy at all.

"I'll get you some water for the Tylenol," she forced out, then turned, walking quickly to the plane's tiny bathroom, stepping inside and shutting the door very firmly behind her.

She leaned back against it for a moment, but then her knees buckled and she slid all the way down to sit on the floor.

Her heartbeat wouldn't slow and the small, terrified animal in her chest was nipping and biting at her in its fear, trying to find a way out.

"Your name is Joanna Lynn."

Something had happened in her head the moment Jacob had said those words. Not her memories returning, nothing like that. But definitely something. As if a curtain in front of a window had twitched in preparation for it to be drawn back.

God, she did *not* want to see what was through that window. *Joanna Lynn.*

Faith shut her eyes tightly. The name echoed inside her like a shout in an empty room, but this time there were no responses, no curtain twitching. The name meant nothing.

She sucked in a breath that was mainly relief.

Maybe it made her a coward to not want to know this stuff and all her talk about wanting control a lie, but that didn't change the fact that there was something inside her, a feeling, a whisper, *something,* that told her she didn't want to know the truth. That the person she was now, Faith Beasley, cool and calm and in control, was the person she wanted to stay.

She didn't want to be Joanna Lynn.

Whoever that was.

But don't you want to know why you were shot at?

The breath she'd sucked in went out of her in a long exhale.

It wasn't hard to guess why. Either they were targeting Faith Beasley and her work with the 11th Hour, which was a possibility. Or they were targeting . . . Joanna Lynn.

A shudder went through her.

This was all too much and if she wasn't careful, it was going to overwhelm her. The psychologist had suggested concentrating on the problem at hand when she had feelings like these, as a way of not letting the weight of everything press down on her, and that had worked well enough.

So perhaps simply concentrating on getting the Tylenol for Jacob was what she could do now. And being clear with him that she needed some more time before he started telling her anything more.

Then again, he wouldn't be telling her anything at all if that wound kept bleeding. No matter what he said about being able to handle it, he'd been white around the mouth as she'd cleaned up the blood and that indicated some level of pain at least.

Carefully she didn't think about how it had felt to lean up against the wild, animal heat of him or to have that long, powerful body underneath hers, all his muscles contracting when she'd started cleaning the gunshot wound. And she very definitely didn't think about how her skin had prickled in response. As if she'd liked it . . .

You did *like it.*

Faith ignored that thought, pushing herself up from the floor and moving over to the tiny basin opposite the door. There was a plastic cup dispenser beside it, so she grabbed one and filled it with water.

Yet her brain didn't want to let it go. Why had he touched her hair? He'd never touched any part of her before, so why now? And why her hair specifically? He'd rubbed it gently as he'd talked, watching her, his gaze sharp and hard and glittering.

She shivered, her skin prickling once more with that odd heat.

Not good, definitely not good. She may have been missing her episodic memory, but she was pretty sure she knew what that heat was and why she found him so uncomfortable to be around. He was compelling, charismatic, and . . . yes, extremely physically attractive. And she wasn't as immune as she pretended to be.

Dammit.

Being attracted to the man who'd brought her out of the hospital and taken care of her for six months was pretty screwed up. Especially considering how much of a stranger he was to her.

Taking the cup of water, she turned back to the door of the bathroom, but paused there a moment.

She was escaping the only city she remembered after being shot at by people she didn't know, in the company of a man she also didn't know. Who'd taken her from the hospital for reasons of his own and had kept her for six months in his house, for yet more reasons of his own.

If she was this woman Joanna, then didn't she have family to come and get her? Or had he kidnapped her and was even now hiding her from her family? And more importantly, why had he taken her in the first place?

Perhaps you should have asked yourself these questions months ago?

Faith gritted her teeth. Yes, she should have, but she hadn't.

She'd been too afraid of everything, too traumatized by the loss of her identity. Jacob had been so certain. He'd walked into the hospital and simply taken charge of her as if he'd known her all her life and she was his.

And she'd found his certainty so reassuring that she hadn't argued. Everything was strange to her so who's to say he wasn't the cousin he'd pretended to be for the sake of the doctors?

Of course, she'd realized that he wasn't over the course of the next few months, but she hadn't asked him any questions about his motivations for taking her. She hadn't asked him any questions at all.

Maybe it's time to start?

Knowledge was power, he'd said, and he wasn't wrong. But the real question was whether she was ready to know.

She was afraid the answer was no.

Swallowing, she pulled the door open and stepped back into the cabin.

Jacob was still sitting in the chair, his attention on his thigh.

Faith blinked as she realized that he was sewing the wound shut himself, pushing a needle through his own skin without even flinching.

Dear God, the man must be made of steel.

"Have you finished sulking?" His voice betrayed nothing.

"I wasn't sulking." Faith crossed over to where he sat, putting the water down on the low table in front of him. "I was having a mild freak-out. Not the same thing at all."

Jacob pulled the thread, the two halves of the wound closing. Blood welled up from the neat stitches. "If you say so." He began tying off the thread. "How's the memory?"

"Still gone."

"Pass me the swab."

She bent to get a fresh one from the kit, grabbing that and a couple of Tylenol, and handing both to him.

He looked up at her as she did so and she met his sharp gaze without flinching.

"You've got some explaining to do," she said.

Faith's stare was steady, meeting his without a flicker for a change.

She had courage, he'd give her that.

He knew telling her who she really was would be difficult

for her. Especially after months of avoiding it. But the time for that bullshit was over. They didn't have the luxury of waiting, not anymore.

His thigh throbbed, but he ignored it.

Instead he downed the Tylenol with the water she'd brought, then leaned forward to get some bandages out of the first aid kit. "Sit down," he ordered. "An explanation might take a while."

She didn't move. "I want this on my terms, Mr. Night. Not yours."

Damn woman. She wouldn't even let him give her information without arguing about it.

Gritting his teeth against the pain, he began cleaning up the wound. "And what terms would those be, Ms. Beasley?"

"I don't want you to mention that name again."

"What name? Joanna Lynn?"

"No need to be an asshole about it."

In spite of himself, he let out a short laugh. The number of people who dared call him an asshole to his face he could count on one hand. No, scratch that. People *never* called him an asshole to his face.

"You do like to push the boundaries, don't you?" He threw the swab onto the floor along with the rest of the used and bloody supplies. "Fine, I won't mention the name again."

Faith gave a small nod as if she'd expected him to agree, which irritated him. "And you'll stop when I tell you, please. Too much information is overwhelming and I'm going to need some time to process it all."

Okay, he could do that. He really *didn't* want any more freak-outs. They couldn't afford any.

"Fair enough." He reached for a thick pad and put it over the wound. "Put your hand here and press down."

She hesitated only slightly before moving in close to him and bending to put her hand on the pad on his thigh. The pressure was painful, but not quite as distracting as her nearness.

Her glossy hair had fallen forward over her shoulders and it was almost brushing his chest, and he could smell her lavender scent under the metallic tang of his own blood.

It wasn't a good idea to be so aware of her, but he allowed himself a moment of indulgence. It was better than pain and did wonders for his mood, though if the hot surge of response inside him was anything to go by, it would be a mistake to indulge himself for too long.

"I'm searching for someone," he began, wrapping the bandage around his leg. He'd never told anyone his motivations for the things he did—knowledge *was* power and he tended to keep that knowledge to himself—but it wasn't as if this woman could use any of that knowledge against him. Not when she was so completely in his power. "I'm searching for my brother. We were separated as young children and I've spent a good few years trying to track him down. A while ago, I managed to get some leads tracing him to the military, the Navy, specifically. But then I lost him again."

"And this relates to me how?"

Faith's voice was cool, but he could see the curve of her cheek as he tied off the bandage. It was pink.

Interesting. Was that him? Being close to him? Several times over the past couple of months he thought he'd caught her looking at him with more than her usual wariness. But he'd told himself it was nothing. Because if it was something then . . .

No. Not going there. He'd already decided.

"I'm getting to that," he murmured. "You can sit down now."

This time she obeyed, moving away from him quickly as if she couldn't wait to put some distance between them. But she didn't sit down. Instead, she began clearing up the first aid supplies.

Well, he wasn't going to argue. He liked a tidy space.

"Then, a couple of years ago," he went on, lifting the cup of water to take another sip, "I found a trace of him again. A black ops operation in Guatemala that had been sabotaged and there was evidence that he'd been involved with the mission somehow."

"Black ops?" Faith finished putting the bloody swabs in the trash, then came back to where he was sitting and began tidying up the rest of the supplies. "How did you manage to find out anything?"

"I have my sources." And they were, unfortunately, expensive. But then he had the money. He'd been paid off very well after the disaster in the Ukraine and a couple of astute investments later, he'd more than tripled his payout. And just as well. Finding Joshua was always going to come at a price.

Faith closed the first aid kit and finally went to sit down in the seat opposite him. "So what about this mission?"

"A number of the team involved were killed. But not my brother. He survived but disappeared."

"You said there was sabotage?"

"The details are sketchy and since it was a black ops mission, locating information about it is difficult. In other words, I don't know." And the not knowing had been as frustrating as hell. But getting any further intel had been next to impossible even with the money he'd thrown at it.

He shifted on the seat, moving to test the stitches. It was painful, but okay. "Anyway, a couple of months ago I got word that my brother had been in South America and that he'd been associated with a gun-running ring being operated out of the States."

It had *not* been what he'd hoped, naturally. That his brother had gotten into the military and had ended up being involved in a black ops mission was one thing. But being associated with the kind of scum who bought and sold weapons? Yeah, he hadn't been that thrilled with the news. Then again, since rumor and hearsay were all he had, he wasn't about to go jumping to conclusions just yet.

Faith's eyes gleamed. "This wouldn't happen to be the same gun-running ring that Kellan's father was involved with?"

Well, she was nothing if not smart.

"Yes." He tilted his head slightly, watching her. "Callie's father had money invested in it too."

Callie's father was a senator and a total prick, but it hadn't been a coincidence that had led Jacob to accepting the senator's job offer. Jacob had needed information from the asshole. The job itself hadn't gone without its hitches, involving Jack going rogue to save Callie from her father's abuse, but it had all worked out in the end. The information Jacob had gotten from the senator led to Kellan's father and the gun-running ring.

"So the last couple of missions were all in aid of finding your brother?" She crossed one knee over the other, the tight fabric of her skirt pulling around her thighs. "How does this relate to me?"

He studied her carefully. There were small lines of tension around her eyes and mouth, though her expression was perfectly composed. She'd always been good at keeping her feelings hidden, and over the past month or so she'd gotten even better at it.

Control. That's what it was all about for her—at least that's what she'd said earlier—and shit, he understood that. Sometimes control over your own choices, over your own feelings, was all you had.

"You? Your name came up in conjunction with that initial black ops mission." The source he'd paid to get him the names of the people on that mission had been expensive and ultimately unreliable, but the intel had led him to find Faith. Which would have been fine if anyone knew her. But even as Joanna, information on her was almost nonexistent.

Faith's eyes widened, but he went on. "I couldn't find out any details other than that you were connected with the mission in some way. I tried searching for you then, to track you down to see what you knew and whether you'd met my brother, but I couldn't find you. Then, a little over six months ago, I got word that a woman matching your description had been found in a hospital in Florida. You'd been transferred from another hospital in South America after you were found badly injured and unconscious in an alleyway. You had no ID, no nothing. No one knew who you were." He paused, studying her yet again, noting those little lines of tension getting more pronounced. "You spoke while you were unconscious apparently, and that's how they discovered you were American."

She said nothing.

"I went to the hospital in Florida hoping to talk to you, see what you knew about that mission, about my brother and whether you could help me find him. And that's when I discovered you had no memory of your former life."

"So you decided to take me and basically adopt me for six months?" There was no expression in her voice.

"Yes." He saw no point in denying it or apologizing for it. "I'd had reports that I wasn't the only visitor who wanted to see you while you were in the hospital. That there were others. I had some sources investigate and it became apparent that the people trying to visit you were associated with the arms ring. Which meant you were associated with it in some way too. I couldn't wait until your memory returned and I didn't want these other assholes getting hold of you either, so yes, I lied and told the staff I was your cousin. I paid a lot of money to get you out and bring you back to San Diego with me."

She looked away briefly, out the window into the sky beyond.

Was she disturbed by this news? Unhappy? Angry? He couldn't tell, not that it mattered. Leaving her in that hospital would have resulted in her death so no, he wasn't sorry in the least.

"And you're certain I'm associated with this arms ring then?"

"Yes. Though in what capacity I have no idea. I was able to get some information from Phillip Blake, however." Kellan's father had not been pleased with his tactics, but Jacob didn't care. He'd spent too many years looking for Joshua to have anyone stand in his way now that he was so close to finding him. "The guy Blake and the others dealt with when selling the guns was a go-between. He managed the deals on behalf of a man called Smith, who ran the whole show. Blake told me you were Smith's lover and that Smith told you everything about the ring." He paused yet again, watching her carefully. "I suspect Smith is my brother."

She was very still, her gaze still fixed to the window. "Stop."

He didn't argue. He had no more to tell her anyway. That was all the information he'd managed to get over the past six months and it was paltry at best.

Nothing but suspicion and rumor, of an arms ring managed by an American called Smith, who was supposedly ex-military. A man whose physical description could have been Jacob himself.

Which was why, even though Jacob had no concrete proof, he thought Smith was Joshua. Because Joshua was his twin.

However, if it *was* true, then it involved a whole lot of implications that Jacob didn't want to think about, not until he had that proof. Such as how his brother had gone from the military to importing illegal arms. And why. And just what the fuck he was going to do about that.

His twin had always been the quieter, more thoughtful, less aggressive one. And Jacob had promised their mother he'd look after Joshua should the breast cancer kill her. It had killed her and so the two boys had been sent to live with Rebecca, his mother's closest friend. That had been the second step in the slow loss of everything Jacob had loved.

As it had turned out, he'd failed in his promise to his mother and he'd lost Joshua, and where his twin had gone, he'd had no idea.

Until now.

Unfortunately though, the only link he had to Joshua was sitting opposite him and she had no memory.

Jacob watched her, but she remained silent, her gaze on the sky. Her hands were gripping the arms of the seat, her knuckles white against the black leather.

This was tough for her to hear, he got that. But it was all necessary and he didn't regret telling her. He'd been searching for Joshua for too long to let her feelings interfere.

Joanna Lynn. Who'd been part of a black ops mission and whose involvement with "Smith" he still didn't have enough information about.

Fuck, he needed her to *remember*.

But she said nothing, not even looking at him, and he knew he wasn't going to get anything more from her. At least not yet. Best to leave her to process this on her own like she'd asked.

He had a plane to fly anyway, plus he needed to get in contact with the 11th Hour team and let them know what had happened. He'd pull them off any jobs they had going on and get them investigating exactly who was after Faith.

Shoving himself out of the chair and only just managing not to wince as the stitches pulled, Jacob turned in the direction of the cockpit.

"That's all you wanted me for? So I could tell you where your brother was?"

He halted, but didn't turn, the question irritating him for some reason. "Of course. Why else?"

But she didn't reply.

CHAPTER 4

Faith carefully thought of nothing as the jet touched down on a tiny private airstrip in the middle of nowhere. Outside there was only forest and what looked to be the remains of a ruined stone building on a rocky outcrop. Grass and other vegetation grew among the crumbling stones. It looked like the place hadn't been visited in years and she couldn't imagine why they were visiting now.

Was this the safe house that Jacob had mentioned? And if so, was he expecting her to camp out in an abandoned building?

"Here?" she asked him as he came out of the cockpit and disarmed the door to the jet. "Really?"

He didn't reply, lowering the stairs, then jerking his head toward the door, clearly indicating for her to get out. There was a glittering look in his eyes that she couldn't interpret.

Inexplicably irritated, she bit down on her questions and moved to the plane's entrance before going gingerly down the stairs and onto the tarmac of the airstrip.

The air smelled of salt and forest, and she could hear the sea crashing against rocks.

She looked around curiously, noting that even though the stone building appeared overgrown and abandoned, and the flat area around the airstrip was full of weeds, overlong grass, and stones, the tarmac itself was meticulously maintained. There was a flat concrete slab not far away that was also clean.

Was that . . . a helipad?

Jacob was moving toward the stone building, his stride in no way hampered by the gunshot wound in his thigh, and Faith had to trot to catch up with him.

Off the airstrip, she kept stumbling over stones, making her wish she'd rethought the stupid high heels she was wearing. Then again, when she'd gotten dressed this morning she hadn't counted on being shot at, then whisked away to some remote location by her mysterious boss.

Or being told who you really are.

Yeah, she wasn't going to think about that. Not yet. Not until she was familiar with where she was and what was happening. Everything was too much to deal with at the moment, let alone having her actual identity thrust on her.

There was a set of uneven, broken stairs leading up to what once must have been the door of the building, but was now a gaping hole. Yet Jacob didn't approach the stairs. Instead he headed to another doorway with stairs leading down into darkness.

The steps were mossy and slippery looking, the rusty iron handrail set into the brick wall sagging, and she could smell damp concrete and wet earth.

Unease coiled in her gut.

But Jacob headed down the stairs without hesitation and so she steeled herself, going down them slowly and trying not to slip.

At the bottom, it was completely dark, and she had to take a couple of breaths to stop from panicking. Jacob had stopped and appeared to be fiddling around with a rusty metal box set on the wall, pulling it open.

As her eyes adjusted to the dark, she saw he was standing in front of another door, this time a metal one. Rust streaked this, too. It looked like it hadn't been opened in centuries.

There must have been controls on the wall, because Jacob did something and she heard a heavy thump. Then he put his hand on the rusty metal door's handle and pulled it.

The door swung open soundlessly.

Okay, so maybe it *had* been opened more recently than centuries ago. It made sense though, the illusion of abandonment. Like the carefully maintained tarmac of the airstrip, it was all designed to give the appearance that nothing was here.

But something was, clearly. The only remaining question was what?

Jacob gestured to the doorway, his eyes gleaming with what looked a little like challenge.

Foreboding twisted inside her, though why that was she had no idea. Ignoring it, she stepped through the doorway.

There was a short hallway, well lit and painted white, in complete contrast to the darkness and damp concrete of where she'd just been standing. At the end of it was another door.

Jacob wouldn't have made her go first if there was danger waiting for her, so she put her hand on the door handle and opened it without hesitation.

She found herself standing in a big room, with a bank of windows opposite her. They gave a view out over the cliff and a blue expanse of sea. The room was painted white and was clearly a living room of some sort, because there were dark leather couches arranged at one end of it, with shelving nearby that contained a multitude of books and what looked like a stereo. A massive flat-screen TV was on the wall near the couch. At the other end of the room were a long, rustic dining table and chairs in dark oak.

There were no pictures on the wall or knickknacks of any

kind, only books and electronics. The floor was polished wood, gleaming in the light coming through the windows.

Doors that must lead off into other areas of the—house? bunker?—were situated at each end of the room.

Faith moved over to the windows that looked out over the water, staring down a sharp cliff face to where the waves threw themselves against the rocks. It was almost as if this place had been built into the cliff itself.

She turned around as she heard the heavy clang of the outer metal door shut, and a couple of seconds later, Jacob came into the room, shutting the door to the short hallway behind him.

"So . . . what is this place?" she asked. "I guess the run-down look is deliberate?"

"Of course." There was an electronic keypad and a small screen beside the door, and with a practiced movement he punched in what must have been a code, the screen flashing red. "It used to be a castle. A rich manufacturing tycoon built it last century for his English wife so she wouldn't get homesick, but she died before he could finish it." Jacob took his phone out from his pocket. "The castle turrets were ruined when I bought it, but the rooms under it were all in pretty good repair so I had it modified. And yes, the run-down look is deliberate." He flashed her a sudden, very white smile. "Wouldn't make a good safe house if people could find it."

"No, I guess not." She crossed her arms, the sound of the sea below the windows making her feel cold all of a sudden. Though that could have been more to do with the unfamiliarity of the whole situation.

Everything Jacob had told her in the plane was pressing in on her and she knew she was going to have to think about it at some point, but right now, standing in this new place and not knowing quite what was going on, she just didn't want to.

Jacob gestured to one of the doorways. "That way leads

to the kitchen, plus other service areas. There should be some food in the cupboards since I keep this place stocked for emergencies. We're on generator power so it's off-grid and there's also a heavily encrypted Wi-Fi signal." He turned and gestured to the other doorway. "Bathrooms and bedrooms are down that way in case you want to go and freshen up. I have to call the team to let them know what's going on, plus a few other people. We're going to need some more supplies so I'll handle that, too."

Faith rubbed at her arms, the cold feeling intensifying inexplicably. "So what? We're going to hang out here? For how long?"

"For as long as it takes to get those fuckers off your back." He lifted the phone, but kept looking at her. "Perhaps even until your memory returns."

Faith eyed him, not liking the sound of that. "It's been six months, Jacob. It won't simply come back on command."

The look in his eyes gleamed. But all he said was "We'll see." He turned away, still holding the phone. "Good morning, Mr. Blake. Yes, it's your lucky day. You get a personal call from your boss."

Faith watched as Jacob moved toward the door that apparently led to the kitchen and went through it, his voice fading. Then she let out a breath.

So. Here they were. In hiding.

She rubbed her arms again, going over to the windows once more, staring out sightlessly.

It wouldn't be too bad. It wasn't as if she'd have to get used to a whole new city and new people. There were only Jacob and her here, no one else. And it looked like it was pretty remote.

Nothing here to do but think . . .

Her fingers dug into her upper arms as what Jacob had told her on the plane came floating back.

An arms ring that she'd been associated with. A man called

Smith. Who'd been her lover. And who Jacob believed to be his brother . . .

A shudder went through her. An echo, though she wasn't sure of what. Was that why Jacob had always felt familiar to her somehow? Because she'd known his brother? And he'd told her that he'd spent years searching for said brother. That there had been a black ops mission. And sabotage and—

She turned from the window abruptly, a rush of panic tightening her muscles. Her brain felt too full, too tangled, the black hole where her memory should be even more terrifying.

All of what he'd told her should have triggered something, but it hadn't. Apart from that weird feeling when he'd told her what her real name was, none of the other information had prompted anything at all. As if the darkness shrouding her memory had swallowed it up or simply absorbed it.

That scared her. It felt like the quiet of an indrawn breath before the scream. A moment of calm before the hurricane hit.

The panicky feeling deepened.

Standing around here waiting for Jacob to tell her what to do was a stupid idea. She needed to occupy herself with something, distract herself somehow. Not think.

Moving over to the doorway that led to what Jacob had told her were the bedroom/bathroom areas, she pushed the door open and went through into another well-lit hallway.

The white walls were broken only by wall lights and a few doors.

She opened the first one and looked into a big room that had a couple of bunk beds up against one wall, the view the same as it was from the living area. A utilitarian bedroom, a big dresser the only furniture apart from the bunks.

She closed the door, then moved on to the door next to it. Another similar bedroom with bunks and a dresser. Was Jacob expecting to provide accommodation for a lot of people or what?

The door at the end of the hallway led to a bedroom that was different. This room was smaller, with only one bed, a big king-size wooden-framed thing that was pushed beneath the sea-facing windows. But there was another window too in the adjacent wall, looking out over an expanse of flat, rocky ground that ended in yet another cliff. Trees hung over the edge of the cliff, leaning and lopsided, their branches shaped by the wind.

She moved over to the window, caught by the view and the movement of the wind in the trees, the glitter of the sea beyond them. There was something bleak about the scene and yet beautiful, too, a wildness that tugged at her heart for reasons she didn't understand.

Near the window was another door and further exploration yielded a bathroom with the biggest shower stall she'd ever seen. It was tiled in dark slate, the glass walls and stainless steel fittings giving it a stark, industrial feel. She liked it though. There was a texture to the tiles that made it feel less stark than it looked.

She abruptly felt sweaty and gritty, the urge to jump into the shower and wash everything away almost overwhelming. But then she'd have to put on her old clothes again and that thought didn't appeal either.

Leaving the en suite bathroom, she went back into the living area and went over to the bookshelves near the TV, examining the small collection of paperbacks stacked there. They were all fiction in varying genres, though mostly science fiction and political thrillers.

Interesting. Was this Jacob's personal collection? Or was it a random selection?

Picking up a thriller, she went to sit down on one of the couches. It was more comfortable than she expected, the leather buttery soft and obviously expensive.

Sitting down and reading wasn't really what she should be doing right now, but quite frankly there wasn't anything else to do. Besides, she'd reached her limit with all the new information clamoring for space and attention in her brain.

Back at the house she shared with Jacob, she watched a lot of TV and movies, as well as reading when she needed to not think. Or she worked like a demon on whatever mission the team were undertaking all the time. She was good at distraction and right now, some distraction was what she needed.

The sun coming through the windows was warm and as she opened the book to the first page, lethargy wound through her.

Not surprising considering how awful her sleep had been lately, full of those nightmares of flames and blood, and running down a dusty street being chased by something. Which made her not want to sleep now.

She tried to shake it off, concentrating on the words on the page, but ten minutes later they were still blurring in front of her eyes and her head felt heavy. After everything that had happened today, she felt exhausted, her brain overloaded and overwhelmed, and she just didn't have any remaining energy to fight it.

Perhaps it wouldn't be so bad if she had a short nap. With any luck the nightmares wouldn't be able to sink their teeth into her if it was short and a rest would give her a bit more energy to cope with whatever Jacob was going to throw at her.

Faith closed her eyes. Just for a second.

"Really?" Kellan Blake sounded deeply skeptical. "She wants all that stuff?"

Jacob moved over to the fridge and pulled open the door, examining the contents. "It's not a question of want, Mr. Blake. It's a question of need. And yes, she needs all that stuff."

He'd given Kellan a brief rundown about what had happened, telling him the bare minimum, then had informed him that Faith was with him and they were going to lie low for a while, at least until whoever was after her had been found. Then

he'd given Kellan a list of things that Faith might need since
there wasn't much in the way of feminine products stocked
here, and although he paid a contact of his a lot of money to
keep the bunker clean and prepared, he didn't necessarily want
them knowing he had Faith with him.

The fewer people who knew she was here the better.

"Okay, fine," Kellan said, then paused. "I'll go to your place
and—"

"Not you," Jacob interrupted, making a mental note to get
his contact to get another few six-packs of beer, just in case.
"Miss Hawthorne can go. I'm sure she'll know better what
Faith may want in the way of clothing."

"Hey, I can choose a woman's clothes. I'm not a total fucking idiot."

"I beg to differ." Jacob straightened and shut the fridge
door, moving over to the stainless steel cupboards. "Besides,
it's not a matter of who can choose the best clothes. Faith likes
Miss Hawthorne and if anyone is going to go through her stuff
without her being present, it'll be her."

It was true, Faith did like Callie, Jack King's fiancée. Jacob
had debated whether to get one of the team to go out and buy
new stuff, but Faith liked familiarity and having a few things
she recognized around her would make this a whole lot easier.

Not that any of it was going to be easy, but there was no
point stressing her needlessly.

"I want Ms. Leighton looking at any security cameras in the
area of that bar," he went on, checking over the contents of the
cupboards. "I didn't spot them so it's not going to be easy but
I want her going over any footage with a fine-toothed comb,
understand me?"

"Yeah, got it." Kellan's voice was uninflected—the soldier
obeying orders and just as well. Jacob didn't want any argument. He wanted whoever was after Faith found and dealt with
ASAP. "Isiah is due back tomorrow so with any luck we'll find

something and be able to go over it with him then too." He paused. "Any suspicions you might want to let us know about?"

Kellan had not been happy when Jacob had told him what had happened and he was even less happy with the information Jacob was prepared to give him. Which was understandable since it was barely anything.

But Kellan would have to live with it. Jacob didn't want to give out any intel to anyone who didn't need to know about it before they had to. Years of experience had taught him that it was better to keep your cards close to your vest before playing them. That way you were more likely to win.

"No," Jacob said flatly. "Just do what I said, Mr. Blake. Get Ms. Leighton to check any footage and we'll go from there."

Kellan was silent a moment. Then he said, "Faith okay?"

"Yes. She's fine."

"Good." Another pause. "Make sure she stays fine, understand?"

There was an edge to his voice and it made Jacob smile. "You're concerned about her?"

"Of course I'm fucking concerned about her. She was shot at."

"Not by me, I can assure you."

"I never said—"

"No, but you're suspicious of me all the same." He didn't make it a question; he knew anyway.

Kellan said nothing.

"Rest assured, Mr. Blake, that Ms. Beasley's continued good health is as important to me as it is to the rest of the team. That's why she's here with me. I don't trust anyone else with her safety."

Another pause.

"Can I speak to her?"

Jacob's grin widened, half-amused at the suspicious note in Kellan's voice and half-pissed at the suggestion he'd ever hurt

Faith. "No. Just do what I asked, Mr. Blake. I'll contact you again this evening." He didn't wait for Kellan to respond, simply hitting the disconnect button.

There were other people he needed to contact, but those could wait. He had to make sure there were enough supplies to last them for however long they were going to be here, check over the generator and the fuel stocks, and lastly disguise the jet before he got to anything else.

Perhaps he should check on Faith first though.

He moved from the kitchen down the short corridor that led to the lounge area, stepping through the doorway and surveying the room.

The sun coming through the windows lay across the couches down one end and there was Faith, a book resting across her stomach, one arm thrown across her face.

Was she asleep? She certainly wasn't moving.

Jacob walked soundlessly over to the couch and stood beside it, looking down at her.

She'd taken one of his thrillers—his favorite title, coincidentally—though perhaps she hadn't enjoyed it as much as he had since she was asleep, from the sounds of her breathing. Then again, after the disturbed nights she'd been having and then a morning full of people trying to kill her, he wasn't surprised. She must be exhausted.

Her hair was spread out on the dark leather, glossy in the sunshine, her pale skin almost glowing.

The first month or so after she'd come to live with him, he'd had a camera installed in her bedroom with her agreement, basically so he could keep an eye on her. And he'd watched her sleep many times.

She always told him she'd slept fine, but both of them knew she didn't. That after the camera was no longer necessary, he still had a monitor in her room so he could hear her breathing, and knew when the nightmares came.

It was never peaceful for her, no matter what she said.

So he was loath to wake her now, when her breathing was regular and she was lying still, sleeping like a normal person.

He bent to pick up the book on her stomach, intending to put it down, then find her a blanket from one of the bedrooms, but as he reached for the book, her hand abruptly shot out and gripped his wrist. Then her whole body twisted, fast and fluid as an eel, her strength irresistible, and he found himself on his knees beside the couch, with his arm twisted up behind his back while she knelt on the cushions behind him, holding it there.

Fuck. What the hell just happened?

Jacob blinked, shock holding him still, for the first time in years completely and utterly taken by surprise. Then adrenaline kicked in and it was only sheer force of will that had him remaining where he was and not twisting out of her hold, breaking her arm in the process.

That move she'd made on him hadn't been intentional, he was certain. It had been instinct. A killer instinct. Which meant . . .

Joanna Lynn had been associated with a black ops mission, but what if she'd been part of it? What if she'd been one of the team members? It had been something he'd considered when he'd first discovered her association, but then dismissed the idea since she sure hadn't acted like any black ops team member. Certainly while she'd been living with him, nothing about her had screamed military.

But Christ, if she could move like that, taking *him* by surprise, then she must have been. Fuck and she was strong, too.

Something lit inside him, catching fire, a heat that he'd always been sure to keep well banked. He liked a strong woman, especially when it came to sex, and if this one could have him on his knees and so fucking easily then . . . shit, he was more than up for the challenge.

You're not going to, remember?

Behind him he could hear Faith panting. The grip she had on his wrist strong and sure. *Oh yeah,* he remembered. *More's the fucking pity.*

With an effort, he shoved away the heat, concentrating instead on the problem at hand which was how a woman with no memory of who she was could have him in a lock with comparatively little effort.

"Any particular reason you're holding my arm behind my back, Ms. Beasley?" he asked calmly. "I wasn't trying to steal your book, I promise."

She said nothing, but her fingers around his wrist didn't budge so he shifted, twisting and using his strength to break her grip. He was half expecting her to move with him, to fight him, but she let him go almost immediately and when he turned, he found her sitting back against the couch cushions, a look of complete shock on her face.

"J-Jacob," she stuttered. "I'm sorry, I don't know . . ." She trailed off, looking down at her hands as if they were someone else's.

Which, in many ways, they were.

But then her shock began to turn to horror and he found himself crouching beside the sofa and taking her hands in his. Her gaze came to his straightaway, staring at him as if he had all the answers to every single one of her questions. "It has to do with my memory, doesn't it?" The edge of fear in her voice was unmistakable. "It's coming back."

Her fingertips were icy so he wrapped his own fingers around hers, gripping tight in reassurance. "I don't know. Did you do that consciously?"

She shook her head, making no attempt to pull away from him, her skin slowly warming against his. "No. I was asleep. And then I . . . I sensed you were there and I just . . ."

"Got me in a lock."

Her eyes darkened. "How could I have done that?"

A fair enough question and one he could hardly answer himself.

"You took me by surprise," he said after a moment. "I wasn't expecting it. And you were very, *very* fast and strong."

"But . . . *how* . . . ?"

"I think you know how." He held her gaze. "You're not just associated with black ops. I think you were part of the mission itself. You moved like you were trained and trained well."

She was silent, searching his face. Then abruptly she pulled her hands from his, looking away and smoothing her hair back.

Jacob didn't move. Because if this was, indeed, a sign that her memory was returning, then perhaps they needed to do more to encourage it. Not that she was going to want to, but Christ, if she was the kind of woman who could get him in an armlock on his knees, then she could handle whatever it was in her past that she was so afraid of.

And then he could finally find out where Joshua was.

"We should experiment," he said calmly. "There's a workout room near the laundry area and it might be a good idea to see if we can re-create what you did to me just then. When you're actually awake this time."

She looked at him sharply. "You're kidding, right?"

"No."

"So you want me to . . . what? Fight you?"

"That's the idea." His blood was pumping a little faster at the thought, and not wholly because it might return her memory. There was a part of him that was *very* interested in the thought of getting close to her physically, of matching her. He liked a fight when it came to sex, liked the whole resistance and surrender deal, though only with women who also got off on it because if they weren't craving him, then there was no point.

Would Faith be like that? Would she fight him? And would she end up surrendering to him?

Why the fuck are you thinking about that? She's not for you, remember?

Of course he remembered.

"I don't think so," Faith said, moving to the edge of the couch and smoothing down her skirt. "You'll probably kill me."

Irritated at himself, Jacob rose to his feet. "I won't kill you, Ms. Beasley. Give me some fucking credit."

"The answer is still no."

"Why not? Scared?"

She gave him an exasperated look from underneath her lashes that did nothing to quell the heat burning in his veins. God, did the woman have *any* idea what she was doing when she did shit like that?

"I'm not a coward, Mr. Night," she said crisply. "And I don't need to justify myself. I don't want to fight you. The end."

"But if this *is* a sign of your memory returning, then don't you want to take charge of the process?" He knew he was pushing, but if her memory was coming back, then maybe she needed the push. Sure, it was mainly self-interest on his part, but also the way she was dealing with it wasn't exactly working for her, not if those nightmares were anything to go by. "Avoidance is not the answer to conquering a fear, Ms. Beasley. Facing it is."

She gave him another one of those long, cool looks before rising to her feet. "I think I might have a shower."

"I thought you said you weren't a coward."

"I'm not."

"Then you didn't hear a word I said about avoidance?"

Her delicate jaw tightened. "I got next to no sleep last night and this morning I was shot at, was involved in a high-speed car chase, then was whisked away by jet to a completely different state, where a mysterious man with who knows what kind of unarmed combat skills wants me to fight him." Her gaze was steady, her voice level. "So you'll forgive me if I take some time out to avoid reality for a little longer."

She was so very cool and calm with him, treating him as if he were nothing more than an irritating child or a bothersome pet.

He rather liked it. Made him want to see exactly how bothersome he could be, which was not at all what he was supposed to be doing.

"You're forgiven." He smiled, letting her see some teeth. Letting her know that he wasn't at all put off or fooled by her apparent calmness. "And I'm not that mysterious. All you have to do is ask."

A flash of surprise flickered briefly over her face and he couldn't help feeling pleased with himself that he'd managed to get that out of her. Again.

"But I thought—"

"You thought what? That I was deliberately keeping secrets from you? No, Ms. Beasley. You simply haven't asked me the right questions."

Another flicker of emotion in her eyes that he thought might have been curiosity. Then she looked away again. "Yes, well, thank you for that, but I've had enough of questions for one day. I want a shower. And some clean clothes might be nice, though I don't suppose you'll have anything like that lying around."

"Oh, you'd be surprised at what I have lying around. I've asked Mr. Blake to get Miss Hawthorne to visit my place and grab some of your belongings for you." He paused. "I thought you'd want something familiar around you, though I'm afraid it'll mean Miss Hawthorne will be looking through your things."

A tinge of red appeared on her cheekbones. "Oh, no, that's fine. And . . . yes, I would like that. Thank you."

Her faint blush satisfied him for reasons he couldn't quite

pinpoint, which probably meant that now was a good time to get on with the stuff he had to do and leave her alone for a little bit.

"Unfortunately, the items aren't likely to get here until this evening, so you might have to be satisfied with whatever clothing I can find in the meantime." He turned toward the doorway that led to the hall and the steps outside. "I have to check on the generator fuel stocks. I'll leave the clothes outside the bathroom."

She said nothing but he could feel her watching him as he moved past her, heading toward the door.

"Questions, Ms. Beasley." He put his hand on the door handle. "You can ask me anything and I'll answer." He turned back and met her gaze. "But only on one condition."

She didn't want to ask him what it was, he could see that, so he waited. Sure enough, eventually she asked, "And what's that?"

He smiled. "You fight me, of course."

CHAPTER 5

The shower was heaven. The water was hot, the pressure divine, and though the only soap available smelled faintly masculine, Faith didn't care. And if she could have washed away the rest of her problems like she washed away the sweat of the day, then it would have been perfect.

Sadly, those problems remained, taunting her as she finally got out of the big, slate shower and went into the bedroom, a big white towel wrapped firmly around her.

A pile of neatly folded clothes was sitting on the bed. Obviously, Jacob had been as good as his word and had found her something to wear.

She stared at the pile and bit her lip, the unease that she'd successfully managed to push aside as she'd had her shower returning once more. And this time bringing with it everything else that Jacob had told her on the plane.

He'd said her real name was Joanna Lynn. That she'd been involved in a black ops mission. That she'd also been associated with an arms ring and a man named Smith. That she'd been his lover.

Before, those things had felt abstract, a series of facts that didn't feel like they related to her at all. But now . . . after what had happened in the living room, they didn't feel so abstract anymore.

She'd been drifting, half-asleep, half-awake, conscious only of a tall presence leaning over her, and something had woken to life inside her. An instinct she hadn't realized was there. And she'd responded to it without thought, her body moving in a way that felt utterly familiar to her. She'd grabbed his wrist and twisted, using momentum to turn him around before jerking his hand up behind his back, forcing him down onto the floor.

She hadn't thought about what she'd done, she'd simply done it. And then a hot burst of triumph had flooded through her, that she could put a strong, powerful man like him on his knees.

The feeling was a strange one and she wasn't sure where it had come from since she'd never had the urge to fight Jacob physically before. But that didn't make the feeling go away.

You like matching wits with him, come on.

Yes, but that wasn't the same as actually fighting.

Her heartbeat had picked up speed at the memory of him kneeling by the couch, his arm drawn up behind his back and his strong wrist in her grip, all his considerable strength at her mercy. Yeah, that had felt good. She'd felt powerful and that had been intoxicating, especially after six months of feeling afraid. But there had been something underlying it too, like an echo of memory, a familiarity. As if she'd done something like this before . . .

Faith took a breath, then let it out.

He hadn't fought back. He'd simply knelt there, letting her hold him. And she'd thought part of that had been sheer sur-prise and the other part . . . Well, she didn't know what. She hadn't had time to examine it, not when she'd realized what she'd done and been horrified by it.

Yes, horrified. Because her body had moved without her conscious thought and that had been frightening. Almost as if she'd been taken over by something else or possessed.

Possessed by yourself. Joanna Lynn.

She took another shaky breath, forcing the thought away, bending down to examine the clothing Jacob had left her.

"Avoidance is not the answer. . . ."

Faith scowled as his voice rang disconcertingly in her head. He was right, of course; avoiding thinking about it wasn't the answer. She'd been doing that for six months and all it had gotten her was a constant feeling of fear and unease. And that wasn't even taking into account being shot at by people unknown and having to go into hiding. Then there were the nightmares and now she'd pulled off some kind of fast unarmed combat move while barely being conscious. . . .

Yes, none of this was good. And it was doing nothing to help her stay in control.

Jacob, the bastard, was probably right in what he'd told her on the plane, that the best way to take control of her life was to get her memory back. Even if she was afraid of what she might find.

And if that meant fighting him . . .

God, she didn't want to fight him. She was afraid of that, too, not so much of him hurting her, but of what might happen if she did. Of what it might uncover about herself.

Don't you want to ask questions about him?

Faith picked up the pair of sweatpants that also accompanied the T-shirt. They were way too big, but luckily, they had a drawstring, plus she could roll them up.

She'd had six months of *not* knowing about him and not wanting to know either, so was his promise to answer questions really that much of an enticement?

Ah, but then she knew the answer to that. No matter how much she'd told herself she didn't want to know, she did. He was a mystery, an enigma, and she had no idea what made him tick. But then in the plane he'd mentioned a brother he'd been searching for and . . .

Yes. She wanted to know.

Pulling the sweatpants on, she drew them up and tied the drawstring before bending to roll up the hems. Then she straightened, feeling marginally better now that she was clean and in fresh clothes.

Though not better enough to want to go racing out to find Jacob and get him in a headlock.

Then again, she was pretty sick of the constant feeling of fear and disquiet, sick of the nightmares, sick of the dread of chaos and uncertainty. Dressing the part, having a routine, and sticking to the familiar really hadn't helped in the slightest. And now she'd been thrown into a situation where there was nothing but uncertainty and unfamiliarity . . . Really, what more did she have to lose?

Yourself.

She swallowed. Would remembering who she'd once been destroy who she was now? Would it change her? Would she become someone else? Someone she didn't recognize?

Her blood went cold, an incipient terror icing her veins.

Clearly, standing around and thinking was *not* good for her. Time to go and find some distraction.

She moved to the doorway and went back out into the living area. There was no sign of Jacob, which she was happy about, since she hadn't quite decided what she was going to do about his offer, so she went on through the doorway that apparently led to the kitchen and service area.

A brief exploration revealed not only a sizable, industrial-looking kitchen, but a room that reminded her of Sabrina's computer area in the 11th Hour HQ. There were a multitude of screens on the walls that looked to be receiving feeds from various security cameras, plus a few more displaying web browsers.

A desk sat before the screens with a chair behind it, currently unoccupied.

Faith also discovered the workout room that Jacob had been talking about earlier, a big space full of different sorts of fitness equipment. There were a stationary bike, a rowing machine, a bench and weights, plus a punching bag suspended from the ceiling. The windows faced the sea, filling the area with light.

She leaned against the doorway, staring into the room, turning Jacob's offer over in her head.

"Still thinking about it?"

His voice, deep and dark, came unexpectedly from behind her and she jumped, unable to help herself. "Could you not?" She turned around sharply, annoyed at being taken by surprise.

He was standing right behind her, looming over her like a mountain. He'd changed too, into a plain black T-shirt that stretched beautifully over his muscular chest and a pair of plain black utility pants. He was a study in darkness: dark clothes, dark hair, and even darker eyes. Like Hades, ready to drag Persephone into the underworld.

Her skin prickled, the curiosity she'd been questioning pulling tight inside her.

What was the story behind that black gaze? And what about the scars on his face, the faint white lines that marred the olive skin of his cheeks. There were more on his strong jaw, too, though they were mainly hidden by the rough five o'clock shadow that dusted it.

A weird urge gripped her, to touch that jaw and feel the brush of his beard against her fingers, to trace those faint scars. Her hand began to lift before she was even aware of it, then she became conscious of what she was doing and lowered it hastily.

He noticed though, damn him, his attention dropping to her hand briefly before returning to her face. "Feel free," he murmured, a rough edge to his voice. "I won't bite."

Her cheeks heated, which irritated her. How the hell did he

know what she was doing all the time? Could the goddamn man read her mind? Well, if he could, good luck to him. While he was there, perhaps he could tell her what he found because she sure as hell couldn't work it out.

"Thanks," she said levelly. "But I'll pass."

His mouth curved in a half smile that had the heat in her cheeks intensifying though she couldn't for the life of her imagine why. "Does that mean you're going to refuse my offer, Ms. Beasley?" His gaze dropped again, taking in her T-shirt and sweatpants. "Pity when you're already dressed for it."

Faith pushed herself away from the doorframe, uneasy with how close he was and how her body seemed to find that terribly exciting. "I think I've had enough for one day. And besides, is fighting really a good idea when you've been shot?"

"I've done more than that with a gunshot wound before." The fascinating half smile deepened. "After all, it's not like you're going to hurt me."

There was a challenging note in his voice and double damn him, she could feel that thing inside her, the mysterious need that always wanted to answer that challenge rise to meet it.

Was that need part of Joanna Lynn? The woman who could take a man like Jacob Night by surprise and force him onto his knees? Because she didn't think it was part of Faith Beasley, the cool, calm, and collected organizer for the 11th Hour.

How would you know?

That was the problem, she didn't know.

Then perhaps it's time you did?

Faith leaned her shoulder against the doorframe, her heartbeat thudding louder in her head. She wasn't seriously contemplating this, was she? "You said you'd answer any questions. That still on the table?"

Yes, apparently, she was.

"Of course." He put a hand on the wooden frame just above

her head, leaning on it. A not-so-subtle dominating move. "As long as you win."

She frowned. "You didn't mention that before."

"No, it's true. I didn't."

"That's hardly fair."

"Why not?" One black brow rose. "Don't think you can beat me?"

He was very close, the hard wall of his chest right in front of her, his heat making her feel like she was only inches away from a roaring fire. It was disconcerting and . . .

Exciting.

She lifted her chin, not wanting him to know what kind of effect he was having on her. "I had you on your knees before. Maybe I can again."

This time his smile was fierce, his deep-set eyes glittering. "You're certainly free to try, Ms. Beasley. Right now if you like."

She shouldn't. She should refuse and go back to the living room, keep reading her book. Or go into the kitchen and fix herself something to eat. Keep avoiding all the frightening things, keep herself safe.

But there was something about Jacob's smile, about the ferocity in it that sparked a response in her. The same one that liked the challenge. It was almost as if she wanted the chance to prove herself to him, which was ridiculous since she didn't have anything to prove.

Yet she found she simply couldn't walk away.

Instead she stared up at him, her heartbeat accelerating, adrenaline surging in her blood. Then without a word she pushed away from the doorframe and backed into the gym.

Surprise flickered through Jacob's eyes, which was gratifying, but then that disappeared, his harsh, compelling face settling into intent lines that made her pulse thud loudly in her head.

He didn't hesitate, coming through the door after her and following her over to the clear area near the punching bag.

A mat had been laid on the floor to provide a bit of a cushion from the bare floorboards beneath, but it was still going to hurt if she fell on it.

Or was thrown.

Faith stopped. God, what the hell was she doing? Yes, she'd taken him by surprise earlier, but he hadn't been expecting her to suddenly be an expert in unarmed combat. And she'd been half-asleep, responding to an instinct she only half understood.

Now, watching him come toward her, tall and broad-shouldered and muscular, moving fluidly and with that deadly predator's grace, she was seriously beginning to question her choices.

She knew nothing about unarmed combat. Nothing at all. Or at least, she knew nothing consciously about it.

But Joanna Lynn does.

Well, Joanna might, but Faith? Not so much.

"I should warn you that I don't know how to do this," she said, hoping she didn't sound as scared as she actually was. "So you might want to keep that in mind."

Jacob came to a stop at the edge of the mat, but she didn't make the mistake of thinking he'd changed his mind. His posture looked relaxed enough, but readiness and tension were in every line of him, his focus completely on her.

It made her breathless.

"I certainly will, Ms. Beasley." He tilted his head, studying her. "Are you ready?"

She gave a nod, ready as she'd ever be.

Then he came for her.

Jacob knew the moment he took that first step toward her that Faith was telling him the truth. She really *didn't* know what she was doing.

That wasn't going to stop him though.

A rush of adrenaline or fear could prompt people to act instinctively rather than logically, and he was hoping the instinct to protect herself would drive her to reach beyond the veil cloaking her memory. And hopefully, that would give them the breakthrough they needed.

Or rather, the breakthrough that he needed.

All he had to do was provide her with the right incentive.

He moved fast, heading straight for her, and her eyes went wide. She stumbled back a few steps, lifting her hands to stop him, but he'd already come to a halt at the edge of the mat.

He'd give her a few moments to understand he wasn't going to hold back, then he'd try again.

"Don't think, Ms. Beasley." Slowly he backed away to the opposite side of the mat again. "Just follow your instinct."

She took a couple of deep breaths and pushed her hair back behind her ears. "Easy for you to say. You don't have a giant coming at you looking like he wants to kill you."

"If it helps, I'm not coming to kill you."

"Then why are you looking at me like you want to?"

"Because instinct happens in moments of pure adrenaline," he said. "When you're intensely angry or afraid. So if I make you angry or afraid enough, maybe you'll connect with the memories you've dissociated from."

She frowned as she cautiously approached the side of the mat opposite him. "I haven't dissociated. It's amnesia."

Just as she'd never asked him about her previous life, she'd never asked him about what had triggered her memory loss. In fact, she hadn't seemed interested in learning more about it at all.

Maybe this was progress?

"Yes," he said. "But it's possibly connected with a traumatic incident. Your brain has essentially forgotten in order to protect you." He paused. "It's likely that's why you don't want to remember."

The look on her face tightened. "So why are you making me?"

If he'd been a kinder man he might have felt sorry for her. Perhaps even reconsidered his position. But he wasn't a kinder man and once he'd made a decision, he seldom changed it. Especially not when it concerned his brother.

He'd lost everything that had ever mattered to him and now he was so close to regaining the last link he had to the family he'd loved, he wasn't going to let anything get in his way.

So all he said was "You know why."

"But I—"

He didn't let her finish, coming at her again without giving her any time to prepare herself. And this time when she backed away hurriedly, he kept on coming, grabbing both her wrists and taking them behind her, holding them pinned in the small of her back.

She gave a soft gasp, but didn't struggle or pull any fancy moves, merely stiffening, her eyes darkening until they were the color of the sky at midnight. Her body was pressed the length of his, breasts, stomach, hips, and thighs all held tight against him. She was warm, *very* warm.

Mistake, you fucking idiot.

The thought flashed through his brain, trailing sparks and fire like a comet. He'd never let himself get this close to her before. He'd never been stupid enough. So what the hell was the matter with him now?

She was staring up at him as if mesmerized, her mouth going full and soft. Her muscles had loosened, no longer so stiff, and she didn't fight him. In fact, if he wasn't much mistaken, it felt like she was relaxing, melting against him instead.

Which was definitely *not* supposed to happen.

"Fight me," he ordered harshly, gripping her wrists tighter.

But she only blinked up at him, the softness of her breasts pushing against his chest as she took a shaken breath in.

His body hardened in response and he nearly growled.

Fuck, this chemistry between them was making everything far more difficult than it needed to be, not to mention making him aware that his control was far more tenuous than he'd thought.

Irritated at himself, he held her even tighter, then bent his head, getting in her face. "Fight me, damn you."

She took a shaky breath. But didn't move.

Jesus.

He bent even closer, inches away from that wide blue gaze, staring fiercely at her. "Fight me, *Joanna.*"

And deep in the endless dark of her eyes, something flickered.

It was the only warning he got.

She surged upward suddenly, her forehead connecting with his and making pain explode in his skull. He tried to retain his grip on her wrists, but she used his split second of shock to twist and somehow get free. Then she moved again, fast, her foot connecting with the gunshot wound in his thigh, sending another burst of agony through him. He cursed, trying to grab her ankle, but it was gone. Instead, her fingers closed around his wrist and with a sudden, fierce strength, she jerked his arm up behind his back, at the same time as she kicked at the back of his leg.

He went down onto his knees for the second time that goddamn day, pain still ringing through his head, his wound throbbing, his arm held up behind him at an agonizing angle.

Holy fuck. Again? Really?

He could hear her breathing behind him, fast and hard, and the savage excitement that had hit him back in the living room when she'd had him down on his knees surged through him once more, overwhelming the pain.

Yes, *fuck* yes.

It might not be her memory returning, but certainly instinct had her in its grip now and he needed it to tighten its hold on her.

So he only waited long enough for the pressure on his arm to loosen slightly, then using his superior strength, he jerked it down, tearing her grip free of his wrist and twisting around.

She danced back, light on her feet. There was an intentness in her eyes that he hadn't seen before, examining him as if he were a mountain to climb or a castle to conquer.

Excitement beat hard inside him as the heel of her palm came up, ready to connect to his jaw. He ducked low, sweeping his arm out to hook around her waist and jerking her off balance. Then he kicked her ankle out from underneath her and brought her down hard onto the mat. She twisted like an eel, but he was faster, flipping her over onto her back, then coming down on top of her.

She struggled, trying to bring her legs up to kick him again, but he pushed his hips between her thighs, letting the weight of his lower body pin her. He held himself braced above her, his hands flat to the mat on either side of her head, ignoring the way she pushed at his shoulders and chest, at the way she wriggled and twisted beneath him.

Her movements were getting him hard, but he ignored that, too, concentrating instead on her face. A flush stained her cheeks, a spark glowing hot in her eyes.

A spark that looked a hell of a lot like fury.

"Get off me." Her voice had thickened, her hands coming to his shoulders and shoving hard. "Get the hell off!"

But he didn't move. Instead he bared his teeth, looking into her eyes, addressing the instinct he saw burning in them. "Make me."

She cursed and shoved at him again before angling her body, trying to bring her knee up so she could jam it against the gunshot wound in his thigh.

He kept still, allowing his lower body to press even harder against her, pinning her more firmly.

"Fuck you," she spat in a voice that sounded completely unlike hers, then shoved her elbow at his face.

He moved his head to the side, avoiding the elbow easily enough, fascinated by the fury that burned hot in her eyes.

Was that Faith? Or was that Joanna? And what exactly was she so angry about? Was it directed at him and the way he was holding her down? Or was it something else? Something more?

She tried the elbow move again, but he dodged it. Persistent, wasn't she?

"Who are you?" he demanded, studying the burning spark in her gaze, utterly mesmerized by it.

She panted, twisting yet again. "Get *off* me!"

"Tell me who you are."

A hand came up this time, the heel of her palm driving toward his face in another lightning fast and savage move. At the same time he felt her muscles tighten, her body gathering itself for yet another break for freedom.

He avoided her palm, letting the full weight of his lower body rest on her hips. She made a sound of frustration, arching her spine and trying to buck him off.

But he didn't move and eventually she stilled, panting beneath him, her face turned away so all he could see was the flushed curve of one cheek and the strands of inky black hair sticking to her forehead.

Then she turned back, looking up at him. The spark of fury that had been burning there before was gone, leaving nothing but blue shadows and darkness.

Unexpectedly, his chest tightened.

Her throat, pale and vulnerable, moved as she swallowed. And then she said, "I'm scared, Jacob."

CHAPTER 6

Admitting to Jacob Night that she was afraid was the very last thing in the world Faith wanted, but now that the words were out, there was nothing she could do to take them back.

But she meant it. She *was* scared.

Something had happened to her. He'd held her hands behind her back and told her to fight him. He'd called her *Joanna* and something had simply . . . taken over.

She'd moved without conscious thought, obeying an instinct she hadn't known was inside her. An instinct that had her shifting and twisting out of his grip, then going for the vulnerable places on his body without hesitation.

God, she'd kicked him in the leg, where the gunshot wound was, not thinking twice about how it would hurt. Knowing only that it was a good area to target to bring him down.

And she had brought him down. Onto his knees for the second time that day.

How the hell had she managed to do that?

This time he hadn't been content to sit there, jerking away before coming at her and forcing her to defend herself. She'd let

that instinct take over then too, feeling the part of her that was
Faith retreat to the back of her mind.

She hadn't paid attention to that part, too busy fighting him
instead, giving herself over to the instinct that had her struggling and trying to get away even when he'd brought her down
onto the mat on her back.

For some reason she'd been furious about that and she didn't
understand why. Whether it was because she'd been beaten or
what she didn't know, but everything had gone out of her head
the moment he'd demanded she tell him who she was, lost under the fear that had taken hold.

Because she didn't know who she was either.

He was braced above her now, studying her with such intensity that she wanted to roll over and hide from him. But he was
stretched out over her, his long, powerful body pinning hers to
the mat, and she couldn't move.

"What are you scared of, Ms. Beasley?" His voice was low
and deep, his eyes glittering like jet. "Is it of me? Because you
don't need to be. You acquitted yourself very well."

She was very conscious of the way he'd pinned her down, of
her thighs spread on either side of his lean hips, of his intense
heat. Lying beneath him was like lying beneath a furnace.

He'd braced himself on his hands, holding his upper body
away so his full weight wasn't resting on her. But even so, her
chest felt tight, like she couldn't take a proper breath.

"You asked me who I was." Her voice sounded weird, thick
and unlike herself. "Why did you ask me that?"

"Why?" He studied her. "Is that what made you afraid?"

She shifted under him, trying to find some breathing space
and failing. "Jacob . . . please move."

"Answer the question, Ms. Beasley. You told me you were
afraid. I want to know why."

God, he was *so* hot. The heat of his body was making it difficult to concentrate on anything at all let alone answering his

question. And there was so much of him. When he'd pulled her close and put her hands behind her back, her brain had shorted out at the feel of him against her. Actually, come to think of it, maybe that was why she'd let that instinct take over. Because it was easier than the reality of him right up close to her.

And now that reality was right up close again, his muscular shoulders blocking out the rest of the room, the black fabric of his T-shirt stretched across the hard expanse of his chest.

Her heartbeat thudded in her ears. She was conscious of his hips resting on hers, of a subtle, insistent pressure between her thighs. It made her face feel hot.

"You asked me who I was," she forced out, trying to keep it together, bringing her attention from the intoxicating heat of his body to the harsh lines of his compelling face. Not that that was any easier. "And yes, that frightened me. Because I didn't know the answer."

"Bullshit." The rough edge in his voice made her shiver inexplicably. "You know who you are, Ms. Beasley. I think you know exactly."

"No, I don't." She tried yet again to take a breath, but his smoky scent invaded her senses, making her feel dizzy. "And don't ask me how I managed to get free," she went on, dropping her gaze to his throat and the strong pulse that beat there, "or how I was able to get you in that armlock because I don't know. I just . . ."

"You let your instinct take over," he finished, the deep rumble of his voice vibrating in her chest and farther down, in her sex. "Your body remembers even if your mind refuses."

She swallowed, her mouth dry. It was getting difficult to focus on what he was saying and she couldn't seem to drag her gaze away from the smooth olive skin of his throat and the steady beat of his pulse.

"That doesn't make me feel any better," she murmured.

Oh God, he had to get off her. If he stayed there any longer, he was going to know what he was doing to her and she *really* didn't want him to know.

Yet the heat of him was insidious and she couldn't seem to ignore that or the aching pressure of his hips between her thighs. He wasn't pressing on anything too sensitive but all he'd have to do was shift a little and . . .

Her cheeks flamed, a burst of panic cutting through the heat. "Can you move, please?" She tried to keep her voice sounding normal. "I can't breathe."

He remained exactly where he was. "You can breathe. You've got plenty of room."

Goddamn man.

She wanted to shove at him, but that would mean putting her hands on his hard chest and something inside of her was telling her that would be a mistake.

So she kept her hands to herself, concentrated instead on his throat and that maddening pulse. "I know, but still. You've made your point."

"If you don't have your memory back then no, I haven't."

"Well, lying on me like this isn't going to help," she snapped, a spark of anger and frustration making her risk a glance up at him.

The expression on his face was intent, his gaze searing.

He knew what he was doing to her. God, he *knew.*

Sensation flashed the length of her spine as the pressure of his body changed and he shifted his hips, pressing down directly on her clit, making a gasp rise in her throat.

Faith choked it back, not wanting to give him any sign that what he was doing was having an effect. But that didn't stop the heat from scalding her cheeks or slow her rocketing heartbeat. Or prevent the restless movement of her own hips against his.

And he must have felt it, because a dark flame leapt in his eyes, burning hot. "You can get away from me easily enough. That is, if you want to."

Do you want to?

Stupid question. Of course she did. Yet the heat and the musky, smoky masculine scent of him were all around her and it was becoming difficult to think of why. Especially when it would be so easy to simply lie there and lift her hips, increase that maddening pressure on her clit. Find some release, some satisfaction.

How long had it been since she'd had an orgasm? She couldn't remember. Not since she'd gotten out of the hospital, that was for sure. Sex hadn't exactly been top of her list of things to do after all.

But now . . . It felt as if every second of those six months without physical pleasure was weighing on her like lead.

She struggled to get some air in her lungs, conscious of the way he was staring at her, so intently, like he could read every thought she had. The darkness of his eyes seemed to swallow all the light in the room.

"You appear to be having some problems, Ms. Beasley." The low, rough sound of his voice rolled over her like a stroking hand. "Anything I can do to help?" His hips shifted again, pressing more firmly against the sensitive place between her thighs, and she broke out into a sweat, a shudder coursing the length of her spine.

"What . . . what are you doing?" She couldn't hide the raw note in her voice.

"What do you think? I'm giving you some incentive to follow your instinct." He shifted once more, his biceps flexing as he lowered his upper body an inch or two, his chest almost brushing the increasingly sensitive tips of her breasts. "You can feel it, Ms. Beasley, I know you can. So stop thinking and take it."

Take it . . .

Did she want to take it? Was that the instinct he was talking about? She didn't know. She couldn't think.

It felt like she was coming down with a fever, the heat building inside her, making her pant. Making her conscious of nothing else but how hot she was and how badly she ached. How badly she wanted to touch that massive, muscular body stretched out above hers and rub herself against the hard ridge pressing between her thighs.

Was that . . . his cock?

She was looking up at him even though she'd told herself she shouldn't, staring straight into the hot darkness of his eyes. And he made no attempt to hide the hunger that burned there, letting her see it.

Yes, he wanted her and she could feel evidence of it in the exquisite pressure against her clit.

Perhaps it had been the fight. Perhaps that had excited him.

No "perhaps." And it excited you, too.

The thought blazed across her consciousness, bringing with it an echo of familiarity, as if somewhere, at some time, she'd fought another man and enjoyed it. A man who was as big and muscular as Jacob and maybe . . . but her mind shied away from the echo before she could nail it down, as if sensing something painful.

"What is it?" The question was sharp, his focus becoming even more intent. As if he knew she'd remembered something.

But she didn't want to talk about it, didn't even want to think it, so she lifted her hands and pressed her fingers to his chest, though whether to push him off or simply to distract him she didn't know.

Until she made contact and then everything became clear.

He felt hard, his skin hot beneath the cotton of his T-shirt, and she didn't want to take her hands away. So she didn't, spreading her fingers out and pressing her palms against his chest. The feel of him was intoxicating, making her breath catch and her heartbeat thunder in her ears.

"Ms. Beasley."

She curled her fingers, pulling at the fabric and watching it stretch across the sharply defined muscle beneath it. Then she let it go, pressing her palms against him once more, relishing the raw heat soaking through the cotton.

"Ms. Beasley," he said again, his voice sounding far away.

"What?" She curled her fingers once more, digging her nails into the cotton, testing his hardness.

"What are you doing?"

Yes, what are *you doing?*

Touching him. Oh God, she was touching him.

"I . . ." She was panting, barely able to speak, and she couldn't seem to drag her hands away from him.

"Don't stop." The words were a rough whisper, winding around her like a caress, inciting her. "Follow your instinct."

"I shouldn't," she said hoarsely, not even sure why she was saying it, not when touching him felt so good.

"Yes, you should." His impressive biceps flexed again as he lowered his upper body another half an inch, his chest now brushing against her hardened nipples, the look on his harsh, scarred face stealing all her breath. "Don't be afraid. Nothing will hurt you while I'm here."

Don't be afraid. . . .

She didn't know why the words echoed in her head or why it felt like he'd opened a door inside her. She only knew that she couldn't fight the desire that had her in its grip, a hunger she'd been denying for a long time now. A hunger that maybe didn't need to be denied anymore.

A sound escaped her, half a whimper, half a groan, and her hands were pulling at the fabric of his T-shirt, clawing it up so she could touch him. She felt starved, desperate. Like she'd been wanting to do this since the moment she'd seen him.

She shoved the fabric up under his arms, staring hungrily at the chiseled expanse of olive skin dusted with curling black hair. He had tattoos, military from the looks of it. An eagle and trident over his right pec—obviously, he'd been a SEAL at one point—and a snarling wolf with the Stars and Stripes behind it over his left. Curving black lines licked around the military designs, indicating the presence of some kind of intricate tat on his back, too.

Her hands shook as she touched him. His skin felt like oiled silk stretched over iron-hard muscle, and he was *so* hot.

A helpless groan escaped her as she spread her fingers and pressed her palms flat against his chest. He felt good, so impossibly good. She couldn't get enough.

There was a deep, hollow ache between her thighs and she shifted beneath him, responding automatically to it, angling her hips against the hardness of his cock, wanting more pressure, more friction.

He remained motionless above her, the expression on his face taut, his eyes hot coals, burning her alive.

"Move," she ordered hoarsely. "Move, please."

"No." He stayed maddeningly still. "You want it, you take it."

Frustrating bastard.

She didn't want to have to do this herself. She didn't want to have to make the choice. Yet it looked like he was going to give her no other option. She either took what she wanted or—

But no. There was no choice, not for her. The hunger inside her was too strong to be denied.

Faith slid her hands up his chest, scratching him with her nails before lifting her head and pressing her mouth to the base of his strong throat.

His flavor burst on her tongue, salt and male musk, and the steady beat of his pulse. God, he tasted delicious, rich and decadent, like the very best chocolate or the very finest wine. It went straight to her head and she couldn't get enough, licking him, tracing his collarbones with her tongue before moving higher, brushing his hard jaw with her mouth, his beard a sensual roughness against her lips.

Desperation was starting to take hold, her hunger deepening.

She clamped her thighs around his waist, lifting her hips, the pressure of his cock against her clit a jolt of pleasure that set alight every nerve ending she had.

Another groan escaped her and she arched her spine, unable to stop herself from rubbing her aching nipples against his chest, frustrated at the fabric that separated them.

"That's it." His voice was soft and impossibly deep, dark heat threaded through it, making her ache, making her burn. "Take what you need, sweet girl. Use me. Rub yourself all over me."

She barely heard, feverish and impatient and so desperate it was difficult to breathe. Clawing at the T-shirt she wore, she pulled it up, then shoved her bra up with it, baring her breasts, needing his skin on hers without any fabric between them.

The raw heat of his skin made her gasp, crisp hair brushing over her sensitive nipples. She turned her head into the side of his neck, licking and biting, wanting his taste in her mouth.

She gave no thought to control. There was nothing but heat and need, the burning desire to touch, to breathe him in, inhale everything about him.

"Jacob." His name was a frantic whisper as she put her arms around him, her hands on his back, sliding down his spine to the waistband of his pants. "Please . . . oh, *please* . . ."

But he wasn't moving, he just wasn't moving. So she shoved her hands beneath the fabric, finding the muscled curve of his ass, digging her nails in as she lifted her hips, rocking herself against the hard ridge of his cock, wanting *more*.

He made a sound, a rumble in his chest like a growl, and finally—thank *God*—he shifted, flexing his hips in a small movement that sent pleasure cascading through her, making her groan yet again.

She panted, her eyes drifting shut, moving against him, faster, harder. Aware of nothing but the pressure that was building inside her, the exquisite pleasure and frustration of it making her want to scream.

Her nipples ached, wanting to be touched, but all she could do was rub them against his bare chest, the heat of his skin scorching her.

He changed the angle of his movements, his hard cock grinding against her clit, and suddenly she was gasping and trembling all over.

She said his name again, wanting this to be over, wanting the delicious agony of it to end and yet not wanting it to, not ever. Because right here, right now, there was no black hole of memory, no chaos. And more importantly, no fear. There was only him, his big, rock-hard body anchoring her to the earth, a shield between her and the rest of the world, a place of safety.

That and the intense, blinding pleasure that scrubbed everything else from her mind.

She buried her hot face in his neck as the pressure released, raw ecstasy flooding through her, making her cry out in relief, tears prickling behind her eyes.

Only then did Jacob finally move. But not away from her.

Instead he lowered himself completely, covering her with his body, wrapping himself around her so she was contained, leaving her to sob in his arms, completely and utterly safe.

Just as he promised she'd be.

It took Jacob all the control he'd learned in his long years of military service not to push Faith onto her back, strip those far too big sweatpants from her body, spread her thighs, and drive himself deep inside her.

He managed it, but barely.

Six months of slow-building chemistry plus a few weeks of no sex had already set him on edge, and her running her hands all over him while rubbing her delicious tits all over his chest and her hot little pussy against his cock had nearly pushed him over it.

But he had a goal and fucking her wasn't it, no matter how badly he wanted to.

She had her face turned into his neck, her breath hot on his throat, and he could feel the hard press of her nipples against his chest.

His cock ached like a motherfucker, the wet heat of her sex soaking through the fabric of his pants, and he had to grit his teeth, fighting the urge to take his own pleasure in turn.

Christ, he had no idea why he'd incited her to use him to get herself off, which was a worry since he always—*always*—had a reason for the choices he made.

He'd been trying to get her to follow her instincts, thinking that maybe her own brain was stopping her from remembering what she needed to. At least, that's what he'd initially intended.

Until he'd become fascinated by the flush that had stained her cheeks and the way she'd kept shifting beneath him. Watching as her resistance to him became ragged, her control fraying, his cool Ms. Beasley transforming into a hot, sensual, hungry woman.

It was mesmerizing.

Plus it was also deeply satisfying to know that he could do this to her. That he could make her lose her mind without doing a thing. She'd been strong too, resisting him valiantly, only to lose out to her own hunger in the end.

He'd never had that happen with a woman before. He chose his lovers for their strength, because if there was no vulnerability, there was no way for them to be hurt. But it also meant they were never desperate for him, never helpless with desire.

And he hadn't realized how intoxicating that was until now.

You're forgetting one little thing. She might be your brother's lover.

Ah, Christ. He *had* forgotten. In which case, should he be feeling guilty about what had just happened between them? Possibly. Then again, guilt was something he'd long since ceased to feel about anything, and besides, it wasn't as if he was going to take this any further with Faith. She was a means to an end, nothing more.

What about her own guilt? When she remembers who she is . . .

Something pricked at him that he'd thought long dead: his conscience. Because what if she was indeed Joshua's lover? And what if she was in love with him? What would she think when her memory returned, knowing she'd done this with him?

What if she's only attracted to you because of your resemblance to Joshua?

That thought caught at him like a briar. He and Joshua were twins after all, and even if she didn't remember his brother, perhaps there was enough of an echo there to make her believe she was attracted to him too.

He didn't like that. *Really* didn't like it.

Another tremble shook her lithe body and he found himself holding her tighter, protectiveness stealing through him. He was a man who kept what was his and kept it safe, and even though Faith wasn't his and never would be, she was his protect right now.

Except there was no threat here, so why he felt the need to keep her safe was anyone's guess.

"You need to keep your promise," Faith murmured unexpectedly, soft and husky sounding.

For a second he didn't understand what she was talking about.

"What promise?"

"You said you'd answer some questions if I fought you."

Shit. That's right, he had. "You have to win, Ms. Beasley."

"I did win."

Jacob lifted his head, looking down at where she lay tucked beneath him. Her cheeks were flushed, her eyes a deep sapphire blue. Strands of ink-black hair were stuck to her forehead, the rest of it spread wildly across the mat they were both lying on.

She'd been lovely all buttoned up in her neat little suits, but now, with the effects of the orgasm he'd given her lighting her up from the inside . . .

It hit him hard that she was the most beautiful creature he'd ever seen.

"Yes," he said, conscious of the huskiness in his own voice. "So you did. For a couple of seconds at least."

Her long black silky lashes lowered, blue gleaming from beneath them, and he felt her hand slide between them, her fingers stroking over the front of his pants where he was hard and aching. "Well, unless there was . . . something else you wanted to do."

Electricity crackled over his skin, the ache in his cock becoming deeper, more insistent. Her touch was gentle and he couldn't figure out quite why that felt so good when rough was his preferred choice.

Perhaps it was because he hadn't had gentle in a long time. So long, he'd almost forgotten what it felt like.

There's a reason for that.

Yeah, there was. Gentle had no place in his life, not now, not ever.

"I think not," he said on a growl, and ignoring the disappointed pull of his body, he pushed himself off her and got to his feet.

Surprise and then a flash of hurt flickered across her lovely face. "What did I do?"

"Nothing."

Slowly she sat up. "So you don't want me to do anything for you?"

Jesus, he'd like nothing better. But he wasn't going to be touching her, not again.

"You might have been my brother's lover," he said, seeing no need to sugarcoat the truth. "And when your memory returns, that will matter to you."

Her mouth opened. Closed. Then she looked away. "Thanks for the reminder." She didn't sound particularly thankful. "I suppose I need to forget about this then."

"Yes, you should." Something that felt an awful lot like disappointment tightened in his chest. He ignored it. "It won't happen again."

She lifted a hand, brushing her hair back behind her ear, keeping her gaze averted. "Why did you do it?"

He didn't need to ask her what she was talking about. "You needed to learn to follow your instincts." It wasn't the whole truth but it was part of it. "A little less control in your life is good for you, Ms. Beasley."

"Right." She got to her feet. "And the questions you were going to answer? What about those?"

Ah, Christ, back to that. Not that he had anything to hide. He simply liked to keep his secrets close, his motivations unknown. Because once people knew what they were, that gave them power over you. And he would never be in anyone's power, not ever again.

Still, Ms. Faith Beasley was a woman without a memory and for six months she'd been supremely uninterested in knowing anything about him anyway. So he was pretty sure it wasn't power over him that she wanted. Besides, there wasn't much she could do with the information. Not when everything she had was what he'd chosen to give her.

She was in his power, not the other way around.

"I'll answer them, but perhaps not right now." He turned

toward the door. "I have a few things to do first." Distance, that's what he needed, not to mention some private time to work out the ache in his goddamn dick.

He was already partway to the door when she said quietly, "You can answer one now."

He came to a stop, but didn't turn. "Fine. One."

"What happened to your brother?"

Of course she would ask about Joshua. It was natural considering she was supposed to be sleeping with him, at least if Phillip Blake was correct.

But he hadn't talked about Joshua with another soul before and it took him a moment to find the words now. Yet he didn't consider not telling her. He'd made her a promise and he kept his promises.

"I lost him," he said, because it was his fault and always had been. "When we were children. We were separated into different foster families. I haven't seen him since I was ten years old."

There was a short, shocked silence.

Then she said, "How could they separate you? I thought they tried to keep siblings together."

"Social services were told we were trouble together. That we should be fostered separately." And all because of that prick Greg, Rebecca's new husband. He was the one who'd told social services that they should be separated, because Jacob had used a knife against him trying to protect Joshua.

One of the greatest disappointments in Jacob's life had been tracking Greg down years later only to find out that he'd died of cancer a couple of months earlier.

Though maybe that had been a good thing. Being tried for murder would have made things difficult.

But she didn't need to know that, just like she didn't need to know the details of why Jacob had taken a knife to his foster mother's new husband. That wasn't his story to tell.

Apart from any of that, it wasn't something he wanted to

think about, just like he didn't want to think about anything from that part of his life. Where slowly but surely he'd lost everything he'd ever loved and everyone who'd ever loved him.

The last thing he'd lost being his brother.

These days, he kept himself to himself, giving nothing, taking nothing. It was easier. Simpler.

"Oh." Her voice was soft. "That must have been difficult."

"Yes." He turned to face her, not letting the sympathy in her eyes touch him. "Was there anything else?"

"No. I—" She broke off, glancing down at his body, frowning. "Wait. Is that blood?"

He looked down too. There was a dark stain on his thigh, where the gunshot wound was. Shit, that's where she'd kicked him. The stitches were still fresh so no wonder it was bleeding.

"Oh my God." Faith took a step toward him. "I'm sorry, that was my fault. Let me—"

"No need," he interrupted, irritated and mostly at himself, because it wasn't her fault, it was his. "I'll deal with it."

He was the one who'd suggested the fight in the first place and that was what had led to her kicking him and him pinning her on the ground. Where he'd watched her come apart beneath him . . .

You knew that would happen. Why else did you suggest a fight? When you know how much it excites you?

"Jacob, please." The cool, controlled Faith was back. "Don't get all tiresomely alpha on me now."

Jacob shoved the insidious whisper of his brain away. "If I wanted a nurse, Ms. Beasley, I would have hired one." He turned toward the door. "Go and find yourself something else to manage. Currently I'm off-limits."

Then he walked out before she could reply.

CHAPTER 7

Faith slept better that night than she had in months.

Jacob had told her she could have the room with the en suite bathroom and she hadn't argued, curling up in the big bed and falling asleep right away. And miracle of miracles she didn't have any nightmares.

Maybe it was the effects of the orgasm or maybe it was simply that she'd been exhausted by the time she'd gotten into bed, whatever, the next morning she woke up feeling good.

At least until the memories of the previous day filtered into her consciousness.

People trying to kill her. Taken in a jet to an isolated run-down castle. Finding out her real name. Fighting Jacob.

Rubbing herself all over Jacob . . .

She turned her head into her pillow, searching for a cool spot as a wave of heat flooded through her.

What the hell had she been thinking? She hadn't been thinking, that was the problem. She'd been pinned beneath that hard, hot body of his and had simply gotten overcome by desire.

Not good. Not good at all. Especially when afterward she'd

touched him, wanting to give him a little of what he'd given her and yet he'd refused her.

And with good reason if she had in fact been his brother's lover.

Slowly Faith turned over and stared at the ceiling.

Jacob had told her what had happened between them would matter once her memory was recovered and she supposed he was right. If she was someone else's lover, then technically she'd just been unfaithful.

Except it hadn't felt wrong yesterday. Yes, there had been faint echoes, like a trip wire being tripped, prompting vague shadows of memory, but nothing concrete.

Mainly it had just felt *so* good and it had hurt when he'd denied her, when he'd told her it wouldn't happen again. It made sense, but . . . She had no memory of making love to anyone, no memory of anyone touching her. No memory of feeling anything for anyone but Jacob. And those faint echoes of familiarity had simply made it all feel even better somehow, safer. More right.

But it's not. In which case it's just another reason you need to remember.

Icy fear wound through her.

Remembering would change things. Change her feelings. Change herself. It would turn her into someone else, turn all the pleasure she'd taken with Jacob into something guilty and wrong.

She didn't want that. For six months she'd had nothing but fear and uncertainty, and yesterday, for a little while, she hadn't felt either. She'd only felt good and quite frankly she wanted more of that, not less.

Pity Jacob didn't feel the same.

The thought of him was a hot current, melting the fear, making her skin feel sensitive and setting up an ache between her thighs. But there wasn't any point in wishing for more. He'd made his position clear and she couldn't blame him. He had all his memories and a clear loyalty to the brother he hadn't seen in years.

She'd probably make the same decision if she'd been in his shoes.

Restless, she pushed back the covers and slipped out of bed, searching for the clothes she'd been wearing yesterday only to find them gone, a black leather bag sitting on top of the dresser instead.

She recognized that bag. It was hers. From the home she shared with Jacob in San Diego. Well, he'd promised her that Callie would get her some of her own things and she was ridiculously pleased that they were here.

She would have texted Callie to thank her but sadly Jacob had gotten rid of her phone to prevent anyone tracking them, so she couldn't.

Moving over to the dresser, she pulled open the bag, digging through a pile of clothing to find her favorite lavender bath gel right at the bottom, plus a few other toiletries and feminine necessities.

The clothing consisted of underwear and a couple of pairs of yoga pants, plus T-shirts and a sweater or two. None of her skirts, jackets, or blouses had made it into the bag and she supposed that was intentional.

It wasn't like she'd be going to any meetings out here.

Then again, not having her usual clothes made her feel uneasy. Yes, they had become a bit of a shield for her, but they also grounded her. Made her surer of her own identity.

They're not Joanna's clothes.

The breath went out of her. She had no idea how she knew that Joanna wouldn't be seen dead in the clothes that Faith wore, she just did. She knew it with certainty.

Her heartbeat thudded and she went still, the fear returning. Was this it? Was this how it would start? Would little bits and pieces of Joanna come back to her like a jigsaw puzzle slowly assembling itself? Or would it all happen at once, like being struck by lightning? Would Faith simply cease to exist one minute and she'd be Joanna the next?

Slowly she made herself move, reaching into the bag and pulling out the clothes. Finding the bath gel and carrying it into the bathroom.

Perhaps if she didn't think so much, everything would be okay. There were no memories battering at the door of her consciousness now so maybe she needed to go with it, be in the moment like her psychologist had suggested.

She had a shower, the feel of the water on her skin grounding her, the familiar scent of lavender calming. Then once she was done, she dressed in a pair of plain black yoga pants and a dark blue T-shirt, before making her way out into the living area.

It was empty.

She didn't know what the time was, but judging from the morning sun coming through the windows, it wasn't much before nine.

Moving through into the kitchen, she found a covered plate on the counter with fried bacon and toast on it, both still warm, a mug of coffee steaming gently to one side.

She smiled.

Last night Jacob had made dinner too, surprising her with a simple meal of steak and salad that had tasted absolutely delicious. She hadn't realized he could cook, but then since he could fly a jet and stitch up his own wounds, that really shouldn't have been so surprising.

They hadn't talked about anything of note and she'd been happy with that. She had questions—so many questions—but she'd been exhausted and not in the mood to push him about them.

He'd been distant, eating with her, then disappearing off God only knew where, leaving her to spend her evening by herself. She'd been happy with that too, deciding that going to bed was the best idea.

Now, she picked up a piece of bacon and crunched on it, wondering whether to go find him, see if there was any update on the people after her.

Or maybe just to see him.

She swallowed the bacon, then picked up the mug of coffee, letting it warm her fingers. Okay, yes, she had to admit that to herself. She wanted to see him.

Taking a piece of toast with her, along with her coffee mug, she left the kitchen and moved along the short corridor to the room with all the computers in it to see if he was in there.

Sure enough, he was sitting at the desk, his gaze intent on the computer screen in front of him, fingers moving lightly over the keyboard.

"Good morning, Ms. Beasley," he said without looking up. "You slept well?"

"I did, thanks." Faith leaned against the doorframe and took a bite of her toast.

"No nightmares, I take it?"

She chewed, then swallowed her mouthful. "Oddly enough, no. Thanks for breakfast."

"My pleasure."

"And for the clothes. When did they arrive?"

"Late last night. Mr. Blake dropped them off."

She blinked in surprise. "How?"

"He flies helicopters. You remember that, don't you?"

"Oh, right. Of course. So he flew all the way up here purely to drop off some clothes for me?"

"Yes." Jacob's attention remained on the screen. "Because I told him to and he follows orders."

"I thought you didn't want anyone to know where we were?"

He sat back in his seat and flicked her a glance, his gaze unreadable. And even though she'd braced herself for it, she still felt the impact of his stare lance through her.

He was wearing pretty much what he'd worn yesterday, nothing special, black T-shirt and black pants. Though presumably these were fresh since there was no bloodstain on his thigh the way there had been the day before. But he looked just as damn hot. Just as damn compelling. All darkness, rough heat, and hard-packed muscle.

She remembered how his chest had felt beneath her fingertips, and how hot his body had been. How delicious the pressure of his cock between her thighs . . .

"I don't," he was saying. "But Mr. Blake is a trusted member of my team. And besides, you needed your things."

Her skin felt scorched and she had to look away from him, not wanting him to know that what she'd felt yesterday was still there. And that she was so hungry for more she could barely pay attention to what he was saying.

"Thank you." She tried to sound normal, hoping she'd succeeded. "I appreciate it."

"Are you worried about Mr. Blake?"

She attempted to get her brain back on track, forcing herself to meet his dense black stare. "No, of course not."

"Good. You shouldn't be. He's loyal."

A memory hit her all of a sudden, of the tattoo on his chest, the eagle and trident.

"You were a SEAL." It wasn't a question. "Like Kellan."

If the comment surprised him, he didn't show it. "Yes. Once."

"But . . . ?"

"Is that another question for me, Ms. Beasley?"

There was a challenging glint in the look he gave her, though she didn't understand why.

"Yes," she said, and this time she didn't look away. "You

owe me, don't you think? Or am I going to have to fight you again?"

A flame lit briefly in his eyes, as if he liked the sound of that very much indeed.

You do too.

Maybe she did, though she wouldn't. She couldn't risk it. Not getting too close to him and certainly not doing anything that might prompt Joanna to take over again.

Jacob swiveled the chair to face her, stretching his long legs out. "Don't you want to know any updates on your situation?"

"It depends. Are there any updates?" She made an effort to lift her coffee mug to her mouth and take a measured sip, struggling against the urge to tell him she didn't want to know.

"Sabrina got a lead on a suspicious-looking car from the security cameras that were in the area. A local rental from the looks of things, but she hacked into their database and found the name of the person who rented it."

Faith stilled. "Oh?"

"It's a name I don't know, but I'm running it by some contacts right now." His look turned measuring. "Michael Campbell. Ring any bells?"

Much to her relief, there were no echoes inside her, none at all.

She shook her head. "Doesn't sound familiar."

"It's unlikely to be his real name anyway." He glanced back at the bank of computer screens. "Mr. Blake also handled Mr. Thomas's untimely death to put the police off the scent."

"Mr. Thomas?" She frowned, then remembered. "Oh, your driver."

"Yes."

A thread of guilt wound through her. She hadn't known the man—Jacob had only employed him a few weeks before—but he'd still died.

Because of you.

The guilt wound tighter, bringing with it the cold edge of fear. A reminder that this wasn't simply a game of car chases and fake identities. Lives were at stake. Her life and those of the people around her.

"I'm sorry." It was trite and ridiculously ineffectual, but it was all she could think of to say.

"I'm sorry too. I've instructed Mr. Blake to make arrangements for his family. They'll be well taken care of."

She took another sip of coffee to ease the tangle of feelings inside her, the hot liquid burning as she swallowed it down. "So what do we do now? Wait?"

He looked at her, something hard and uncompromising in his face. "No. Now we try to get your memory back."

Faith ignored the shiver that went through her. "These things don't happen just because you want them to."

"I realize that. But there are steps we can take to encourage things."

The chill settling over her deepened. Turning, she placed her coffee mug down on the shelf closest to the door, along with her piece of toast, the movements calming her.

Then she turned back to him. "Such as?"

He tilted his head, watching her. "Did you know that my brother and I are twins?"

Something flickered in the back of her head, a kind of shock.

Jacob had always felt familiar to her and what if that familiarity was because he reminded her of someone? His twin brother, for instance.

She stared at his strong jaw and high forehead, the blade of his nose, his deep-set eyes. It was strange to think that this charismatic face had a twin somewhere, because it didn't seem possible. Jacob Night was one of a kind. Yet, searching it now . . .

"That's not a surprise to you," he said very quietly. And it wasn't a question.

"I . . ." She stopped, unable to deny it because no, it didn't feel like a surprise to her at all.

Quite suddenly, Jacob pushed himself out of his chair, unfolding to his full height, which had to be well over six-two, then came toward her, closing the distance between them in seconds.

She froze, her heartbeat thudding, every muscle in her body drawing tight in what felt horribly like anticipation.

He came to a stop in front of her, the intentness in his gaze making her breath catch. "You knew, didn't you? How did you know, Ms. Beasley?"

"I didn't," she said thickly. "It's just . . ."

"It's just what?" He put his hands on the doorframe above her head and leaned down so his eyes were inches from hers, his powerful, muscular body leaning over her. "Tell me what you remember."

Faith had gone very still.

She knew something, he was certain. The moment he'd mentioned that he and Joshua were twins, he'd seen recognition flicker in her gaze and he'd gotten up from the chair and gone over to her before he'd even realized what he was doing.

Dimly, he knew getting close to her was probably a mistake, but this was too important to let go. If something had been triggered in her memory, then he had to know.

"I don't remember anything." Her lashes fell, veiling her gaze. "It's more that you were familiar to me. I wasn't surprised when you said you were my cousin because . . . I felt that I knew you somehow."

He reached out, gripped her chin, and turned her face up to him, wanting to see her eyes, wanting to see the truth. "What kind of familiar are we talking about here?"

She stiffened but didn't pull away. "I can't put my finger on it exactly. It was like . . . I had met you before. Even though I had no memory of it."

Her skin was soft beneath his fingers and she was very warm. He could smell lavender, too, which must have meant that Callie had put the shower gel she liked into that bag of belongings.

Christ, he should not be thinking about how she felt or how she smelled. He'd already decided he wasn't going to touch her.

And yet you've got her chin in your hand. What the fuck are you doing?

He felt a muscle leap in his jaw. Perhaps getting this close was a bad idea, but still, he wasn't a fucking teenage boy. He could get close to a woman without ripping her clothes off. Hell, he'd managed to do it for six months so far, including how he kept his hands to himself while she rubbed herself all over him yesterday.

It might even be a good thing. Maybe proximity would prompt a memory for her.

Yes, of your brother. You okay with that?

Why wouldn't he be okay with it? As he'd told himself yesterday, she wasn't his. He had no claim on her. Finding Joshua had consumed him for years and now he was so close . . .

Fuck, he'd try anything.

She was the only link he had and for six months he'd taken the softly, softly approach, hoping that given time and space her memory would return. But it hadn't. And now that time was running out.

Excellent justification you've got there.

Jacob ignored the thought and firmed his grip on Faith's delicate chin. "You'd met my brother," he said flatly. "That's why. You were his lover so no wonder I felt familiar to you."

The color of her eyes had darkened into a deep midnight and stiffness had bled out of her. She was looking at him now as if she was searching for something—perhaps to try to see Joshua in him?

He found he didn't like that thought, which was strange

since didn't he want her to? That was how she'd potentially remember after all.

"I suppose that's true." A crack ran through her voice. "And when I look at you, what I'm seeing is him. That's why you felt safe to me even though I had no idea who you were."

Safe? She'd felt safe with him?

He didn't know why that hit him the way it did, hard in the chest. Or why the thought of her looking at him and seeing Joshua made something inside him twist.

He ignored both sensations. The focus had to remain on her memory, not whatever the hell bullshit feelings he was having about it.

"What else," he demanded. "What other things did you feel around me?"

She flushed. "I'm sure you know one of them already."

Ah, yes, their physical attraction.

"You want me," he said, naming it.

Her flush deepened. "Yes."

"Because of Joshua."

She blinked. "That's his name?"

He studied her, watching the shadows in her eyes shift, watching for anything that looked like recognition. But there was none. "It is. At least, that's what he was called when we were kids. Like I told you, I suspect the name he uses now is Smith."

"Joshua doesn't . . . sound familiar." She was searching his face now as if she was looking for someone. Someone who wasn't him.

He didn't like it.

Jacob dropped his hand from her chin and before he quite understood what he was doing, it had settled around her throat.

Faith's eyes widened and her breath caught. She stiffened.

He could feel the beat of her pulse against his palm, her skin like silk.

It was fine to touch her. A test. A prompt to jog her memory, that's all. Joshua would have touched her like this and maybe if he did, too, with his resemblance to his brother, she might remember something.

You fucking idiot. That's not why you're touching her.

Anger shifted inside him, formless, a constant flame that never went out. Rage for everything he'd lost, furious at the world for taking what it had from him and leaving him with nothing.

Even this chemistry with Faith was nothing. It was based completely on her memories of another man—his own fucking brother, for God's sake.

She didn't want *him*.

Why should that matter to you?

No, it shouldn't matter to him. At all.

Yet he didn't remove his hand.

She said nothing and he could feel her pulse getting faster and faster. Her delicate face was pink and her pupils had dilated, making her eyes look almost black.

"It's for him, isn't it?" His voice had lowered into a growl and he couldn't seem to stop it. "What you're feeling right now. It's all for him."

"I . . . don't know." She swallowed and he felt the movement of her throat against his palm, making him want to tighten his grip a little, impress the warmth of her into his skin. "I can't remember him."

"It is." He didn't know why he was so insistent. "You can't remember how to fight, but you did."

She leaned her head back against the doorframe, looking up at him, the expression in her eyes searching. "Does it matter?"

His fingers flexed against her throat, reminding her of who he was. "Of course it fucking matters. Especially if I'm going to help you remember."

"What's that got to do with it?" There was an edge in her

voice this time. "No, wait, I think I understand. You think your getting close to me will remind me of him? Prompt a memory?"

Smart woman.

He stepped even closer to prove his point, stroking his thumb up and down the soft skin on the side of her neck. "Naturally. Why else would I be doing this?"

Her gaze hid nothing. "I don't remember anything, Jacob. And I didn't yesterday, either, and you were *very* close then. So why would today make any difference?"

The delicate scent of lavender filled the space between them, goose bumps rising on her skin where he touched her. Was that him? Or was that Joshua?

His anger twisted and coiled like a cut snake, made even worse by the fact that he didn't understand what exactly was making him so annoyed.

You want her but she wants your brother, that's why you're annoyed. You want it to be you.

Why the fuck should that matter? When the only important thing was getting her memory back?

He tried to ignore the anger, baring his teeth in an approximation of a smile. "Perhaps we didn't try hard enough."

"We?" There was a glint in her eyes, a hint of challenge. "You're assuming I'm okay with this."

Christ, he liked the fight in her, the way she questioned him. He thought it was probably her true identity bleeding through, glimpses of Joanna Lynn, the badass woman who'd fought him yesterday.

It turned him on, got him hard. Which meant that pursuing this was a bad idea. Then again, if it helped her remember, then he'd be stupid not to keep going. Fighting didn't only mean beating someone up or trying to kill them. A struggle for dominance could include pleasure as well.

"You were okay with it yesterday." He stroked the side of her neck again, enjoying her shiver of response much more than he should have. "Besides, you want me. You told me so yourself."

"Do I?" The challenge in her gaze was much more than a hint now, the hard note of it in her voice. "How would you know? Because I certainly don't. Maybe it's your brother I want after all."

Emotion glowed blue and hot in her eyes. Anger.

She'd been angry with him yesterday, too, as he'd gotten her on the ground and held her down. Why? Was it the warrior in her not liking to be bested? Yet they weren't fighting now and she could easily get away from him. So what was the issue?

"You're pissed with me," he said. "Is it not wanting to remember? Because if it is, we've had that discussion."

"It's not that," she snapped. "My objection is your using my desire for you to essentially reboot my brain."

He frowned, not understanding. "Why should that make any difference?"

Another expression flickered across her face, gone too quickly for him to work out what it was. "Because it does." Her voice had gotten cool, but the look in her eyes hadn't. "I have no memory of being with anyone, Jacob. I have no memory of making love at all. I mean, I know I must have at some stage and if it's true about your brother, then yes, I must have been to bed with him. But right now . . . well . . ." She flushed. "I might as well be a virgin again. And that . . . matters. It just does."

He hadn't thought of it like that. He'd assumed it wouldn't be that much of a big deal.

Really? After yesterday? When she tried so hard to hide what being close to you was doing to her?

He gritted his teeth. Okay, so he got it. But this was more important than her feelings. This was about recovering her memory and possibly finding out which bastards were sent to kill her, not to mention locating Joshua. And he couldn't afford to let something as irrelevant as emotions get in the way of saving her life or finding his brother. Also, there was no forgetting the fact that his driver had got caught in the crossfire, and he didn't want that to happen to anyone else.

"We need your memories, Ms. Beasley," he said. "You know that."

"Yes, I do know that." The challenge in her eyes had returned but there was something beneath it. Something vulnerable. "You want my memories, but do you want me?"

"What are you talking about?"

"I wasn't lying when I said I wanted you, Jacob. There's no memory of anyone else, not even an echo. Right now, in my mind, there's only you." Unexpectedly, she lifted a hand and touched his cheek, her delicate fingertips resting on his skin, burning like embers. "And I want you to want me back."

Her honesty was a punch to the gut, hooking into something inside him. The hungry, possessive part of him that he tried to lock down as much as he could.

He'd never wanted anyone in his life, because he knew himself too well. After the kind of childhood he'd had, anything that became his stayed his, and that included people. *Especially* people.

And people generally didn't like to be kept.

He couldn't afford for Ms. Faith Beasley to become his and certainly not if she was his brother's.

Yet . . . the way she was looking at him, so direct, so honest. Hiding nothing. He'd spent six months looking after her, taking care of her, and the thought of denying her something as simple as an admission of a desire he already felt seemed . . . churlish.

After all, desire wasn't anything more than desire. And he had to admit, he was caveman enough that he liked that she remembered nothing about any other man. That all there was in her head was him.

Even if these feelings she had for him were prompted by his

brother, she wasn't thinking of Joshua. She wasn't remembering Joshua. Or anyone else for that matter.

If he touched her that's what she'd remember. Him and *only* him.

Unless she gets her memories back.

There was that. But there was only one way to test that theory.

He pressed his fingers to the satiny skin of her neck, firming his grip, meeting her gaze, letting her see the hunger in his. "And if I did want you back? What then, Ms. Beasley?"

Her eyes darkened, her fingers trailing down the side of his face, down to his jaw, a caress that had his breath catching. "Then I think you should kiss me, Mr. Night."

He didn't need to be told twice. Her mouth was right there, full and red, and he'd been wanting to kiss it for months now.

So he bent his head and brushed his lips over hers.

It was only supposed to be a test. A small taste to see what would happen.

But she gave a soft, helpless moan, and at the sound all the frustrated desire of the day before returned suddenly and full force, wrapping its fingers around his throat, choking him. Setting alight a fire inside him that burned white hot.

Her scent, the feel of her skin. The softness of her mouth opening under his, letting him in as if his kiss had been what she'd been waiting for years for.

As if it truly was him turning Ms. Cool and Controlled Faith Beasley inside out with desire.

The deep satisfaction that filled him in that moment should have made him pull back, because this wasn't meant to be personal. This wasn't supposed to mean anything at all.

But she'd lifted both hands to his face, cupping his jaw, and he could feel her fingertips trembling against his skin. Pulling away would hurt her and that's not what he wanted to do.

So he didn't pull back.

Instead he gave her what she wanted, slowly beginning to explore the sweet heat of her mouth, tasting her and gently coaxing her to taste him in return. She gave another of those soft moans in the back of her throat, kissing him back at first tentatively then, as he encouraged her to kiss him deeper, with more desperation.

There was no finesse to her kiss but somehow that only made it more erotic, his cock hardening painfully, demand rising inside him. Wanting more of her. Wanting her surrender.

He spread his fingers out on her throat, slid his hand down so his fingertips traced the fragile dips and hollows of her collarbones.

Such vulnerability and yet such strength. She was a woman of so many contrasts and mysteries, and she tasted like them too, sweetness with a dark edge that made his own darkness want to roar.

He took the kiss deeper, not meaning to, yet unable to help himself, demanding more and getting it as her head fell back to allow him greater access. Her hands moved from his jaw and up, her arms winding around his neck, her body arching into his.

This was only supposed to be about getting her memory back, about giving her something that she'd asked for, but it was difficult to remember that when the heat of her mouth and the delicate press of her body were making him want things he shouldn't.

She'd asked him for a kiss, that was all. And he'd given it to her.

But now he couldn't stop.

He wanted more than that. He wanted her under him the way she'd been yesterday, except with nothing between them this time but skin. He wanted her naked and wet for him, panting his name. Desperate for his cock. Desperate for anything he'd give her.

Because no one had ever been desperate for him like this.

He'd never let anyone get close enough to be desperate. He kept everyone at a distance, kept himself a stranger, a mystery, and he preferred it that way.

It was an isolated kind of existence, but he didn't let himself want anything more, because losing it was way too easy.

But then Faith had turned up in that hospital and he'd taken her home, cared for her. Let her into his life—at least to a limited extent. She knew him better than anyone ever had and now she wanted him too . . .

He'd never thought that would be such an aphrodisiac. But it was. It just fucking was.

He broke off the kiss, ignoring her soft cry of protest. Then gently he shoved her up against the doorframe and pinned her there.

She gave a sharp intake of breath, her eyes widening as she stared up at him. Her gaze was hot and full of hunger.

That made him even harder.

He kept one hand around her throat, the other on the doorframe above her head then, slowly, pushed his thigh between hers, watching her face as he did so.

She gave a little groan, her legs opening, letting him push the muscle of his thigh right up between them until he was pressing against her pussy. She wore yoga pants, the thin fabric doing nothing to stop the heat he could feel soaking into him.

Fuck, it felt good.

Her eyes glowed brighter and she lifted her hands to his chest, spreading her fingers out over his T-shirt and pushing lightly at him. Testing him.

The pressure was delicious and he was very tempted to strip his T-shirt off and let her touch him skin to skin. But no, not yet. He wanted more of her hunger for him first. He wanted to drive her into a goddamn frenzy.

He'd needed her for six months, needed her memories, all the while taunted by the chemistry that burned between them. He'd controlled it ruthlessly because he'd needed her trust more than anything else, but it had taken its toll even if he hadn't truly admitted it to himself. Now control seemed irrelevant, especially since she was burning too. And holy shit, it was intoxicating to see her want him as badly as she did. To need him. To see her usual self-containment break apart under the pressure of her desire.

He wanted more of that, so much more.

She angled her hips, trying to push against him, her breathing getting faster.

Demanding, wasn't she?

He let the hand around her throat drift down her body, his fingertips trailing over the curve of her breasts, brushing the button-hard tips of her nipples and making her gasp, but not lingering. Tantalizing her. Then he let his fingers trail lower, over the flat plane of her stomach, and farther down, to where his thigh was pushing between hers.

She shuddered as he eased his hand into the tight gap, until he was cupping her pussy though the fabric of her pants, the damp heat burning against his palm.

Her mouth opened and her pupils dilated, her breath catching audibly.

"Who are you thinking of, Ms. Beasley?" He stared into her eyes, not hiding the rough sound of his voice. "Tell me who you're thinking of right now."

"You." There was no hesitation and the way she was looking at him . . . as if nothing else existed for her but him. "I'm thinking of you."

"No one else?" He shifted his thumb, pressing lightly over her clit. "No glimmers of memory?"

"No." She took a ragged breath, her hips lifting against his hand. "N-nothing."

"Hmmm." He moved his thumb, tracing a light circle around

the hard bud he could feel beneath the damp fabric, watching pleasure unfurl across her lovely face. "What about now?"

She gave her head a shake, arching her spine restlessly against the wood of the doorframe, trying to move against his thumb. The material where his hand pressed was wet, the delicate musky scent of her arousal filling the air between them.

He fucking loved it. Loved how she panted and twisted and moved, wanting more of his touch. More of him.

It made him feel savage. Made him want to draw this out, push her higher. Make her beg the way she had the day before.

He rubbed his thumb across her clit back and forth, relishing the way she groaned. How her head fell back against the frame, her lashes falling with it, her fingers curling in the fabric of his T-shirt and gripping on tight.

"J-Jacob . . ." Her voice was thick and he loved the slight stutter as she said his name too. "What are you d-doing?"

"What does it look like?" He leaned down even farther so her face was inches from his, so he could study the fine grain of her skin, all pink with the pleasure he was giving her, and see the glint of blue beneath her black lashes. "I'm going to make you come, Ms. Beasley."

And he stroked her again, moving his thumb rhythmically, unable to tear his gaze from her face.

"Look at me," he ordered roughly, wanting that midnight gaze on his when it happened, wanting to see it burn with ecstasy. "Look at me *now*."

Her lashes lifted as if she'd been waiting for his command. And as he pressed his thumb down on her clit, curling his fingers against the soft heat of her pussy, the look in her eyes began to ignite.

It was one of the most erotic things he'd ever seen.

She gripped his T-shirt even harder, pulling on it as her hips shifted against his thumb, against his hand. And she trembled and gasped, and then cried out as he increased the pressure on her stiff little clit.

"Harder," she said raggedly. "Faster. I need m-more."

He smiled, the demand in her voice making everything that much sweeter. "You're very bossy when you're about to come, Ms. Beasley." He bent and brushed her hungry mouth with his, purely to tease her. "I like it."

She tried to kiss him back, giving a frustrated moan when he pulled away, not giving her what she wanted. Not yet.

"And you're a b-bastard." She panted, twisting the fabric of his shirt in her hands. "P-please . . ."

"Since you asked so nicely." He slid his hand beneath the waistband of her yoga pants.

She went still as his fingers touched the smooth, hot skin of her stomach, her breathing ragged, then began to tremble as he pushed his fingers farther, under the lace of her panties, finding wetness and heat and soft, damp curls.

Jesus, she felt good.

Her eyes went huge and dark as he stroked through her slick folds, caressing and exploring a little before he eased a finger inside her.

"Oh . . ."

The sound she made was husky, throaty as he slid his finger deeper, and he felt her tremble. She was so wet, so hot, her inner muscles clamping down hard on him. Tight too, so very, very tight.

She had no memory of any other man touching her like this; to her, he would be the first. And he liked that. No, he fucking *loved* that.

Possessiveness clenched hard inside him.

"Is this mine?" he demanded. "Is this wet little pussy all for me?"

Faith's chest heaved, her breasts pushing against the fabric of her T-shirt, the hard outlines of her nipples visible. "Y-yes . . ."

"No one else's." He slowly eased another finger inside her, stretching her gently. "Only mine."

She gasped, lifting her hips, trembling. "Yes."

"Say it," he ordered. "Say it, Faith."

But at the sound of her name she jerked, her pussy convulsing around his fingers, and whatever she'd been going to say was lost in her desperate cry of release.

So he covered her mouth and took what he wanted anyway.

CHAPTER 8

Faith could barely stand, the after-effects of the orgasm sweeping through her making it difficult to concentrate on anything as mundane as standing. Only Jacob's hard thigh kept her upright along with the big, hot hand that lingered between her legs, his fingers still buried inside her.

She panted through the aftershocks that pulsed in time with the beat of her heart, the intense pleasure making her feel boneless and heavy.

She didn't want to move. In fact, she didn't think it was possible for her to ever move again.

Jacob had lifted his mouth from hers and was looking down at her, eyes glittering, the intent expression on his brutally handsome face sending shivers up and down her spine.

He'd never looked at her that way before, not with such open hunger, and it left her breathless.

Being honest with him and telling him that she'd wanted him to want her back had been a risk, but it was one she was glad she'd taken. So *very* glad.

Because then he'd crowded her against the doorframe with his big, hard, delicious body and turned the kiss she'd asked for into a touch that had set her on fire. The feel of his fingers pushing inside her had made her come almost immediately and shockingly hard.

She'd told him the truth when he'd demanded to know whom she'd been thinking about. There had been no glimmers of anyone else, no echoes of memory. As far as she was concerned the hot kiss he'd given her had been her first, just like the touch of his fingers between her thighs.

And then there had been his sudden burst of possessiveness. *Only mine . . . Say it, Faith.*

Her name. He'd never said it before and the sound of it in his rough, deep voice had sent her over the edge almost before she was ready.

That and the demand with which he'd said it.

He was possessive with things he viewed as his, he'd just never gotten possessive with her. And the fact that he had . . . well . . .

That means you're his, doesn't it?

The thought made her shiver all over.

He was such a mystery, a black-eyed enigma who'd held himself separate from her for a long time and now that he'd purposely closed the distance between them—very, *very* purposely—it was as if he'd handed her the keys to the kingdom.

She had no idea what this would mean or where it would lead, but she didn't much care. He'd been her anchor in the frightening days after she'd come out of the hospital, had provided her with a calm, safe space, had allowed herself to find an identity.

She trusted him. And perhaps that was simply an echo from his brother and perhaps it wasn't, but it was Jacob whom she was with now. Jacob who was kissing her, touching her.

Jacob and no one else.

His fingers inside her shifted, pulling out slowly. Then he lifted that hand in front of her face.

"Look," he said in a low, rough voice. "See how wet I made you."

His skin glistened and she went hot all over.

Then before she could say a word he licked his fingers.

The rawness, the sheer dirtiness of watching his tongue lick her moisture from his skin had the breath catching in her throat. She couldn't take her eyes off him.

He made a deep, very male sound that caused yet more heat to wash over her. "Delicious." His voice was a purr. "I've had breakfast and yet now I'm starving." He dropped his hand and then leaned in again, pinning her with his dark gaze and his hard body. Pinning her with the desire she felt building inside her once more, making her acutely aware of how hollow she felt, how empty.

"What do you think I should do about that, hmmm?" He lowered his head, his beautiful mouth millimeters from hers. All she'd have to do would be to reach up and it would be on hers.

God, she wanted it to be on hers.

She was starting to feel desperate again, which was shocking considering the first orgasm she had was still making its presence felt. Yet that didn't stop her from trying to rise up on her toes, seeking his mouth. Only to have him pull back and out of reach the way he had before. "Don't do that," she murmured, frustrated.

His eyes gleamed, as if he knew exactly what he was doing to her and, more, was enjoying it. "Don't do what?"

Breathless with impatience, she jerked on the soft cotton of his T-shirt. "Don't pull away."

He smiled. Oh yes, he was enjoying this, the bastard. Like he had yesterday, too. Looked like he got off on it.

"Demanding," he said softly, approvingly. "I like that in a woman."

She tugged at him harder. He still had his thigh thrust between her legs, and the heat and the pressure were starting to drive her nuts. "Jacob, stop. You're being a tease."

"You didn't answer the question, Ms. Beasley."

"Question?" She couldn't stop looking at his mouth, at the shape of his full bottom lip. It had felt soft on hers and yet hard as well, and so, *so* hot. He'd tasted like whisky, strong and rich and wickedly alcoholic and she wanted more. She wanted to drink the whole damn bottle. "What question?"

"The question of what's mine."

He stood there unmoving, obdurate as a rock wall, while she tugged at his T-shirt like a kitten clawing at a curtain and just as ineffectual. It was frustrating as hell.

She felt like she had yesterday, trapped under his massive, iron-hard body, wild with desire and frustration while he did nothing.

He called you sweet girl.

She blinked at the memory. Yes, so he had. Whatever that meant, if it meant anything at all.

"What do you mean what's yours?" she asked, dismissing the thought. "I really think you need to stop talking now."

The hand he'd just licked moved again, down to her mouth, his thumb stroking along her lower lip. "This, for example," he said. "Or maybe . . ." His hand dropped lower, fingertips brushing over her breast, grazing her sensitive nipple and sending sparks of sensation racing along her nerve endings. "This."

The look in his eyes was fierce, sharp, demanding a response from her whether she wanted to give him one or not.

She shuddered. "Why do you want those?"

"Because I do. Because you wanted me to want you back and that's a dangerous thing to say to a man like me."

"It's not dangerous." Her mouth felt sensitized, almost bruised, though his touch had been featherlight, and she was desperate for him to stroke his thumb along it again. "Why is it dangerous?"

"You should know by now." One blunt-tipped finger circled her nipple, a light caress that had her shivering all over. "I keep what's mine and I never let it go." Another aching circle, another rush of sensation arrowing straight between her thighs. "So be very careful about how you answer, Ms. Beasley."

But she was getting tired of him toying with her. Tired of his questions. She didn't want to talk anymore. She wanted his hands on her and hers on him, and she didn't much care how it happened, only that it happened now.

So she pulled his T-shirt hard and rose up again, hooking one hand around his neck so he couldn't lift his head, seeking his mouth . . .

Only to find herself jammed up against the doorframe with both arms above her head, pinned at the wrists by one of Jacob's powerful hands.

He gripped her chin hard with the other, giving her an intense black look. "You think it's a joke?" There was a note in his voice, a certain ferocity that felt like it was stealing all the air from the room. "That I'm saying this for fun?"

Her heart began to hammer in her chest. She'd seen this side of him before on the odd occasion, when an operation wasn't going to his liking or he'd been thwarted by something. He'd never lose his temper. He'd only become dark, an intensity gripping him that bordered on savage.

People called him frightening and yes, when he was like this, he was.

But she wasn't scared. Right now, looking up into his face and the darkness in his eyes, she felt nothing but excited. And turned on.

There was something thrilling about having all that intensity turned on her, and it made her want to test him, see how far he would go.

Which was probably a really crappy idea. But something in her couldn't leave it alone. The same thing that loved fighting him and always had.

Her body knew what to do and maybe it was another of those echoes, a muscle memory, but she let it do its thing, using the way he was pinning her wrists to lift her legs and wrap them around his lean hips. Then she pulled him in tight against her, feeling the hard ridge of his cock press against her aching clit, a delicious flare of sensation like a match being struck.

"I don't think you're saying it for fun," she said huskily, staring into his eyes. "I think you're serious. But if you're trying to scare me, it won't work. Nothing about you scares me. You being a possessive asshole least of all."

He didn't say a word, his gaze dense as a black hole, sucking in all light.

She almost stopped breathing under the weight of it.

Then suddenly he took her chin in his hand once more, and his mouth was on hers, and in that moment she realized just how much he'd been holding back earlier.

Because this wasn't a kiss, it was a conquering.

His tongue pushed deep inside her mouth, taking it as if it were his, exploring like she was new territory he was hell-bent on claiming. And claim he did, demanding and hungry, devouring her as if she were the first bite of food after weeks of starvation. Taking all that feverish heat inside her and building it up into an inferno.

The taste of him was like nothing she'd ever experienced in her life and she tried to kiss him back, just as starved as he was, but he wouldn't let her, forcing her head back so he could explore even deeper. He became more demanding, hungrier, biting her, licking her, changing angles, his fingers pressing hard against her jaw as he made the kiss his and her along with it.

It was like a storm breaking over her or watching a hurricane hit. With the winds roaring in her ears and the rain soaking her skin. Except the winds were the beat of her own heart and there was no rain, only desire, an endless, desperate well of hunger that only he alone could feed.

She tried to pull against his hold, because she was dying to touch him, but his grip was unbreakable. So she clamped her legs tighter around him instead, lifting her hips against the tantalizing ridge of his cock. She didn't care if she got off that way, she had no shame where he was concerned.

Besides, when it came right down to it, this excited her. The storm force of his will, of his hunger, was an insane aphrodisiac. After months of distance he'd finally unleashed himself and behind that enigmatic black gaze lay a passion she'd never imagined.

She wanted more of it. She wanted it all.

She bit him, sinking her teeth into his bottom lip as she arched her back, pressing her breasts against the granite wall of his chest. He made a growling sound deep in his throat and then the hand on her chin shifted, moving down to the waistband of her yoga pants. She felt a hard, sharp jerk, heard fabric ripping, and then the material was falling away from her; he just tore it away. He did the same with her panties and then there was nothing between her bare, heated skin and the material of his pants.

She shuddered as he uncovered her, fabric brushing against the sensitive folds of her sex as his mouth ravaged hers, making her breath come in short, hard gasps. His hand moved again and she heard the sound of his zipper.

Yes. *God, yes.*

Her spine bowed as she wriggled and shifted, trying to push herself against him. Then what little breath she had left went out of her in a rush as she felt something smooth and long and unbelievably hot brush against her stomach.

His cock.

Her hips bucked, a blaze of sensation arcing through her as he brushed the slick head of his dick against her clit. She gasped against his mouth, the sound blending with his own rough growl in a vibration that stroked between her legs like a touch.

He pulled his mouth from hers once more, saying nothing, black flames burning in his eyes, intent written all over his scarred, compelling face.

"Let me go," she said thickly. "I want to touch you."

But he remained silent, the fingers around her wrists not budging an inch. His free hand went to the pocket of his pants, hauling out his wallet. And then, one-handed, he extracted something from it, leaving the wallet to fall carelessly on the floor.

When he lifted his hand again, something gleamed in his fingers. A silver packet. Without a pause he ripped the packet open with his teeth, getting rid of it with an easy motion. Then her gaze was drawn relentlessly downward as he began to put the condom on.

Faith's breath caught.

She must have seen a man's cock before, but of course she had no memory of it and therefore no frame of reference. So there was only Jacob's. Smooth skin and crisp black hair. Long and very thick, it curved upward toward his chiseled stomach, making her mouth go dry.

It was as beautiful as the rest of him.

"Let me," she panted, watching as those capable, blunt-tipped fingers rolled the latex down, desperate to touch him. "Please. I want to."

But again, he said nothing, and once the condom was on, he took her chin in his hand once more and covered her mouth, silencing her with another of those savage, hungry kisses.

Then all thought vanished as the blunt head of his cock

pressed against the entrance of her body and she felt herself stretching around him, impossibly tight.

She groaned into his mouth, shivering as he began to push into her, sensitive tissues burning at the massive stretch of him.

The feeling was . . . strange. Intense, almost painful. And yet so insanely good, she could hardly breathe.

Too good. She was on the edge of orgasm already and he wasn't even fully inside her.

She jerked in his grip as he pushed in by gradual increments, so achingly slowly she wanted to scream. Wriggling and twisting, she tried to take him even deeper, feverishly attempting to push herself over the edge.

But it was as if he was in control of her orgasm and was holding it just out of her reach, giving her nothing but the relentless push of his cock as he pressed her against the wooden frame of the door, his kiss turning slow yet somehow no less savage. She tried to pull away from it, wanting to look down to see what was happening, but he wouldn't let her, his grip on her unbreakable.

She pulled harder, feeling like there was no air in her lungs, like she couldn't take any more of him inside her and yet at the same time wanting more. Wanting that heavy pressure and burning stretch, painful and yet so delicious she couldn't get enough.

Then he stopped, so deep she didn't think she could handle it. She bit his lip again, trying to angle her hips to get some relief, but he remained still, not letting her go, not doing anything but kissing her on and on, now lazy and slow enough that she wanted to weep.

Only when she was nearly sobbing did he draw his hips back, the slide of his cock the most exquisite thing she'd ever felt in her entire life, drawing it almost all the way out before sliding back in, another slow, relentless glide.

She cried out against his mouth, the sensation nearly too

intense to bear, her whole body shaking under the weight of the pleasure that was filling her. Then his hips flexed and he was moving yet again in another smooth motion, thrusting in and pulling back, deep and slick and so hard she couldn't stop shaking.

Her orgasm hit unexpectedly, a white burst of light behind her eyes, tearing a sob from her as it detonated throughout her body, her inner muscles clenching around his cock as she trembled and shook against him.

And he didn't stop. He kept on going as if he could do it all day, driving into her, harder this time, faster, slamming her against the wood of the doorframe. Then he changed his angle, so the base of his cock hit her clit every time he thrust back in, changing the aftershocks of her orgasm into pulses of building hunger.

Jesus. He was going to kill her. She was going to die from sheer pleasure.

Finally, he took his mouth off hers, trailing it along the side of her jaw and down her neck, his teeth closing on the fragile tendons there, the sharp pain as exquisite as the relentless drive of his cock.

He released her jaw, gripping the material of her T-shirt instead, pulling at it, jerking hard, the fabric ripping there, too, baring her. He shoved her bra up and aside, his massive, hot hand cupping one bare breast, his palm scorching like a brand against her skin.

She groaned, then cried out, as his fingers took her nipple between them and pinched, adding bites of pain to the sensations tangling and knotting inside her. There were too many, the pleasure and pain so tightly woven she'd never be able to tell which was which. Not that it mattered when the whole was so much more than she'd ever thought it would be.

He pinched her once more, slamming back into her as he did

so, overloading her nerve endings with so much sensation more light burst behind her eyes. Then he bent his head and that hot, wicked mouth of his covered her nipple, sucking hard, biting with just enough pressure to send her entire central nervous system into the stratosphere.

She shut her eyes tight as another orgasm crashed over her and a sob escaped her aching throat. Stealing her awareness of anything but the pleasure that blinded her.

Dimly she was aware of the movement of his hips, picking up speed, slamming her even harder against the doorframe. Of his breath against her breast and the harsh grunt he made every time he thrust in deep. And then his own harsh cry as he buried himself one last time inside her.

Jacob felt like someone had hit him over the back of the head with a brick. No, not a brick. A fucking jumbo jet.

He couldn't remember the last time he'd had an orgasm that powerful, that intense. Couldn't remember the last time he'd given in to his latent possessive tendencies and taken a woman the way he'd taken Faith, either.

But fuck, the way she'd writhed against him, demanding and hot, trying to take back the control. Trying to fight him . . .

He hadn't been able to resist her or his own need for her surrender. And he'd gotten it. Jesus Christ, how he'd gotten it.

She'd thought he was joking about the things he considered his.

He wasn't.

There had been a reason he'd held back from her all these months and he'd told himself a lot of stories as to what that reason was. But they weren't the truth.

The truth was that some part of him knew that once he touched her, that was it. He wouldn't want to let her go until he'd had his fill. And he'd been right.

She was *his* lover now and he was going to make sure he

explored every single aspect of her. And he wasn't going to let her go until he had.

She'd unleashed him and now she had to face the consequences.

He lifted his head, looking down at her, examining her flushed face. He'd been rough and demanding, and he'd been fully aware of that. But he'd thought she could take it and she certainly had.

Yeah, she liked a fight as much as he did.

Her mouth looked swollen, her blue eyes almost black. It was such a delicious sight though, her pink cheeks and red mouth, and then farther down, the pale skin revealed between the ragged edges of her ripped T-shirt. Smooth and silky, her pink-tipped breasts still glistening from his mouth.

He let himself look farther, between her thighs to where they were still joined, where soft black hair curled and she was pink and glistening and stretched around his cock.

It was the most incredibly erotic sight, made even more so by the fact that he was the one who'd done that to her. Who'd stripped her down and gotten her so hot that she'd begged him.

After years of anonymous hookups this—with Faith—was different. This was more real somehow and certainly ten million times hotter.

Who'd have thought?

Yeah, but don't get too excited. Don't let it become something more than it is.

Oh, no fear of that. He knew exactly what this was.

Hot, raw sex. That's all.

He stared down between her thighs, remembering the flavor of her when he'd licked her fluids off his own fingers, salt and sweetness with a maddeningly delicious dark edge.

He wanted more of that. And he was going to have it.

"Sooo . . ." Her voice was thick and scratchy sounding. "When am I going to get you with your clothes off?"

"Good question. Probably when I can trust myself not to ravage you the moment you put your hands on me."

A little smile turned her lovely mouth. A very satisfied smile. Clearly, she liked being wanted by him as much as he liked being wanted by her.

Shit, even now the thought of those delicate fingers touching him the way she had yesterday was enough to make him want to push her against the doorframe yet again for another round.

But no. Not quite yet. The wood was hard and no doubt her wrists and arms would be hurting from having had them pinned above her head.

"You did very well holding back yesterday," she pointed out.

Slowly he drew himself out of her, liking the way she shivered as he did so, then very carefully lowered her to the ground. "I've been in special ops for years," he murmured. "Controlling myself around one lovely woman wasn't all that difficult."

"Liar."

He flashed her a grin, liking her challenge. "Put it this way. It was slightly more difficult than sitting in a box for two days without food or water. Slightly less difficult than a fifty-mile ruck march."

"I don't know if I like being compared to special ops training."

"Deal with it, Ms. Beasley."

Once she was steady on her feet, he released his hold on her wrists but didn't let go of her completely. He held them in his hands, chafing her skin to get the blood flowing.

She leaned back against the frame, watching him sleepily from beneath her lashes. "You called me Faith just before."

So he had and that had been very deliberate. He'd wanted an answer from Faith the woman, not the identity of Ms. Beasley that she'd created. Plus he'd never called her Faith before—he hadn't allowed himself—and part of him had simply wanted to taste the sound of her name.

But that's not her name.

No, but that's who she was right now, right here with him.

"So I did," he murmured. "Don't get used to it."

"Why not?"

"You're talking too much." He let go of her wrists, dealt with the condom into a nearby wastebasket, and then very matter-of-factly, he pulled her torn clothes from her body. "And I'm not interested in chatting."

She gave another delicate little shiver as the rest of her clothing fell away, goose bumps rising on her pale, pretty skin. "Well, that's obvious."

He reached for her, lifting her into his arms before she could protest. Her weight was slight, the warmth of her body settling against his chest making him start to harden already.

Her head tipped back against his shoulder, her eyes still slightly glazed. "I can walk on my own, you know."

"If you can walk then I haven't done a good enough job of fucking you senseless." He began to make his way toward the bedroom area. "But don't worry, I'm going to rectify that right now."

She gave another of those self-satisfied smiles. "You can certainly try."

A thrill went down his spine and he looked down, meeting her glowing blue gaze. "Is that a challenge I hear, Ms. Beasley?"

"It is."

"In that case, I accept."

Jesus, this woman. He should be checking his contacts, seeing if any had come back to him about this Campbell guy, or checking in with Isiah. But . . . Well. They could wait a couple of hours. After all, who knew when he'd get this chance again? Her memory might come back at any moment and when it did there was no telling what she might do.

She won't want to find herself in bed with you.

Not if it was his brother she wanted. And that meant that taking advantage of her memory loss in the way he was made him a fucking bastard of the highest order.

But he didn't care. He'd wanted her for months and she wanted him, and in this moment she was his.

Because moments were all he'd ever had back when he'd been a kid and he'd learned to appreciate them whenever they'd come along, few and far between as they were. And now that he was an adult he did the same thing, relishing those instants of satisfaction. Of pleasure.

And taking them for himself when he could.

He carried her into the room that she'd chosen for herself, the one with the massive king-size bed, because there was no way he was going to screw her in a fucking bunk.

Setting her on the edge of the bed, he then went into the en suite bathroom, pulling open one of the drawers and getting out the box of condoms he knew were stocked there—he always kept his bathroom stocked for every and any eventuality—and came back out with it.

Dropping it on the nightstand, he went over to the bed and stood in front of her. She'd leaned back on her hands, apparently at ease with being naked. Her creamy skin was silky-looking and smooth, but here and there was the evidence of the injuries that had put her in the hospital. Scars from a gunshot wound on one shoulder and what looked like knife cuts on her torso and arms. There were older scars too, from what he had no idea, though if she'd been special ops like he thought, then she must have gotten them on different operations.

Curiosity burned inside him, a curiosity that would remain unsatisfied because she wouldn't know how she'd gotten those scars or what operations she'd been on. She knew nothing at all.

"So do I get to see you naked?" she asked. "Or are you just going to stand there and look at me?"

"You're mine, Ms. Beasley. Remember that. Which means you only get whatever I choose to give you."

"And what if I don't like that?"

"Then you get nothing at all."

She pouted. "That doesn't seem fair."

"Perhaps you should have thought about that when you told me you were mine." He smiled, white and sharp, stepping toward her and reaching out, casually taking some of her inky hair in his fist and tugging her head back. "I meant what I said, by the way. I'm possessive and territorial, and once you're mine I will take advantage of that mercilessly."

She took a small breath, her color rising beneath her skin, her gaze darkening as she looked up at him. Desire was starting to glow in her eyes, her nipples tightening even as he watched.

She liked this. She liked being held like this.

"And do I get any choice in the matter?" She didn't sound scared, only curious.

"Of course. But if you don't want to do what you're told like a good girl, then you don't get nice things."

Something flared in her eyes, a hint of a fascinating darkness that burned like electricity in his blood, and made his cock even harder than it was already.

"But I'm not a good girl." Her voice had quieted, now almost a whisper, yet he heard the note of challenge in it anyway.

He tightened his fist, drawing her head back farther. "Oh, don't worry, Ms. Beasley. I know that already. And I'm not unhappy about it either, not at all. Because I'm not a good man." He reached for his zipper. He hadn't bothered to fasten his pants properly from before so all he had to do was pull it down a little way so it was open. "I'm a prick and an asshole, and the quicker you understand that the better."

Her mouth was slightly open, the darkness in her eyes growing deeper with every second that passed. "Please." She didn't hide the desperate note in her voice. "Please be naked. Please be naked with me."

The raw need in her expression calmed something inside him, though he had no idea what it was. The nights he'd had with other women, when he'd taken them hard and rough, when he'd made them scream . . . none of them had been as desperate to touch him, see him, as Faith had. None of them had looked into his eyes and let him see it.

He couldn't resist that so he didn't.

"You beg so beautifully." Slowly he loosened his fist, let her go, and stood back from the bed. "So why not?"

Reaching for the hem of his T-shirt, he drew it up, then off over his head in one movement, dropping it negligently on the floor.

Faith's eyes went wide, her gaze roaming over him with such avid hunger it stole his breath. "I want to touch you," she whispered hoarsely. "Can I?"

"Of course, but you have to earn it first." He kicked off his boots, then shoved his pants and underwear down around his ankles before kicking those off too.

Her eyes went wider as her gaze dropped down to where his dick stood out from his body, hard and ready. "Why do I have to do that?"

He came back to the bed and reached for her hair once more, tangling it in his fingers and drawing her head back. "Because I said." Carefully he studied her expression, looking for any signs of fear or discomfort. But there were none. "And because I think you like taking my orders."

A blush made her already pink cheeks an even deeper rose. "That's not true."

"Seems like we're both good at lying." He smiled and gripped her tighter. "But I think you'll like my next order." And she would. He'd been planning on simply shoving her back onto the mattress and licking her out immediately, but there was something about her scars. They told a story that the woman who wore them didn't remember, but the story was there all the same. It was part of her and he suspected that it was a terrible part.

A terrible part he was trying to force her to remember, even though she didn't want to. Yeah, he was going to be ruthless about that, but that didn't mean he couldn't give her something she actually did want. Give her a good moment among all the bad.

"Open your mouth, Ms. Beasley," he murmured.

CHAPTER 9

Jacob's hand in her hair was the most delicious pressure, making her whole body feel sensitized and needy. She was conscious of the air moving over her skin and of the insane heat of his body inches from hers. Of his black eyes that seemed to see into her soul.

She didn't mind that. Because if there were things in there she needed to hide, she didn't know what they were anyway.

But she did know some things.

She knew that being held like this made her breath catch and her heart race. That the way he'd told her that she was his and that he could do whatever he wanted with her made her sex throb.

She knew that his naked body was a god's and that she'd do anything he wanted—anything at all—for a chance to explore it.

And she knew that he was right, she probably would love his next order because if he wanted her mouth open, then it was probably because he was going to put something in it. And if that something was his cock, then she'd probably die. Of happiness.

You're insane.

Or drunk. Jacob-drunk. And hell, she didn't mind that either. She didn't mind any of the things he'd done or the things he'd said. Not being his or having to follow his orders, or even being told to be a good girl.

Maybe because she knew he didn't really want her to be a good girl. She'd seen the glitter in his eyes when she'd said she wasn't good. Yes, he'd liked that very much.

He wanted to be challenged. He wanted to be tested. And she was up for that—more than up for it.

Her heartbeat raced. She hadn't thought it would be possible after two such intense climaxes to be all ready to go again so soon, but apparently, it was.

Perhaps now wasn't a good time to test him, especially considering she desperately wanted what he was going to give her—if he was indeed going to give her what she was hoping it was.

Perhaps now was the time to prove what a good girl she was.

Slowly, Faith opened her mouth.

He didn't smile, but his stare became blacker, denser. "Very nice." His voice had gotten impossibly deep, impossibly rough. If she could have rolled naked in that voice, rubbed the thick, velvet roughness of it all over her skin, she would have. "My sweet girl knows how to take orders."

My sweet girl.

She shivered at the words, an echo of something that felt like longing whispering inside her. But she didn't want any hint of memory to disturb what was happening right now, so she ignored it.

"I think you want what I'm going to give you, don't you?" Jacob's hand in her hair tightened, sending delicate prickles of pain sparking all over her scalp.

She nodded wordlessly, trying to force down the demand rising inside her. Trying to be patient.

And he must have seen that too, because amusement glinted suddenly in his eyes. "You're desperate, Ms. Beasley. I know. I can see it. But good things come to those who wait and since you've waited so beautifully, you've earned a reward."

Keeping one hand in her hair, he gripped his cock with the other.

Her breath caught, her gaze now riveted to where his fingers wrapped around the long, thick length of his erection. His skin was smooth, the blunt head glistening with moisture, and the deeply chiseled plane of his stomach flexed as he moved, taking a step right up close to the bed.

She began to tremble as the hand in her hair slipped to the back of her neck, easing her forward, then applying pressure, pushing her head down.

Then he was feeding the head of his cock into her mouth, the taste of salt and musk lying heavy against her tongue.

She shuddered. Who knew he'd taste so good? That having him between her lips would be so damn delicious?

He pushed in deeper, going slowly, and she angled her head to take more, because she wanted more, Holy God, she wanted whatever he could give her.

A sound broke from him, a low rumble of pleasure that felt like a long, slow stroke down her spine. "Good girl. You're being such a very good girl for me. Now . . ." He took a breath and it sounded ragged, and right then and there she decided that she was going to turn him inside out the way he'd done to her. "Do you know what to do from here?"

She gave a sharp shake of her head, unable to speak since the head of his cock was brushing the back of her throat.

"No, of course you don't." His thumb rubbed along the side of her neck and it felt like a reassurance. "Well, I'm in the mood to be indulgent and considering how good you've been for me, I'm going to let you figure it out for yourself. I'm sure you'll suck my cock like a dream, Ms. Beasley."

Yes, God, *yes.*

He reached for her hand and despite what he'd said about letting her figure it out, he guided her fingers to the thick base of his dick and wrapped them around it, showing her how to grip him. Then he let go.

And he was hers now, oh yes, he was. He might think she was his—and she was and wanted to be—but it went both ways. In fact, a very female part of her was telling her that now she had him, quite literally, in the palm of her hand.

The rush of power that came with that thought was heady, dizzying. And she had to hold him and not move for a moment simply to get used to the idea.

Did he know that? Did he know what he'd just given her? Did he know what it meant for a woman like her, who had no power over anything, not even her own brain, to be given power over a man like him?

Well, if he didn't know, she was certainly going to show him.

Experimentally, she gripped him tighter, then began to explore the hard length of him in her mouth with her tongue. He gave another low rumble in his chest, his thumb continuing to stroke the side of her neck.

He liked that, clearly.

So she did it again, drawing her head back to lick him, then swallowing him in deep. At the same time as she squeezed with her fist.

Jacob made another of those rough, growling sounds and she wanted to look up and see his face, see what she was doing to him, but with his hand on the back of her neck, she couldn't. There was only the hard, flat expanse of his stomach and the powerful width of his thighs in front of her.

Not a bad view. But she wanted more. She wanted to touch him, run her fingers across the fascinating corrugations of his abs, feel all that cut muscle flex and release as she stroked him. Feel his smooth, hot skin . . .

She pulled her head back and slid off the bed before he could protest, shoving at him so she could go down onto her knees in front of him. He let her, his fingers sliding into her hair and fisting tightly, a warning. Not that she needed it. Nothing on earth was going to drag her away from him now.

She opened her mouth and took him in again, deeper, until he was brushing the back of her throat, and she kept him there as she slid her hands up his thighs, glorying in the feel of his skin under her palms.

The grip in her hair became tighter, holding her exactly where she was, then he began to thrust into her mouth, slowly, rhythmically.

She groaned, the heat and taste of him rich and heady, the scent of male musk making the pulse of desire between her thighs beat harder, with insistence.

His rhythm picked up speed and she slid her hands up his thighs and around to the strong curve of his ass, loving the feel of his muscles flexing beneath her palms. She dug her nails into him and he grunted, thrusting harder.

Clearly, he liked that, too, so she did it again, scratching him, pressing her body against his legs, her fingers coming to stroke at last those hard-cut abdominal muscles that had been fascinating her for so long.

He felt so good and this, kneeling in front of him with his cock in her mouth, felt right. More right than anything else had since she'd woken up in that hospital bed. There was a peace inside her, as if in this moment she was finally, at last, in her own skin. She was herself in a way she hadn't been before now.

And then she wasn't thinking anymore, she was touching him everywhere she could while he thrust deeper, harder, his hands in her hair almost painful. But she didn't care about the pain. She didn't care about the discomfort.

Right now, right here, she was where she needed to be.

For the first time in six months.

She lost herself. Drowned herself in him and when, at last, he threw back his head and roared, she swallowed down everything he gave her, every inch of her own skin sensitized, the heaviness between her legs almost overwhelming. When he drew himself out of her mouth, it felt like a loss, and she found herself clutching him tighter.

He didn't leave her alone for long though.

Before she even had a chance to miss him, he was bending and picking her up in his arms, then he took her to the bed and tossed her onto the mattress, following her down, prowling like a lion up her body.

"Hold on to the headboard, Ms. Beasley," he growled. "And don't let go."

So she did, holding on tight, trembling with anticipation as he slid his big, warm palms up her thighs and lifted them, throwing them over his heavily muscled, tattooed shoulders. Then he gripped her hips and lifted those too, right up to his mouth, holding her like she was a cup he was going to drink from.

Then he pushed his tongue through the slick folds of her sex, found the beating heart of her, and made the entire world burst into flame.

Her body convulsed, the orgasm crashing down on her so hard she barely had any time to scream. And he didn't stop, didn't give her any time to even breathe, licking and exploring, pushing his tongue inside her, tasting her. He lifted her hips higher, angling his head so he could go even deeper, the feel of his whiskers on the sensitive skin of her inner thighs and the hungry, male noises he was making driving her insane.

He was driving her insane, period.

She didn't think she could come again, but then he shifted his grip and used his fingers as well as his tongue and she was crashing over the edge of the universe again.

It was bliss.

There was nothing to think about, nothing to worry about, nothing to fear. There was only the vast wave of unrolling pleasure and his touch, his heat, the powerful, enduring presence that had been her anchor for months and continued to anchor her, holding her fast as the chaos of ecstasy tossed her up, then left her to free fall.

Back down, into his arms.

Jacob rolled out of bed finally around early evening. Faith was asleep and he decided not to wake her—he was planning on giving her another workout much later that night so she was going to need to catch up on as much sleep as she could.

They'd spent most of the day in bed, venturing out only to grab food and for Jacob to check on any replies from his contacts. Frustratingly, there were none. Which on the upside meant he could take Faith back to bed. After all, it wasn't as if they didn't have anything to keep them occupied.

Pulling on some pants, he then headed out of the bedroom, making his way to the control room to do another check on his intel.

He had a couple of e-mails waiting for him, but all they'd turned up on the Campbell guy was a big fat nothing. The trail went dead, just stopped. Which meant that whoever Campbell was, he had pretty good people hiding his tracks.

Jacob sat back in his chair and glowered at the screen.

Fuck, they should have been able to turn something up. What was the point of paying all this money if people couldn't give him what he wanted?

Briefly, he debated paying another visit to Kellan's father, see if he couldn't get any more details about the gun-running ring and confirmation that it was indeed these people who were after Faith. But then he discarded the idea. Phillip Blake lived in New York State and he wasn't going to leave Faith here by herself while he flew across the country. He didn't want to take her with him either. It was too risky.

Jesus, this was taking too long. The more time it took to find whoever was after her, the more time it gave them to plan and move against her, and maybe get sneakier this time. Maybe threaten other people, such as their team. He didn't think they'd be able to find his bunker out here in the middle of the wilds of Washington State, but he didn't like to assume they wouldn't either.

And if they did? Well, he had a whole armory here and the place was well fortified. He could hold it by himself if necessary. As for the rest of the 11th Hour team, well, their HQ was hidden, plus it wasn't like the rest of them didn't know how to defend themselves. Jack, Kellan, and Isiah could more than handle any direct physical aggression.

With any luck, though, those assholes would be out of commission one way or another before they even got near either Faith or his team.

A slow-burning rage smoldered inside him at the thought.

They'd killed his driver and he was pissed enough about that, but if they even so much as touched a hair on her head he wouldn't be responsible for what he might do.

Restless, he pushed the chair back and stood up, reaching for his phone in his pants pocket. Then he put a call through to Isiah.

"Any updates?" he asked brusquely.

"No," Isiah answered, just as brusque. "Sabrina tried to get a clear pic of the guy from the car rental security cameras but the angle was wrong. And he was wearing a cap."

"Show me."

"The video quality is shit—"

"Show me," Jacob repeated, in no mood to dick around.

Isiah—showing he knew what was good for him—didn't

argue again and two seconds later a video file showed up on Jacob's phone.

The 11th Hour commander hadn't been lying; the video quality was shit and the angle was wrong. The man coming in to rent the car wore a cap pulled down low over his eyes and a plain black jacket that could have come from any one of a number of clothing stores.

The transaction lasted all of a minute and there was no sound.

Jacob kept Isiah on the phone as he watched it once, twice, and then another couple of times more.

"See anything?" Isiah asked. "Because I sure as hell—"

"Shut up." Jacob hit pause on the video as something caught his eye. The man was handing the car rental guy some money and there was . . . something on his hand. A ring of some kind. "Thirty seconds in," he said. "Get me a still. And get Sabrina to see if she can do anything with the resolution if I want to blow it up."

There was a brief silence.

"Sir," Isiah said, then disconnected.

Jacob waited. He hadn't needed to tell Isiah he wanted it now because Isiah knew that if Jacob hadn't specified a time frame it meant he wanted it immediately. And he did mean immediately.

Sure enough, a minute or so later, the still appeared on his phone with a message from Sabrina letting him know that the quality was as good as she could get it.

He stared down at the picture, focusing on the hand reaching out with the cash in it, zooming in to the glint of something bright around the man's finger. Yes, it was a ring and not a wedding ring. Worn on the middle finger of his hand and with some engraving.

Jacob tried to zoom in closer to see what the engraving was

but the resolution wasn't good enough. Not that he needed to anyway. Not when his gut was telling him all he needed to know.

That ring was familiar and it was familiar because he was pretty sure it was the same one as he had sitting in a box in his study back in his house in San Diego.

The ring with a snarling wolf's head engraved on it.

There were only six people in the entire world who knew what that wolf's head meant and he was one of them. The rest . . .

The rest were supposed to be dead.

The Wolf Pack, a special ops team that had imploded after a disastrous mission in the Ukraine had led to the deaths of five team members.

His team members.

His jaw got tight as he stared at the ghost in the picture, shock pulsing through him along with a wave of unwanted memory. Bad intel that had led the team into a trap, a deliberate sabotage by some higher-up who'd wanted them all dead.

He'd never been able to figure out who that higher-up had been or the reasons for the sabotage, nor how he himself had managed to get out of the trap alive. But he had.

After, he'd headed back home, determined to find out the truth about what had happened, only to discover that all evidence of his team had been swept from the records. They no longer existed and neither did he.

The government had given him a massive payout for his troubles, which he'd taken because he hadn't any other choice, and then he was told that if he wanted to remain alive, he needed to disappear.

So he had. Once again, left with nothing.

Nothing except his mission to find his brother.

Jacob gritted his teeth, staring at the phone screen.

142 / Jackie Ashenden

Apparently, though, he had something left after all. One of his teammates he'd thought was dead. Who appeared to be in-volved with a gun-running ring and who was now after Faith.

Fuck, this was getting worse and worse, and he'd hit a brick wall with his sources. The only thing he had was Faith and the contents of her head, and she couldn't remember.

Which meant he had to make her. Except he was running out of things to try to prompt it with because he didn't know anything about Joanna Lynn, other than she'd been ex–special ops and potentially his brother's lover.

Fighting hadn't worked and neither had sex, so what the fuck else did he have?

Tossing aside his phone, he put his hand on the keyboard and sent a quick e-mail to the contact who'd found him the initial info on Joanna, then he shoved himself out of his chair and strode back into the bedroom, intending to wake Faith up and have a serious chat.

But she was lying there still asleep, all curled up with her head resting on the pillow, black hair spread everywhere, her hands folded beneath her cheek like a child's. She looked vul-nerable and beautiful, and possessiveness hit him like a gut punch, even stronger than it had been earlier.

She belonged here. She belonged to *him.*

Faith might, but does Joanna?

His chest tightened, something painful constricting inside him.

Once she remembered her past, this would all be over. She would hate herself for what she'd done with him, for betraying his brother, and maybe she'd hate him, too. And this moment he'd had—this one precious moment where she'd given him not only her body but her trust as well—that would be gone.

And he didn't want it to be gone.

The night's not over yet.

No, it wasn't. And taking it, keeping Faith for the duration of it, wouldn't change anything. He could take a night. Just one.

He went over to the bed and reached out a hand, gently touching the fine-grained skin of her cheek, feeling softness and warmth.

She'd been such a generous lover, both with her body and her trust. She hadn't hidden her desire for him or the pleasure she took in his touch, and even though she'd eventually given him her surrender, she'd given him enough of a fight to make that surrender sweet.

Physically, she really was perfect for him in every way. An exquisite combination of strength and beauty and fire, and a sweetness that stole his breath. Eager and honest and brave, too.

He hadn't had a woman who suited him so well in such a long time, if ever.

She didn't wake as he touched her, but her head turned slightly toward his hand, as if she knew he was there and wanted more of him.

Christ. That shouldn't have made him want more too, but it did, the tightness in his chest winding tighter, even as his cock hardened. But he didn't want to wake her so he took his hand away, the warmth of her skin lingering on his fingertips all the same.

Yes, if all he had was tonight with her, then he'd take it.

He'd fucking take it *all*.

But that didn't mean he wasn't going to give. Because he did have something of his own that she'd wanted and maybe it was time to offer it to her.

Information. The questions she'd wanted to ask. The things he'd never told another soul.

She'd trusted him enough to let him make her his. It was time to show her that trust went both ways.

Why? Don't you know how dangerous that is? What the fuck

144 / Jackie Ashenden

do you think she'll do with that information when she becomes Joanna again?

He didn't know, which he guessed made telling her a really stupid idea. Maybe nothing would happen. Or maybe she'd use it against him in some way. Or maybe it would stay with her, a little part of himself that she'd always carry.

"I suppose, Ms. Beasley," he murmured very quietly, "one way or another, we'll eventually find out."

CHAPTER 10

Faith woke up after a dreamless sleep feeling boneless and heavy and unbelievably sated. Jacob wasn't there, which was disappointing, but he couldn't have gone far, and for a moment she simply lay there enjoying the sensation.

They'd spent all day in bed and it had been so good that she'd have been quite happy to remain there for the rest of the night too.

Jacob had been . . . well, quite simply, Jacob had been magnificent in every possible way there was and she knew—even without having any other frame of reference—that she wouldn't find another man to match him.

Even though she was supposed to be his brother's lover, it was difficult to know how his brother could possibly give her what Jacob had given her over the course of the day. So much pleasure. Like he could see inside her and anticipate her every desire. Even some she didn't know she had.

It had been . . . revelatory.

She stretched, then glanced toward the window. It was dark outside so obviously she'd been asleep awhile.

Time to get up.

Slipping from the bed she debated the merits of another shower, then decided not to. She liked the scent of sex and Jacob on her skin and she thought he might like it too.

Going over to where her bag sat on the dresser, she dug around inside it, then pulled out a clean pair of panties and a loose white T-shirt, and put them on. Since her yoga pants were in pieces back near the control room and she had no desire for Jacob to rip up another pair, she didn't bother with pants, heading straight out of the bedroom as she was.

But when she got to the living room, she stopped dead.

The only light was warm, flickering, and she realized it was coming from the multitude of candles that had been lit and were standing in bottles placed at different points around the room.

The candles were of the plain white emergency kind and the bottles looked to be old wine or beer bottles, but the light they gave off was beautiful.

There was another candle sitting on the table, the glow softening the hard edges and brutal lines of the man sitting near it, his gaze on hers.

Jacob.

She stopped in the doorway, a breathless feeling sweeping over her.

Were all these candles for her?

And then she noticed something else. The table was set and there was food on it, plus an open bottle of wine.

"Is this for me?" A stupid question when she was the only one here.

His beautiful mouth settled into a half smile. "Of course it's for you. I thought you might like to join me for dinner, Ms. Beasley."

Her throat constricted. She didn't know why a simple roomful of candles should make her so breathless or her heart feel like it was swelling up in her chest, but it did.

"I would," she said, not caring that her voice was all scratchy. "I would very much like to join you for dinner, Mr. Night."

That half smile deepened into something warmer and brighter than all the candles in the room put together. He had such an amazing smile. How had she not noticed?

He gestured to the seat beside him. "Come sit."

So she did, but not where he indicated.

Instead she went straight to him and stood next to his chair, looking down at him meaningfully.

His gaze made a slow journey down her body, lingering on her breasts, making her nipples get hard, before moving down farther, to her panties and her bare legs. He made no effort to hide the heat in his eyes, and when they came back to hers, the flames in them nearly burned her alive.

He said nothing. Merely pushed his chair back.

She didn't need any further invitation, straddling his lean hips, then settling down into his lap so she was facing him. He was hot and powerful beneath her and she was sad he was wearing a T-shirt, because she very much wanted to touch his bare skin. But she lifted her hands and put them on his chest anyway, purely so she could feel his heat and his strength, so satisfyingly hard beneath her palms.

He watched her, that half smile playing around his mouth. "I didn't mean you could sit on me."

She arched a brow. "Is that a complaint?"

"Hardly. I approve of your T-shirt, by the way."

"Thought you might." She'd known it was vaguely see-through when she'd put it on. That was the whole point of wearing it. "And I approve of the candles and dinner. You're quite the romantic."

He gave a soft, deep rumble of a laugh that she found so

sexy she wanted to kiss him. "Not quite. The candles are from the emergency stores, the wineglasses are glass tumblers, and I'm not sure the wine is even drinkable. But the steak, at least, should be good."

"Well, I like the thought at least." She stroked him like she was petting a big cat. "What's the occasion?"

"You need a nice dinner after all the exercise we've done today." His smile became sensual. "Plus, you also need to build up your strength for tonight."

A shiver ran the length of her spine.

"But there's also another reason," he went on, the heat in his gaze dampening slightly. "I wanted to give you some time to ask your questions."

Surprise moved through her. She'd thought he'd forgotten about that. Hell, she certainly had—until now at least.

"Why?" she asked bluntly.

"Because you're mine and I want you to know." His gaze was very direct. "And because you gave yourself to me this afternoon. You gave me your trust. So now I'm going to give you mine."

Something in her chest shifted again, her throat tightening.

She hadn't expected this. Yes, he'd told her that all she had to do was ask and he'd answered a couple of her questions already, but . . . Well. He wasn't a man who'd give his secrets to anyone lightly, and now, here he was, promising them to her, a woman with no past and no memory.

A woman who wasn't even sure who she was.

"Is that wise?" she asked softly. "You don't know who I am, Jacob. Even I don't know who I am." Then another thought hit her. "Are you sure that you want Joanna to know these things?"

His obsidian eyes gleamed. "I don't know. What do you think?"

A little pulse of some emotion she couldn't name went

through her and she wanted to tell him yes, that he could tell her, that he could trust her. But the reality was she didn't know.

"I think," she said thickly, "that you should be careful."

His mouth twitched. "I'll keep that in mind."

"Jacob, I . . ." She broke off, not really sure what she wanted to say. So she slid her palm up his chest, over his left pec, to where his heart beat strong and sure. And she kept it there. "Are you really sure about this?"

"Yes." There was no hesitation. "Ask any question you like, Ms. Beasley."

A thousand questions instantly jostled for position. "Okay, so." She pressed her hands against him, testing the firm muscle of his chest. "How did you and your brother get to be in foster care?"

"You don't start with the easy ones, do you?"

"I thought I'd start at the beginning."

"It's not a happy story, Ms. Beasley. Are you sure you want to hear it?"

"You were in foster care." She smoothed her hand over him. "Of course it's not going to be a happy story."

"I suppose not." He was silent a minute. "Believe it or not, it starts out happy enough. Dad was a sergeant in the army so he and my mom lived with us on base until Josh and I were about six years old.

"Then Dad went on deployment, going missing soon after on a routine patrol. They never found his body, he simply vanished. I don't remember much else about it, just Mom crying whenever I asked her when Dad was coming home." He paused, the look in his eyes turning distant. "About a year later, Mom got sick. Aggressive breast cancer. It was terminal and she had no other family except a great-uncle in a nursing home in Florida, which made figuring out what to do with Josh and me difficult. But she had a very good friend who offered to take us when the time came and so, when she eventually died, Rebecca took us to live with her."

Faith swallowed. His voice was deep and measured, and there was no pain in it, but she could feel the tension in him. The muscles of his thighs were tight, as were his shoulders. And no wonder, losing his parents so young and both so quickly must have been dreadful.

She said nothing, because she couldn't think of anything to say besides banalities. So she stroked him instead, trying to loosen that tension, give him whatever comfort she could.

"It was okay at first," he went on. "Rebecca was kind and even though she wasn't Mom, she was good to us. But a couple of years after, she fell for a man named Greg. Initially, he seemed like a good guy, but gradually . . . Let's just say I noticed things about him I wished I hadn't."

Foreboding settled down inside her. Jacob's expression gave nothing away, but she could tell that whatever it was he was going to say, it wasn't going to be good.

He must have picked up on her own tension because he said softly, "You might not like this next part, Ms. Beasley. Shall I continue?"

She looked into his strong, battered face. "Is it important?"

"Very."

"Then yes, continue. If you can say it then I can listen."

Something glittered bright in his gaze. "Greg liked Joshua. But in a way he shouldn't."

Cold crept over her skin. "Oh God. Did he . . . ?" She stopped, unable to actually say it.

Jacob's gaze had become very black, the lines of his face hardening. "I'd taken to carrying around a little pocketknife Rebecca had given me for my tenth birthday, and the day I found Greg trying to hurt Josh, I stabbed him with it." His deep voice was stripped down and rusty-sounding, with an icy edge to it that made her shiver. "The knife wasn't very big so

I didn't hurt him much, but it was enough for him to call the cops. A fuss was made and even though I tried to tell everyone what that prick had done, no one believed me." Jacob smiled, very white and very sharp. A shark's smile or a tiger's. "He hid his demons well, I'll give him that. So well not even Rebecca believed I was telling the truth."

The righteous, protective anger that gripped Faith in that moment surprised her with its strength. "How could they not believe you?" she demanded. "I mean, why the hell would you make something like that up?"

"Greg told them that I was making trouble because Rebecca was pregnant and I was jealous of the new baby. He then convinced Rebecca that the pair of us should go into foster care since he and Rebecca didn't have the skills to look after us properly."

Faith stared at him, horrified. "Oh my God, seriously?"

"Yes. He told her he thought it would be for our own good and for the good of the new baby." Another of those white, menacing smiles. "I was dangerous, apparently. Too dangerous to be around other children."

She shook her head, her heart aching for him. "Did no one stick up for you? Not even one person?"

"Of course not." He said it like that was unsurprising, a self-evident fact. "Rebecca was tired and sick with her pregnancy and she was so securely under his thumb she believed everything he told her. So into foster care we went. Greg told me that if I kept to myself what he'd done to Josh, he'd ensure that we stayed together. So I kept it to myself." Jacob's expression became suddenly, terrifyingly dark. "But he lied. And we were split up in the end."

A terrible sadness turned over inside her. His expression gave nothing away, but she could see the glitter of old pain in the depths of his eyes. And no wonder. He'd lost everything. He'd gone from having a mother and father and twin brother, a family who'd loved him, to having nothing. It had all been slowly and inexorably stripped from him.

He must have been so alone. And she knew how that felt, didn't she?

Unexpectedly, Jacob lifted his hand to her cheek, his palm warm against her skin. He was frowning, but the darkness had lifted from his expression somewhat. "Don't look so sad, sweet girl." His thumb stroked along her bottom lip. "It happened a long time ago."

Sweet girl . . .

A whisper of electricity chased over her skin and she found herself leaning into his palm like an animal wanting to be petted. "I can't help it," she said. "It *is* sad. You lost everything. At ten years old."

"I did. But I survived it."

Of course he would have. Jacob Night was nothing if not a survivor.

She looked straight into his eyes. "I know what it's like to be alone. I know what it's like to have nothing and no one."

His expression didn't soften. If anything it became fiercer, though the touch of his thumb upon her lip was still gentle. "You're probably the only one who would. You and Joshua."

"Is that why you want to find him so badly?" she asked. "I mean, I know he's your brother, but you haven't seen him for a long, long time . . ." She broke off, realizing how stupid the question sounded.

Jacob's thumb pressed gently against her bottom lip as if testing it. "I'm the older twin. It was my job to take care of him. I was supposed to save him from that asshole Greg, and I was supposed to keep us together. And I failed in both of those things. So yes, it's important to me that I find him."

She understood, oh she understood all too well.

Jacob Night, for all his darkness, for all his healthy disregard for the boundaries of law and order, was a protector at heart. Why else would he have looked after her for six months? Why else would he have an entire business based on helping people with various difficulties?

"So what happened next?" she asked, suddenly desperate to fit all the pieces of the fascinating jigsaw that he was together. "When did you go into the military?"

"Not till I aged out of the system. I was in many different foster homes before that, though 'home' was a very loose term for them. The first thing I did when I came of age was to enlist in the Navy."

"But why the military?"

"Because I failed school and there was nothing else I wanted to do. Because I was angry and needed a focus for it."

And he was still angry, she knew that much. She'd seen it smoldering in his eyes sometimes when he thought no one was looking.

"You didn't go into the Army?" she asked. "Like your dad?"

"No." The word was flat. "Dad's career was his own. I wanted a fresh start."

"So . . . what happened after that?"

"I had a Navy career. Became a SEAL." There was a sharp, glittering expression in his gaze now. "I was then asked to join an elite black ops unit, which I did for a few years. The missions were classified so I can't tell you where or why, but during one there was a disaster which involved the deaths of many of my unit."

Something shifted inside her, like the ground settling after an earthquake. And she caught her breath. But there was no abrupt flash of memory or even an echo.

How strange.

Jacob's relentless black stare was on hers. "You okay?"

"It's nothing. Go on."

The expression on his face told her that he didn't believe her. Nevertheless, he continued. "I was given a substantial payout following that particular mission and my affiliations with the unit were dissolved. They made me go underground, made me disappear. And that's when I decided I had to find Joshua."

She studied him. His voice gave nothing away and yet there was more to that story, she was sure of it. Why would he be paid for his silence? Why would he be made to disappear? She knew better than to ask him those questions though, especially as the information was classified.

Not that the reasons would make a difference to what happened. He'd lost everything when he'd been a boy, and then, as a man, it had been done to him again.

No wonder he's so angry.

And no wonder he was trying to find his brother. Joshua really was the only thing he had left.

"So why the 11th Hour?" she asked. "Was that part of finding Joshua too?"

"Yes. I soon realized that doing things myself could only take me so far and that I needed a team to help. My initial investigations into Joshua's whereabouts led into some dangerous territory and I needed some cover. The 11th Hour is my cover." Dark humor flickered briefly in his eyes. "Plus, doing jobs that other people don't want to do, especially if they're not quite legal, is lucrative. And money is very, very useful in getting people to talk."

"You're helping people too, Jacob," she pointed out. "All the jobs you take on are to help people or protect them."

The humor vanished as quickly as it had come. "You're ascribing some very noble motives to me, Ms. Beasley, but don't go imagining I'm some kind of secret Good Samaritan or a saint. The jobs I take on are all for a reason. Protecting Senator Hawthorne's daughter, for example, was purely so I could get intel about Smith and the gun-running ring. Sending Mr. Blake and Ms. Leighton to get information from Mr. Blake's father was again purely for intelligence purposes." His tiger's smile made a reappearance. "I want to find my brother and maybe get a little revenge while I'm at it, nothing more."

Revenge? Interesting, he'd never mentioned that before. "Revenge? Revenge for what?"

"That's classified." His thumb that had been pressed to her bottom lip dropped away. "It's time for dinner, Ms. Beasley."

It was clear Faith was not happy to break for food, but right now, Jacob didn't care. He was done answering her questions.

He hadn't thought it would be so difficult to tell her, not about his childhood, because it had all happened so long ago. And yet when the time came to say it, he'd found it . . . hard.

Perhaps it was having her warmth and softness pressed against him, making him even more acutely aware of everything that he'd lost. Or maybe it was simply the fact that he hadn't told anyone the story before.

Certainly, the way she'd looked at him, an unexpected understanding in her eyes, had for some reason brought into sharp relief the isolation of his current existence.

When was the last time he'd been able to talk to someone like this? Not ever. He kept everything to himself, every single fucking thing. And he'd been okay with that, telling himself he didn't need to tell anyone anything. That he didn't need anyone, period.

But the day he'd taken Faith home from the hospital, everything had changed.

He had someone in his keeping now and even though that someone was a woman who didn't know who she was, it was still someone. Then over the space of a few months, he'd come to know her, and had discovered how fascinating she was. How much of an enigma and yet, to some extent, how much of an open book.

Whether his fascination was merely proximity or something to do with the link she had to his brother, he didn't know. But one thing he did know was that right now, he didn't regret telling her what he had, even though it was hard. Even though he had no idea what would happen once she remembered who she was.

It had been worth it just to have someone look at him as if they understood.

It's not proximity. It's her.

No, it couldn't be her. He couldn't afford for it to be her. Not when he needed her to remember who she was so he could find Joshua. And not when the moment she remembered . . .

You'll lose her.

He shoved the thought from his head, reaching for the wine bottle and pouring some wine into the tumbler beside her plate. She was sitting now in her own seat, which he hadn't wanted. He would have been quite happy for her to remain in his lap, but then if he'd kept her there, he would have ended up eating something else and regardless of whether he needed actual food himself or not, she certainly did.

So. Food first and then her, preferably spread across the table so he could feast on her naked body at will.

Faith had attacked the steak without hesitation, obviously hungry, and it gave him a certain amount of satisfaction to see her take pleasure in the food he'd brought for her.

They ate in comfortable silence for a couple of minutes, which he allowed to stretch a little longer than he should have, mainly because he didn't want to disturb it. But disturb it he must, so eventually, he put his fork down and said, "Are you going to tell me what was wrong?"

"What do you mean?"

"When I told you about the death of my unit."

She stared at him a second. Then she looked down at her plate. "There was nothing wrong."

HARD NIGHT / 157

"Yes, there was. You went very still and your eyes became glassy."

A lock of hair had fallen over her shoulder, the inky length of it in stark contrast to the white of her T-shirt. He remembered how that hair had felt in his fist as she'd sucked him, how silky and soft it had been.

"It really was nothing." Slowly she lifted her gaze back to his again. "A strange . . . shift. But no echoes of memory or anything. I can't describe it any better than that."

"But it was talking about my unit that prompted it."

"I couldn't say." She reached for her tumbler and took a hefty sip. Then pulled a face. "How long did you say you've had this wine?"

Jacob was unsurprised. The wine had been in the bottom of one of the cupboards for a long time and it had been cheap. "Not sure. And don't change the subject."

Faith put the glass down. "Fine. But find me something else to drink first."

He eyed her. She was stalling, he'd lay a thousand bucks on it.

Then again, it wasn't as if he was in any rush to talk about this himself. He'd been searching for Joshua for years; one more night wasn't going to make much difference.

It might to her. It might to him. Don't forget who they are to each other.

An emotion he thought he'd long since ceased to feel twisted in his gut. A painful, poisonous emotion. Guilt.

Fuck, he'd thought he was done with that. For years after he and his brother were split up, guilt was all he'd felt. Guilt for not protecting Josh from Greg. Guilt for screwing up what family they'd managed to find after their mother had died. Guilt for promising him they'd stay together only for them to be split up.

Guilt. So much fucking guilt.

Jesus Christ, what was happening to him? It was Faith getting under his skin, making him feel things he hadn't felt for years. Faith, the only person he'd let even a little into his life.

Faith, whom he'd fucked and made his, completely and totally.

What would his brother think about that when he found out? They'd never had a competitive relationship because they'd both liked different things. Jacob had always been more into physical pursuits, while Joshua had preferred reading and playing computer games. Maybe if they'd grown up together as teenagers that might have changed. Maybe they would have had problems with liking the same girl.

Or maybe they wouldn't have.

It was all a moot point anyway because that's not what had happened.

If he's anything like you are now though, he's going to be angry as fuck with you.

Jacob shoved his chair back and stood up. "I'll get the vodka," he said brusquely, and strode out of the room, guilt like acid in his gut.

He found the vodka at the back of one of the shelves in the kitchen. It was unopened and dusty, but he pulled it out and took it back into the living area.

Faith had finished her meal and was over by the banks of electronics beneath the TV screen on the wall, fiddling with some of the buttons. As he put the vodka down on the table, music abruptly flooded the room.

"You found the stereo, I see," he said, sitting back down in his chair.

She turned and gave him a grin. "Internet radio. Do you mind?"

"Not at all."

Slowly she came over to where he sat, giving his lap another meaningful look.

He didn't bother waiting, gripping her hips and tugging her

down. She put her hands on his shoulders, the warmth of her settling onto him and making his cock twitch.

Fuck it. The conversation about what she remembered or didn't remember could wait. She was here in his lap and she was warm, and he could see her nipples hardening into tight points beneath her T-shirt. The pulse at the base of her throat was beating fast and he wanted to put his mouth on it, make it beat even faster.

As if on cue the music changed from some upbeat nineties pop song to the slow, familiar strains of "Unchained Melody."

He lifted his palms and cupped her breasts, brushing his thumbs over her nipples. She shivered, arching her back, pushing herself against his hands. Then she turned and grabbed the vodka bottle, twisting off the cap and lifting it to her mouth, raising it to drink.

The move was so unlike Faith that for a second he forgot about touching her, watching as she took a swallow, a kernel of ice slowly hardening in his gut.

She choked a little on the alcohol and he took the bottle out of her hand before she dropped it, putting it back on the table. She'd bent forward coughing, her hair falling down and into her eyes.

He pushed it back to see her face, the silky strands drifting over the backs of his hands. Her cheeks were pink, her lashes veiling her gaze.

"Are you all right?" he demanded, rougher than he'd intended.

She didn't reply, taking her hands from his shoulders and pressing them over her eyes.

"Faith." He said the name he'd given her deliberately, the kernel of ice getting larger. "What's wrong?"

"The vodka and . . . this song." She shivered, her shoulders hunching.

A web of ice began to wrap around him and before he knew

what he was doing, he'd grabbed her wrists, pulling her hands away from her eyes, wanting to see her face.

The midnight blue of her eyes had darkened into black and she'd gone very, very pale. She stared at him as if she'd never seen him before in her entire life.

He gave her a searching look, the worry inside him beginning to deepen into fear. Fear for her. "What about the vodka and this song? Are you sick? What?" He let go of her wrists, cupping her face between his palms. "What is it, sweet girl? Tell me."

And he saw it then, swirling like clouds in the depths of her gaze.

Fear.

"Faith," he said again, an order this time. "Faith, tell me what's wrong."

She kept staring at him, fear black in her eyes. Then suddenly she twisted in his lap and was off him, heading straight toward the door to the bedrooms.

He followed like a shot, reaching out to grab her, but somehow she avoided him, the door to the hallway slamming in his face.

With a growl he flung it open, only to see her disappear through the door to the bedroom she'd been using. He tried to pull that one open too, but she'd locked it behind her.

Adrenaline flooded through him and he jerked at the door handle, but it remained stubbornly shut. "Faith!" he shouted hoarsely. "Open the fucking door!"

But there was no answer.

The web of ice froze solid, encasing him in cold. Because he knew what was going on. Deep down, he knew.

"Faith," he ground out, hammering at the door. "Open the door. *Now.*"

Nothing happened.

He took a step back, ready to launch his boot at the door

and kick it the fuck down when suddenly it jerked open and Faith stood on the threshold.

She was dressed completely in a T-shirt and a pair of tight-fitting black pants, black boots on her feet. Her hair had been pulled into a ponytail high on the back of her head and the expression on her face was utterly impenetrable.

She was sleek and sexy and so fucking beautiful that for a second he couldn't breathe.

"Not Faith," she said in a voice he didn't recognize. "Not today."

Then her fist came back and flashed toward him.

Taken by surprise, he tried to dodge, but she was too fast and it smashed into his face with surprising strength.

Pain exploded in his head, dizzying him, but old reflexes kicked in and he shook it off, moving in for the attack. Except she was moving too, and faster than he was, lifting her foot and slamming it without mercy between his legs.

He dropped like a stone as agony burst through him, barely conscious as she bent down next to him.

"I'm sorry, Jacob," she said in that unfamiliar voice. "But I was never yours. And now I have to go."

Then something else smashed into his head and blackness claimed him.

He came to again sometime later to find himself lying in the hallway where she'd dropped him, his groin still a fucking agony.

Painfully he levered himself to his feet and began a systematic search of his ruined castle.

A pointless exercise when he knew already she'd gone, but he had to be thorough.

He'd thought that maybe she'd have found the jeep he kept covered with camo netting and used that to escape.

But she hadn't.

And that's when the truth that he'd been trying to deny since the moment she'd taken a sip of that vodka came crashing down onto him.

Because there was one vehicle missing in the little fleet he maintained here and it certainly wasn't the jeep.

It was the small Dynali, a light, maneuverable one-person helicopter that he kept for emergency getaways.

Which could only mean one thing.

Faith had finally remembered who she was.

CHAPTER 11

It had been a while since Joanna had flown a helo and her skills were a bit rusty, but the Dynali was a solid machine and she managed to get herself to Seattle without incident.

Pity there hadn't been a bigger helicopter that would have gotten her back to San Diego in one hit, but it was either the Dynali that would get her to Seattle or the jet. And the jet would have meant refueling and she didn't have time for that.

So the Dynali and Seattle it was.

Luckily, she had a contact in Seattle who was then able to get her down to San Diego on another helo, no questions asked.

Good thing too since questions were the last thing she wanted.

She spent the journey determinedly not thinking about anything, trying to hold back the wave of memories that threatened to swamp her by sheer force of will.

She had a lot of that as it turned out.

Her contact in Seattle had given her a burner phone and by the time she reached San Diego she'd organized a car to take her from the airport out to Jacob's cliffside home in La Jolla.

Probably a mistake to go there since it would no doubt be the first place Jacob would come looking for her, but she needed weapons and the house had an impressive armory.

She just wouldn't linger. It would take him a while to get back down here anyway, presuming he managed to fix the tires on the jet after she'd slashed them.

Then again, she couldn't assume anything about Jacob Night.

He was dangerous and she'd known that right from the start.

Jacob's large, airy, modern home was a set of boxes constructed of glass and stone, set on top of a cliff overlooking the Pacific, and was as heavily protected and fortified as he was. But it wasn't any drama getting inside. That had been a risk, that he would have changed the facial recognition software on all the locks so she couldn't get in. But he hadn't and they unlocked for her like the cave before Ali Baba.

It might have been a bad sign, of course, but it wasn't like she had a choice. There wasn't anywhere else she could get a weapon at short notice and without drawing attention.

She should have headed straight to the armory once she'd gotten inside, yet she didn't, veering off to the set of rooms on the east side of the house.

Clothes. Yes, she needed more clothes. That's why she went to the rooms she'd once lived in.

Faith's rooms.

Her heart was beating faster than it should have been as she stepped into the bedroom, the pressure of all those memories beating against the doors of her mind.

But she couldn't let them in, not all at once. She had to take this slow, pace herself, otherwise she'd crack under the weight like she nearly had back in the bunker with Jacob.

It had been the taste of the vodka and that fucking song, an unmistakable combination, that had opened the door a crack, memory following on behind it, muscling through that crack and pushing those doors wide open.

A run-down bar. "Unchained Melody" playing on the old, cracked jukebox and bad vodka. And a man sitting opposite her. A man with black eyes and an unscarred face. Raising a glass to her and smiling, and she was drinking too, relief coursing through her because she'd made a decision.

She wasn't going to kill him after all.

Josh Smith. Who wasn't her lover and never had been. Who'd once been a good friend and teammate, and whom she'd been sent to kill.

And whom she'd had to—

No, she couldn't think about that, not yet.

Forcing the memories back, she went over to the dresser, trying to ignore the blackness of the night beyond the windows. She'd loved that view. Loved looking at the ocean, the sun glittering off the waves . . .

No. No, she hadn't. That was Faith who'd loved that and she wasn't Faith anymore. Alone and scared Faith. Terrified, vulnerable Faith.

She wasn't that woman. She was Joanna again.

Riffling through the drawers in the dresser, she grimaced at the pretty, filmy underwear. Impractical and ridiculous. Jesus, what had possessed her to think that's what she liked?

Cotton, plain and practical for her bottom half. Sports bras for her top half. Anything else was an indulgence. A waste.

Her mother had told her a long time ago that nice things weren't for girls like her and she knew that was true. Killers didn't wear pretty lace and silk. They weren't allowed to.

And she was a killer. She'd accepted that.

People shouting. Pulling the trigger. Josh's face blank with shock as he'd fallen, knocking over the table. Blood had bloomed red against the white of his T-shirt. She'd killed him after all? Hadn't she?

Joanna sucked in a breath and closed her eyes, trying to shove the memories aside.

But then another face loomed in her mind. A mirror of Josh's, but stronger somehow and scarred, yet just as blank with shock.

She'd hit him and hard, because holding back was never an option with Jacob Night. He'd stop her if he could and if she didn't take the advantage immediately, he would. And then she'd never find out . . . she'd never know if . . .

Jesus, if she could just *stop* thinking for one fucking second.

She slammed the drawer back in without taking anything from it, then straightened to rifle through the things sitting on top of the dresser. Little bottles of makeup and decorative trinket holders for jewelry. All the girly shit that Faith seemed to like that Joanna had never allowed herself.

Her hands were shaking as she shoved things aside, not even sure what she was looking for until she saw it, sitting neatly in the little box that held all her special items.

A necklace. A delicate platinum phoenix on a chain that rested in the hollow of her throat. She'd been out with Jacob one day and she'd seen it in a shop window and for some reason had been caught by it.

It was expensive and she couldn't have said why she'd liked it, only that the phoenix rising from the ashes had spoken to her. And Jacob must have seen her looking at it because the next day, when she'd gotten up in the morning, she'd found a little box beside her cereal bowl in the kitchen. And inside the box was the necklace.

He'd gotten it for her.

That morning, as she'd taken it out of its box and put it around her neck, tears had pricked her eyes and she hadn't known why.

She did now.

No one had ever bought her jewelry before.

When she'd been a little girl, she'd wanted to be a princess, with pretty dresses and sparkly necklaces and glass slippers. But her mother had told her she didn't deserve nice things and besides, princesses were for princes and there were no princes left in this world.

Not since Joanna had killed the last one.

She'd never been allowed to forget that and she hadn't. Except for the past six months, when she hadn't remembered anything at all.

Memories of a past she didn't want, a past she'd been trying to escape pushed against her mind. Her mother's face, lined and aged by alcohol and disappointment and grief, telling her she had to be good for this new stepfather. Because he had money for a change and it was worth a few slaps to have a warm bed and food in the cupboard. And that if Joanna ruined it for her this time, her mother would call social services and get them to take Joanna away.

She leaned against the dresser, a crushing weight descending on her chest.

No. *Fuck*, no. She'd left her mother and that pathetic, lousy existence behind. Found herself a new family in the military, a family that appreciated her and her skills. Who *liked* that she was a killer through and through.

Something dug into her palm and when she looked down, she realized she was clutching something in her hand. She opened her fingers slowly to find the little phoenix on its fine chain glittering there.

Jacob had given her that. The only person in the whole world to have ever gotten her something pretty.

Put it back. You don't need that shit.

Yeah, she should. She knew who she was now and that wasn't Faith, with her ridiculous pencil skirts and the high heels she'd

had to practice walking in. With all that stupid, girly, feminine bullshit designed to make a target out of a woman. Faith,
who'd cried over a fucking necklace some man had given her.

Not "some man." Jacob.

Her heart shuddered in her chest, as if the thought of Jacob
was painful somehow, so she ignored the sensation.

She wasn't Faith anymore. She was Joanna. A soldier. A
killer. Just like her mother had always told her she was. And
she didn't fight it these days, no, she embraced it. Became it.

Her inclination was to throw the little phoenix back into
the box it had come from. Yet, for reasons she couldn't have
explained even to herself, she stuffed it into the back pocket of
her pants.

Then she went to find the armory.

It was down in the basement, behind a steel door that had
the kind of locks on it that would have done a Swiss bank vault
proud, but she had no problems getting inside. Another retina
scan and the door unlocked for her beautifully.

Inside there were metal lockers standing against the walls
with yet more locks, and she opened all of them.

It was an arms dealer's paradise, with enough weaponry to
supply a small army.

She looked wistfully at a rocket launcher but since that was
something she could hardly keep tucked away at the small of
her back, she moved on. She needed something smaller. Much
smaller.

One locker was full of ARs and she picked up a Remington,
examining it. Thinking.

The plan she'd gone with on the journey to San Diego had
been half-formed at best, because she hadn't wanted to face the
memories, not just yet. But if she wanted to find out what had
happened to Josh, then she was going to have to.

She needed to figure out how to find him.

If he isn't dead. If you haven't killed him.

Grief and pain waited for her, she could feel them gathering like vultures, but she kept her thoughts firmly on the present. There would be plenty of time to think about what had happened and how she'd potentially killed the first real friend she'd ever had. Plenty of time.

Right now, getting armed, then getting a decent plan together, was more important. And quickly. There was no telling how fast Jacob would follow her and he'd definitely come here first. She needed to get a move on.

So. She'd take the AR and a couple of handguns; that should cover every eventuality.

Calmly, she disassembled the AR and put it in its case before finding a bag she could put the case in, along with a good supply of ammo. Then she chose a couple of handguns—a Sig and a Glock—putting one in the bag, the other in the waistband of her pants at the small of her back.

Then she tossed the bag over her shoulder and got out of there.

She was on her way out of the house when an idea came to her.

Finding Josh was always going to be the difficult part. She had some idea of who might have taken him, but no certainties. And that didn't leave her with much choice about what to do next.

If the people after her were the same as the people who'd taken Josh, then she needed to let them find her and once they did, perhaps she'd be able to negotiate an exchange of information. That was if they didn't kill her outright first.

But that was a problem for the future. Right now, she had to find them and the most logical way to do that was to let them find her first.

Or rather, let them find Faith.

She made another detour back into Faith's room and grabbed some clothes at random, stuffing them into the bag along with the guns. That done she finally headed to the door and let herself out of the house.

There was no one waiting outside—thank God—so she made her way down the sidewalk until she was well away from the house. She ordered herself an Uber and got them to take her first to a 7-Eleven for some supplies, then to a motel well away from La Jolla.

It was a crappy place that looked like it hadn't been updated since the nineties, but the reception was open and it was quiet and off the beaten track, which was all that mattered.

Once she was in the room, she locked the door, kicked the bag of weapons under the bed, then headed to the shower. Ten minutes later, feeling a little better now she was clean, she went over to the low coffee table where she'd dumped her paper bag of supplies and took out the whisky bottle. Finding a semi-clean glass, she poured herself a generous couple of fingers, then took out the protein bar she'd also bought and sat down on the couch.

She ate the bar quickly, letting the food settle her stomach, then she took a sip of the whisky.

It was cheap and raw, and burned on the way down, but it got the taste of vodka out of her head at least.

She closed her eyes, trying to calm her racing heartbeat.

This was always going to be hard. The moment when she stopped moving and planning and not thinking. The moment when she'd have to face the return of the memories inside her. Memories she'd been running from for six months.

She took another sip of the whisky, knowing she was going to have to do it, the alcohol doing nothing to melt the ice sitting in her gut. Of course, her mind kept wanting to protect her, telling her she had to get up, make sure her weapons were in good working order, to watch out the window in case anyone had followed her, to do anything else but face what she had to face.

But it had been protecting her for too long and she couldn't run from it anymore.

She had to face what she'd done to Josh.

She had to remember.

The shitty bar was full of cigarette smoke—no one cared about anti-smoking laws down in this part of South America—the fan turning the dead air only slowly. Tinny music played on an old jukebox and the dirt floor was dusty, something crunching under her boots as she'd stepped inside, but the light was too dim to see what it was so she ignored it.

Josh was there at one of the tables, obviously waiting, and as soon as she entered, he kicked his chair back and stared at her. A challenge.

Her heart leapt even though she'd told it not to—she hadn't seen him for two years and she'd missed him, God, so much—because she wasn't here for old times' sake. She was here with a mission.

And her mission was to take him out.

Yet she didn't go for her Sig. She walked over to the table and sat down instead. Because she'd promised herself that she'd find out why first. Why he'd betrayed the team the way he had done.

"I know why you're here," he said, pushing a glass over the table toward her, then filling it up with some kind of clear liquid from the bottle in front of him. "You're here to kill me, aren't you?"

The Beach Boys were playing on the jukebox. "Surfin' USA." Such a strange counterpoint to his blunt statement.

She wasn't surprised he knew. He'd never been a stupid man and he would have guessed their superiors wouldn't let him go without some kind of comeback.

So she didn't waste time denying it. Instead she picked up the glass and sipped. Vodka. Cheap vodka, the taste sharp and raw.

She drained the glass without a grimace, then put it down with a click. "I just want to know why, Josh."

His eyes gleamed. He looked good, if thinner, not that that detracted in any way from his looks. Six-four and built like a linebacker, with a strong jaw and high cheekbones, deeply set black eyes, and a mouth to die for, he was devastatingly attractive.

When he'd first joined the team, she'd found him distracting, but liaisons were forbidden among team members and she hadn't wanted anything to do with men anyway, so she'd never gone there. But emotionally . . . well, that had been a different story.

Her mother had told her there were no princes left in the world, but her mother hadn't met Joshua. He was the first man she'd met who seemed good. Decent. Kind. He'd gotten past her defenses and made a friend of her—the first she'd ever had—which was why his betrayal had hit her so hard.

It was why she was here in this bar, ready to talk and not taking out her gun and finishing her mission.

He was her friend and he'd betrayed her and their team and she just . . . wanted to know why.

He watched her silently. He'd never been a man who spoke unnecessarily. "Why do you want to know?"

"Why do you think?" She reached around and took out her Sig. Laid it down on the tabletop. "Yes, I was sent here to kill you."

"And yet you haven't."

She met his dark eyes. "You're my friend. Or at least, you used to be." Her throat felt tight, though she refused to give in to the feeling of grief. Anger was easier, always had been. "Tell me why the fuck you betrayed us, Josh. Give me one good reason why I shouldn't kill you right here and now."

He glanced at the Sig, then back at her, his expression giving nothing away. "You wouldn't understand."

She didn't bother to hide her anger. "Jesus Christ, how many missions have we done together? How often have I saved your ass and you saved mine? We've been through hell together so many times I've lost count. So don't give me that bullshit about not understanding."

He was silent again, lifting his glass and draining it. Then he put it back down and poured himself another measure, refilling her glass in the process.

"Why should I tell you a goddamn thing?" he asked. "You're going to kill me anyway."

She couldn't believe he even had to ask. "You're really going to ask me that question? After everything we went through?"

He had the grace to look away at that. "Fuck, Jo," he said at last. "You really want to know why? Money." He looked back at her and there was something very, very dark in his eyes. "They offered me money. A lot of it. And power. I'd be their go-between, the negotiator. All I had to do was sabotage our mission because it was getting too close to their operations." He picked up his glass. "You know what it's like to grow up with nothing. With no one on your side." Tipping it up, he took a swallow. "It makes you weak. Vulnerable. Money, on the other hand, is a whole lot of power right there. It won't abandon you. It won't betray you." He drained the glass. "It gives you respect. And I have to say, I like that. I like that a lot."

She blinked, not believing the words that were coming out of his mouth because . . . this was not the friend she knew. The man who'd been kind to her when she'd first joined the team. Who'd shown her the ropes and who'd shared missions and whisky bottles with her. Whom she'd shared her shitty childhood with and learned about his in the foster system. Whom she'd thought had her back.

Except he didn't have her back, did he?

"So respect and money meant more to you than our friendship?" she demanded. "It meant more than the team?"

"*Fuck the team,*" he spat suddenly, anger crossing his face. "*You want to know what the fucking team was really all about?*" He said the word team like it was poison. "*Cornwall told me they wanted me out. That mission was the last one I'd be on and then I'd be given my marching orders. After five fucking years of loyal service that was it.*" There was rage in his eyes this time, not mere anger. "*That was my military career over, Jo. And there was nothing else for me. The payout they were going to give me was pathetic and I . . .*" He stopped, looking down at his empty glass. "*I couldn't go back to civilian life. I couldn't. So when they offered me money and power and shit . . . just a little fucking respect, I couldn't say no.*" He glanced back up at her. "*They were going to make it so that everyone died, but I told them no. That having an entire black ops team disappear would mean no one would ever stop hunting them. And then I showed them how I'd sabotage the mission so no one died or drew it back to them.*"

She didn't know what to say to that because she'd had no idea they wanted him out. That made his anger understandable, but still, to go so far as to betray the whole team?

"*I didn't know,*" she said thickly. "*Why would they want you out?*"

His expression twisted. "*I have no fucking idea. They wouldn't tell me. Yet another reason for me to give them a big fuck-you on the way out.*"

"*Josh . . .*" She stopped, not knowing what else to say.

There was a heavy, loaded silence.

"*I didn't want to hurt you, Jo,*" he said at last. "*And I'm sorry I did.*"

"*I'm sorry too.*" She lifted her glass, took another sip of the vodka. "*They want you dead because of what you did.*"

"*What made them choose you?*"

She stared at him, not hiding anything. "*I volunteered.*"

For the first time, he smiled, a glimpse of the friend she re-membered. "You must have been really *fucking angry then.*"

The tightness in her chest eased, but she didn't return the smile. "You could say that. Plus, I wanted a straight answer."

"Fair enough." *He drained his glass again and poured yet more vodka into it.* "So now you've gotten it, what are you go-ing to do?"

She let out a breath. It had always been a question with only one answer. "How good are you at pretending to be dead?"

He laughed. "Excellent, as it happens. No one knows my name here. I just go by 'Smith.'"

"Good. We might also need a doctor who can fake a good death certificate." *There was one thing though that niggled at her. One thing she was* not *happy with.* "You going to stay working for them?"

He knew who she meant. The smile faded from his face, something harder appearing, something colder. "Of course. They'll never let me go anyway. And I'm okay with that."

"What you're doing is not okay, though. Those guns will lead to innocent people dying, Josh. And that's not what we set out to do."

He was in the unit to protect people, that's what he'd told her. And she'd agreed. Though for her, it was more that there were only two places a killer could safely be and that was ei-ther in jail or in the military. Since she'd only been six years old when she'd picked up that gun and shot her mother's abuser, jail was not an option for her. So the military it was. And she'd felt good there. She'd felt wanted. Safe. She liked feeling that she was protecting people too. Doing something good for a change.

Josh looked down at his glass cradled in one large hand. "In-nocent people will always get hurt," *he said quietly.* "No matter what you do."

She hadn't known what to make of that statement since it

had a ring of something personal about it, and she was on the point of asking him what he meant, when his head lifted and he turned toward the door. "Someone's coming." His black gaze came to hers. "Were you followed?"

She frowned. "No. I—"

But she had no chance to say more because the door burst open and a couple of guys came in, weapons drawn already.

Guys she knew. They were from her team.

She made a grab for her Sig, on her feet in an instant. "Craig?" she demanded. "Vincent? What the fuck are you doing here?"

But they weren't looking at her. They were looking at Josh.

"Out of the way, Lynn," Craig said curtly. "We fucking knew you couldn't do it. But don't worry. We will."

She knew what had happened then. Cornwall hadn't trusted she'd be able to complete the mission and so he'd sent a backup. To finish it.

Josh upended the table with a crash, but she was already moving, knocking away Craig's gun at the same time as she swept out a foot and took Vincent down. They weren't expecting her to move on them and in another couple of seconds she had them both on the floor unconscious.

"Shit," Josh said from behind her. "You've gotten good."

"I was always good." She turned around, her Sig in her hand. "Come on, we have to get out of here. They won't be alone, I'm sure of it."

He'd come out from behind the table holding a Glock. His eyes were glittering and there was a half smile on his face. He liked a fight, did Josh.

He moved over to her and she turned toward the door, but he wasn't coming after her. He was standing above the two prone men on the ground, his Glock already pointed at Vincent's face.

Again, she moved without thought, punching him hard in the arm. His shot went wide, slamming into the wall. Luckily, what few bar patrons there had been were all gone now.

"What the fuck did you do that for?" That darkness was back in his eyes.

"You can't kill them. Not like that."

"They were going to kill me." A muscle jumped in the side of his jaw. "Besides, I can't let them live, not now they know where I am."

Her heart clenched. "Don't be stupid. You don't want a couple of dead American soldiers here. Think of the consequences."

But that hard thing was in his expression, the hard thing that hadn't been there before. "They're black ops. No one'll know they're here anyway." He lifted his gun. "And if I go for the face—"

"No." She reached out and gripped his arm, holding him still. "Don't. They're part of our team."

"Not my team." His mouth pulled in a half snarl. "Not anymore."

"Josh—"

"Take your hand off my arm, Jo." His voice was flat and cold. "You led them here. If you want someone to blame, it's yourself."

Pain sliced through her, unexpected and raw.

She'd expect something like that from her mother, not from him, and it got to her, no matter how hard she tried not to let it.

"Don't put this on me," she snapped. "I didn't know Cornwall would send another team after me."

Josh lifted a shoulder. "Whatever, it's time these two were out of the picture." And he raised his Glock again.

But she couldn't let him do it, not shoot a couple of people in cold blood. So she made a grab for the gun.

Only to have something come down hard on the back of her head, pain exploding around her. Blackness descended for a moment and when it cleared, she found herself on her knees, her head aching. Someone was holding her hands behind her back in an iron grip.

In front of her was Josh, talking to someone in Spanish on his *cell, his voice hard and cold. Of Craig and Vincent there was no sign, only a pool of blood where they'd been lying.*

Oh shit. Josh had done it, hadn't he? He'd killed them.

And now someone was holding her and she was . . . a prisoner? What?

The taste of vodka sat sharply in her mouth, the cheerful sounds of the Beach Boys that had been playing on the jukebox replaced by the Righteous Brothers and "Unchained Melody."

She looked at Josh as he spoke, and she understood enough to know that he was relaying information about her. That killing her was a mistake, that she'd make a good hostage.

And she felt the knife slide deeper inside her, betrayal cutting her open.

Your mother was right all along. There are no princes left in this world.

Anger was a dark fire in her heart, burning hot and bright.

She'd thought she'd found a friend, someone she could trust. Someone who understood her, but of course she hadn't. All she'd found was yet another man who lied. Who'd sucked her in with kindness, then betrayed her.

She'd been a fool to believe he cared about her.

The grip on her wrists shifted minutely and that's when she moved. Fast. Hard. No hesitation. Springing straight up from her knees, the back of her head striking someone's jaw. There was a crack, a curse, and the grip on her wrists fell away. Her head rang like a bell, pain spider-webbing everywhere, but she ignored it, spinning around and kicking the man who'd been holding her, a foot direct to the chest. There was another guy standing next to him who had his knife out already and she took a couple of cuts to her arms as he lunged at her, but a roundhouse kick to the head brought him down easy enough. There was a gun wedged into his jeans in the small of his back and she was able to snatch it as he fell.

"Jo, stop," Josh said coldly.

But she didn't, spinning around, lifting the gun and aiming at the man she'd thought of as her friend.

To find his Glock pointed directly at her heart.

"You don't want to do that." There was no mercy in his eyes. Only that darkness. "I can't let them find me. And that means I can't let you go."

She wanted to ask him whether the friendship between them had all been a lie. Whether he'd cared anything about her at all. But that would be giving too much away and she'd already given enough away as it was.

The Righteous Brothers sang about lonely rivers and hungry touches and needing love.

But Joanna did the only thing she could.

She pulled the trigger and shot him.

Joanna shuddered and opened her eyes, her heart beating so fast she thought she might pass out. She didn't want to remember the next part but it was there in her head all the same.

His gun had gone off at the same time as she'd pulled her trigger, and she'd felt a tearing pain as the bullet took her in the shoulder. She'd gone down, gasping, lying there on the dirty floor of the bar as pain filled her entire world.

Somehow she'd managed to drag herself over to where Josh lay. His eyes were closed, his T-shirt covered with blood, a hole in his chest where her bullet had hit him.

He looked dead, but before she had time to check, she'd heard shouts from outside the bar. His friends, no doubt, and if they found her, they'd kill her.

So she'd hauled herself to her feet and had escaped out the back, blood covering her, shock both physical and emotional like an icy ocean dragging at her.

It was a successful mission and yet she'd failed in every way that mattered.

She'd been responsible for the deaths of two of her own

team, but that wasn't even the worst part. The worst part was that she'd picked up that gun and fired in anger.

She'd shot her best friend and probably killed him, because he'd betrayed her.

Because her mother had been right. She was a killer after all.

She'd stumbled down the alley behind the bar, bleeding from the gunshot wound in her shoulder, from the knife cuts on her arms and from where they'd hit her on the back of her head, wondering why she was even bothering to run when there was no escape from the past that kept following her around wherever she went.

No escape from the pain. It would always be there, deep in her soul.

So she'd stopped running and had just lain down in the dirt.

And when the blackness had come, she hadn't fought. She'd simply let it take her . . .

Someone was breathing very fast and very hard and she realized it was herself. Her cheeks were wet and she was clutching something in her hand, the edges digging into her skin.

She opened her fingers and looked down to see the phoenix necklace that Jacob had given her sitting in her palm.

Jesus, why was she holding that like a goddamn security blanket? It was just a stupid piece of jewelry.

Yet she didn't drop it. She kept it in her hand as she downed the rest of her whisky, a reminder of the six months when she'd been free.

When she didn't have the knowledge of who and what she was hanging over her head.

When you found out that there maybe are *still princes in this world all the same.*

No. Jacob Night wasn't a prince. He might have taken care of her for six months, he might have given her jewelry, but that was all for a reason. He wanted her memories. He wanted to know what had happened to his brother.

Well, she could tell him.

She'd killed him.

Something slipped down her cheek. Another fucking tear.

A formless, dark fury twisted in her blood, but she pushed it away. Giving in to it was a mistake, hadn't she learned that? No, it was better to ignore it. It was better to not feel anything at all.

She poured herself another whisky and downed it. Drank a third glass for luck, then pushed herself off the couch.

The phoenix necklace was still in her hand and she didn't know what to do with it. The logical thing would have been to throw it in the trash, but she couldn't bring herself to for some reason. So she put it around her neck instead.

After a brief check at the windows to see if there was anyone lurking around outside—there wasn't—she went over to the bed, pulled back the quilt, and got into it.

The mattress was uncomfortable, and she thought she wouldn't sleep, but it was three a.m. and she'd come to the end of her strength.

Sleep pulled her down, black and gritty, and she went with it, falling into the old nightmare, of running down that alleyway with flames following her, a nameless dread pulling at her.

Only to wake with a start, feeling something large and heavy and hot lying on her.

Because she was disoriented from the whisky and the dreams, her heart leapt like a frightened rabbit and for a second she was Faith again, memory-less and tormented by nightmares. She opened her mouth to scream only to have a large, warm hand cover it, silencing her.

"Caught you, sweet girl," a deep, rough male voice murmured in her ear.

CHAPTER 12

Faith had gone still beneath him and he could feel the shudder that went through her. But he didn't make any effort to shift his weight off her or release her.

She was dangerous and he wasn't going to let his guard down around her, not again. Not while Joanna was in charge.

Silence filled the small motel room, but he was ready.

Sure enough, she tried to twist out from under him, her body lithe and strong. He'd been expecting it and moved, shifting to let his superior weight pin her to the mattress and pressing down against her face with his hand so she had to let go or else break her own jaw.

"We've done this before," he said, not bothering to hide the amusement in his voice. "And I won then so I don't know what makes you think you're going to win now."

She didn't reply, simply brought up her knee, but he was ready for that too and shifted to straddle her, trapping her thighs between his knees so she couldn't move her legs.

She wasn't done then, either, rearing up to slam her forehead into his nose. Easy enough to avoid it though, then settle his weight on her more completely, his fingers wound around her slender wrists and pressing them hard onto the pillow.

She said nothing, her eyes dark as she stared up at him. There was no fear in her expression, but that lovely mouth was set and hard, and she was breathing very fast.

Yeah, he'd lay money on the fact that she was furious, and no wonder. She probably thought she'd escaped him.

He smiled, a savage kind of anticipation gripping him as her familiar scent wrapped around him, feminine musk and lavender, while her sweet heat soaked through the quilt and into him.

Fuck, he wasn't done with her. Not nearly done. And that wasn't even including the memories he was going to drag from her. No, there was more, a lot more that he wanted.

"You can run, but you can't hide from me, Ms. Beasley. Or is that Ms. Lynn now?"

"Get the fuck off me." Her voice was hard and yet he didn't miss the breathless quality to it.

"Language, Ms. Beasley." He smiled wider. "I'd tell you to make me but as I said, we've done that already. Though feel free to try again. As I recall, it involved you rubbing yourself all over my cock."

She bared her teeth at him. "Been there, done that. And it really wasn't all that exciting the first time around."

He gave a rough laugh. "Bullshit. You loved it. I watched you come, remember? In fact, I'd go so far as to say that being under me is your favorite place to be."

"Faith might have. But I'm not her." She'd relaxed, her muscles going loose. "How did you find me?"

Hoping to lull him into thinking she'd given up the fight, no doubt. Sadly for her, she was mistaken in thinking he could be lulled.

He loosened his grip, giving the impression that he was distracted. "Easily enough. I had your clothes bugged." It had been an added precaution for her safety, so that if anyone took her, he could track her. He just hadn't expected her to run off of her own accord.

She said nothing to that, but her jaw was tight, the gleam of fury in her eyes leaping higher.

He understood. In addition to being supremely pissed with him, she'd no doubt be angry at herself that she hadn't thought of that. Then again, there was no reason for her to know since he hadn't told her.

Too bad about all the rest of the things you told her.

He ignored the thought. No, the whole situation hadn't been exactly ideal, but he'd tracked her down in the end. Though that had been the easy part. Getting away from the bunker had been a mission since she'd slashed the jet's tires. However, he kept his safe house supplied for every eventuality and that included a spare set of tires plus all the equipment needed for a solo tire change, including a pneumatic jack.

Even so, it had taken him the better part of three hours to get it done.

Landing in San Diego, he'd then tracked her to his own house in La Jolla, which again, he'd been expecting. He'd gotten there just in time to see her come out the front door and he'd debated grabbing her right there and then, but had decided against it in the end, curious to see where she might go.

So he'd followed her to the shitty little motel, waiting until he was sure she'd fallen asleep before making his move.

The lock on the door had been easy enough to pick and she hadn't stirred when he'd entered the room. He'd thought she might be more aware than that, but apparently not.

She hadn't even woken when he'd climbed onto the bed and lain down on top of her, pinning her so she couldn't get away.

No wonder she was pissed.

"So what now?" Her voice held none of Faith's warmth, only a flat note. "You want a fuck before you get down to interrogating me?"

Oh, yes. She was *extremely* pissed.

"I'm easy." He loosened his grip even more to encourage her. "Though if you're offering, I certainly wouldn't say no."

"Yeah, well, like I said. Been there, done that." She turned her head on the pillow sharply, looking toward the door as if she'd heard a sound. Probably hoping that he'd look too.

He obliged her.

Sure enough, as soon as he did, she jackknifed on the bed, her body moving powerfully beneath his. Fuck, she was good. She managed to get one hand loose, her knee getting perilously close to his groin, and he had to shift fast to avoid it. Unfortunately, that meant having to take a strike that made his head ring like a bell, but he ignored it, rolling with her, using momentum to take her back down under him again.

They were lying across the bed now, the sheets and quilt tangled around their legs. He had her wrists pinned on either side of her head, his thighs on either side of hers, keeping her trapped.

She was breathing fast, her breasts brushing against his chest. And it did not escape his notice that her nipples were hard.

Anticipation swept through him, along with a dizzying rush of desire.

Faith had always been strong, but now that she'd remembered who she was, there was another facet to her, a physical strength and skill that he found absolutely fucking intoxicating.

Christ, he hadn't thought this woman could get any more perfect than she already was and then she went ahead and did so.

"Nice move." His voice had gone gravelly with a heat he didn't bother hiding. "Pity it didn't work."

Her expression gave nothing away, her chest rising and falling fast and hard, the softness of her breasts pushing against him.

Then her body shifted again as she arched herself up, lifting her hips against his, the damp heat between her thighs pressed to the hard ridge of his dick.

He hissed as pleasure licked up his spine and then she did it again, pressing against him even harder.

Fuck. Little witch was trying to use his own tactic against him.

And Jesus, it was working.

She twisted, grinding against him, not holding back, and his breathing changed, getting faster, shorter.

He tried to avoid the lift of her hips, settling down more heavily on her so his weight would pin her to the bed, but that only seemed to make her writhe like a goddamn eel.

It was . . . exquisite.

"Stop that," he ordered roughly.

But she didn't. Instead she lifted her head and her mouth found his, hungry and hot.

The kiss was like a match to a tank of gas and he went up in flames, sliding his tongue deep into her mouth in an effort to take control. But she wouldn't let him, angling her head to kiss him harder, biting at his bottom lip as her hips lifted rhythmically against his painfully hard cock.

Holy fuck. If he wasn't careful he was going to forget that she was only doing this to distract him and that the moment he dropped his guard, she'd no doubt try to get away on him.

But Jesus, this was one hell of a distraction technique. And she had one hell of an advantage too, because she knew what he liked. She knew all too well.

She moved beneath him, writhing and twisting, grinding that hot little pussy of hers against his dick as she sunk her teeth into his bottom lip. The slight pain only added to the pleasure that was building inside him, making him want to growl. To move so he could tear those pants down her legs and get inside her.

Mother*fuck*, how had she managed to get him so close to

the limits of his control? Because he was. And that was a shock because two days ago she'd done the same thing and he'd been able to hold back, no problem.

You've had a taste of her now, though, and that's made it worse.

It wasn't supposed to be like that. One fuck and the desire was gone, that's what happened every other goddamn time. But not apparently with her. No, one fuck and he wanted more.

You dumb bastard. You should never have told her all that stuff. She'll use that against you like she's using your own cock against you now.

Jacob growled and tore his mouth away. Then he drove his thigh between hers. She gave a gasp and he could feel it, the dampness soaking into the fabric of his pants.

She was wet.

He looked down at her, conscious that his breathing was way too fast. "Been there, done that, huh?" His voice was thick and rough-sounding. "You're awfully wet to be sounding so bored."

In the dark he couldn't tell if she was flushed or not, but the wet heat between her thighs didn't lie.

"Fuck you, Jacob," she panted.

"Sadly for you, not tonight."

"Get the hell off me."

"What? And have you kick me in the balls again? Not a chance, Ms. Beasley."

"Don't fucking call me that."

"My mistake, Ms. Lynn." He put a little weight on his thigh, nudging it against her pussy, watching as her lashes fluttered and her breath caught. "Hmmm. You like that, don't you? Are you sure you don't want to continue?"

She blinked, then looked straight up at him, that fury glittering in her eyes. "Faith might have, but I don't."

Something shifted inside him, a tightness that hadn't been

there before. He'd wondered if the return of her memories would change her, would make her different from the woman he knew, and clearly, that had happened.

Don't forget Joshua.

The constriction in his chest got more intense, along with that possessiveness he couldn't quite shake.

Was she thinking about his brother right now? Had they been lovers? Were they still? And did she regret sleeping with him?

He hated the thought of that. *Hated* it.

"Were you lovers?" he demanded, unable to stop himself. "You and Joshua?"

This time it was her turn to study him, her gaze sharp. Then, as if she'd spotted something in his expression that pleased her, she gave him a maddening smile. "Wouldn't you like to know."

Oh no, she wasn't doing that. Not here, not with him.

He opened his mouth to issue yet another demand and then stopped, seeing something gleam in the hollow of her throat. It was the phoenix necklace he'd bought Faith after he'd seen her mooning over it in an expensive jewelry store. She'd pretended she hadn't wanted it, but he'd bought it for her anyway, because it had seemed so appropriate.

She was rising from the ashes of her old self, with a new identity, a symbol of magic and hope.

She'd teared up when he'd given it to her even though she'd tried to hide it from him, and then had tried to refuse, telling him she couldn't possibly accept anything so expensive. He'd insisted and afterward had noticed that she wore it virtually every day.

Just like she was wearing it now.

The tightness in his chest shifted, became something else, less painful yet somehow no less intense.

She must have gotten it when she went back to his house and she must have picked it up specifically.

Even now that she'd remembered who she was, it meant something to her, didn't it?

They can't have been lovers. She wouldn't be wearing your gift if she was Joshua's.

Maybe. And perhaps she didn't even know it herself or realize what wearing that phoenix meant, but he did.

"You weren't," he said with absolute conviction, feeling the truth of it echo inside him. "You were always mine."

An expression that looked like shock flickered briefly over her face, before it morphed back into anger. "Yours?" She gave a laugh that had nothing to do with amusement. "Seriously? You're one arrogant son of a bitch, you know that?"

He ignored the dig. "You're wearing the necklace I gave you."

Another flicker of surprise, once again swiftly masked. "So?"

"So you must have picked it up from your dresser. Deliberately."

She didn't like that, not one bit, and showed it by making yet another attempt to get free. Twisting harder. But he only moved his grip and kept her weighted down with his body.

"What's wrong?" he murmured as she quieted. "You don't like thinking of yourself as Faith, do you?"

"Because I'm not her!" She virtually spat the words at him.

Interesting. She *really* didn't like that.

"You are. You're the same person, sweet girl. Accept it."

"Fuck you and your sweet girl bullshit." Fury burned in her eyes. "You're not here for that. You're here for my memories."

Oh, she was angry with him. So *very* angry. Why? Was it only because he'd found her and captured her? Or was it about something more? It was almost as if she was pissed at him that her memories were the only reason he'd come after her, which was strange because he'd never made a secret of the fact that he wanted them.

But that's not the only reason you came after her.

No, it wasn't and he knew it.

He'd come after her because as far as he was concerned, she was still his. Yes, he wanted to know where his brother was and what had happened to him, but that wasn't the only thing he wanted.

He wanted to know about the woman he'd slowly become more and more fascinated with over the last six months. About the past she hadn't been able to remember and all the little secrets that had been locked inside her brain.

He wanted to know who Joanna Lynn was and how different she was from the woman he knew—if they were different, and he didn't think they were, no matter what she was trying to tell him.

So many things he wanted to know. In fact, for the first time in years, it felt more important that he know about her than he did about what had happened to his brother.

You could at least know if he's alive.

But he shoved that thought from his head. If his brother was alive, then another half an hour wouldn't make much difference, not at four in the morning. And if his brother was dead . . . well, nothing he did would make any difference now anyway.

"No," Jacob said softly. "I'm here for you."

He was lying. He had to be. He'd spent six goddamn months making a big deal of wanting her to remember, yet now he was trying to tell her he was here for her?

Bull*shit*.

Not that it mattered, because it wasn't like she cared. She was pissed, yes, but that was all due to how he'd caught her off guard. That she'd had that whisky and then hadn't woken up the way she should have when he'd crept into her hotel room. That he'd pinned her and she couldn't escape.

Nothing to do with the fact that he wasn't wrong about you enjoying being under him.

Yeah and *that* was the most terrible part about all of this.

She'd thought that with all her memories intact, she wouldn't have any feelings at all about Jacob Night. Yet it turned out she did.

Or at least her body did. And she hated it.

But it didn't seem to matter whether she hated it or not. The feel of him pressing down on her, that powerful thigh pushed between her legs, reminded her of when he'd shoved her up against the doorframe and kissed her. Touched her. Pushed inside her. And how she'd wanted him. How desperate she'd been for him. How hard she'd come for him and how badly she wanted to do it again.

It wasn't supposed to happen. She wasn't supposed to want a man like him that badly. She wasn't supposed to want a man like him at all.

Yet here she was, lying under him, staring up into his hard, scarred face, so familiar and yet so unfamiliar at the same time, and all she could think about was that thigh thrust between hers and the fact that he apparently was here for her too.

Men lie. Haven't you learned anything?

"You think I'm lying, don't you?" he said, lifting the thought directly out of her head. "Don't deny it, Ms. Lynn, I can see it in your eyes."

He *was* lying. He wasn't here for her. Jesus, he didn't even know her.

God, she wanted him *off.* She couldn't stand the relentless pressure between her thighs, the way parts of her body softened for him while other parts hardened. It brought back memories she didn't want in her head, feelings she didn't want in her heart.

Joanna. She was Joanna now, not Faith. Joanna didn't care about Jacob Night, and she certainly wasn't attracted to him.

She gritted her teeth, ignoring her body, looking up at him and trying to see Joshua, her friend, not the man who'd taken her apart so sweetly and completely with his hands and his body.

The man who took you in and looked after you for six months after you lost your memory.

Yeah. But not out of the goodness of his heart. He'd done that because he'd wanted that memory and he was prepared to do anything to get it. He was as bad, if not worse, as all the rest of them, men who wanted something from women and took what wasn't theirs. Who lied and cheated and stole and hurt.

Her mother was right and had always been right. There were no princes here, only demons.

"I'm not denying it," she bit out. "You *are* lying."

He shifted, the movement of his body causing lightning strikes of pleasure to pulse along her nerve endings. "What makes you think that?"

"How about six months of you harping on about how I need to remember what happened to me because you want to know about your brother."

"I do want to know about my brother." His eyes gleamed in the dark, not as flat and depthless as Joshua's, but brighter somehow. Like the light reflecting off a shiny black surface. "But I also want to know about you."

"Why?" Subtly she tried to pull against the hold on her wrists but his grip was very strong. If she was going to get out from under him, she was going to have to do better than that.

"Because you lived with me for six months and you fascinate me."

"Faith fascinates you. Not me."

"I'm curious. Why do you persist in thinking of yourself as two different people?"

"I'm not two different people. I was Faith for six months

because I had no memory of who I was, but I remember now, and I'm not Faith. She doesn't exist anymore."

His mouth curved in a smile and she couldn't drag her gaze from it. Joshua's smiles were friendly, nonthreatening. Not edged and full of challenge the way Jacob's were.

Joshua's smile would never make you feel the way you do now.

No, it wouldn't. Because she'd never been attracted to Joshua. And she wasn't attracted to Jacob, either, not at all.

Now who's lying?

Oh God, she *had* to get him off her.

"And yet you're wearing my necklace," he murmured, his weight settling down on her even more heavily, as if he knew that she'd been trying to figure out how to get out from under him and was planning on stopping her. "Faith really liked that necklace."

If her hands had been free, she would have ripped that necklace away and thrown it as far as she could. But she'd been stupid and had put it on, and she still didn't even know why.

Jewelry was for silly little girls who'd never picked up a gun and taken a life with it.

"It's not going to stay on, believe me." Maybe if she spread her legs she could wrap them around that muscled thigh between hers, then twist. If she did it quick and hard enough, his grip on her wrists might loosen. "First chance I get it's coming off."

"You don't like jewelry?"

"I fucking hate jewelry." She let her legs fall open, encouraging him to press his thigh harder between hers. Which of course he did. It hit her clit, giving her enough of that lightning pleasure to make her breath catch. Goddammit.

"Why? Tell me about yourself, Ms. Lynn."

"I thought your brother was more important?"

"He is. But he can wait ten minutes."

"And if he's dead?"

Jacob's gaze sharpened, his big, hot body tensing.

Then, much to her shock, he let go of her wrists and with a simple, elegant movement, rolled off the bed, moving over to the door of the room and standing in front of it.

It took her a moment to process that she was free.

"What are you doing?" she asked, sitting up slowly.

"You wanted me to get off you. So now I'm off you." He folded his arms over his impressive chest. "My brother. Is he dead or not?"

She swallowed. Her body still felt hot, an ache pulsing between her thighs. Damn him.

"No," she said. "Not when I left him." It was a lie, of course. She had no idea whether he was alive or not. She had no idea why she'd lied either, it just . . . slipped out before she could stop it.

Jacob's expression didn't change, though she thought she caught a slight shift in the set of his wide shoulders, as if the tension had gone out of them. "Let's talk about you then."

It was that slight shift that caught at something deep inside her.

All this time and she hadn't considered how this must be for him, searching for the brother he'd lost all those years ago. She didn't want to consider it now, because his feelings didn't matter to her, not one fucking iota.

And yet . . . he'd loved his brother, hadn't he? He'd cared for him. And this . . . this must hurt him.

And you killed him. You killed Josh.

Ice wound through her veins.

She couldn't sit here talking to fucking Jacob Night. She had to get out. She had to find out what happened to Josh.

"You don't want to know about me." She slid over to the edge of the bed. "If you don't mind, I have shit to—"

"You're not going anywhere, Ms. Lynn," Jacob interrupted calmly. "Not until you tell me what I want to know."

Her guns were under the bed. Maybe if she—

"Thinking about these?" He reached behind himself and pulled out the Sig. *Her* fucking Sig. Then, without any hurry at all, he moved over to the coffee table and picked up her goddamn AR. And smiled. "I took the liberty of securing them for you. Hope you don't mind."

Asshole.

She took a long, slow, soundless breath. Then let it out.

Okay, so he'd taken her weapons. Fine. She didn't need them anyway, not when she had the best weapon of all to use against him.

Herself.

He wanted to know about her, well, she could use that. Could use his obvious desire for her too. Men were simple creatures at heart. Get them by the cock and they'd do anything you wanted.

Yet another lesson she'd learned from her mother. Of course it hadn't saved her in the end, but that was because her mother didn't have the strength that she'd had. She was the one who'd picked up that gun and pulled the trigger. Shot the last prince.

Joanna leaned back on the bed, arching her back slightly, letting the black T-shirt she wore pull tight across her breasts.

His gaze flickered. Good.

"Okay, what do you want to know?" Joshua was the only one she'd told about her background and the shitshow that was her childhood. He'd shared his, too—except he'd never told her he was a twin. He'd never told her he'd had a brother. A brother who'd tried to protect him . . .

Men lie, don't forget.

Of course. Joshua hadn't told her about any of it, and who was to say that Jacob wasn't lying either? She believed he was Josh's brother—the physical resemblance couldn't be denied—but the rest? Who knew what was the truth and what wasn't?

She couldn't trust him. She couldn't trust any of them.

"What do I want to know?" Jacob was a tall, dark wall at the end of the bed. "I want to know everything."

CHAPTER 13

Faith sat on the edge of the bed, her long, glossy black hair tumbling down her back, the fabric of her T-shirt tight across her lovely breasts. She tilted her head, the expression on her face giving nothing away.

"Everything?" she echoed. "That's going to cost you."

He was hard. Still. Which made getting off of her a good thing. But that hadn't been the entire reason. Doing the unexpected was the best way to get under people's guard.

"What's your price?" he asked, ignoring the ache in his groin.

"I tell you about me. You let me go. Easy."

Yes, easy. If he wanted to let her go and he didn't. He could give her a head start, though. "Done."

Her gaze flickered. Clearly, she hadn't expected him to agree. Good. This might take less time than he'd anticipated.

"Okay," she said after a moment. "I lived on the East Coast, then my mom moved to California. Nothing much to report. I was a beach bunny, liked hanging out with the surfers. Had the same kinds of teenage drama that everyone else had. When

I was eighteen I enlisted. Army. Became a Ranger. I was good and eventually I was approached to join a special unit dealing with the cartels in South America." Her blue eyes were guileless. "Seemed like fun so I agreed. That's where I met Josh. We got on well, eventually hooked up and—"

"Stop." He said it quietly, but with enough authority that she did as she was told, like the good little soldier she was. "That's a great story. If it was true." And it wasn't, he knew deep in his bones.

The lie was there in the necklace she wore, the necklace he'd given her. No, she and his brother hadn't hooked up, he was sure of it. And as to the rest, the Army stuff he'd believe, but hanging out with surfers? A beach bunny? And the "usual teenage drama" . . .

No. There was too much anger in her eyes for it to be as simple as that. There was too much anger in her, period. It poured off her like heat off a rock after a day in the hot sun.

People didn't get to be that angry without good reason and it wasn't due to the "usual teenage drama."

"It is true." She pushed herself off the bed. "Now . . . How about you get out of the way. I have shit to do."

He didn't move.

She scowled. "You said you were going to—"

"You lied, Ms. Lynn."

Her chin came up. "Like you would know."

"I do know." He wasn't angry with her. In her place he would have lied too. Then again, surely she would know by now that she could trust him. She certainly had back in the bunker.

She didn't remember who she was then.

So? Faith and Joanna were the same person and remembering who she was didn't suddenly change the six months she'd spent in his care, or what they'd shared between them. At least, it shouldn't. And if it did, well . . . He wanted to know why.

"I thought you trusted me," he said quietly.

"Faith might have. But I don't."

"I told you my story."

"Oh, so this is a quid pro quo now?"

"No." He held her gaze, letting her see the truth in his eyes. "Just a reminder that you had my trust and that you still do."

"Then you're a fool." Bitterness laced the words. "And you should never have told me what you did. Not when you had no idea who I really was."

Ah, but she didn't understand and, shit, if she kept thinking of herself as two different people then she wouldn't.

"I know you, Faith Beasley."

"I'm not—"

"And I know you, Joanna Lynn. I've watched over you, lived with you, worked with you for months now. And remembering your true identity doesn't change things."

Tension was gathering in her, he could see it in the set of her shoulders and in the still way she was standing. Her expression was guarded, but those dark eyes . . . he could see the anger in them.

"You have no idea what you're talking about." Her voice was sharp, like a knife. "You think I'm like Faith? Girly and pretty? Tearing up over stupid things like necklaces? Sitting there happily in your lap while you told her sad tales of your childhood?"

He ignored the derision in her tone. "You *are* Faith, sweet girl."

"Don't call me that. I'm not fucking sweet and I'm definitely no girl."

Ah, that sounded personal. Very personal indeed.

"What are you then?" he asked softly. "Tell me."

She didn't respond immediately, her eyes shadowed. Then abruptly, she came over to him, walking with purpose, lithe and graceful.

She stopped right in front of him, folding her arms over her chest and tipping her head back to look up at him. "You really want to know?"

He heard the note of challenge in her voice. It delighted him. No doubt she thought she was going to shock him with tales of violence and death. In which case, silly girl. How could she have forgotten what he was? It wasn't as if he hadn't told her. If she was black ops the way she'd said she was, then she'd know nothing she could say would shock him.

"I wouldn't have asked if I didn't," he said.

"I'm a killer." The words were as flat as the look in her eyes.

"Of course you are." He raised a brow. "Is that it?"

"When I was six years old, I picked up a gun and shot my mother's boyfriend with it. He died."

Ah, now *that* sounded like truth.

"Did you?" He studied her lovely face, pale in the shadowed room. Her delicate jaw was tight, lines of tension around her mouth, and deep in her beautiful eyes, fury glowed like a fire. This was what hurt, wasn't it? This was what she was so angry about.

"Yes." She bit the word out like it tasted bad.

Smiling would be a bad thing now, so he didn't. But he wanted to. Because seriously, if she thought this made her any less a sweet girl to him, she was wrong. Very, *very* wrong.

"I'm sure he deserved it," he murmured.

"You think this is a joke?"

"A joke?" He dropped his arms and stepped forward, towering over her, letting her see the darkness inside of him. And then he did smile, white and savage. "No. You thinking that would matter to me is the joke. Or have you forgotten what I am?"

She didn't back away even though he was a full head taller than she was and probably outweighing her by a good hundred pounds.

"I meant to kill him," she said and there was satisfaction in her tone, he heard it. "I wanted to. I knew where he kept his gun so I went and got it, and I shot him with it. And I was glad he was dead."

"Why?" He searched her face, seeing the rage there and also the pain that lay underneath it. "What did he do to you?"

"It doesn't matter why."

"Wrong. It *always* matters why." He lifted a hand to cup her jaw, because she was hurting and he didn't like that one fucking bit.

But she jerked her head away, refusing his touch. "I killed him. *That's* the only thing that matters."

Jacob ignored her. "He hurt you, didn't he?"

"No. Not me." Her throat moved as she swallowed, her gaze flickering. "He hurt my Mom."

Jacob lifted both hands and took her face between his palms, not allowing her to pull away this time. "Good," he said. "I'm glad you killed him in that case. He deserved to die."

She'd gone stiff in his hold. "I was six."

"So? I was ten when I pulled a knife on Greg. And to this day I wish I'd managed to kill him with it." He could feel the tension in her jaw so he started to stroke her fine-grained skin with his thumbs.

But she wasn't having any of that, twisting out of his hold and turning away, her hair falling over her shoulder and veiling her face. "I gave you what you wanted. You can get the hell out of the way of the door now."

He let his hands drop, yet didn't move. "The rest of it, Ms. Lynn. If you please."

She let out a breath, then turned back to him, her expression guarded once more. "What else do you want to know? That my mother blamed me for his death? That she never forgave me for it? That she spent the rest of my childhood going from man to man trying to find him again? Telling me over and over again that our shitty situation was all my fault?" Faith threw the questions at him like knives. "He told her that he loved her, that he didn't mean to hit her, and she believed him, even though he hit her more than once and after he promised not to again." A bitter laugh broke from her. "Men lie, that's what she told me, except the one I killed, obviously. But she wasn't wrong. Men *do* lie. They promise you all kinds of shit and then . . ." She broke off, her jaw going hard. "Jesus, why the fuck am I telling you all of this? You're a liar like all the rest of them."

Anger gripped him, but not at her. Someone had betrayed her, that was obvious. Some man had lied to her and it had hurt her. Badly.

Closing the distance between them, he reached for her, his hands on her hips, turning her to face him. "Who lied to you?" he demanded.

She tried to twist away from him, but he pulled her in close, holding her tight. He wasn't going to let her have any distance, not this time. "Was it my brother?"

"Let me the fuck go!"

Jacob wound an arm around her, then gripped her chin in his free hand, tipping her head back so he could see her face.

Rage glowed deep in her eyes.

"It was him, wasn't it?" He didn't bother to keep the edge of authority out of his voice. Fuck, he wanted answers and he wanted them now.

He expected her to fight him, but she didn't. She went still in his grip, staring at him. "Josh was supposed to be my friend. But he wanted to use me."

"Use you how?"

"He got a better offer of employment. They were going to get rid of him from the unit anyway so he sabotaged one of our missions. Then he disappeared. I volunteered to track him down because I wanted to know why he'd betrayed us. I found him eventually and that's when he told me they'd been going to get rid of him." She didn't fight, her eyes suddenly glowing bright. "I didn't know that I'd been followed though. Two of our team had been sent to find us and they did. They ambushed us and Josh . . . killed them." She bared her teeth. "He was going to take me too, use me as a hostage. I don't know exactly. But I was to be his prisoner. So I . . ." She stopped.

Something cold solidified slowly in Jacob's gut. "You what?"

Faith smiled, a bitter, cold kind of smile. "So I shot him."

She waited for that strange reflective light to die in his eyes. Waited for the moment when he'd finally see her for what she truly was.

Because surely now he would. She'd killed his brother, her only friend. She'd shot him down in anger, because he'd betrayed her.

Joshua Smith deserved a lot of things, but he didn't deserve to die. Yes, he'd lied to her, but the finger on the trigger had been hers and she hadn't hesitated.

Neither did he, remember?

She ignored that, staring up into Jacob's black eyes. Staring up into the face that, now she was studying it, looked nothing like Josh's. There had been an easy warmth in Josh's face that was absent from Jacob's.

Jacob's was hard. Fierce. Savage. No warmth, no, but there was heat. There was fire. A passion that his brother didn't have, a kind of granite strength and determination.

She'd always been drawn to his strength though, hadn't she? His absolute certainty had been what she'd clung to after she'd gotten out of the hospital, his strength her anchor—

No, shit, that had been Faith who'd liked that. Not her.

And yet . . .

His fingers were digging into her hips, his grip nearly painful.

But that light in his eyes wasn't dying. It was growing brighter.

"I thought you said he was alive," Jacob said, enunciating every word.

Why was he looking at her like that? Why wasn't he throwing her to one side and grabbing those guns? Pointing them in her face?

"I lied," she spat, wanting to goad him, make him angry. Make him lose his temper with her. Make him see that she wasn't Faith anymore, she was Joanna. "I don't know whether he's alive or not. All I know is that he pulled a gun on me and so I—"

Jacob lifted his hands and grabbed the front of her T-shirt. Then he ripped it open.

Instantly she shifted her weight onto the balls of her feet, curling her fingers in toward her palm, driving it into his stomach. But he was shifting too, moving fast, dodging her fist at the same time as he hooked an arm around her waist, then turned her, slamming her up against the nearest wall.

He didn't speak, jerking aside the ripped halves of her T-shirt. Her breath caught and for some reason she didn't stop him when he lifted a hand to her chest, her heart beating hard with what she had a terrible suspicion was excitement, not the fury it should have been.

Almost as if she wanted him to touch her.

And then he *did* touch her, his fingers brushing the skin near her right shoulder, so gently, so lightly.

That was . . . not where she'd been expecting him to touch her. Or so gently. What the hell was going on?

His gaze burned as he stared at the place his fingers were touching.

And then she realized what he was looking at.

Her gunshot wound.

Goose bumps lifted all over her skin. Why was he looking at that?

His gaze came to hers as if he'd heard her unspoken question. "He shot you, didn't he? This . . ." His fingers brushed over the angry red scar. "This was from him."

She couldn't read the look in his eyes. Was he angry with her? Because he should be. He should be furious. He should be wanting retribution. Revenge for the life she'd taken.

Yet he was staring at her as if . . . well, she didn't know. She didn't understand the way he was looking at her or what he wanted.

"So?" She shifted against the wall, unease filling her. "I shot him, Jacob. And I don't know whether he's alive or dead, and that's the truth."

He shook his head, as if he was trying to clear it of something, his gaze returning to the scar on her chest. "Josh shot you." He said the words as if they tasted strange in his mouth.

She shivered as his fingers touched her again, featherlight. And her unease deepened. "Jesus, don't you understand? I was there to *kill* him. Our handlers wanted him gone and so I volunteered. I was there to end him."

Slowly he looked up at her and that light was still in his eyes. It wasn't dying and she didn't understand that, not at all. She'd maybe killed his brother and he was still looking at her like he didn't see the darkness inside her. "You wanted an explanation for the sabotage, that's what you said." His voice was rough, a vibration she felt deep in her soul. "You wanted to know why. He was your friend and he betrayed you."

"I shot him. I didn't even hesitate—"

He grabbed her chin, forcing her head back. "Why didn't you tell me he'd pulled a gun on you? Why didn't you say he'd shot you?"

His body pinned her to the wall, his heat scorching against

206 / Jackie Ashenden

her bared skin. So much power there, so much strength. And passion, too, it blazed from him. Anger and something else she didn't understand.

"Why does that matter?" she demanded, her own anger rising to meet his. "I was the one who was there to kill him. And I'm pretty sure I did."

His fingers tightened, his eyes searing as they stared down into hers. "I know what you're doing, don't think that I don't. You're trying to goad me. Why?"

Shock pulsed down her spine. "I'm not goading you. I'm only trying to make you see, you fucking idiot."

"See what? That you're a killer? Tell me something I don't know already, Ms. Lynn."

Her throat closed. Because it wasn't only that, was it?

"You don't know I'm not Faith," she said hoarsely. "You keep thinking I'm her and I'm not."

He said nothing, staring at her, into her, as if he could see everything she was. Everything she was trying to hide. "And what is so very wrong with being Faith?"

"Because she wants things she can't have!" The answer wasn't the one she'd meant to say, but now it was out, she couldn't take it back.

Something shifted in Jacob's gaze. His stare was no less fierce, but the grip on her chin eased, his thumb stroking along the line of her jaw. "What things, sweet girl?"

Jewelry. Pretty clothes. Passion. Pleasure. A prince. *Him.*

Things she couldn't have because she didn't deserve them. That's what her mother had always told her and somewhere in her heart, that's what she believed too. Even though she tried hard not to.

But there was no way she could tell him that. And there was no way she was going to let him get any closer to the truth than he already was. Oh, she could tell him more lies, but he'd never let her get away with them, which meant there was only one option left for her.

She was going to have to fight him.

And there was only one way she could fight Jacob Night.

Joanna lifted her hands and pushed her fingers into his thick black hair and held on to it tightly. Then she pulled his mouth down on hers.

It wasn't so much a kiss as a declaration of war.

She sunk her teeth into his bottom lip, biting down hard, fisting her fingers in his hair as he tried to pull back. Then she pushed her tongue into his mouth, the flavor of him going straight to her head.

Fighting him this way was always going to be a risk, but it wasn't as if she hadn't had sex before with men. Faith might have been a virgin, but she wasn't and sex didn't have to mean anything if you didn't want it to. It was just another weapon in her arsenal, nothing more.

Except with Jacob she was going to have to be careful. He was so big and so powerful. So hot. Everything she admired physically in a man. And that edge to him, that darkness. That strength. Yeah, she liked that far more than she should.

He remained still as she kissed him, his body a hard wall at her front, so she bit him again, wanting a reaction. And this time she got it.

He gave a low growl and his hand was at her throat, long fingers wrapping around it and holding her as he jerked his head back and free from her grip.

There were flames in his eyes but she didn't give him a moment for any more goddamn questions. She reached for the fastening of his pants, ripping them open, then shoving her hand down and into his boxers, her fingers circling his cock. He was hard and ready for her, just as she knew he would be.

"You want a fight?" His voice was as rough and dark as her

heart. "Is that what you're after? Because if you do, believe me, I have no problems with that at all."

The thrill that grabbed her was thick and hot. Yes, a fight. That's exactly what she was after. That way she could show him who she truly was and it wasn't pretty little Faith, who seemed to think she could have everything she'd always wanted without any consequences at all.

She tightened her grip on his dick, running her thumb down the smooth, hard length of it, then squeezing, watching the bonfire in his eyes leap higher. "You've got no idea what you're taking on."

He laughed at that, the bastard. A deep, dark laugh that felt like it shook her right down to her foundation. Then the powerful hand around her throat tightened, pressing her against the wall, and he leaned in so his mouth was right next to her ear, seemingly not caring that she still had her fingers wrapped around his cock. "You seem to be suffering under a delusion, Ms. Lynn. You seem to think that I couldn't possibly handle Joanna. That maybe, even, I wouldn't want her."

She opened her mouth to deny it, but quicker than a snake striking, his hand left her throat and came down over her mouth, silencing her.

"Maybe you even think that it's Faith I'd prefer," he went on, his warm breath brushing over the side of her neck, making her shiver. "The truth, sweet girl, is that yes, I want Faith. But I want Joanna, too, and I don't care what she's done. I don't care that she shot my brother, maybe even killed him. The truth about that will come out eventually. But until it does, make no mistake. *Both* of you are mine."

His smoky scent was everywhere, his heat burning through her clothes, his palm against her mouth searing.

And those words, those rough, possessive words hooked into a vulnerable place deep in her soul. A place where she was weak. Where she was Faith, wanting things she couldn't have and didn't deserve, because she would only break them.

She couldn't be that weak. She couldn't want those things. She couldn't afford to believe him when he said she was his either, because men lied. *People* lied.

They said they wouldn't hurt you, but they did. All the time.

The only person you could trust was yourself and sometimes not even then. Not when it was your own feelings that were suspect.

Joanna opened her mouth, bit his palm hard.

He didn't make a sound, nor did he remove his hand. "A fight then? Is that what you want? To push me away? Stop me from getting too close?" He smiled, white and sharp in the dim room. "Well, it's too late for that, Ms. Lynn. Too fucking late."

Excitement deepened, that wild thrill pulsing through her, and it must have shown in her face because he gave another of those dark, sexy laughs. "I know, you like that, don't you? You're desperate for a fight. You want to see how far you can push me before I'll let you go, see what my limits are." He leaned down, his forehead resting on hers, his gaze filling her entire world. "Well, I'll save you the trouble. I have none. And if I want you, I'll take you. And I'll keep you, understand?"

She didn't know why she was standing there letting him keep his hand over her mouth. Letting him pin her to the wall. Letting him say all these things to her, things he didn't mean. Because no one else had meant them, so why should he?

Jesus Christ. You do *want him.*

No, that was the whole point of this, wasn't it? She *didn't* want him. She just wanted to get the fuck away from him.

She squeezed the hard length of his erection, then ran her thumb around the sensitive head of his dick, a subtle reminder of her power.

Yet that smile of his only got wider. "If you want the fight

you only have to tell me, sweet girl. But you *do* have to tell me."
His hand lowered, giving her an opportunity to speak.

She took it. "I want it."

The black bonfire in his eyes burned high, and she could feel
it burning inside herself, too. Heat and that wild excitement,
that thrill. The anticipation coiling tighter than a clock spring.

Here it was, fucking finally. The chance to prove that all his
arrogant assumptions about her were wrong. That she didn't
want him and didn't care if he wanted her or not. He wasn't
going to take her and he wasn't going to keep her.

Time to show him what Joanna was really made of.

CHAPTER 14

His heart was beating very fast, adrenaline starting to build, along with an anticipation he could see mirrored in her eyes.

Yes, she wanted it. And he did too. *God,* how he wanted it.

Her T-shirt was hanging half-open from where he'd ripped it, exposing her plain black sports bra. But it wasn't the sight of her bare skin or the bra that was driving him crazy. It was the angry red scar near her shoulder.

Joshua might be dead and she might have killed him, yet all he could think about was that his brother had shot her. She'd said he'd been her friend and yet he'd pulled a gun on her, tried to take her prisoner.

He'd betrayed her.

Jacob had tried not to think about his brother turning into a bad guy, not even when it had become clear that Joshua was linked to this arms ring. It had been the search that had consumed him, the finding of Josh that had mattered, not what he'd find when that search was over.

But he should have thought about it, because now everything had become infinitely more complicated.

She was everything he wanted and every damn thing she said, every damn move she made, was further proof of that.

Faith with her passion and her heart. Joanna with her fury and her iron determination. She could deny it all she liked, pretend to herself that he'd never want Joanna, but she was wrong.

Joanna was the armor she wore. Tough and spiky and hard, protecting the softness and heart that was Faith.

It was a combination that intoxicated him, fascinated him.

He'd always found Faith's emotional honesty intriguing and now that was mixed with Joanna's physical strength and will, well, fuck . . . He was gone.

She was never getting away from him, never ever.

But that was the complicated part. Because Josh had hurt her and Jacob's first reaction to that was rage. Even though she was the one who'd shot Josh. Even though he might be dead.

You don't care that she might have killed him?

Of course he cared. But there were extenuating circumstances.

She might have been sent to kill his brother, yet she'd wanted to talk to him first. Yes, she'd shot him in the end, but that was *after* Josh had shown his true colors. And then there was the fact that she hadn't even mentioned that the gunshot wound in her shoulder had come from him.

He could only guess that was because she was so fucking hell-bent on showing him what a bad person she was. Letting him think that she'd been the one to take that shot, all the while never mentioning that she'd been shot too.

That mattered for some reason. That mattered a great deal.

Not that she gave him much of a chance to think further about it.

He saw the shift and change in her eyes, felt the tension in her body gather tight.

She could hurt him right now and badly, seeing as those long, delicate fingers were wrapped tightly around his dick. But he didn't think she would. She might be furious and hurting, but he trusted that she wouldn't do anything to permanently maim him.

Maybe that was stupid. He guessed he'd find out soon enough.

She didn't leave him wondering long.

Jerking her hand from his pants, she dropped down, sliding to the floor, then darting sideways.

He had no time for relief or satisfaction that he'd been right, whirling around in time to find a punch being launched at his gut. He blocked it and the one she aimed higher, at his throat, then ducked the roundhouse kick at his head.

Her recovery was quick, but he was quicker, delivering a short, hard kick at the inside of her knee to put her off balance.

It connected, but she went with it, turning a fall into a roll that had her coming up and facing him, fists ready.

A savage excitement burned hot in his veins, made all the more intense by the hunger mixed in with it. She was so fucking beautiful. So fucking lethal, standing there with her cheeks flushed, the same kind of excitement that gripped him glowing in her eyes.

He came at her, but she dodged his punches and avoided his kicks, her movements athletic, graceful. Christ, he could watch her in a fight all goddamned day.

She was faster than he was, but she didn't have his reach or strength. Not that she wasn't powerful—shit, she'd knocked him out cold after all—but she was smaller than he was and had less bulk. Still, she used it to her advantage, getting in a couple of strikes he wasn't fast enough to block.

It hurt, but he didn't give a shit about the pain. It only added extra spice to his desire anyway.

He was getting impatient though.

Letting his guard drop on his left side, he took a punch to the gut, but before she could pull back, he snatched her wrist from the air and turned hard, using her momentum to pull her forward against him, then twisting her around so her arm was held up against her spine.

A soft gasp of pain escaped her, but he didn't release her.

Instead he hooked his arm around her neck, dragging her head back against his shoulder.

"Enjoying this, Ms. Beasley?" he asked conversationally. "Because I'm fucking loving it."

As he'd hoped, the use of her name made her twist in his grip, an elbow shoving hard into his gut. Good. He'd never wanted this to be easy.

He tried to drag her arm higher, but her head came back all of a sudden, at the same time as she rose on her toes, aiming at his nose.

Avoiding the head butt, he laughed and released her. Only to grab her by the hips as she tried to turn to face him, lifting her, then throwing her bodily onto the bed next to them.

She was already springing up again, agile as a cat, but he was heavy and powerful, and she couldn't quite avoid him as he came down on top of her, pinning her on her back on the mattress.

"This is getting old." Her voice was breathless, the look in her eyes electric.

"I don't agree." He flexed his hips against her, pressing into the heat between her thighs. "This is just starting to get interesting."

"You wish." She wriggled, somehow managing to get her knees up, her feet planting themselves hard in his stomach, the whole force of her body in her kick as she shoved him back.

"Clever." He reached for her as she turned, trying to get off the bed, catching her by the ankle. "But not quite fast enough."

She kicked at him, but he dragged her back, getting her under him again and this time straddling her so she couldn't move her legs. Her fists rose, but he grabbed her wrists and shoved them down hard on either side of her head.

But even then she didn't give up. She lifted her head instead, finding his mouth and delivering another of those hard kisses, her teeth against his lip.

Ah . . . yes. *Fuck* yes.

He kissed her back, pushing his tongue deep into her mouth, tasting the heat that was Faith and the fire that was Joanna, a flavor he'd never get out of his head and never wanted to.

She made a soft, hungry sound in the back of her throat in response, her body arching, pressing herself to him. He could feel the bare skin of her torso soaking through the cotton of his T-shirt and the hard points of her nipples against his chest.

Jesus. Whether she liked it or not, she wanted him and it was obvious. He just didn't know why she was so determined to push him away.

No doubt, it had something to do with her childhood and the man she'd shot. His brother's betrayal wouldn't have helped either. He was interested to know why she was so certain people were lying to her, because he knew how that went. It had happened to him as well.

Still, there was a truth she needed to understand first and that was that he didn't lie. And he meant what he said when he'd told her he never gave up what was his; it didn't matter how hard she pushed him away, he wasn't letting her go.

And second, she was allowed to have what she wanted. She was allowed to have him.

He broke the kiss, looking down at her. "Are you done? Can we get to fucking each other now?"

She looked back, panting. Then her whole body gathered itself, her wrists twisting out of his grip, a fist headed straight for his face.

"I'll take that as a no." He dodged the punch and shifted his weight, trying to pin her once again.

But she was too fast, wriggling away and rolling off the bed, heading for the door.

Oh no. She wasn't going fucking anywhere.

He caught her just as she was pulling the door open, slamming it shut again with one hand while the other gripped the back of her neck, pushing her face first against the wood.

She turned her head so her cheek was pressed to the door, her breathing wild. He probably shouldn't get too close, not when she had such painfully sharp elbows, but he couldn't resist.

Sure enough, as soon as he stepped up behind her, she tried to jab him in the gut, but he took the hit, pressing the entire length of his body up against hers. She struggled a little, which was pure heaven since it involved the softness of her butt grinding against his hard dick.

"Keep doing that and I'll fuck you up against this door, right here, right now," he growled in warning. Then with his free hand, he pulled her hair away from the side of her neck and brushed his mouth over her heated skin, lightly in contrast to the firmness of his hold. "Unless that's what you want, in which case by all means continue."

She shuddered, the sound of her breathing loud in the silence, but didn't speak, so he gave her another featherlight kiss, adjusting his grip on her nape so he could graze the sensitive area where her neck met her shoulder with his teeth.

Her breath caught sharply, so he bit down to intensify the sensation, and she gave another shudder, a soft groan escaping her.

Fucking excellent.

"I don't want you." Her denial was hoarse. "I don't."

"If you don't like people lying to you then maybe you should stop lying to yourself." He nuzzled against her neck, touching his tongue to her damp skin, tasting salt. "You want me, sweet girl. Doesn't matter who you think you are, Faith or Joanna, you want me."

"No. I—"

He bit her again, running his free hand down her side, then over the curve of her ass, squeezing her. "Stop denying it. You know I don't believe you." He let his hand move farther down, adjusting his stance so he could push his fingers between her thighs, trailing them along the seam of her pants, applying pressure, feeling heat and damp fabric.

Her hips jerked and she gasped, trying to pull away, but he kept his hand right where it was, pressing a little harder.

"You see?" He began to trace the soft folds of her pussy through the material. "This excites you the same way it excites me. And now you're so fucking wet for me it's soaking right through the fabric."

She made another attempt at a struggle, but he pinned her harder with his body, sliding his fingers farther between her thighs so he could get at her clit, circling and stroking.

A low moan escaped her, her hips lifting against his hand.

Yes, Christ, she wanted this. And he was going to have that admission from her one way or another. He wanted her to tell him, out loud.

He wanted her to beg.

He wanted her surrender.

He'd gotten both from Faith. Now he'd get them from Joanna.

He tightened his hold on her nape as he kissed the side of her neck, nuzzling and biting at the same time as he increased the pressure of his strokes between her thighs. "Do you want me to force you, Joanna?" he murmured against her skin. "Do you want me to take the decision away from you? Because if you do, you're shit out of luck." He took his hand from between her thighs, then pushed it down under the waistband of her pants

218 / Jackie Ashenden

and her panties, sliding his palm over the smooth skin of her ass, cupping her. "I want the words, sweet girl. Or you don't get me."

She was still a moment. Then she reached around and grabbed his wrist, jerking his hand from her pants before twisting around to face him.

He didn't fight her this time, curious to see what she'd do.

The look in her eyes was burning as she shoved hard against his chest, making him take a few steps back. She didn't look behind her at the door that was now unguarded or the guns sitting discarded on the coffee table. She looked only at him, stepping up close and shoving him back a few steps once more, until he felt the bed bump up against the back of his knees.

There was fury in her gaze and heat, and when she shoved him a third time, he gripped onto her hips and pulled her down with him as he fell onto his back on the mattress.

She didn't make any move to get away this time. Instead she grabbed his hands and put them down on the mattress on either side of his head, straddling him the way he'd straddled her.

Then she bent and kissed him again, hungry and hot, feverish and desperate.

Jesus, she was fighting dirty.

He wanted those fucking words and if she thought she could get away with not saying them, she could think again.

Time to stop holding back.

Time to take what was his once and for fucking all.

Finally she had him beneath her, his powerful body coiled and tight, like a big cat about to pounce.

Adrenaline and hunger pulsed like a giant heartbeat inside her as she lifted her mouth from his, looking down at him. Wanting to see his face. Wanting to see if he felt this too.

But she needn't have worried. The same hunger was blazing in his eyes and in his strong, compelling face.

There was a moment of absolute stillness as they stared at each other, disturbed only by the sounds of their breathing, loud and fast.

And she experienced a second of pure wonder that he was still here. That he was still looking at her the way he was, as if he wanted to eat her alive, even after what she'd told him about his brother.

Even after she'd punched and kicked and fought.

What could she do to get rid of him? What would it take?

But then there was no more thinking, because he moved without warning, his big hands coming up to rip the rest of the T-shirt from her, then rolling, taking her down onto the mattress beneath him.

She wanted to continue fighting, to not give in, because she didn't want to give in. She didn't want to give him the admission he demanded.

But what's the point continuing to fight it? He knows anyway and so do you.

That was the problem. Her head might not want to give up, but her body did. It was tired of fighting. It was tired of being denied.

She ached. She burned. And when his hot, muscular body pinned her down, the weight of him a delicious pressure, she knew she wasn't going to be able to keep holding out.

She lifted her hands, wanting to grab him, and tried to spread her legs so she could wrap them around his waist, but it soon became clear that she wasn't the only one who'd had enough.

He flipped her over onto her front with an easy strength that told her just how much he'd been holding back earlier, and held her down with one hand on the back of her neck, while with the other he jerked her pants down her legs and her panties along with them.

Her fingers dug into the mattress, everything in her gathering into a tight, hard knot.

"Lie still," he ordered roughly. "If you keep fighting me, if you even fucking move, I'll spank you like the bad girl you are."

A shock pulsed through her, a kind of raw electricity.

God, was he serious?

You want him to be.

She swallowed, her mouth dry. "Try it and I'll fucking kill you."

He only laughed. "No, you wouldn't. In fact, I think you'd like a spanking. Should appeal to the masochist in you."

"I'm not a—"

Without warning his palm cracked across her ass and she went rigid with shock. Not at the pain—that was minimal—but at the pleasure that came along with it, unexpected and primal, that left her panting, aching, her fingers gripping onto the mattress for dear life.

She panted, half of her ready to go on the attack while the other half trembled, waiting for more. Wanting it. All her muscles coiled tight, but before she could make a decision either way, his palm descended again in another sharp strike. She gasped, her hips lifting helplessly.

It stung yet felt so insanely good and she couldn't work out why.

Surely, she shouldn't like this. Not lying naked while he spanked her. That was . . . wrong, wasn't it? A warrior like her should be fighting or at least defending herself, right?

But she didn't move and Jacob gave another of those soft, deep, rumbling laughs as his palm cracked across her butt once more, and this time staying there, cupping her stinging ass cheek and massaging the pain away.

"There, I knew it." He sounded so satisfied, she wanted to hit him. "You liked that, didn't you?"

She didn't hit him. Instead she turned her face into the cool sheets beneath her, ashamed of how much she'd liked the weird combination of pain and pleasure, and embarrassed that she'd lain there and taken it. Shocked at herself that she hadn't gotten up and broken his goddamn arm.

"Fuck you, asshole," she whispered against the sheets, trembling as his massaging fingers curved down and slid between her thighs, cupping her throbbing pussy and pressing gently against it.

"All in good time, sweet girl. First of all, you have to give me the words I want to hear."

"No." She groaned as his fingers slipped through the folds of her sex, stroking, teasing, finding her clit and circling lightly. Her hips shuddered, the need to lift them to encourage him to touch her with more pressure becoming nearly overwhelming.

But then his hands left her body and the mattress dipped. She heard the rustle of fabric, the thump of something heavy hitting the floor, the crinkle of foil, and she turned her head, trying to see what was happening.

But his palm struck her ass again and she jerked, the delicious pleasure/pain sending fire through every single nerve ending she had.

"You moved," he growled. "I told you not to move."

"But I—"

He spanked her once more and she couldn't hold back her moan of pleasure or stop herself from spreading her knees wide and lifting her hips, presenting herself to him, wanting his touch.

She forgot to be ashamed of herself. She forgot to be embarrassed. She forgot about everything except that she needed more.

The mattress shifted beneath her and she felt him move, searing heat suddenly against her back and her ass as he forced her down onto the bed, covering her with his body, the hard length of his cock sliding between her thighs.

A familiar feeling crept through her, one she'd had before, in the bunker. When she'd been beneath him and she'd felt so safe, his powerful body between her and the world, protecting her from harm.

She didn't want to feel that again, not now that she'd remembered who she was and that she was strong enough to protect herself. Yet for some reason, the feeling of him against her, broad and hot and strong, pressing her down, made her want to relax. Let him do whatever he wanted to her, anything at all. But most especially, let him give her the pleasure she so desperately wanted.

Pleasure you don't deserve.

Joanna shut her eyes, trying to shut out the voice in her head and him, too, but it was impossible to shut out Jacob. He was everywhere. The smoky, bonfire scent of him and the heat he put out. The rock-hard chest that pressed against her back and the powerful arm that slid around her waist, catching her beneath her hips and lifting her slightly.

His mouth brushed over the back of her neck, giving her one of those gentle kisses that contrasted so painfully and beautifully with the raw strength of him.

"The words," he whispered in her ear. "Give me the words, sweet girl. Say them and I'll give you everything you've ever wanted."

"Liar." Her voice was hoarse and thick. "You won't."

"I've never lied to you and you know it." His hips shifted, the head of his cock sliding through the folds of her pussy, the hardness and scorching heat making her jerk. "Tell me, Faith."

She shuddered at the name, so familiar and yet so wrong. She didn't know why she was still holding out either. All she had to do was tell him she wanted him. That wasn't so difficult, was it?

It's difficult because it's the truth. And you don't want it to be.

She didn't. But there was no point in hiding it now, no point in fighting. And sometimes in order to win the war, you had to lose the battle. No shame in that, was there?

"I want you." Her voice was croaky and ragged, but the words were surprisingly easy to say. "I want you, Jacob."

"Yes, sweet girl," he murmured. "I know."

Then he pushed into her deep and slow, and she squeezed her eyes shut tight, her mouth opening as the pleasure began to expand inside her, impossibly bright, impossibly sharp.

Even then there was a small part of her that wanted to keep fighting, but that was soon lost, crushed beneath the feeling of Jacob Night inside her.

He was big and hot, and she felt stretched wide, her cheek pressed to the pillow. And she didn't think he could get any deeper, but then the arm around her tightened and he slid in even farther, making her cry out.

He felt so good, so perfect. Right.

The connection was already intense, but she wanted more, so she lifted one hand and reached back, gripping on to one of his powerful thighs. Feeling the muscle flex as he drew his hips back, his cock sliding out, then pushing in again.

The burn of her stretched flesh was exquisite and she broke out into a sweat, gasping, her free hand fisting in the sheets beneath her.

He began to move, hard and deep, his rhythm almost brutal. The sound of his flesh hitting hers was loud in the room, the bed knocking against the wall with each powerful thrust, sending shockwaves of pleasure through her.

She couldn't stay still anymore, bucking her hips, shoving herself back on him, arching for more sensation, wanting it, desperate for it.

"You like that, don't you?" His voice had a savage edge that rasped deliciously over her skin. "You like me fucking you with my hand on the back of your neck and that pretty ass pink." He thrust harder, deeper. "You like me fighting you. You like me winning, too."

She panted, digging her nails into the hard muscle of his thigh, even now fighting him. "It was the only way I could get you to shut the fuck up."

His laugh was darkness itself. "Bullshit. You wanted a fight because you wanted to make me work for it, to see how badly I wanted you. But that's okay. I don't mind that." His breath whispered over the top of her spine, his mouth brushing her shoulder. "Not when you surrender so sweetly to me."

"I didn't—"

"You did." He bit down at the same time as he slammed into her, making him grunt and her gasp aloud. "You're mine, sweet girl. You're mine and you know it."

Yes. Yes. That's exactly what you are.

The whisper was all Faith's, which immediately made it suspect. But now she was lying beneath him, feeling him deep inside her, all around her, and . . . she didn't want to deny it.

She wasn't allowed nice things, that's what her mother had always said, but surely, she could have this moment?

Surely, she could have Jacob, just this once?

But then he began to up his pace and her brain simply refused to work any longer.

She began to crack slowly, coming to pieces as he moved faster, deeper, harder. Slamming her into the mattress, the pressure of his body against her spine and his hand on the back of her neck making everything sharper, more intense, and somehow even more perfect than it already was.

And at the same time, safer.

No one could hurt her here, no one could betray her.

If she was his, she was protected, which was a strange thing to think when she could and had killed men before.

Perhaps it was a mistake to let go, but she did anyway, throwing herself into the maelstrom of pleasure, giving herself up to it in a way she'd never done before, not with anyone.

It should have been frightening, but it wasn't.

Because when the orgasm came for her at last and she broke, screaming into the mattress as she shattered into a million pieces, Jacob was there, holding her together.

She wasn't conscious of much else after that, only that his thrusts got wilder, deeper, and he pounded himself into her as if he was trying to break the goddamn bed.

Then she felt him give one last deep thrust as he roared her name and stiffened, the climax coming for him, too.

She kept her eyes shut tight, waiting for him to pull out and leave the bed, but he didn't. Instead he curled himself around her, surrounding her in heat and granite-hard muscle.

The way he held her made tears prickle against her closed lids and she made a cursory attempt to get away, hating the feeling. But then his palm settled on her spine, stroking gently. "Settle," he ordered, the word quiet.

And she did.

"Now." His arms came around her. "Tell me what your mother said to you. I want to know every fucking thing."

It was not at all what she'd expected him to say.

He'd been searching for his brother for years. Had kept her for six months in the hope of her memories returning so she'd be able to tell him where Josh was. Yet now all he wanted to hear about was her mother?

"Don't you want to know about your brother?" She had to force herself to ask the question, because talking about Josh was the last thing she wanted to do. But ignoring it wasn't going to make the subject go away.

"That'll keep," he said shortly. "Tell me about your mother, Ms. Lynn."

She didn't want to talk about her mother, either, but the

aftereffects of the orgasm had left her boneless and heavy, and she simply couldn't be bothered fighting.

"What's there to say? She blamed me for Carl's death. Told me that I'd destroyed her life and that she wasn't going to let me forget it." For some reason it was easier to talk about this with Jacob's arms around her, as if he were insulating her from the sharp cuts of guilt and blame. "And she never did. I wasn't allowed . . . things I wanted, because she told me I didn't deserve them."

"What kind of things did you want?"

"I . . ." She hesitated, not wanting to tell him. "Silly things. Girly things."

"Details, Ms. Lynn, please."

The crisp way he said it reminded her of the six months she'd spent employed by him, sitting in his limo or in the kitchen of his home, giving him the latest rundown on whatever project they were working on at the time.

She'd liked working for him, she realized now. She'd liked it very much. He challenged her, made her think, exercised her intellect rather than her body, and she hadn't even known that's what she'd been missing until now.

"I wanted a princess dress," she said before she could think better of it. "And a crown. And pretty shoes. Jewelry. I wanted to be a princess."

God, if he laughed, she would kill him. She'd just fucking—

"A princess." He said it as if that was the most natural thing to want to be in the entire world. "Of course. You were a little girl."

That's exactly what she'd been. A little girl who'd shot a man.

"Mom said I couldn't, that I wasn't allowed. And that I couldn't be a princess anyway since I'd killed the last prince."

"What prince?"

She swallowed, remembering her mother's grief-stricken voice talking at the wake after Carl's funeral. Joanna hadn't been allowed to go to the funeral itself and she was forbidden to show her face at the wake, too, but she'd crept out of her bedroom at the top of the stairs and listened to the people talking. To her mother crying. Knowing that all of this was her fault.

"That's what she called him," she said thickly. "Her prince."

"After he beat her?"

"It was just a couple of slaps. That's what she said. She told me it's what people who love each other do."

There was a silence and for a second she was conscious only of his arms around her, strong and tight. She'd never been held like that before and it felt so good.

"No," Jacob said at last. "That's not what people who love each other do. I was only six when Dad disappeared and I don't remember much about my parents' marriage. But I do remember that they argued. It was never physical, only shouting. And they always made up afterward. Neither of them ever hit me either." His arms tightened. "Your mother was wrong."

Of course, she knew that. Didn't she?

"But you hit me." She couldn't stop herself from saying it. "Just then."

"Let's be clear. I spanked you because you enjoyed it. Because it got you off. That's something entirely different."

Was it? Maybe it was. She certainly *had* enjoyed it, that much was true.

"Plus, I gave you the opportunity to get away," he went on. "And you didn't. You lay there waiting for me to do it again."

A kind of peace stole through her, making every muscle in her body relax, and she couldn't remember the last time she'd felt like that.

Yes, you do. It was back in the bunker, when he was in bed with you.

Oh yes, so it was. Some part of her—the Joanna part—wanted to protest that it wasn't her, that it was Faith who'd felt that, but right now, she just couldn't find it in her to listen to that part.

"How do you know so much about me?" she asked softly.

He brushed another kiss over her shoulder, making her shiver. "I cared for you for six months, sweet girl. I made you my study. That's how."

"But I was . . . different then."

"No. You just weren't wearing your armor." He shifted slightly, pulling out of her, one hand sliding up her arm to her shoulder, then moving down her back, stroking her like a cat. "That's what Joanna is. She's your armor, your protection. And you need her. Because this world is a dangerous place."

Huh. She'd never thought of it like that before.

She wriggled a little to get him to release her and he did so, clearly reluctantly. Once she had some room, she turned over onto her back and looked up at him. He was lying half on her and half to the side, his forearms flat to the mattress on either side of her head.

The look on his face fascinated her for reasons she didn't understand.

"What's your armor then?" She stared up into his eyes, trying to see the man hidden in the depths. "And who are you without it?"

His mouth curved, but something glittered in his gaze. Something sharp. "You don't want to know."

"I do. Tell me."

He was silent a long moment.

"I don't need armor," he said quietly at last. "I need a cage."

Perhaps she should have been afraid of the knife-bright edge in his voice and the darkness that threaded through it. But she wasn't.

No, if anything, she was desperately curious.

"A cage?" She searched his face. "What do you mean?"

"Joanna Lynn protects you from other people." He reached out and brushed her hair back from her forehead, a tender gesture. "Jacob Night protects other people from me."

CHAPTER 15

It was just daylight when Jacob woke and considering he'd only had a few hours' sleep, he was feeling pretty good.

Faith was still asleep, so he eased himself out of the bed without waking her, dressing quickly, then letting himself out of the room.

A half hour later, having stocked up on a few essentials—such as coffee and a few breakfast pastries that he knew she liked, plus a pit stop at the drugstore to get more condoms—he came back to find the room empty.

Leaving her alone had been a risk, but he didn't think she would leave the way she'd bolted from the bunker the night before.

And indeed when he closed the door behind him and set the breakfast treats down on the coffee table, he noted that both guns were still there. She wouldn't leave without those, he'd bet his entire fortune on it.

Then he heard the shower going and smiled.

Moving over to the bathroom door, he opened it and stepped inside.

The room was full of steam but not enough to hide the shower cubicle in the corner or the naked woman standing inside it.

She had her back to him, her skin gone pink from the heat, and as he watched, she tipped her head back and pushed her hands through her black hair, water streaming down her spine and over the perfect curve of her ass.

Instantly he was hard, but he made no move, content to stand there and watch her. Because she was eminently watchable and he hadn't done it nearly enough.

He would have preferred to do a lot more of it the night before—or rather very early that morning—and a lot more fucking too, but they'd both needed some sleep and so he hadn't pushed it.

He couldn't really push it now, not when the situation that had brought them here still hadn't been addressed. Then again, another half hour wouldn't make much difference.

That's what you said last night and you still haven't dealt with it.

Yes. His brother and his whereabouts, and the issue of his continued existence. Not to mention the fact that he might not be the man Jacob thought he was.

Also not forgetting that she might have killed him.

That also.

Emotion shifted inside him, black anger and a deep, possessive hunger. But they weren't useful and weren't needed, so he pushed them down back where they came from.

What he wanted and needed was right here, standing in the shower cubicle. And she was naked.

"I hope you're not being shy," she said without turning around. "Because I can't think of any other reason you're still standing there fully dressed."

"Shyness is not my problem, I assure you. I'm simply admiring the view."

"This view is getting bored."

He laughed and reached for the hem of his T-shirt, dragging it up and over his head, dropping it onto the floor before taking a condom out of his pants pocket and getting rid of the rest of his clothes. Ripping open the packet, he took out the condom, then rolled it down, enjoying the anticipation building inside him. Then he moved to the shower and pulled open the door.

The shower stall was tiny, barely enough room for him let alone both of them, but he didn't care, stepping inside and pulling the door shut after him.

Then he put a possessive hand on the back of her neck, getting a kick out of the way she shivered as he touched her.

"Why do you do that?" she asked as he pushed her gently against the wall of the shower in front of her. "Hold me . . . there?"

"Because you like it." He kept his hand where it was and moved behind her, pressing his body against the length of hers.

She was wet, slippery, and already he was finding it difficult to think.

He tightened his grip and bent to the side of her neck, trailing his mouth from below her ear and down to where her neck met her shoulder. "And because you're mine," he added, then bit her the way he had the night before.

She shivered in response, angling her head to bare her neck to him. "I'm not yours."

"Yes, you are." He bit her again, harder this time, the edge of his teeth against her skin, tasting salt and Faith. "And you want it, I know you do."

The breath went out of her as he trailed more kisses over the side of her neck and shoulder. "Jacob . . ."

"What is it, sweet girl?" He slid an arm around her waist, drawing her up onto her toes, then flexed his hips so he could slide his cock between her thighs. "I hope you're not going to continue arguing with me. It's unseemly in a princess."

A tremble shook her as he nudged against all that soft, wet heat. "I'm not a—"

"Oh yes, you are." He pushed himself inside her, a hard, deep thrust that forced her against the wall of the shower. She gasped, her hands slapping down onto the tiles in front of her.

He paused, not moving, not moving just yet, dipping his head to nuzzle against her neck. "Your mother lied to you. You were a princess then and you're a princess now. A warrior princess. How else could you handle me?"

She was breathing fast, her body trembling. "So . . . w-what does that make you? A prince?"

He massaged the back of her neck with his thumb as a burst of intense possessiveness gripped him. And he didn't fight it. He embraced it.

Christ, he loved how she was shaking. Loved how her pussy was gripping him so tightly, as if she didn't want to let him go. *Mine. Fucking mine.*

"I told you I'd give you everything you ever wanted. And if you want a prince, then you'll have one." Slowly he slid out of her, then thrust back in, sharper, harder.

"J-Jacob . . ." His name was a low moan, her fingers pressed to the tiles, her knuckles white. "Oh . . . *God* . . ."

He kept her off her toes, so she had nothing to hold on to but him, thrusting again, short, hard strokes that had her writhing against the shower wall, gasping with each push of his hips.

Dangerous to let himself go like this, but it had been a long time since he had. And she could take it. He tended to frighten people when he was full-on, but she wasn't frightened of him. No, she was arching against him, grinding that perfect ass of hers against his groin, wanting more.

Just like she wanted to be his, even though she tried to deny it.

You could be hers, too.

Ah no, that wasn't going to happen. He'd never belong to

anyone. Jacob Night was his own man and that's how it would stay. How it *had* to stay.

He'd never be Jake Foster again.

Her nails scraped across the tiles as his rhythm intensified, and he lost himself in the tight heat of her cunt and the slippery wet feel of her skin. She was panting now and so was he, their breathing harsh, mingling with the warm water and the steam.

"You *are* mine," he whispered roughly against her skin. "Tell me."

She gave a little sob, squirming and arching into him, desperate for release. "Yes . . . y-yes . . . please . . . Jacob, *please* . . ."

"Whose are you?" He paused, deep inside her, wanting the words. He'd had them from Faith, but he wanted them from Joanna, too, so there could be no argument. So both of them were absolutely clear.

"Yours." She twisted in his grip, trying to move, but he held her off her feet and she couldn't get any purchase. "I'm yours, J-Jacob."

"Are you sure?"

"Yes . . ." Her voice was thick, breathless. "Please, God, just fuck me already."

An intense, primitive kind of triumph shot through him and he smiled, his teeth at her neck. Oh yes, she was perfect. Just fucking perfect.

"My pleasure," he murmured.

He began to move again, slamming into her, driving her against the wall of the shower, each thrust making him grunt and her gasp.

It was hard, brutal, because that's what he was. And he loved it that she took him. And when she dropped her hands to where his arm circled her waist, and dug her nails into his skin, scratching him, he loved that, too. Just like he loved the way she begged for more, for harder, for deeper, as if she wanted everything he did.

But there was no "as if" about it. She *did* want what he did.

So he gave it to her, everything she wanted. Releasing the back of her neck, he slid his hand down over her stomach, finding her clit with his fingers, stroking her relentlessly, until she screamed against the tiles, her pussy convulsing around his cock as she came.

Then he released the hold he had on himself, driving into her, the shower stall shaking with the force of his thrusts, until the climax took him like a hammer blow, making his head ring and the room echo with the sound of her name.

Afterward he leaned against the shower wall, still holding her, his face turned into her neck, her wet hair silky against his skin. He'd never felt unsteady on his feet before, but he did now, and he wasn't sure if he'd ever fucking move again.

Certainly he was never going to let her go. That just wasn't going to happen.

"How are you feeling, Ms. Beasley?" he asked eventually, having to force his voice to work.

"Like I can't stand." The words were slurred, as if she were drunk. "Did we break the shower?"

"Sadly, no."

"You'll have to up your game in that case."

"Clearly." He put one hand on the shower wall, leaning on it as he gently pulled out of her and lowered her back onto her feet. "I didn't hurt you, did I?"

She shook her head, standing now, but obviously in no hurry to go anywhere as she leaned into him. "I think I hurt your arm though."

He looked down over her shoulder to where his forearm lay over her stomach. There were scratches there and a thin line of blood.

The sight hit him weirdly. She'd left her mark on him, like a claim, and there was a part of him that found that deeply satisfying. Which it shouldn't. He didn't want anyone claiming him, because he wasn't anyone's to claim.

Oblivious, Faith made a small, contented sound, her head falling back against his shoulder, water streaming down her naked body. "You can probably stop calling me Ms. Beasley though. It's getting weird."

Distracted from the scratches, he smiled and reached for the soap, keeping his hold on her. "Would you prefer Ms. Lynn?" He began to wash her gently. Not that she needed it since she was already clean, he just wanted to touch her.

"No." She gave a sensual little stretch, then twisted her head slightly so she could look up at him. Her face was flushed, blue eyes gone midnight. "I think you can drop the 'Ms.' and call me Faith."

Emotion caught in his chest. This meant something and he knew it, but he didn't understand what, and for the first time in years, he couldn't think of one fucking word to say.

Instead he dropped the soap and curled his hand around her lovely throat, holding her turned toward him, then he kissed her. Hard.

She made another of those sensual sounds, then twisted around so she was facing him, sliding her arms around his neck and arching her body into his. Her mouth was hot, open, and sweet, and he wanted to keep kissing her all fucking day.

But after a moment, she pulled away, leaning back in his arms so she could look up at him. She didn't say anything right away, keeping one arm around his neck, while with the other she touched him, stroking her hand over his shoulder and down over his left pec. Her fingers lingered on the snarling wolf's head tattoo he had over his heart, her gaze lingering there too.

"You said Jacob Night was there to protect other people

from you," she said at last, glancing up at him. "What did you mean by that?"

Ah, yes. That. He hadn't replied the night before, not wanting to get into it, distracting her easily enough with his mouth and his hands.

But he could tell that wasn't going to work now.

Or maybe you don't want to distract her now. Maybe you just want to tell her.

It would be a mistake to let her know too much. Then again, he'd already told her things he shouldn't have. And there was a part of him that chafed at his isolation. That wanted more. Even having one fucking person to talk to . . .

But Jake Foster wanted that. And he killed people.

No, fuck it. Talking to Faith didn't mean he was back to being Jake again. He'd been Jacob too long, his control was all good. He was fine.

"I've done bad things, sweet girl," he said. "You know what I'm talking about. All those tours . . . They change people and usually for the worse. But I was fucked up going in, angry and full of hate. I had no control, no off switch. And I channeled all that bad shit into my Navy career and into the enemy."

She said nothing, but there was understanding in her eyes. Of course there would be. She'd been there too.

"Then my career ended and I was made to disappear. But you can't live like that in the civilian world. You can't view every single person you meet as a target. So I had to become someone different, find a way of living that didn't put people at risk. I had to channel all that anger into something else."

Slowly she pressed her palm to the wolf's head, the warmth covering his skin. Over his heart. "The 11th Hour."

"Yes."

"And does that work?"

"Most of the time."

"What do you do when it doesn't?"

He smiled. "Target practice. Punching bag. Running on the treadmill."

"If you need a partner, I could help." The look in her eyes turned smoky. "I'm very hard to hurt."

Yes, physically. But emotionally?

She's vulnerable. Too vulnerable.

He put his hand over hers where it rested on his chest. "I'll take you up on it, believe me. But until then, we have a mission to complete."

One dark brow arched. "We?"

His smile deepened, because she was beautiful and imperious and he wanted to fuck her again. "You had a plan for finding Joshua, didn't you?"

"Maybe." She flexed her fingers on his chest. "Not sure I want to tell you about it though."

He laughed, then pushed her gently up against the back wall of the shower. "You're going to tell me. You're going to tell me everything I want to know."

"Oh really?"

"Yes, really. My interrogation skills are excellent." He cupped her breast, rubbing his thumb over her rapidly hardening nipple. "Let's see how long you can hold out, hmmm?"

Faith—yes, she could think of herself as Faith now—smoothed her black pencil skirt down over her knees and grimaced at the pinch of the high heels on her feet. She hadn't noticed how irritating it was wearing such restrictive clothing a week ago—she hadn't realized it even *was* restrictive—but she certainly did now.

Then again, a week ago she hadn't been planning on using herself as bait to get a very shady arms ring to come out of the woodwork.

"Okay," she said, doing a last-minute double check to make sure the Sig was resting securely in the waistband of her skirt, at the small of her back. "I'm ready."

She turned to find Jacob at the motel window, angling himself to look out through the drawn curtains.

His massive figure was very still, the set of his broad shoulders tense. He was dressed once again in a black T-shirt and black combat pants, every inch the lethal weapon he was.

Goose bumps rose on her skin, her heart beating faster.

Jesus. Now was not the time to be contemplating all the things she'd like to do to this man given another couple of days of complete privacy and an extra big bed to do them in. Not that she needed the bed.

Though it was weird to still be so completely obsessed with him when their shower/interrogation session had ended with her—unsurprisingly—telling him everything he wanted to know about her plan to locate Joshua. Admittedly, she hadn't tried very hard to hold out and he had been *very* persuasive. In fact she was surprised the shower stall was still standing after he'd finished "interrogating" her.

The memory of his hard, almost brutal brand of fucking left her mouth dry. Who'd known she liked it rough? Not that it came as any great surprise, all things considered.

They both liked a fight and in the end, she liked to surrender while he liked to win. It worked perfectly for both of them, since essentially, they both ended up winning.

They'd had to get serious after that though, because he hadn't liked her plan, hadn't liked it one bit. Being bait for a bunch of shady motherfuckers running guns—his words—was not what he had in mind for her. He preferred to wait since there was a lead he was following up, that he should hopefully get more intel on soon.

But she didn't want to wait.

Impatience and worry were beginning to eat away at her, the stress of not knowing whether Josh was alive or dead making her restless.

She had to know. She had to know whether she'd killed her friend.

Teaming up with Jacob on this had seemed logical, though there was still a part of her that wasn't sure about it. Trust was something that was difficult for Joanna and even though Faith trusted Jacob, she wasn't sure that Joanna did, even now.

But she didn't have a choice. She either let him in on her plans or she tried to get away from him again, and since another escape attempt would only waste more time, including him seemed the best option.

She'd planned on returning to the 11th Hour HQ as Faith, to get the people after her out in the open, but he'd flatly refused, not wanting to give away the rest of the team's location or put everyone else at risk.

She understood that, but unless they spent the day ostentatiously driving around San Diego in Jacob's very distinctive limo, there wasn't much else they could do to announce her arrival back in the city.

"Problem?" she asked, when he didn't say anything.

"Maybe." He didn't turn. "There's a car out on the street that wasn't there last night. And there's a guy in it reading the paper."

She moved over to the other window, peering out through a gap in the curtains and immediately spotting the car Jacob was talking about.

A nondescript silver sedan, the driver seemingly absorbed in the sports section of the paper.

Nothing out of the ordinary.

Except that every so often the guy would look up and glance out the window. He was wearing sunglasses, which made it difficult to spot where he was looking, but she'd bet a million bucks it was at the motel.

Where they were.

"I was sure I wasn't followed last night." Jacob's voice was low. "Clearly I was wrong."

She didn't question his instincts about the car, mainly because she was getting the same vibe. It wasn't anything tangible, just a sense of threat that set every military instinct she had on high alert.

"I didn't see anyone at your house," she said quietly. "I checked."

"No. They must have tracked me from the airport."

She squinted at the car. "They want to see if you're going to lead them to me, I guess."

"Undoubtedly."

"Why do you think they left it this long? They could have taken us while we were sleeping last night."

Jacob stepped back from the window. "Probably waiting for reinforcements." His smile was full of menace. "They won't want to tackle me without a small army at their back."

She grinned. "You're not that dangerous. I took you on all by myself."

He went over to the coffee table, picking up the assault rifle she'd liberated from his house, and checking it over with practiced movements. "And who was the one screaming in the end?"

Annoyingly, she felt her cheeks heat. "Next time it's your turn."

"You can certainly try." He lifted the AR. "You brought more ammo, I assume?"

"Naturally." She moved to the bed and bent to pull the bag she'd brought with her out from under it before dumping it on the mattress. "It's all in there."

Jacob gave a short nod. He stared down at the AR a second, then came over to the bed, putting the weapon in the bag. "I'm going to go out to talk to our well-read friend. You stay here."

"Wait." She reached out and put a hand on his arm, her heart beating weirdly fast for some reason. "Let me go. It's me they're after, remember?"

Jacob's deep-set eyes glittered. "Yes. Because they want you dead. He might shoot you on sight."

"And they won't shoot you?"

The feral smile on his face faded, became something warmer. "Concerned for my safety, Ms. Beasley?"

It was strange to discover that actually, yes, she was. But there were other things she was concerned about too.

Such as her initial plan. It had involved using the only leverage she had to prevent them killing her outright and that was gambling on the fact that they would want information about Jacob Night.

Information only she had.

But she wasn't so sure she wanted to do that now. He'd trusted her and betraying that trust felt . . . wrong. Yet what else did she have that would preserve her life and at the same time get her the information she wanted about Josh?

Unless Jacob had another plan.

"I might be," she said. "I might also be concerned about what you might say."

"Why? You think I'd give you up in return for Joshua?" He asked the question so casually, she almost didn't quite understand it.

And then she did.

Something inside her went very tight and still. Was it a good thing that the thought he might betray her hadn't entered her head? Or was that a bad thing? A sign of naïveté?

His expression gave nothing away.

Damn him. She didn't want to ask, she really didn't. Not when asking it would reveal so much.

Yet she couldn't help herself. "I don't know, would you?"

Unexpectedly, his hand came out to cup her cheek, his palm warm. "You're forgetting something, sweet girl. You're mine. And what's mine, stays mine."

Her chest was tight, tension gathering inside her.

How can you trust him?

The whisper in her head was soft, but it was there and she heard it. The part of her that was Joanna, who trusted no one and most especially not a man.

He'd sell her out, because they all did in the end. The men her mother attached herself to, who said they'd never hurt her and yet did. The superior officers who were supposed to treat you like any other soldier yet didn't. And the friends who said that you could trust them, but you couldn't.

Something in her hardened. No, she couldn't trust him.

But maybe there was a way around it. A way that would get them what they both wanted. Jacob wouldn't like it though. Then again, they didn't have a lot of choice.

"I have an idea." She put her hand over his where it rested on her cheek. "But you're not going to like it."

He gave her an assessing look. "If it involves me giving you to them then no, it's not—"

"Wait," she interrupted. "Hear me out."

"Give me one good reason."

"This is the quickest way to find out what happened to Joshua."

The look in his eyes was impenetrable. He said nothing.

"The bug you put in my clothes," she went on, determined. "How easy is it to detect?"

"Almost impossible. It's new tech and you need special scanners to find them." His gaze narrowed. "If you're going to tell me that—"

"I want to go with my original plan," she interrupted. "I want to give myself up to them."

His expression hardened, his hand dropping from her cheek. "Not happening," he said, his voice flat with certainty. "I'm not sending you—"

"*You're* not sending me anywhere," she interrupted yet again, irritated. "This was what I was going to do anyway."

"No."

Goddamn stupid man.

She shoved her annoyance down. "Think about it, Jacob. Going straight for them is the fastest way to get information. And I have information they're going to want. I can make them listen."

"No." The word landed as heavily as a boulder dropping off a ten-story building. "I'm awaiting confirmation of a particular man's identity. One of those pricks after you might be someone I know. In which case you're *not* going anywhere near him."

It was her turn to narrow her gaze at him. "Who?"

"Not yet. I need confirmation first. But if it is who I think it is, then this whole situation is a lot more complicated than we initially thought. And that means you need to stay clear."

Jesus. The man was the most stubborn asshole she'd ever met.

"I'm not *just* Faith, remember?" She stared hard at him. "I was a Ranger, Jacob. I know what I'm doing."

He moved, lightning fast and fluid, her jaw suddenly gripped in one powerful hand, his black eyes inches from hers. "And you're *mine.*" His deep voice was full of rough darkness and heat. "Which means you stay out of this where I can keep you safe."

She knew that look on his face. Once he'd made a decision about something he never changed it. And it was obvious he'd made a decision now.

Well, luckily for her she didn't need his permission.

What she needed was to find Joshua and going straight to the people who'd employed him seemed the most obvious answer. Dangerous, yes, and sure, that's why Jacob was being a dick about it. She got that. Protecting people was always what Jacob Night had been about, whether he realized it or not. But she wasn't one of those who needed his protection. Faith, yes, but this was a situation that called for her armor.

This called for Joanna.

"Fine," she snapped, and didn't need to manufacture the anger in her voice. "I guess I'm staying here then."

"Damn straight." He bent his head, covered her mouth in a hard kiss that left her breathless. Then he let her go, turning to the bed. "Now, where are the—"

She didn't pause for thought. Surprise was the only advantage she had when it came to a fight with him and she took it without hesitation.

Drawing the Sig from the small of her back, she hit him hard over the back of the head with it. The strike would have put a lesser man out cold, but Jacob only jerked, cursed, then began to turn. So she hit him again, harder, and this time he dropped down onto the bed and didn't move.

Shit. Had she hit him *too* hard?

Her heart hammering, she bent and laid her fingers over the warm skin of his throat. His pulse beat there, strong and sure, making relief curl through her. Ah, God, but there was blood in his black hair from where she'd hit him.

Pain tightened in her gut, but she pushed it aside.

"I'm sorry," she said aloud, even though he couldn't hear her. "I know you don't want me to do this, but I have to find Joshua. I have to know whether I . . . killed him or not." Her fingers moved to his cheek, stroking over the rough prickliness of his morning beard, unable to resist the urge to touch him. "And if he's alive . . . Well." Her fingers stilled. "I'll bring him back to you, I promise."

For a second she remained there, staring down at him, the pain in her gut moving outward, morphing into a heaviness in her chest that she had no idea what to do with.

But she had to move. Once he woke up, he'd make sure she wouldn't get this opportunity again.

So she turned and headed straight to the door of the motel unit and pulled it open. Then, keeping the Sig held down low at her side, she moved quickly toward the car with the man reading the newspaper inside it.

He looked up, saw her, began to reach for something, but by that stage she was at the car, the muzzle of her gun pointing directly at him.

She smiled and gestured to the window.

There was a pause and slowly the man rolled the window down.

"Tell your employers I want to talk to them," she said shortly. "Tell them I have information they might want. Information about Jacob Night."

CHAPTER 16

Jacob woke up with a crashing headache and the sense that he'd done something really fucking stupid.

He was lying on the bed in the motel unit and he knew pretty much instantly that he was alone.

Faith fucking Beasley, that beautiful little bitch, had knocked him out for the second time in twenty-four hours.

Christ, he could get away with it once. But twice? Yeah, that was starting to look like carelessness.

He cursed under his breath, rolled over, then pushed himself up.

Sure enough, the room was empty. She was gone.

And he didn't need to think too hard about where she might have taken off to.

Gritting his teeth against the pain in his skull, he pushed himself off the bed and strode to the window, pulling aside the curtain. Sure enough, the car that had been waiting in the street was gone.

His heart squeezed painfully tight.

He'd told her that she wasn't going to act on her stupid plan

248 / Jackie Ashenden

and she'd gone ahead and done it anyway. And now she'd given herself up to those fucking assholes and he wasn't there to protect her.

Fuck.

His chest began to ache, but he couldn't afford to think about that right now. What he had to think about was his next move, because the quicker he acted the better.

Luckily, he had an idea about what he was going to do already.

He got out his phone and opened the tracking app, trying not to pay any attention to the dread that curled around his heart. An image came up, a map of San Diego with a red light blinking in the middle of it. The red light was Faith and she must be in a car since the light was traveling at speed.

She was alive. There were the heart rate and body temperature readings and they were completely normal. The bugs he'd put in her clothing were operating, feeding him back information the way they'd done when he'd followed her after she'd escaped the bunker.

The relief that caught at him almost stole his breath, but he didn't allow himself to give in to it.

Instead he kept moving, packing up all the personal shit he could find in the unit, then doing a quick check of the outside to make sure no one else was lurking around. Seemed clear so he pulled on a hoodie, tugging the hood down low, then stepped out of the unit. He went and paid the bill, then took the bike he'd arrived on early that morning and headed straight into the city.

He parked in a hidden back alley, doing another check around to make sure the coast was clear, before moving to a heavy steel door that was locked and chained shut. Quickly he undid the chains—they were purely for show—then pushed aside a faded poster sticking to the brick wall, uncovering the camera and keypad that unlocked the door.

One retinal scan later and the door opened.

Jacob strode through, shutting it behind him before moving down a short, dim corridor to another door. This one was also locked and needed another retinal scan to open it.

Once he'd unlocked it, the door opened soundlessly and Jacob stepped through it into a huge, vaulting space. The interior of a building that had been gutted, nothing but air between him and the ceiling four floors above him.

The space had been sectioned off with furniture, a gym area with all the equipment to his left, a living area with couches and chairs to his right. Ahead of him was a cluster of desks covered in computer screens and keyboards and various computer-related paraphernalia.

The 11th Hour HQ.

A small group of people clustered around one of the desks, looking at a computer screen. A woman with long, curly brown hair was seated in the middle of them directly in front of the screen, while a tall blond man stood just behind her, his hand resting possessively on her shoulder. Sabrina and Kellan, the 11th Hour computer hacker and one of his top field agents respectively. Another woman, small and blond and pretty, stood on Sabrina's other side frowning at the screen. A second tall man was standing behind her, resting his palms on her head, which seemed to irritate her intensely. The man was dark and scarred, and paid no attention to her irritation. Jack, a former marine, and his fiancée, Callie, the ex-socialite he'd rescued.

Right behind Sabrina stood another man, older, with a salt-and-pepper beard and a hard cast to his face. Isiah, the 11th Hour commander.

His team, all present and accounted for.

Except for Faith.

The ache in Jacob's chest grew deeper. He ignored it.

Suddenly Isiah glanced around in his direction, even though

Jacob hadn't made a sound coming through the door, and went absolutely still.

Everyone else seemed to pick up on it, all of them turning and looking at Jacob.

A deathly silence fell.

"Good morning, team," Jacob said, lifting his hands and pulling back his hood. "I have a job for you."

They stared at him, varying degrees of shock on their faces.

No one bar Kellan had ever seen him so they wouldn't know what he looked like. But they knew his voice. Oh yes, they knew.

"Night," Kellan said, moving to stand protectively in front of Sabrina. "What the fuck—"

"All other jobs are on hold," Jacob interrupted, in no mood to fuck around. "The 11th Hour now has a new mission. We need to locate Faith Beasley." He stared at them all, each one in turn, so they knew, so they understood just how fucking serious he was. "And then we need to save her."

The car pulled up outside a massive house to the south of the city, built rather like Jacob's, on a bluff overlooking the sea.

The guy driving didn't turn around. "You're to go straight in," he said. "Door's open."

Joanna—because she had to be Joanna to get this done—stared at the house, her fingers tight around the gun in her lap.

Getting here had been surprisingly easy. The driver hadn't even argued when she'd instructed him to contact his employers—not that arguing with the gun she'd pointed in his face would have been a good idea anyway—but still, he'd taken his phone out and called his boss without a word of protest.

She'd expected a little more argument from his superiors though, she had to admit, and hadn't got that either. No, they'd simply agreed.

Almost like they wanted to meet you rather than kill you.

Interesting thought, and there could be a few reasons for that.

And once you find out, what then?

Then she'd cross that bridge when she came to it. She was good at thinking of stuff on the fly. No doubt she'd come up with an exit strategy when the time came.

Joanna pulled open the car door and stepped out.

The house was protected by a high wall and a gate, which opened as she approached.

Huh. Friendly of them.

She walked through the gate and along a small path that led to some stone steps and the front door, her Sig in her hand and at the ready.

She didn't let herself think about anything else except what was going on right now, and what to expect when she finally met whoever was after her. With any luck her suspicions would be correct and this would lead her to Joshua.

The front door opened, another flunky in a dark suit standing there as she came up the steps. His gaze flicked to her Sig but he didn't give her any instructions, simply turning around and moving into the house.

Clearly, she was supposed to follow.

The house was all blank white walls, hard angles, and chrome. The furniture was minimal, the art on the gallery-like walls abstract, the floors cool tile. An obviously expensive place, but even the light shining through the windows seemed hard and far too bright.

Joanna followed the suit up a flight of stairs and into a big living area furnished with uncomfortable-looking white couches. The wall facing the ocean had sliding windows that had been rolled back to let in the sun and air. Through the windows was a terrace with an outdoor table and some chairs arranged around it. A man sat on one of the chairs, a small white cup at his elbow, a newspaper on the table in front of him.

A couple of other men in dark suits stood on either side of the terrace, radiating threat. Security, obviously.

The suit she was following gestured toward the terrace but didn't make any move to take her gun, so she kept it loosely in her hand as she walked through the living room.

The man at the table didn't look up as she stepped outside onto the terrace, the security guys shifting on their feet but making no move toward their own weaponry.

Whoever this guy was, he was confident.

"Joanna Lynn, I presume?" the man said finally, lifting his head and looking at her. "I hear you have something you want to talk to me about. Take a seat."

He was handsome, in his late thirties, dark-haired, with the coldest gray eyes she'd ever seen. His clothing—T-shirt and jeans—had a lived-in look to them, his hands tattooed and scarred. On the middle finger of his left hand was a ring with a wolf's head on it, the metal glinting in the sun as he folded the paper neatly and put it to one side.

Ex-military, she'd have laid money on the fact.

"I'll stand, thank you," she said, still casually holding her Sig.

"Suit yourself." The man tilted his head. "My name is Frost."

"So, Mr. Frost. I guess you don't want to kill me now?"

He gave her a cold smile. "Let's just say I've changed my angle on that. Especially since it depends on what kind of information you have on Jacob Night. And naturally what you want in return."

She was conscious of a certain satisfaction, mixed with not an inconsiderable amount of relief. Looked like her gamble had paid off.

"With regard to Jacob, I can tell you anything you want to

know. I worked closely with him for six months. I have his security codes, his passwords, all the details about the 11th Hour operation. I also know things about his past that he's told no one else."

"How . . . interesting. And presumably you'll want something in return for this information." Frost's cold eyes gleamed. "Not that I need to ask what that is."

There was something icy in her gut, a fear she didn't want him to see, so she made sure he didn't see it, giving him nothing back but Joanna, her armor. "No, I'm sure you don't. Joshua Smith. Where is he?"

Frost nodded slowly. "Before any of that, there were rumors that you lost your memory. Has it returned?"

What could she say? Denying it now would be futile.

"Yes." She lifted a brow. "Does that mean I'm back at the top of your shit list?"

He gave a laugh. "It would if I was a simplistic kind of man. But I'm not. In fact, if people are generally useful to me, I'd rather not kill them if I don't have to. There are, after all, ways of getting people to do what you want with the minimum amount of fuss."

"You sound like someone I know," she muttered. "What does that mean?"

"It means that you're someone who could be useful to me. Especially with what you have on Jacob Night, not to mention your other military skills."

Okay, so how did he know about those other skills? He couldn't. He wouldn't know her from a bar of soap. Unless someone had told him . . .

Something surged in her. "He's alive," she said. "Isn't he?"

"Who? Your friend Joshua?" Frost nodded. "Yes."

Her heartbeat was loud in her ears, a steady, strong beat.

She *hadn't* killed him. She hadn't shot her best friend and left him to die. He was alive. . . .

And if he's alive, what's the plan now? You tell this asshole everything you know about Jacob?

Her breath hitched.

"Smith told me a lot about you, Joanna," Frost went on. "He's keen to have you on board, become part of our team."

Wait, what? They wanted her to join them?

She was caught off guard. "I thought you wanted to kill me."

"Sure. We couldn't have you running around free, not when your connection to Smith could have been used by people who'd make life difficult for us. But that was then. This is now. And let's just say that Smith persuaded me to change my mind." He leaned forward all of a sudden, sunlight glinting off the metal of his ring as he clasped his hands in front of him. "Now, let's have a little chat about Mr. Night."

Something was going on here, she could feel it. She'd thought that using her connection to Jacob would become useful, but there was a sharp glint in Frost's eyes. This felt like it was . . . personal almost.

She knew this had always been personal for Jacob because Jacob had been searching for his brother, involving other members of the 11th Hour team in his search. Information from Callie's father and then from Kellan's. All in aid of tracking down this arms ring . . .

But what if there was another connection here? One neither Jacob nor she had seen? Because why else would this man want information about him? Not when no one else knew Jacob Night existed.

She stared at him. "First things first. I want proof Smith is alive."

"He's alive," a deep voice said behind her.

For a second the world seemed to shift weirdly on its axis, because that voice was familiar. It was her friend's.

It was also her lover's.

She turned around sharply and this time the weird shift hit

her doubly hard. Because there was a man stepping out onto the terrace, massively tall and muscled, dark-haired, dark-eyed. And a rush of adrenaline spiked in her blood.

Jacob.

But it wasn't Jacob. The man coming toward her didn't have scars on his face and he held himself differently, moving more heavily than his brother did.

Josh.

And despite herself, she felt the disappointment like the twist of a knife. Strange. She shouldn't be disappointed, should she? She should be ecstatic, thrilled that her friend was alive and that here he was, right in front of her.

Except for the fact that you shot him. And that he shot you, not to mention he was planning on taking you prisoner.

Prisoner . . . yes, he'd mentioned that. He'd told his superiors she'd make a good hostage.

How wonderful that you turned up here then. And all without him having to lift a finger . . .

A cold current washed through her.

Josh didn't smile. He simply stared at her and it was only now that she'd known Jacob that she could see it. There was something hollow about him, something brittle. He was missing the fire that his brother had, an iron strength and determination. Jacob was folded steel, but she had the sense that his brother had a crack in him, a flaw. And at the slightest blow, he would shatter.

"Josh," she said thickly. She made no move toward him, because the sense that something was happening was getting stronger and stronger.

"Jo," he said. "I knew you'd come."

There was a tension in the air, a certain electricity that comes before a storm, and she couldn't work out where it was coming from.

She tried to ignore it. "I'm sorry. I'm sorry about—"

"Hey, it's okay." Josh stuck his hands in the pockets of his jeans, his expression oddly neutral. "I'm alive, obviously."

"So . . . what happened?"

"After you shot me? Frost came and got me out." His gaze sharpened. "And you? I hear you lost your memory. Started working for my brother."

"You know about him?"

"Of course I know about him."

Shock swept through her. "But you never said anything about him to me."

"No, because it didn't concern you." He took a step toward her. "But it concerns me now. I know he's trying to find me, Jo. So I need you to tell me everything you know about him."

There was a feverish kind of light in his dark eyes now, an intensity that reminded her of his brother. Except, Jacob's intensity excited her. Josh's made her feel cold.

He's already betrayed you once. What's to say he won't do it again? And you came alone. You fucking idiot.

She took a slow, silent breath, trying to keep her heartbeat regular. Her military senses were already taking in any potential threats, such as the security guards on the periphery of her vision. Two of them, plus Frost and Josh, assuming Josh would stop her if she tried to get away. If she was right. If this was all a trap.

You should have thought about how you were going to get out if it all went badly.

Yes, she should have. But she hadn't. She'd thought only of finding Josh, not what she'd do afterward.

Of course, Jacob would be tracking her and no doubt heading straight for her location since he was likely to be extremely pissed at the way she'd knocked him out. So she had some backup. No reason to get too worried yet.

She kept her gaze on her erstwhile best friend, shoving aside the feelings of hurt and loss and betrayal. It wasn't time to get emotional. She was here, in the enemy's stronghold, so maybe the thing to do now was a little reconnaissance. Figure out what they wanted to do with Jacob.

"How do you know he's trying to find you?" she asked casually. "How do you know about him at all?"

An expression she didn't understand flickered over Josh's face, but it wasn't he who answered.

"Good question," Frost said from his place at the table behind her. "He's basically a ghost. No one's been able to find a trace of him anywhere. But I have people in various places. And when you disappeared from the hospital . . . Well, we figured out who it was then."

She turned back to the table, meeting Frost's cold gray eyes.

"He's been trying to derail my business for months now," Frost went on. "And it's annoying. It needs to stop."

So, right. This *was* personal. But it went deeper than simply Jacob derailing Frost's business, she was sure of it. Because the same gleam that was in Josh's gaze was in Frost's.

Josh's connection to Jacob was obvious, but Frost's? Where did he fit in? He was ex-military clearly, so maybe it had to do with Jacob's past. Had they been in the same unit?

Sunlight fell across the table, glinting off the ring on Frost's hand, with the snarling wolf on it.

She'd seen that wolf before. The tattoo on Jacob's chest . . .

Yes. They *had* been in the same unit. And she'd bet everything on the fact that it had to be the special ops unit Jacob had told her about. The unit that had been nearly wiped out, with him being the only survivor.

Except he wasn't the only survivor. There was Frost.

So, okay. This changed things. Two men, both with a personal connection to Jacob. Frost's motivations around his business were obvious, but there was also something else there, something more personal. And Josh's?

She looked at Josh. "He's looking for you. He's been searching for you for years."

"Years, huh?" There was an edge in his voice. "Exactly how many years are we talking?"

She frowned. "He told me that he—"

A screech of chair legs on tile cut her off. Frost had shoved back his chair and was standing. "You can have your little family reunion later, Smith," he said coldly. "All I'm interested in right now is finding out where the hell Night is."

Surprise crossed Josh's face. "But you said that—"

"I don't care what I fucking said." Frost came around the table, moving in Joanna's direction. "She can tell us where he is and that's all that matters."

All her muscles tightened automatically. The tension in the air was close to the snapping point and now that she knew where the threat was coming from, she could prepare.

"I don't know where Jacob is," she said, with complete honesty.

"Of course you don't." Frost paused in front of her. "I gave you what you wanted, Joanna. Now it's time for you to uphold your end of the bargain." He reached for one of the chairs and pulled it out. "Sit down and tell me everything. Now."

Yesterday, she might have. Because what loyalty did she have to Jacob Night? He'd looked after her for six months, yes, but only because he'd wanted her memories, regardless of whatever else he'd told her. He'd wanted to find his brother, that was the beginning and end of it.

But that was before he'd told her that he'd be whatever she needed and if she needed a prince then he'd be that for her. Before he'd told her that she was his warrior princess. Before she'd seen the blood on the back of his head after she'd hit him and had felt it like pain herself.

Before she'd felt vulnerable and yet protected in his arms.

Now, the idea of betraying his secrets was . . . terrible.

You're his. He claimed you. And that's exactly what you want, what you've always been looking for. He and the 11th Hour are the home you never had.

The truth of it settled deep in her soul. Because it *was* true. She'd never felt such a sense of belonging, not even in the military. Being a female Army Ranger hadn't exactly made her fit in, and even the special ops branch she'd been part of, where she'd thought she'd found family, hadn't trusted her. Her superiors had thought she wouldn't be able to do the job and had sent in people after her to finish it.

Jacob is the only one who's ever truly trusted you.

And he had. He'd trusted her with his secrets. With his past. With his identity. He'd had no idea who Joanna was, no idea whether she'd change once she remembered who she was, and still he'd trusted her with everything.

That was a gift. She couldn't betray him.

But Frost didn't need to know that, did he?

Getting out of here was going to be tricky without backup but Jacob would know where she was. And he would come for her, of that she had no doubt. All she had to do was stay here until he came.

She lifted a shoulder like she didn't care one way or the other and sat down, leaning back in the chair. "Sure," she said. "What do you want to know?"

CHAPTER 17

"You've got to be fucking kidding me," Kellan muttered. "She's actually special ops? Seriously?"

Everyone was sitting in the living area of HQ, all staring at Jacob, gobsmacked after hearing him tell them the truth about the woman they'd been working with for six months. About how she was a special ops soldier who'd lost her memory and how, because the gun-running ring the 11th Hour had been chasing for a couple of months now had been after her, he'd decided to take care of her until her memories returned.

He did not tell them about his brother. That was information they didn't need to know.

"No, I'm not fucking kidding you, Mr. Blake," he said shortly. "But your questions can wait. We need a plan to get her out and we need it now."

But Kellan was clearly not going to leave it alone. "So let me get this straight. You took her out of the hospital and looked after her for six months, purely because she had information you needed to nail these bastards?"

"Yes." There was no point telling them about his fascination with her. That was something else they didn't need to know. "She also needed my protection considering those same bastards were trying to kill her."

Kellan was on the couch, his arms folded, scowling. "What about her team? Where were they?"

Jacob debated whether to tell Kellan he'd made sure they couldn't find her either, then decided not to, especially since that would only provoke yet more questions and he had no damn time for that.

A certain desperation was growing in his gut, a gnawing ache.

He had to get to her. He had to get to her *now*. Because if he was right in thinking who was behind this mission, then . . . Jesus. No, that didn't bear thinking about.

Fuck, why had he come here first? He should have simply followed her straight there. Then again, heading in without backup or a plan, without knowing what kind of situation he was getting into, wasn't something he did anymore. That was for Jake Foster, the fucking tool who simply obeyed, a slave to his fury.

Jacob wasn't that man. He planned. He strategized. That's why he'd created a team.

"Like I said, those questions are irrelevant." He kept his voice expressionless, allowing nothing of his impatience or, more importantly, his anger to show. "Right now she's—"

"I've got the address," Sabrina interrupted, staring down at the laptop on her knees. He'd told her about the bugs he'd placed in Faith's clothing, and she'd instantly downloaded the program he'd used to track Faith so she could use it too. "Big place on the cliff to the south. Lots of cameras."

Cameras. Yes. Excellent.

"Can you hack into them?"

"Sure. Easy enough." Her fingers were a blur on the keyboard. "There." She got up, moving over to the computer area. "I'll hook this up to the screens so you can see better."

A minute later they were all gathered around some of the big computer monitors, staring at a whole bunch of security camera feeds displaying different empty rooms.

Except not entirely empty.

There was one showing an outdoor terrace, currently occupied by a couple of what were obviously security and two other men. And one woman.

She was sitting at a table, while one man stood nearby looking down at her, while the other one had his back to the camera, watching the other two.

His heartbeat slowed down, nearly coming to a dead stop.

Because he knew the man standing next to Faith. A man who should be dead. Frost.

A man you betrayed.

Jacob gritted his teeth, ignoring the thought. Because he had a horrible feeling he knew the other man standing there too. Not that he needed to see the guy's face, not when his height and his build gave him away.

Joshua. Alive.

Another you betrayed.

Anger filled him, deep and hot, and for a second he held on to it. Yes, sure, he'd betrayed his brother. Hadn't saved him when he should have, hadn't stopped what was happening to him. And the one action he'd taken had gotten them both split up and sent to different homes.

So yes, that was betrayal.

But then his brother had betrayed Faith. He was supposed to have been her friend and then he'd shot her, intending to take her prisoner. He'd hurt her and now she was Jacob's, that complicated things.

"What the hell is happening?" Isiah growled. "Is she negotiating with them? What?"

On the screen the man who should be dead and yet wasn't, moved quickly all of a sudden, taking Faith's wrist and forcing it onto the table. She tried to struggle, but then the two security guards were there and they were holding her hand firmly to the tabletop.

Josh stood there, making no move.

Then Frost reached down and took something from his boot. A knife.

Someone—Callie—gasped.

"Oh, hell no," Jack said viciously. "Blake? We on this or what?"

But Jacob wasn't listening. Something inside him had shattered and he was already moving, nothing in his head but the need to protect what was his. Protect them at all costs.

"Night!" It was Kellan yelling. "Where the fuck are you going?"

But he didn't respond, heading straight to the door he'd come in through.

He had his Glock. He didn't need anyone else.

Waiting had only led to this, to Faith at a table being held down while his ex-teammate got out a knife. And Jacob knew exactly why that was happening. He remembered.

Frost wanted answers for what had happened all those years ago.

For the mess that Jacob had created. For the deaths that were solely Jacob's fault.

Well, if Frost wanted answers, then Jacob would provide them. With his gun.

Joanna took a long, slow breath. Then another. She shoved Faith right down inside, ignoring the fear and the pain as the two security assholes held her wrist down forcefully on the table.

She hadn't been expecting Frost to lose patience quite so quickly. But he hadn't been satisfied with her answers. Though maybe it wasn't any wonder, seeing as how they were a pack of lies.

Perhaps she'd given herself away somehow, or perhaps he'd simply gotten tired of waiting. Whatever, she hadn't been able to avoid it when he'd suddenly yanked her wrist from the arm of the chair and had pressed it down on the table in front of her.

He was holding a knife now, the blade as sharp and metallic as his gray gaze. "Listen," he said flatly. "I know you're lying. I know you're protecting him. Though for what reason I have no fucking idea since he's a lying sack of shit." He waved the knife casually. "I don't want to have to do this. I mean, I presume you like having your fingers where they are, but unless you start giving me some answers, I've really got no choice."

Breathe. Just breathe. Remember your training.

Yes, she remembered. She'd been in torture simulations before. Physical pain was nothing. The trick was not to fight it, to embrace it, let it pass through you and that way it would leave the rest of you untouched.

It was fear that finally got to you in the end, not pain.

"But I already told you I don't know where he is," she said levelly, ignoring the hold they had on her wrist. "I knocked him out and came straight here. Sure, he'll be trying to find me, but he won't know how."

Frost's jaw hardened. "You underestimate him."

"Oh?" She met his gaze steadily. "Do you know him then?"

"That's none of your fucking business." The knife glinted in the sunlight. "What did he tell you about my little operation?"

"Nothing," she lied. "I just did what he told me. I handed out his orders, that's all."

The knife descended, the blade resting against the knuckle

on the middle finger on her right hand. He didn't press down, it was just resting there, but she felt the sharpness against her skin.

Her heartbeat began to get faster, fear knotting in her gut.

You could tell him. Let Jacob handle it. It's not as if he couldn't, right?

It would be so easy. To open her mouth and tell Frost all about Jacob. To let slip everything he'd told her as he'd held her in his arms. To betray that trust. But she knew, deep in her soul, that she wasn't going to do that. That she couldn't.

There were many people in her life who'd betrayed her. Who'd said they cared about her, only to do things that said they didn't.

But not Jacob. He was the opposite. He'd never said he cared about her, but everything he did told a different story. From the bath gel he'd bought her, to the phoenix she wore around her neck. To the things he'd told her, giving her his trust when he didn't have to, telling her about himself, things he'd never told anyone else.

He could have given her up for his brother and he hadn't.

So she wouldn't give him up now.

No matter what this man did to her.

"Frost," Joshua said from behind her, a warning.

How had she ever mistaken his voice for Jacob's? They were so different. There was something lacking in Joshua's, a kind of richness, a warmth. A passion maybe. Whatever it was, it made her ache. But it was a good kind of ache, reminding her of good things. So she held on to it, thought about that instead of the knife against her skin.

"What?" Frost snapped, his attention over her shoulder.

"Don't fucking hurt her."

"Hey, you were the one who shot her in the first place. Don't go getting squeamish on me now." Frost's gaze came back to hers. "Last chance. Where is he?"

She waited, just on the off chance Joshua might have something more to say about the fact that this man was about to cut her finger off. But he was silent.

Her heart twisted as the last shreds of their friendship died, but she shoved it aside. There would be no help from that quarter and she should have known that all along. Right from the moment he'd pulled the trigger and shot her in the chest.

Instead she looked into Frost's eyes. "I don't know where he is."

"Jo," Joshua said. "You should tell him the truth."

"That is the truth."

Frost lifted a shoulder. "Well, okay. Your choice."

She could fight this, she knew she could. But not three men, all armed. Fighting would also put her life at risk and might mean she'd have to retreat in order to stay alive, which wouldn't help Jacob trying to find her and his brother.

No, she was going to have to stay here and endure whatever Frost was going to do to her.

"Fuck you, asshole," she said.

He smiled. And pressed the knife down.

Jacob parked his bike in a street about a mile away from the address where Faith was being held and ran there. Sabrina—without being asked—had sent him plans for the house, not to mention numbers of security staff. She'd also texted him that she'd disabled the locks on the doors and the camera feeds so he should be able to get in without any drama.

Unfortunately, she'd also told him that Kellan, Jack, and Isiah were on their way as backup.

He texted back that they were to wait until he gave them the word to move, which he had no intention of doing.

Faith was his. Which meant this was his show and he wanted no interference.

There was a time to plan and to strategize, and then there was a time to act.

He was acting now.

Rage burned inside him as he approached the house, his silenced Glock in his hand. If they had hurt her, if they had even so much as put one single bruise on her body, then by God there would be hell to pay.

Judge, jury, and executioner had nothing on him.

Frost, that fucker, would suffer and as for his brother . . .

The memory of that security camera feed loomed large in his head. Of Faith having her hand held down while Frost pulled a knife and Joshua . . . did nothing.

What kind of man had his brother turned into? What kind of man had he really been searching for all these years?

He grimaced, shoving aside the thoughts for the moment as he pushed open the gate that led to the house. There was no one around so he strode straight up the path to the front door. It opened as soon as he twisted the knob so he went right in.

A man in a suit was standing near the door, leaning against a wall, reading a book. He looked up as Jacob entered, shock on his face. His mouth opened, ready to shout for help, but Jacob was faster. He shot him before the guy could get a word out. The man fell to the ground and didn't move.

Jacob ignored him, waiting, listening.

The house was silent.

According to the plans Sabrina had sent him, the terrace was up the stairs, so up he went, soundlessly.

There were more guys at the top, but clearly, they hadn't heard a thing downstairs because they weren't at all ready for him.

Then again, no one was ready for Jacob Night when he was on a mission.

He put them down easily and without a sound, then moved

through into an airy living area. Big windows faced the sea and led to an outside terrace.

"Fuck's sake," a deep, rough voice was saying. "Don't hurt her too badly, okay?"

Three men were gathered around a woman in a chair. Two of them were holding her down with what looked like considerable force, while a third was bent over her, doing something he couldn't see.

She wasn't making a sound, though her breathing was harsh. A small rivulet of blood was dripping off the tabletop and onto the tiles below it, pooling around the table leg.

Faith's blood.

A grenade went off in Jacob's head and blew everything all to hell.

He didn't think. He simply acted, moving through the living area, heading straight for the men holding Faith down. He shot them both without hesitation, making the third man's head come up sharply.

Frost. His teammate. A friend. His second-in-command.

Who'd told him the intel they'd been given was shitty and whom Jacob hadn't listened to, because he was supposed to follow orders. That's all they were there to do. Follow orders, don't think, and kill whoever they told you to kill, that's all.

Frost, whom he should have listened to and hadn't. And so had led his team into a situation only he had survived.

Frost, who was hurting a woman who mattered too damn much.

"Jake," Frost said, smiling as if Jacob were an old friend he hadn't seen for a long time, and not the commander who'd betrayed everyone. "I knew you'd get here eventually."

He reached for something—another weapon probably—but Jacob had always been faster. In a couple of strides he was at the table, grabbing Frost by the neck of his T-shirt and hauling him off the tabletop. Shoving him back against the balustrade that bounded the terrace. Pressing him against it, over it, so that half his body was suspended in the air.

There was so much anger inside him, a red veil of it. He remembered that anger from his military days, a berserker rage that had earned him a fearsome reputation, among both his own men and the enemy. No one wanted to get on the bad side of Jake Foster. No one.

Jacob bent his head so his face was close to Frost's. "You should have died back in Europe," he said, his voice so low and guttural it was almost unrecognizable. "It would have saved me the trouble of killing you now."

Frost bared his teeth, not even looking at the ground below, as if he didn't give a shit that all Jacob had to do was open his hands and he'd fall. "You'd have liked that, wouldn't you, motherfucker?" he panted. "Especially since you killed the rest of our fucking team."

Something shuddered inside Jacob, a knowledge he'd been trying his damndest to forget.

Your team was sabotaged and you were the one responsible for those deaths. You were the fucking saboteur.

"You think I'm going to let you off that easy?" he demanded, the truth hollowing him out inside. "No, you prick. You hurt her, which means I'm going to cut your fingers off one by one, followed by any other appendage that looks interesting, and *then* I'll kill you."

Frost reached for Jacob's hand fisted in his shirt, trying to pull it away and failing. Then he laughed. "She doesn't matter. She was only a tool I wanted to use to get to you. And it worked. I die here and she dies too. So you'd better choose, asshole. Which is it going to be?"

At first he didn't understand, because the only thing between Frost and a three-story drop was his hand clutching the prick's shirt.

Then Faith said in a voice sharp with pain, "Jacob."

Slowly, without letting go of Frost, he looked behind him.

Faith was still sitting in the chair. Her face was white, one hand cradled protectively in the other, blood seeping out from between her fingers.

And his brother, standing behind her. With a gun to her head.

Jacob's line of vision narrowed to the woman in the chair and the man standing behind her.

He remembered those black eyes, so like his own. That had used to look at him with awe and admiration, because Josh had loved his twin once. Eyes that had turned dark and scared the moment Greg had come into their lives. And then didn't look at Jake at all.

Jake, who'd failed to protect his brother and now that brother was holding a gun to the head of the woman who'd come to mean far more to him than she should have.

And that's your fault too. All of this is your fault.

And it was, wasn't it?

Perhaps if he'd saved Joshua from Greg, then his brother wouldn't have become the type of man who ran guns for a living. Who'd betray a friend and stand by while that friend was tortured. Who'd hold a gun to that same friend's head and for what?

If he'd saved his brother, they wouldn't have been split up, and he wouldn't have turned into the ball of rage he'd become. Wouldn't have headed into the military so he could focus that rage, become the killer he'd turned himself into. He wouldn't have been there to take the order that had led his team into death, which meant Frost wouldn't have been there to survive it. Frost, who'd turned into a gun runner and recruited his brother. Who'd then hurt Faith purely to get to Jacob.

Faith, who'd gotten caught in the middle and been hurt by all of them. Hurt badly.

Yeah, and that was his fault. All of it was his fault.

He was supposed to be different, supposed to be Jacob Night, who didn't do shit like that anymore. Who saved people, protected them. Not Jake Foster, who destroyed them.

But that past . . . He couldn't escape it. That past had led to this future and now he was reaping what he'd sown.

His gaze met Faith's, her eyes dark with pain and something else he couldn't decipher.

She'd been hurt. She'd been *hurt*.

"Are you okay, sweet girl?" His voice was as hoarse as hers.

"Not really. I've still got my finger though, if that's what you want to know." Then, weirdly, she smiled. "Seems a fair swap for me hitting you over the back of the head."

Jesus. This woman. She was so fucking strong.

There was an ache inside him and it deepened.

"Let him go," Joshua ordered, ignoring Faith. "You can't kill him, Jake."

Jacob focused on his brother. "You'd shoot her to save this prick? She's your friend."

"And you're my fucking brother." There was something familiar in Joshua's eyes. The same thing he'd seen in his own eyes every goddamned morning for years. Anger. "But I guess you'd prefer killing that asshole and saving her than talking to me."

What? What the hell was he talking about?

Frost tried to struggle, but Jacob ignored him, his attention squarely on his brother. "Do you know how long I spent looking for you? Do you have any fucking idea?"

But at that moment, without warning, Faith abruptly leaned forward and shoved back the chair she'd been sitting in, sending it cannoning back into Joshua's legs.

Taken by surprise, he cursed, stumbling, the gun going wide. Faith had gone down into a crouch but, quicker than she had any right to considering she'd just had her finger nearly cut off, she twisted and sprang, one foot catching Joshua in the chest, kicking him hard. He went down and she went with him.

A surge of adrenaline pulsed inside Jacob. Fuck, he could watch her beat people up all day, even if it was his own brother.

Sadly, he had other business.

Frost was cursing and trying to get away, so Jacob turned, drew back his fist, and punched him in the face. Once, twice, and a third time because he was just so fucking angry and the asshole had hurt Faith.

Frost went out like a light, so Jacob dropped him in a heap onto the tiles. Then he turned back to where Faith was to find her standing over Joshua, the gun now in her hand. Her other hand was held at her side, dripping blood onto the ground.

The sight of that blood made the pressure in his chest get worse, that feral rage squeezing him tight. He wanted to get his Glock, shoot Frost in the face for what he'd done to her. For the pain he'd caused.

Fuck, he'd do it right now.

He gripped his weapon and turned back to where Frost lay on the tiles.

"Jacob," Faith said, her voice quiet yet strong. "Leave him. He's handled. I think it's time you talked to your brother."

She's right. Don't let the anger win. You know how this ends when you do . . .

Yeah, he did. With everyone dead.

He took a breath, for some reason focusing on that cool note in her voice, the one that she used when she was organizing the team or giving him an update on whatever job was happening. Sometimes even when she was arguing with him about something. Businesslike, calm and competent. An antidote to the heat inside him.

The red mist faded and when he'd managed to get himself under control, he said, "One minute, Ms. Beasley." Then he bent down to Frost and without hesitation, ripped a strip off the T-shirt the guy was wearing. Once he had a decent-sized piece, he moved over to where Faith stood.

Her hand was steady where it held the gun, but her face had gone deathly pale. Gently, he took her injured hand in his, shoving aside the howling rage as he saw the white flash of bone, then bound it up tightly to stem the flow of blood.

The only sound she made was a soft exhale as he pulled the fabric tight, but she shook her head sharply as he reached for the gun. "No," she bit out. "I survived a gunshot wound. A cut finger is nothing."

He ignored her. "Sit down. This is my fight. I need someone to cover the rest of those assholes anyway."

She glanced at him and after a moment, nodded, relinquishing her grip on the gun.

Joshua hadn't moved, simply lying there, the look on his face unreadable. Except the gleam in his eyes. Jacob could read that perfectly.

"What the fuck is wrong with you?" he demanded. "I've spent five years looking for you only to find you with a fucking arms dealer and holding a gun to the head of one of my employees." He stared hard into Joshua's eyes. "That's not the brother I thought I was looking for."

"What the fuck did you expect?" Joshua shoved himself up, then stood. Jacob kept the gun trained on him, not trusting him for a second. "That I'd be married and settled down? With a white picket fence and a day job, and a whole bunch of kids? After what happened to me?"

Jacob felt his muscles go tight, the words hitting like blows. Truth was, he hadn't thought about the kind of life his brother had had, or about what kind of person he'd turned into. He'd assumed Joshua had coped, like he'd had to cope, and focused only on the search.

But he shouldn't have.

"Joshua," he began.

"Five years," his brother went on before Jacob could finish, his voice dripping with bitterness. "Five years you've spent looking for me. But what the fuck happened to the last twenty? Did you suddenly just remember that you had a brother or what?"

What could he say? That when he'd finally aged out of the system, he hadn't felt fit to be a proper brother to anyone, let alone him? That he was ashamed for how his mistake had cost them a home? Ashamed for not having protected him?

"No," he said at last. "It wasn't until five years ago that I felt ready to find you."

Joshua gave a hollow-sounding laugh. "Oh yes, I know all about that. Frost told me. About the Wolf Pack. About how you sabotaged your unit and how they all died. And then you were handed a nice fat payout and got to live the rest of your life in peace."

He went cold. Absolutely fucking cold. And he had no answer.

Because it was all true.

He'd taken the order. He'd caused the death of his whole team and there was nothing he could do to change that. And as to peace . . . Was there any peace to be had when you were a traitor?

"And what about me," Faith said suddenly, anger bleeding into her voice. "What's your excuse for selling me out?"

Joshua glanced at her. "Do I really need to explain? You were sent to kill me."

"I wanted an explanation, Josh. I told you that. I never meant to hurt you."

"Yet you shot me anyway."

"Because you betrayed me! Just like you betrayed our entire team, right?"

Joshua sneered. "Hey, just following along in the footsteps of my brother here."

There was nothing but bitterness in Joshua's voice and it was there in his eyes, too. Bitterness and anger and pain.

There were going to be no easy answers here.

"We need to talk," Jacob said. "Alone."

Joshua gave a laugh that held no amusement. "Yeah, I don't think so."

Jacob did not lower his gun. If Josh thought that he was going to simply let him walk away, his brother needed to think again.

"I can't let you go, Josh, if that's what you were hoping. You've done some bad shit, which means you have to take responsibility for it."

Joshua looked at the gun, then back at him. "Like you took responsibility for the 'bad shit' you did? With your payout and your anonymity?"

So his brother was angry. He got it. Joshua wasn't wrong. He *had* gotten a payout and in a way, losing his identity had been a good thing.

It had meant he could start over, with a new life and a new code. A better code. But that didn't erase the past. And if Joshua didn't see fit to take responsibility for his own actions, then Jacob would take responsibility for him. It was the only thing he could do.

"I'm making up for what happened in the Ukraine," he said flatly. "And I'll continue to do so, believe me. But that's got nothing to do with you. What has, is the information I've collected on Frost and your goddamn arms ring. Information that I'll be passing along to the authorities."

Josh's expression hardened, his whole body tensing.

"Don't," Jacob warned very softly, just in case his brother was planning on doing something really, really stupid. "I won't kill you, Josh, but I have no problem with putting a bullet in your thigh if you're planning on running out. Be a fair swap given what you put Faith through."

"Faith?" Josh was derisive. "Her name is Joanna, asshole."

But there was no more opportunity for talking because Jacob caught movement out of the corner of his eye, the distinctive sound of a bullet humming past his ear and embedding itself in the balustrade.

Shit. Looked like Frost's reinforcements had arrived.

Faith was already moving, upending the table to give them some cover. But as she leapt over it, he heard her gasp and jerk, blood blooming up high on the sleeve of her shirt.

His whole world slowed to a stop.

"Jake," Joshua said, low and harsh.

Jacob was already moving in the direction of the table, desperate to get to Faith, but he risked one glance at his brother because there was something in his voice that caught him.

Joshua's dark eyes held his and for a second the anger in them shifted and flickered.

Then abruptly Joshua turned as one of the security guards stepped out onto the terrace, the muzzle of an AR aimed directly at Jacob, and before the guy could get a shot off, Joshua grabbed it, twisted it out of his hands, and elbowed the guy in the face.

There was no time to wonder what the hell his brother was doing, not when Faith was injured, so Jacob dove behind the upturned table. The sounds of guns firing came from beyond it, but no bullets hit, which was weird.

Then he stopped wondering as he gathered a pale-looking Faith up in his arms. She was breathing fast, lines of pain around her mouth.

"You know what?" she said tightly, her head falling back against his shoulder. "I'm getting really sick of being shot."

He said nothing, the pressure in his chest too much for

speech. Instead he pulled at the fabric of her T-shirt to get a look at the wound. It was clean, the bullet having passed right through her shoulder.

"Josh?" she asked faintly.

"I don't know," he forced out. "He turned on them, took a gun . . . I think . . ." He stopped for a second, then went on. "I think he was trying to protect us."

She frowned, her mouth opening to say something. But before she could a familiar voice said, "Night? Where the fuck are you?"

Kellan. The goddamn cavalry at last.

Jacob rose, holding Faith in his arms.

Kellan, Jack, and Isiah were standing at the entrance to the terrace, all of them fully armed and all of them looking puzzled.

And no wonder. Every single one of Frost's security seemed to be lying on the ground.

"Jesus," Kellan said, his eyes widening as he took in Faith. "Do we need an ambulance?"

"No." Jacob tightened his grip on the woman in his arms. "The coast clear?"

Kellan blinked. "Uh, yeah. We got in here and basically everyone's dead. Nothing left for us to do. What happened?"

Joshua must have happened. Christ.

Ignoring the question, Jacob stepped over the table. "Did you see anyone? Anyone at all?"

"No," Jack said curtly. "Not a damn thing. You take them all out yourself?"

He hadn't told them about his brother and he wasn't about to now. They didn't need to know.

Joshua had gotten away somehow and he was . . . well, he wasn't going to go running after him right now, that was for sure.

"I had help," he said gruffly, and looked down at Faith. "We need to keep this on the down-low, sweet girl. You okay with that? I have a doctor on my payroll who'll stitch you up, no questions asked."

She gave him a faint smile. "Of course. Stupid bullet wound didn't kill me before. It's not going to kill me now."

Realizing that his team was staring, no small amount of shock on their faces, Jacob gave them a glare. "Well?" he demanded. "Presumably someone brought a car?"

CHAPTER 18

Two days later, Faith sat on the couch in the 11th Hour HQ, her shoulder all strapped up, her finger stitched, feeling exhausted from the past couple of hours of answering the team's questions about her memory loss and her identity as Joanna Lynn.

She hadn't known how they'd react to the truth, but apparently, fascination was the order of the day, especially about how her amnesia had worked and the moment she'd remembered who she was. She hadn't wanted to talk too much about what had prompted her dissociative state and they were sensitive enough to let that alone, though they did want all the details about how she'd managed to knock Jacob out not once but twice. Kellan in particular seemed to find that very satisfying.

Naturally, their questions soon circled around to what was going to happen now she remembered who she was, but luckily, at that point, Jacob arrived and told everyone in no uncertain terms to get the hell out.

As soon as they were gone and he'd shut the door after them, he came over to where she sat and stood in front of her, arms folded across his massive chest, his black brows drawn down.

She hadn't seen much of him in the past couple of days. He'd been debriefing the team on what had gone down with Frost—leaving Joshua out of it from what she'd managed to discern—and dealing with the fallout from what had happened at Frost's.

The information on the arms ring he'd collected—plus the names of the various high-ranking men involved—had been handed in to the authorities, along with Frost himself. To keep Jacob, not to mention the team, out of the public eye, much of it had been handled anonymously, with Sabrina's hacker skills hiding any digital tracks, and Jacob's network of informants handling anything that needed a physical presence.

The 11th Hour would stay in the shadows.

As for herself, she'd been seen by Jacob's doctor, and had been instructed to take a couple of weeks' bedrest.

Which was fine. Except she didn't feel in the least bit tired.

Her brain kept going over and over the issue of her future and what she was going to do now she'd remembered who she was. Whether she was going to return to her unit—though whether she could or not was another story—or go and do something else.

Or stay with the 11th Hour.

Stay with Jacob.

The thought terrified her for reasons she couldn't articulate so she hadn't thought about that aspect too much. Instead she'd decided to talk to him solely about her position with the 11th Hour and not so much about their relationship.

If they even had a relationship, which they probably didn't. He'd said she was his, but only while they'd been in bed. It was likely to be a heat of the moment thing, nothing he'd meant to continue.

"I never say anything I don't mean . . ."

She shoved his voice from two days ago out of her head and stared at the man standing in front of her now, his gaze impenetrable, giving nothing away.

"Hey," she said. "Hope the rest of them didn't mind being ordered out of their own HQ."

"Since I own the building, I can do whatever the hell I goddamn well please." His voice was rough, which wasn't a good sign.

"Okay." She shifted on the couch. "You want to sit down? Looks like you have something to talk about."

He made no move to sit. "The deal with Frost is handled," he said shortly. "Joshua has disappeared. I can't find him anywhere."

"Oh." She took a silent breath, not wanting to think about Joshua or what had happened out on the terrace. The fierce pain of Frost's knife hadn't been nearly as sharp as the realization that Joshua was not going to stop it from happening. That he was going to stand there and let her be tortured.

That, more than anything else—including the bullet wound—had hurt. But a source of pride to her over the past day or so was that she hadn't told Frost anything about Jacob, not one single damn thing.

Of course, Jacob had arrived before things had gotten too bad and she wasn't too proud that she could admit to loving how he'd simply picked Frost up and nearly thrown him over the edge of the terrace. One-handed. God, she wished she'd caught it on video so she could replay it over and over again.

"Yes," Jacob said. "'Oh' is a good word for it."

She studied him for a second. "You don't want to find him, do you?"

His expression was guarded, which hurt because she was hoping for a bit more trust from him by now. Then again, considering how many times she'd knocked him out, maybe not.

He was silent, though when at last he did speak, it wasn't to answer her question. "I haven't talked to the team yet, but you should know that I'm handing over control of the 11th Hour to Isiah."

Cold shock washed over her. "What?"

"My run is at an end." His voice was flat. "And I've . . . lost my taste for it. I'll still bankroll it but I won't be otherwise involved in it in any way."

His face was set, his jaw hard. A cold light glittered in his eyes.

He was serious about this.

She struggled to think of what to say, because this was the very last thing she'd thought he'd do. "Jacob . . . I don't understand. Why?"

He straightened minutely, as if steeling himself. "You heard what Joshua said, didn't you? About my team? About how I led them to their deaths?"

She'd heard, but she'd simply discounted it because the thought of Jacob somehow betraying his men was ludicrous. "Yes, but that's a lie."

"It's not a lie." His gaze was steady, direct. "I did lead my team to their deaths. And Frost was one of them. I thought he'd died along with everyone else, but he hadn't." His voice could have chipped granite it was so hard.

"What happened?" she asked, straight out. "Tell me."

"We were given orders to attack a building sheltering some militia. We knew from our sources that the place was crawling with the enemy and that we didn't have enough men. I wanted to get in and get out, because we were pressed for time and orders were orders. But Frost disagreed. He thought the orders were wrong. Going in there would be like heading into a meat grinder." Something burned in his expression, a kind of ferocity. "I ignored him. We weren't paid to think. We were paid to get the job done. And so that's what I did. I ordered them in there and they all fucking died." Suddenly his gaze was focusing on her, sharper than razors. "I told you Jacob Night is the cage that protects people from who I used to be. And there's a reason for that."

She shook her head, not understanding. "You were a soldier following orders. You can't hold yourself responsible for—"

"Can't I?" he cut across her, hard and cold. "You don't understand. Frost, Joshua . . . All of that was because of who I was five years ago. Jake Foster, who didn't give a shit about anything. Who didn't want to think. Who lived for the kill. If I'd listened to Frost that day, then my team wouldn't have died. Frost wouldn't have gone on to set up that arms ring and maybe he wouldn't have used my own fucking brother to do it." Something else entered his eyes, black ice. "And you wouldn't have gotten hurt."

But she kept shaking her head, because she still didn't see it. "You made a call based on the information you had. It's not your fault that it was wrong. And as for taking responsibility for everything else . . . Jesus, Jacob, that's not your fault either."

"Frost told me the intel was bad," he said flatly. "And I didn't listen. Because I wanted the fight. I . . . needed it."

Then she heard, beneath the granite in his voice and the black obsidian of his eyes, notes of pain. Rage.

Her throat closed and she had to force out the question, even though she thought she knew the answer already. "Why?"

"I should have protected him." Jacob stared at her but she had a feeling it wasn't really her he was seeing. "I should have protected him better and I didn't."

Joshua. He was talking about Joshua.

She pushed herself out of the couch and took a step toward him. "You did, though. God, you were ten years old and you pulled a knife and—"

"And it got us split up. It got me ten years of being alone. And I hate to think of what happened to Josh after what Greg did to him. What kind of foster experience he had. Because if it was anything like mine . . ." He stopped. "If I hadn't pulled that knife, it wouldn't have happened. But I was angry and I didn't think."

284 / Jackie Ashenden

"Jacob. You were ten years old. How could you—"

"Enough." The weight of the word was like an anvil falling direct from the sky. "I've made my decision. Isiah will be managing the 11th Hour while I leave the country."

It felt weirdly as if he'd pulled out a gun and shot her with it the way Joshua had.

"W-What? What do you mean you're leaving the country?"

"I have too much of a past and it draws too much attention." He paused, his gaze focusing on her. "It's also become . . . personal. And I can't have that. It's why I preferred to run the team anonymously. I don't want any personal connections—I can't afford them."

The bullet wound in her shoulder suddenly didn't hurt as much as the hole that had appeared in the middle of her heart. "Personal connections," she echoed, her voice hoarse. "You mean me."

"Yes," he said quietly. "I mean you."

The look in his eyes had softened, but she didn't think it meant he was going to change his mind. He never did.

She swallowed, her throat tight. Everything tight. "So you're leaving because of me? Is that what you're saying?"

"You were hurt, Faith. And if there's one person in this world that doesn't deserve to be hurt, it's you. And that's on me. I put you in harm's way and I can't have that."

Anger glowed hot, a sudden rush of it, and she took a step forward, getting right in his face. "What? You think a couple of bullet wounds and a cut finger is anything to write home about? Jesus Christ, I've had worse. And I can handle myself, you know I—"

"*You* might be able to handle yourself," he interrupted harshly, "but I sure as hell fucking can't." The blackness of his eyes was as dense and dark as the void of space. "I can't protect the people I should," he bit out. "They get hurt. I get angry and they fucking get hurt. And I'm not doing it anymore. I can't.

It's better if I keep myself to myself. Go and start over some-where else."

"Why?" she demanded, too loud and too shrill, but she didn't care. "So people get hurt. So people get angry. You can't stop that, Jacob. And you can't take responsibility for every goddamn thing that happens."

But his expression closed up. "No, but I can take responsi-bility for myself. And that's what I'm going to do."

Right, so he was going to leave. He was going to leave her.

Since when did you care so much?

She had no idea. What she did know was that it hurt. For some reason she didn't understand, it hurt worse than the gun-shot wounds. Worse even than Josh's betrayal.

"You said I was yours." The words betrayed far too much and yet she was powerless to stop from saying them. "You said you'd give me everything I ever wanted."

His gaze reflected nothing but her own desperate face. "Yes, Ms. Beasley. You *are* mine. But I'm afraid I can never be yours."

This wasn't a gunshot wound. This was like he'd reached into her chest and ripped her heart out with his bare hand.

"Why not?" she asked, because she couldn't stop herself. "Am I not worth it? Don't I deserve it?"

Something flickered in his eyes. And then it was gone.

"Maybe," he said, his voice devoid of all emotion. "Or maybe neither of us deserves anything at all."

That was the knife in her gut, the one that twisted and ripped her apart.

She wanted to tell him that she didn't believe him, that they both deserved to have *everything*, and why shouldn't they? They were good people. Yes, they'd done bad things, but they *were* good. Weren't they?

Maybe you're not. Maybe he's right. He's never lied to you before, remember?

Agony coiled tight around her heart, but she covered the

pain like she always covered it and covered the fury, too, because letting that out, letting him know how deeply it hurt, would be giving away too much and she just couldn't do it.

But she had to say something. She couldn't leave it at that.

"I thought you might be a prince," she said. "But you're not, are you? You're just another fucking man I have to shoot."

And then she walked out.

Faith sat in Mac's Bar, a glass of whisky on the table in front of her, the bottle sitting beside it. The bar was empty, closed for the night.

Or at least, she thought it was empty. Until a small figure sat down in the seat opposite her, a wealth of blond hair giving away who it was.

Callie. Jack's fiancée.

"So," Callie said. "Are you okay?"

"Sure." Faith didn't want to talk. She didn't want to talk ever again.

"Yeah, nothing says 'I'm okay' like a bottle of whisky and a shot glass."

Faith stared at her. "You here for a reason?"

Callie leaned her chin on the heel of her hand. "The others are worried about you and I said I'd go talk to you."

Jacob had clearly not broken the news that he'd be leaving the country yet. He might not even tell them until he'd gone. That would be just the kind of thing he'd do. Because he was a fucking prick.

"Well," Faith said. "I appreciate it but I'm really not in the mood."

Callie tilted her head. "You know, a couple of months back, you helped me with a certain stubborn and hard-headed man. And I'm wondering if maybe you'd like me to return the favor."

Faith went still. How the hell did they know . . . ?

The shock must have been evident on her face because Callie gave her a grin. "I don't think Jacob Night calls just anyone 'sweet girl.'"

Oh yes. While she'd been in his arms with the bullet wound in her shoulder . . .

He was a liar like all the rest of them. You were never his sweet girl.

She looked away from Callie's amused blue eyes, her chest aching. "Like I said, I'm fine. And whatever is between Jacob and me has got nothing to do with anyone else."

"Okay, I get it." But Callie didn't move and after a moment, she added, "I just want you to know, that if he's being a tool and let's face it, men are always being tools, it'll be because he's afraid. And he'll be afraid because he cares."

Faith reached for the shot glass and swallowed her whisky. The alcohol burned warmly going down, but it didn't touch the ice in her soul. The ice that would probably be there forever now, because she was starting to think that nothing could warm it up.

Nothing except Jacob.

And he thinks you don't deserve it.

Did he really think that? Or was Callie right? Had that been simply him pushing her away out of fear?

Shit, what did it matter anyway? He'd made his decision.

"Whatever," she said. "That's his choice. I'm not going to go running after him."

"Why not?"

Faith blinked and looked at her. "Because I'm not. It's his decision. And you know he never changes his mind."

"He changed it when he allowed Jack to come and rescue me," Callie pointed out. "And anyway, why should he get to make all the decisions? Don't you deserve to make one too?"

Something twisted in her heart at that.

*"You killed the last prince in this world, Joanna Lynn, so
don't talk to me about wanting to be a princess. You don't deserve it."*

Her mother's voice echoed in her head, thick and grief-
stricken.

No, she didn't deserve it. And Jacob thought so too. Which
meant it had to be true, right? Because he'd never lied to her . . .

She poured herself another drink. "I don't care."

"Right. So that's why you're sitting alone drinking whisky
and there are tears on your cheeks."

Bullshit. She wasn't crying, was she? But when she raised
her hand to her cheek, her fingers came away wet.

Callie reached out and put her hand over Faith's bandaged
one where it rested on the tabletop. "I don't know your past and
I don't know what went on with you and Jacob, but if there's
one thing I do know it's that everyone deserves to make their
own decisions when it comes to love. You can't let your past tell
you what to do. And you certainly can't let some shady asshole
have the last word on what you deserve." Her hand was a warm
pressure, her gaze very open and honest. "It's worth it, that's all
I wanted to say. It's *so* worth it."

Faith had no answer for that, but then she didn't need to
have one anyway, because without another word, Callie calmly
rose and left her alone in the bar again.

She stared at her whisky, thinking about the decisions she'd
made and the past that had shaped her. A past that had taught
her that she couldn't ever have what she wanted, because she
didn't deserve it.

But who got to say what she did and didn't deserve? Not
her mother, that was for damn sure, and not her superiors.
And maybe Callie was right, maybe not Jacob fucking Night,
either.

He thought she was worth giving everything to and yet in
the end he'd let her go.

Except she knew, deep in her heart, she didn't want that. She didn't want to go. She wanted to be his.

He was a protector. A caregiver. And yet he also respected her strength. More, he got off on it. He thought she was a princess.

He thought she was *his* princess and he'd told her so.

But he'd also told her that maybe neither of them deserved anything. So what was the truth? And what was the lie?

"He'll be afraid because he cares. . . ."

Slowly Faith picked up her glass, swirling the alcohol around inside it, Callie's voice echoing in her head.

She hadn't thought Jacob Night would be afraid of anything, but . . . maybe he was. And people did all kinds of stupid shit when they were afraid. Such as say things they didn't mean. Lie. Lie to themselves . . .

Understanding broke over her all of a sudden, freezing her in place.

That's what she'd been doing, wasn't it? Jacob had told her back in the motel that she was lying to herself and she had been. But not only lying about wanting him, she'd been lying to herself about other things too. Telling herself she didn't deserve to have what she wanted, when in reality, she'd just been too afraid to take them.

Just like she'd been afraid back in HQ, when he'd told her he would never be hers.

The ache in her chest grew stronger, deeper.

It didn't matter whether he lied to her or not, did it? What mattered was that she'd been lying to herself. *She* was the one who'd believed she didn't deserve it. Which meant that if she wanted to have everything, *she* had to believe she did deserve it.

She had to believe in herself.

Her hand closed on the shot glass and she lifted it, knocking the rest of the whisky back. Then she slammed the glass back down on the table.

290 / Jackie Ashenden

"I am worth it," she said aloud to the empty bar. "I'm a warrior fucking princess."

She was. And warrior fucking princesses got everything they wanted.

Including their princes.

CHAPTER 19

Jacob walked into his clifftop house and it felt like a stranger's. He'd bought it because he'd liked the security, plus the view of the ocean was good. It was also nice that he couldn't see his neighbors.

But right now all he was conscious of was the fact that it was empty. So very empty of the woman who'd once lived there.

The woman he'd walked away from earlier that day and would in all likelihood never see again.

Which was good, wasn't it? That's what he wanted. That's what his decision had all been about.

Keep her safe. Keep the rest of the team safe. Keep everyone safe.

From him.

Starting afresh in another country was what he should have done five years earlier, but he hadn't. Because he'd wanted to track Joshua down, and now that had happened and . . . Well, it had all turned to shit.

Just like what had happened with his team.

Yeah, it was a good thing he was going. A very good thing.

And he didn't know why he should feel so very shitty about it, but he did.

Maybe something to do with the fact that you told her she didn't deserve to have you?

A crappy thing to say to her and a dick move. But he'd had to say something to get her to go, hadn't he?

He walked into the big living area with the plate glass windows that looked out over the darkened sea. It was night outside and he didn't bother with the lights, so he didn't see the woman sitting in the armchair by the window.

Not until she abruptly switched on the light.

He stilled, staring at her.

The lamp bathed her in light, glossing her long black hair and illuminating her creamy skin. Glinting off the necklace she wore at her throat.

A phoenix on a chain. The one he'd bought Faith a few months ago.

His heart gave one hard beat.

Her face was pale, the light making the midnight blue of her eyes glow, and there was a very familiar expression in them.

Determination.

"What are you doing here?" It was an effort to keep his voice level. "How did you get in?"

"You never changed the codes to the locks," she said calmly. "And I'm here because we haven't finished our conversation."

"Yes. We have." He moved over to the liquor cabinet that stood in one corner because he had to do something with the strange heat and fury that was filling him.

And yes, it *was* fury. He'd made a decision and it hadn't been an easy one. But it was for the good of everyone around him and for the good of himself, too. And he was comfortable with that.

So why the fuck she was here he had no idea. He wasn't going to change his mind if that's what she was hoping.

Getting a bottle of his favorite brandy out of the liquor cabinet and a crystal tumbler, he poured himself a measure, keeping his movements slow and deliberate. "And I thought I'd made my position clear." He put the bottle down and straightened. "I'm not changing my mind, if that's what you're hoping."

She didn't answer, an assessing look in her eyes, as if he were a fortress she was preparing to mount an assault on and was studying his defenses.

Anger twisted inside him, hot and desperate, along with that ache in his chest that just wouldn't fucking go away.

Yes, she was his and he would always view her as such, but he couldn't give himself to her in the same way. Which meant he couldn't keep her. She had such a loving, generous spirit, while his . . .

His was stunted. Suffocated. And that was for the best. Jake Foster was nothing but rage and she deserved more from him than that.

She was a woman with a vulnerable heart at the center of her core of strength, something that had struck him hard when he'd seen her in HQ earlier that day. She'd been sitting on the couch, all pale and bandaged up, injuries that were his fault, and yet she'd looked at him with such hope. As if she was expecting something from him, something good.

He'd known in that moment that he couldn't give her whatever it was that she wanted. There was too much anger in his heart to leave room for any other kind of emotion. Especially the kind of emotions she needed and deserved.

He wasn't that type of man. Maybe once he had been, but that had been before he'd lost everything.

Which had made his decision to leave an easy one.

He had to stay Jacob Night. And Jacob Night worked best as a lone wolf.

"Your position," she said, finally, "is bullshit."

She was sitting there in that chair, so very calm, so very together. Everything that he wasn't, and he could feel the man he'd used to be straining at the cage he'd set around him. Roaring. Clawing at the bars to get to her.

Jake Foster remembered what it was like to have someone. And now he wanted Faith Beasley. Wanted her so badly. She was everything he'd ever wanted in a woman. Strong. Ballsy. Intelligent. Warm. Generous. Protective.

But Jacob Night remembered what it was like to lose someone. And he wasn't doing that again. Anger was the only thing no one had ever been able to take from him and he was keeping that.

It was all that kept him going.

"I suggest you leave." He was aware he was holding his glass far too tightly and if he put any more pressure on it, it would shatter. "I have nothing more to say on the matter."

She didn't speak, simply staring at him, then she put her hands on the arms of the chair and pushed herself out of it. And he was conscious of a hollow feeling growing inside him, a loss, an absence. And that the absence had a shape. And that the shape was her.

She was leaving, like he'd told her, and now his life would go back to normal.

Normal? Fuck, you're an idiot. It'll never be the same again. It'll be darker. Lonelier. Safer.

The glass in his hand creaked as his grip tightened. Why was he thinking this shit? This was what he'd wanted, wasn't it?

Yet Faith didn't walk out.

She came toward him instead, moving slowly and with purpose, her midnight eyes glowing, until she was right in front of him.

He'd never been the kind of man who retreated from a fight for any reason, but he found himself almost taking a step back now.

She was so close. All feminine heat and the scent of lavender, the pulse at the base of her throat, where the phoenix rested, beating fast.

You're fucked.

He took a breath, trying not to crack the glass he was holding.

"Is that what you really want?" The question was soft, her gaze searching.

"Yes." It took all his considerable will to stand still, to beat down Jake Foster, who wanted him to toss aside the stupid brandy and take her in his arms. Hold her. Never let her go.

"You've never lied to me before," Faith said. "But I think you lied to me earlier at HQ. And I think you're lying now."

It was nothing. A simple question from a woman who'd been lied to and betrayed many times in the past. And it would have been so easy for him to tell her he wasn't lying. That of course leaving was what he wanted.

But that wasn't what happened.

It was as if the question were a lighted match to a tank of gas and he simply went up in flames, the cage he had on Jake Foster cracking, all the rage he had inside him exploding outward.

Hardly aware of what he was doing, he flung the brandy glass at the wall where it shattered, liquid splashing everywhere. But he didn't look at it. Instead he took Faith by her upper arms, propelling her back until she hit the windows, and he held her there, his heart feeling like a grenade about to go off.

Faith only looked at him. There was no fear in her eyes. It was as if she knew exactly what was going on with him.

"I have lost everything I ever loved," he said hoarsely, too loud and too rough, words spilling out of him, words he'd never meant to say. "*Everything!*" He gave her a little shake, to emphasize his point, make her see. "My family, my home. The person I thought I was. Every single fucking thing!" He dug his fingers into her upper arms, lowering his head until her face was inches from his, her blue eyes filling his vision. "I'm not doing it again. I can never keep what's mine. *Never.* It's easier not to have it." He bared his teeth, fury alive in his veins, the truth coming out whether he wanted it to or not. "Yes, I lied to you back at HQ. And if that makes me a coward, then yes, I'm a fucking coward. But no one else is there to protect me, so I have to. I have to fucking protect myself!"

He was breathing fast and hard, the sound of it hoarse in the room, while she looked at him, her face full of something he couldn't bear.

He wanted to push away and push away hard, take himself out of her vicinity before he did something he regretted, but before he could move, her hand came up, delicate fingers cupping his cheek.

"You're wrong," Faith said. "You have me. I'll protect you, Jacob."

It was like that touch was a knife, cutting through his soul.

"No," he said roughly. "You're too vulnerable. You've lost so much and you're—"

"We've both lost too much." Her voice sliced through his effortlessly. "And we're both too vulnerable. But why can't we be vulnerable together? Why can't we protect each other?"

Deep inside him, the part of him that was Jake Foster shuddered. Howled. And then went quiet.

For the first time in his life, Jacob truly felt the fear.

He was afraid of this woman who seemed to be two people and yet wasn't. Who had armor and yet who'd survived six months without that armor. Who'd lost her whole identity and yet had learned to live without it. Be at peace with it.

He couldn't. How could he ever be at peace with Jake Foster? The angry boy who'd failed to protect his brother and had ended up getting them split apart. The isolated, sullen teen who'd withdrawn into himself, nurturing his anger until he was finally able to let it out safely, in the Navy. The furious man desperate to release that anger on the enemy. Any enemy . . .

Under her armor, Faith Beasley was a loving, warmhearted, caring woman. Under his was darkness. Rage. Nothing good.

He hadn't lied about one thing back at HQ. She might deserve to get what she wanted, but he didn't.

"I can't," he bit out. "I fucking *can't*. The man I was is dangerous. I told you, Jacob Night is the cage I need to—"

"I didn't come here for Jacob Night," Faith interrupted. "I came for Jake Foster."

It felt like he'd taken a crossbow bolt straight to the chest, knocking him down.

Piece by piece he'd lost his family. First his father, then his mother. Then his brother. Everyone who'd ever known him and loved him. He'd used to fantasize that his father hadn't gone missing, presumed dead. That he was alive and one day he'd come back. One day he'd find Jacob and bring him home. But that had never happened.

No one had ever come for him. No one.

And he'd come to think that there was a reason for that.

No one wants you . . .

"You don't fucking know Jake Foster." His voice was scraped raw.

Her fingers were cool on his skin, gentle. Unlike his as they gripped her, pushing her against the glass. "I do. He's angry, yes, but only because he cares. And that's why he's so very, *very* angry. Because he cares so very deeply." She touched his mouth. "He's a protector and it hurts when he can't protect the people he cares about the way he should. He blames himself. Because it matters."

His rage shifted inside him, howled. Like a beast.

She's right. And you know why you're angry.

"Faith," he said desperately. "It's not that simple."

She ignored him. "You've been alone a long time, haven't you?" Her voice had gotten thick and there were tears in her eyes, and she was touching him as if he was precious to her. "And you want to belong to someone, I can see it in your eyes, Jake. You want to belong to me."

He felt like he was falling into pieces, like a pane of glass slowly cracking, and each piece was jagged and sharp, lethal to anyone they cut.

Except she wasn't being hurt. She was the one hurting him. Giving him visions of what he wanted. What he'd *always* so desperately wanted.

His throat was tight, his chest sore. And he couldn't breathe. Why couldn't he fucking breathe? Why couldn't he let her go and walk away the way he should?

He'd learned a long time ago to deny himself the things he wanted so this shouldn't be difficult. And yet . . . Belonging to her . . .

"You don't understand," he ground out.

"Of course I understand. You think I haven't denied myself? That I haven't done exactly the same thing? You know what I wanted to be as a kid, I told you. I wanted to be a princess." A tear slid down her cheek, glittering in the light. "But I thought I could never have it, that I didn't deserve it. Until you told me that I already was a princess, a warrior princess. And that you'd give me everything I wanted." She searched his face. "I believed you back in HQ. I believed you when you said that maybe neither of us deserved anything. But you lied. The first lie you ever told me."

Ah, Christ.

"Faith—"

"I know. I get it. You were afraid. And then I realized something. I realized that it didn't matter whether you thought I deserved it or not. What matters is that *I* believe it. And I do, Jake. I believe I deserve to have what I want. And I believe that you do too."

He struggled to get a breath, to get some air in his fucking lungs. "It's not the same. You *do* deserve those things. But I . . ."

"It *is* the same." Her fingers moved into his hair, stroking. "I've done bad things, like you have. I've killed people. Hurt people. But I'm not a bad person, I'm not. And neither are you."

How could he argue with that? With the belief that shone in her eyes?

His chest heaved and he pressed her harder against the glass, wanting to deny it with everything in him. Except he couldn't, not without hurting her.

"Damn you," he whispered.

Her fingers curled in his hair. "It's not your fault, Jake. None of it is your fault. Your dad, your mom, Josh . . . They would never have left you if they'd had the choice, you *know* that. You were a kid and it was all just shitty, shitty luck."

"Stop," he said, his voice shaking. "Fucking shut *up*."

But she didn't. She just kept on going. "I think . . . I'm in love with you. That's what I came here to say. And also that if I'm a warrior princess, then I get what I want. And I want a prince."

"Faith—"

Her fingers tightened, the hold on his hair painful. "No, you don't get to tell me you're not my prince. *I'm* the one who makes that decision. And if I decide you're my fucking prince, then you are." Her blue eyes glowed, fierce and hot. "I need a strong man at my side. I need a good man. An honest man. A caring man. And you're all those things, Jake Foster. You're every single one. And if you can't believe that for yourself, then believe me. Trust me."

He didn't know what happened inside him. Whether those cracked, jagged pieces of himself simply shattered completely or whether they simply ceased to exist at all.

But he was suddenly tired. Tired of fighting himself. Tired

300 / Jackie Ashenden

of the guilt and the pain. Tired of the rage. Tired of pretending he didn't care when he did.

He cared too fucking *much.*

She hadn't gone when he'd told her to and more, she'd come back. The *only* person who'd ever come back for him in his entire goddamn life.

He couldn't resist that. Couldn't tell her she didn't deserve to have what she wanted, because she did. Couldn't tell her he didn't trust her either, because he did. And if that meant accepting that she was right, that he did deserve to have what he wanted too, then maybe he'd just have to suck it up.

Whatever the case, the longing inside him was getting too big to ignore. Too wide. Too deep. Too intense.

He wanted her. She was his.

And even though he wasn't all the things she'd said he was, she'd come back for him anyway, which meant that maybe, despite that, he deserved to be hers after all.

Maybe there was room in his heart for more than rage, too.

Jacob bent his head and covered her beautiful mouth, kissing her with a desperation he'd never allowed himself. A hunger that he couldn't keep inside any longer.

Her fingers knotted in his hair and she was kissing him back, just as desperately, just as hard. And it wasn't enough. He wanted her closer, he wanted her next to him, skin on skin. Wanted to be inside her, part of her.

Tearing his mouth from hers, he grabbed her shirt, pulling it up and over her head, his hands shaking with the effort to be gentle since she was still all bandaged up. She had no such issues, pulling at his clothing roughly, demanding.

By the time they were both naked, they were panting, shaking. There was no time to get to his bedroom, no time for anything but to get close, as close as they could. As close as two people could be.

He rolled down a condom and lifted her against the glass,

his hands sliding beneath her taut ass, holding her. She needed no prompting to wind her legs around his hips, hers tilting back to receive him, and then he was pushing inside her, her pussy clenching around his cock, squeezing him.

Bringing him home.

He pinned her to the window, found her mouth, hungry and desperate. And he moved, hard, deep. Burying all his anger and his pain, burying his loneliness, letting it all just disappear, crushed into dust by the weight of the pleasure, by her heat, by the feel of her arms around him, holding him.

He kissed her and he kissed her, and then he tore his mouth away, looking down into her eyes, holding her gaze. Watching the pleasure build, letting her see how it built in him, too, and then, as they fell into ecstasy together, he whispered, "You win, Ms. Beasley. I'm yours."

She held him tight, the glass cool at her back, his body a furnace at her front and between her thighs. His face was buried in her neck, his breath warm on her skin, and she didn't want to move. Didn't want to let him go.

This stubborn, forceful, powerful man. Who was nevertheless also angry and lonely and in pain.

The man she'd been in love with for a while now and hadn't realized it. Not until he'd pinned her against the glass, fury and desperation in his eyes, his own vulnerability laid bare in that moment.

She'd known then that she'd do anything to take his pain away, make him feel better. Make him feel good. That she'd fight for him. That she'd die for him. That she'd never walk away from him.

That feeling unfurled inside her now, fierce and hot, a pressure in her chest, and she embraced it, held tight to it, the way she was holding him.

He *was* hers. And she would never let him go.

Eventually though, he lifted his head and moved, pulling out of her to deal with the condom. Even then she didn't want to release him and it wasn't until he whispered to her that he wasn't going anywhere that she allowed him to gather her in his arms and take her over to the long sofa upholstered in soft, battered brown leather, laying her on it and following her down.

Then he pushed her beneath him, wrapping her up in his arms, surrounding her.

"You better not still be leaving," she said fiercely, looking up into his depthless black eyes. "Because if you do, after that, I'll hunt you down and kill you."

"So bloodthirsty." His mouth curved. "I'm almost tempted just to see if you'd do it."

Faith dug her fingers into the hard muscle of his chest. "You do and I'll—"

"Settle down," he interrupted gently, before she could finish. "I'm not going anywhere."

Her heart pressed painfully against her ribs, but it was a good pain, a sweet pain. She spread her fingers out on the oiled silk of his skin, loving the feel of it. "I thought you never changed your mind."

"I don't. Seems you engineered a miracle."

"How?"

"You came back for me." His arms tightened around her, the look in his eyes becoming fierce. "No one's ever come back for me, sweet girl. No one but you."

Her eyes prickled with tears. Because of course no one had. He'd lost people and had never regained them.

"Are you sure this is what you want?" She had to force the question out, because she didn't want to ask. But she had to know.

The slight curve of his mouth became a smile that set something inside her on fire. "Yes. Absolutely fucking sure."

"Jake . . ."

"You stood up to me. You fought me. And then you fought *for* me." He shifted so one long-fingered hand could touch her cheekbone. "That changed everything." The fierce expression in his eyes intensified. "You're everything I ever wanted in a woman. Strong. Brave. Challenging. Yet you gave me your trust and your vulnerability without even a second's thought. That's a gift, Faith. And I can't throw that gift away. I don't *want* to throw it away."

Her heart was full, the tears in her eyes sliding down her cheeks and she let them, her throat too tight to speak.

"You were right," he went on softly. "I was a coward. I thought I was afraid of hurting you, but it was myself I was afraid for. Being alone is easier, safer. Because the thought of losing you . . ."

"You won't," she said. "You called me Faith because faith was all you had. And you still have it. You'll always have it. I'll never leave you, Jake. Not ever."

His fingers moved into her hair, curling into a fist, the hot look in his eyes burning even fiercer. "Try it," he murmured. "See how far you get."

Sparks ignited in her blood, answering his challenge because it seemed that she was hard-wired to do so.

"Maybe I will," she said, just to mess with him the way he'd messed with her.

"You won't get far." He leaned down, pressing his forehead to hers. "This is it, Ms. Beasley. You'll never leave me, because I won't let you. So the real question you should be asking is: Are you sure this is what *you* want?"

She slid her hands up his chest, to his broad, powerful shoulders, and farther, into his silky black hair. "Didn't you hear me say I'm in love with you, you stupid man? What does that tell you?"

"It tells me that you're a very poor judge of character." He lifted his head slightly and brushed his mouth over her cheek,

304 / Jackie Ashenden

kissing away her tears. "I, on the other hand, have been in love with you for months, which makes me an excellent judge of character."

She gave a half laugh, half sob. God, who knew you could cry from happiness? "Months?"

"Yes, fucking months. I guess I was too stupid to realize it."

Faith pulled at his hair. "If that's a declaration, then you need to try harder."

His smile deepened. "How about this then? I love you, Faith, my warrior princess. I trust you. I'm not sure I'm the man you think I am or that I deserve the trust you've given me, but if you believe I deserve it, then I'll believe it too. But mainly, I'd be honored to be your prince. And most importantly of all, to fight at your side."

She tightened her grip and pulled his mouth down on hers, giving him the only answer she was capable of.

Because as it turned out, there was one prince left in this world.

And he was hers.

EPILOGUE

Jacob watched as Faith got in the limo and pulled the door shut. Then she sat opposite him and kicked her feet up, resting her boots on the seat next to him.

Three months of them being together and his heart still leapt at the sight of her coming back to him after a mission. It still leapt at the sight of her, period.

His one regret was that he couldn't go on the 11th Hour missions himself, just to help keep her safe, but they'd both agreed that the team worked better if he remained in the background, being the power behind the throne.

Too much testosterone in one room, Faith had told him, or some such bullshit. He preferred it when she called him their secret weapon, only to be deployed in emergencies.

Pity there weren't more emergencies, but then you couldn't have everything.

"Really, Ms. Beasley?" he murmured, shaking his head at her muddy boots. "Give some fucking thought to my upholstery."

She grinned, looking at him from underneath her lashes in that way that never failed to make his blood run hot.

Clearly, the operation she and the rest of the team had just completed had gone well, since she always got horny directly after a successful mission.

Lucky, lucky him.

"I don't care about your fucking upholstery," she said. "I *do* care about fucking, though."

Jacob lifted an eyebrow. "It went well then, I take it?"

"It did."

"Well, don't be shy." He spread his legs. "Come over here and show me—" His phone buzzed in his pocket and he broke off. "Christ."

"Answer it," Faith murmured. "You know you won't be able to concentrate until you do."

It was, alas, true.

Sighing, he took his phone out and stared down at the screen. It was a text from an unknown number and all it said was:

I didn't do it for you. I did it for her. J.

And for a second he had no idea what it meant. Then he did.

"Fuck," he murmured.

Faith must have heard the shock in his voice, because she sat up suddenly, taking her boots from the seat and coming to sit next to him. "What is it?"

Wordlessly, Jacob handed her the phone. Because it was a message for her as well as himself.

"Josh," she murmured, looking down at it. "He did save us in the end."

"No, sweet girl," Jacob said quietly. "He saved you."

Faith looked at him and for a brief moment there were tears in her eyes.

They had, by mutual agreement, decided not to try to find Joshua. It had been a hard decision to make, but it was the right one.

His brother had demons enough chasing him without Jacob

adding to them as well. As long as he kept himself away from anything illegal, at least, and so far he had.

But this was the first contact he'd made. And it wasn't for Jacob, but for Faith. His friend.

"I don't know what to say." Faith kept staring down at the screen. "I'm sorry, Jake, I didn't . . ."

Of course. She was thinking about him. But that was her all over, wasn't it?

"It's okay," Jacob said, and it *was* okay. "I don't begrudge you, if that's what you're worried about."

She said nothing, but took his hand, twining her fingers through his.

"Joshua made his choice." He rubbed his thumb against her palm. "He had some loyalty left for you."

"But not his brother."

"No, but maybe one day he will." It didn't hurt, it really didn't. And he knew why that was.

He reached out and slid his fingers along the delicate line of her jaw, turning her face gently toward him. "Until then, I have you."

In her blue eyes was everything he'd ever wanted.

In her smile was everything he'd ever dreamed.

They weren't alone. Neither of them was.

Not anymore.

Acknowledgments

Thanks to everyone involved in the production of this book, my editor, my agent, and my support crew.

Most particular thanks go to my husband, whom I pestered endlessly with questions about fugue states, TBIs, and sensory triggers. Honey, you deserve a drink.

Once they were soldiers. Now they answer only to honor. . . .

The 11th Hour is made up of men and women who are no longer deemed fit to serve their country, but still need to fight a war. They work in shadows, keep their secrets—and follow their hearts. . . .

Be sure not to miss all of Jackie Ashenden's
11th Hour series, including

TOTAL CONTROL

Helicopter pilot Kellan Blake has always hated being told what to do, so being discharged from the Army for insubordination doesn't come as much of a surprise. What does surprise him is that when he joins up with the elite, underground 11th Hour squad instead, they send him straight home. The nest of vipers that calls itself his family is the next target for the team's tech unit, so he'll either have to brave their traps and deceptions himself—or watch his sweet, shy friend Sabrina walk into them alone. . . .

Sabrina's no femme fatale, but since there's no one else with the tech skills to get the info they need, she'll put on a party dress and take one for the team. But whoever decided she should pretend to be Kellan's new fiancée hit a little too close to home. How can she concentrate on a dangerous mission when she's worried about giving away what she really feels for her loyal, passionate, smoking hot partner? At least she isn't likely to blow their cover. Until she's in the line of fire, and neither Kellan's demons nor his heart are hers to tame. . . .

Keep reading for a special excerpt.

A Kensington trade paperback and e-book on sale now!

PROLOGUE

"I thought you said that you could fly this thing."

Kellan ignored Ian's growl from behind him and tried to keep a tight grip on the joystick, the helo bouncing around in the air like a ball in a pinball machine.

Of course he could fly this thing. He'd been a Night Stalker once, a member of the elite helicopter unit who dealt with the insertion and extraction of military black ops teams. But that had been a couple of years ago and he'd gone from green to blue, leaving the Army and joining the Navy, becoming a SEAL instead. And although he'd tried to keep up his flight skills, he hadn't had as much practice as he would like.

Certainly not for a mission like this, where the team's extraction point had been compromised, which meant they had to rely on him, his chops as a pilot, and a helo with a bullet-damaged rotor to get them out of here.

"Fucking hell," Ian muttered, grabbing at his seat as the helicopter lurched again, almost brushing the tops of the heavy fir trees below them.

"Jesus," one of the other guys in the back said, amid

more cursing from the rest of them. "You need more practice, Kel."

Kellan tuned them all out. He had to. If they were going to
survive this, his concentration had to be total.

Keeping a helicopter in the air was bad enough at the best
of times, but with a damaged rotor? Fucking thing was like a
bumblebee with only one wing and those things shouldn't have
been able to fly with two.

Impossible in other words.

The helicopter lurched again as something hit it, the joystick
in his hand jerking hard. He could feel the machine become
even more unstable and then more fire hit, taking another piece
of rotor out.

Shit.

His last thought before the helicopter dipped, then began to
tip, the skids brushing the tops of the trees, was that his father
was going to be *really* pissed with him for fucking this up.

Then the world turned upside down and there was a massive
bang, and the darkness and the heat came for him.

CHAPTER 1

"We suspect your father's been associated with an illegal arms ring, Kellan." Faith Beasley's blue eyes were coolly sympathetic. "I'm sorry, but we're going to need to investigate."

Kellan Blake, former Night Stalker helicopter pilot, former SEAL, now member of the "special projects" semilegal 11th Hour team, and still total badass motherfucker, laughed.

He liked Faith. She was the one who gave the team their "jobs" on behalf of Jacob Night, the shadowy figure who'd set up and basically owned the 11th Hour. She was cool, calm, and collected, a complete professional, and he had a lot of respect for her.

But this? This was bullshit.

They were sitting in the gutted building that comprised the 11th Hour's San Diego HQ, a massive wall-less space that had been divided off into various areas with furniture.

The area Kellan was in was the "living area." There was a couch, a couple of armchairs, a coffee table, and a floor lamp with a fringed shade. In his opinion all they needed was a large screen TV so he could watch the Giants play and it would be fucking complete.

316 / Jackie Ashenden

Sadly no one else was a football fan. Philistines.

In the recliner near the couch sat Isiah, the grizzled former Army Ranger who was the ostensible CO of the team. He wasn't laughing.

In fact, no one else was laughing. Not Jack, a former Marine who'd joined a few months earlier, not Faith, and not Callie, Jack's fiancée, who'd somehow become part of the team along with Jack, even though she wasn't ex-military.

Then again, Sabrina, his best friend, wasn't ex-military and she was also part of the team. And she wasn't laughing either.

Her wholesome freckled face was pale and her big hazel eyes were full of what looked a hell of a lot like worry.

Kellan stopped laughing. "Jesus Christ," he said to her. "Please don't tell me you believe this arms dealer bullshit?"

She shifted on the couch beside him, glancing at Faith, who was sitting in one of the armchairs opposite, then back at him again. "I . . . don't know. Do you think there might be . . . you know . . . something in it?"

Kellan was aware of a deep kind of shock seeping through him.

Sabrina had lived with the Blake family since she'd been ten years old, after her father—the Blakes' gardener—had walked out and left her behind. She knew his parents. Sure, she was closer to his mother than he was, but surely—*surely*—she didn't believe this gun running crap?

The Blakes were an old money New York family and his father had been one of the top brass in the Army. He'd had a well-respected career and was still incredibly well thought of even after he'd retired.

Kellan had wanted to be just like him.

Until the helicopter accident had put an end to that.

Best not to dwell on *that* failure. Best to think about what was happening now. Sabrina and her reaction, which was . . . weird.

He laughed again, because that tended to be his general response to shit that didn't make any sense. "You're kidding, right? Come on, Bree. Dad? Five-star general Dad? Running guns?"

But Sabrina didn't laugh along with him the way she normally did. Instead, she glanced down at her hands where they clutched her favorite laptop and said nothing.

Okay, this was getting weirder by the fucking second.

Kellan looked at Faith. "So this is according to who? How? Why?"

"Mr. Night has reason to believe—"

"Mr. Night can go fuck himself."

Faith didn't even blink. "As I said, Mr. Night has information that implicates your father, along with a number of other high-ranking members of the military, in a black ops mission that went wrong two years ago. A mission that was deliberately sabotaged."

Kellan grinned, pushing his shock and anger way down deep the way he did with every emotion he didn't like. "Do you know how fucking crazy that sounds?"

"We think that this mission was sabotaged because it was getting too close to uncovering an illegal arms ring providing guns to various drug cartels in Central America. An arms ring that was being run by these high-ranking military members."

"Including my father, presumably?" He grinned wider. "Because Dad really likes guns and loves selling them to people who shouldn't have them?"

No one smiled.

Isiah's hazel eyes were sharp. "This isn't a joke, Blake."

"Yes, it is." Kellan flicked a glance at him, then back to Faith again, skewering her with it. "It's a massive fucking joke. Dad gave forty years of his life to the military. He was a general, for fuck's sake. He wouldn't throw that all away to sell a bunch of guns."

"The information Mr. Night has is—"

"Wrong," Kellan interrupted. "The information Mr. Night has is wrong."

Faith opened her mouth again then shut it. She let out a breath. "Then consider this a chance to prove your father's innocence."

A bolt of pure fury shot down Kellan's spine and he could feel his smile become edged and sharp. "I don't need to prove Dad's innocence." He had to fight to keep his voice steady. "I *know* it."

And he did. Phillip Blake would *never* turn traitor. The man who'd raised him, who'd taught him how to learn from his mistakes and move on, who'd protected him, shown him what it was to be a good man, to aim high and to never accept anything less than complete success . . . Yeah, the idea of a man like that being associated with a secret and highly illegal arms ring, along with a whole lot of high-ranking friends, was ludicrous.

Beside him, Sabrina shifted and he felt her hand come down on his thigh. She squeezed his leg in reassurance and, he thought, as a warning.

Both of which he ignored.

"Well," Faith said in her usual calm way. "Mr. Night disagrees. Your father is implicated. So your choice is to either accept the job of investigating and discovering the truth yourself, or he'll find someone else to do it."

The job . . . what a goddamned joke.

He and Jack, with the support of the rest of the team, had just finished up a mission dealing with a scumbag drug lord when yet another job had come in from Night. Usually the jobs involved protection or handling threats, and most of them barely legal, though he'd never had a problem with that.

He had a problem with this.

"We need you, Kellan," Faith went on when he didn't say

anything. "Mr. Night wants the contents of a computer file apparently in your father's possession."

"What file?"

"Well, that's it," Sabrina muttered. "We couldn't find it. There was nothing on his computer when I hacked in to take a look."

Kellan gave her an incredulous look. "You hacked into Dad's computer?"

She flushed and opened her mouth, probably to explain, but Faith answered before she could.

"I asked Sabrina to," Faith said. "She's the best hacker in the business and your father had some heavy firewalls."

Jesus. What the fuck did Faith think she was doing getting Sabrina to hack into Phillip Blake's computer?

"Regardless of the fact that Sabrina didn't find anything," Faith went on, "Mr. Night is convinced that the file is there. Either on another computer elsewhere or stored on a portable hard drive. All of which means that we need you to search for it personally." She paused. "You *and* Sabrina."

Well, shit. Bad enough that it involved his family, but Sabrina too? Christ, no. Just . . . No. She never went physically to jobs since that wasn't her strength, and there was no reason for her to go now.

"Why Sabrina?" he asked, making no effort to keep the demand from his tone. "She doesn't need to be part of this."

Beside him Sabrina stiffened, but he ignored her.

"Why?" Faith glanced at her. "If the file is anywhere, it'll be heavily encrypted, plus, if it's on another computer, there's likely to be all kinds of other protections in place to keep it safe. Which means we need her skills."

He hated that it sounded so . . . logical.

"Fine," he said curtly. "But find someone else."

"Easy enough." Faith's blue gaze was steady. "We have others who can be Sabrina's backup."

The fury inside Kellan seemed to solidify at Faith's deliberate misunderstanding. "No, you don't get it. If I'm not going, then she's not going either. We're a package deal."

Sabrina stiffened even further, removing her hand from his thigh as if she'd burned herself. "Hey, wait a second—"

"Sabrina is nonnegotiable," Faith said before Sabrina could finish her protest. "As I said, she's the only one with the necessary skills. Your family connection would make the job easier, but we can do without it if necessary. Sabrina knows your parents. Jack could easily pose as her friend or boyfriend—"

"What?" Jack interrupted from his position near the armchair Isiah was sitting in, at the same time as Kellan let loose a growl, not liking that thought *at all*.

Faith merely looked back at him. "A friend, then. Jack could pose as her friend."

Kellan gritted his teeth, fighting to get a handle on himself and keep that fucking smile on his face. But for the first time in years, it was difficult. Anger—or indeed any extreme emotion—was unproductive and didn't get you what you wanted, or at least, that's what his father had taught him. Charm. A smile. And action. Those were the three keys to success according to Phillip Blake and Kellan had found that to be true.

He'd certainly gotten everything he'd wanted by employing them.

Not quite everything.

Well, no. But the two other things he'd wanted and hadn't gotten didn't matter anymore. Not since he'd decided he didn't want them after all.

"I could," Jack said after a moment. "It wouldn't be that hard."

Kellan only just stopped himself from snarling. The scarred former Marine was good, and since he'd joined the 11th Hour team three months earlier, he'd gotten even better. And if there was a guy he needed at his back or to protect those he cared about, Kellan would have chosen Jack King.

But only if Kellan himself were dead. And since he wasn't, the only person who was going to be protecting Sabrina was him.

"No," he said flatly. "Not happening."

There was amusement in Jack's green eyes, which was annoying. Especially seeing as the guy hadn't had a sense of humor at all when he'd first joined the team. That seemed to have changed since he'd hooked up with Callie, the pretty socialite he'd been guarding for an 11th Hour job and had subsequently gotten engaged to.

But it turned out that Kellan didn't have a sense of humor either, at least not when it came to Sabrina's safety.

"Oh, for God's sake." Sabrina's voice was tight.

He turned sharply to meet her green-gold eyes, glowing with anger. "What?" he demanded. "You don't think your safety's important?"

"I like my safety, believe me. What I do not like is you being a territorial asshole about it."

He raised a brow in surprise. "I'm not being territorial. I just don't want—"

Isiah cleared his throat loudly. "Perhaps you two need a moment to discuss this?"

Kellan's attention snapped round to the older man. "No, I don't," he began at the same time as Sabrina said, "Yes, that's a great idea."

There was a silence.

"Seems like Sabrina has a different opinion," Isiah pointed out. Needlessly.

Fuck.

Kellan turned back to her, trying not to let his anger show. Her familiar freckled face with its small upturned nose was set in lines of determination and there was a mulish slant to her chin.

She almost never disagreed with him. Almost never got angry with him either, at least not like this. It was as if a friendly kitten had suddenly grown razor sharp teeth and bitten him.

"Bree," he said. "What's the problem? You can't possibly—"

Sabrina suddenly pushed herself off the couch, not giving him a chance to finish, presenting him with her long, slender back and the bouncy ponytail of dark curls that ran down the length of it. "Tell Mr. Night I'm in," she said to Faith.

Then before anyone could say another word, she strode to the door and walked through it.

Sabrina headed straight down the corridors that led from the 11th Hour HQ to Mac's, the bar that fronted the place. The bar was kept deliberately seedy to discourage too many patrons: cracked linoleum and vinyl seats, crappy TV above the bar, the scent of cigarette smoke from the decades before the first smoking laws imbued into the very walls.

When she'd left her job at an Internet start-up in Silicon Valley in order to join the 11th Hour, she'd taken on some of the Mac's bar work when there was some downtime, and she'd found she'd liked it. Pouring drinks and listening to sob stories from the few patrons that Mac's did have didn't require any brain power and neither did wiping down the bar and messing around with the bottles stacked on shelves behind it. She found both tasks soothing.

But she didn't find it particularly soothing today as she slammed the door that led to HQ behind her and stormed into the empty bar.

Not that she would have found anything particularly soothing if she was honest with herself.

Her hand was shaking as she reached for the least crappy of the bourbons, pulling the bottle off the shelf and grabbing a glass, pouring herself a hefty measure. Then she picked the glass up and downed it.

Drinking was another thing she didn't do very often, but shit, after what had happened in there, needs must and all of that.

She poured herself a second glass, then put her hands flat on the bar and stared down at the bar top, taking a few calming breaths.

Fear and shock sat like small hard stones in her gut, the rush of alcohol doing nothing to dissolve them, along with a flickering anger that didn't help either.

The moment Faith had gotten her to hack into Phillip Blake's computer a day or so earlier, Sabrina had felt that fear touch her, and it had only gotten worse now Faith had made the latest mission clear. And the more Kellan had protested, the angrier and more afraid she'd gotten.

It wasn't fair to get angry at him, not when she knew how much of a shock finding out about this latest job had been to him. He idolized his father—always had—so it was no surprise that he hadn't reacted well to the news.

And that was part of the problem.

His father wasn't the man Kellan thought he was, as Sabrina had good reason to know. And if there was one thing she didn't want, it was Kellan finding that out.

He'd already been through so much after the helicopter crash that had effectively ended the military career that had given him his identity. Physical pain from the burns he'd suffered. Emotional pain from the medics' decision that he wasn't fit to resume military service and wouldn't ever be.

Now this.

She stared down at the amber liquid in the glass, pain twisting inside her. Then there was him getting all territorial on her. It made her think things she shouldn't be thinking, feel things she shouldn't be feeling.

Friends. That's all they were. Just friends.

She'd been telling herself that for years, but it never made any difference to her poor stupid heart. Her poor stupid heart had been in love with him since she was ten years old.

But that was beside the point.

The point was the potential of this mission to uncover a lot of skeletons in Phillip Blake's closet. Skeletons that Sabrina had been trying to keep secret from Kellan for years. She didn't know for certain that Kellan's father was involved in the things that Faith said he was, but she knew he wasn't the fine, upstanding former general that everyone thought so well of either.

She also knew that Kellan couldn't find out, not ever. He was a man who protected people, but someone had to protect him, and she'd decided years ago that someone was going to be her. Because she'd do anything for him.

Anything at all.

Besides, she'd made a promise to Charlotte, Kellan's mother, who'd been a mother to Sabrina too, after she'd lost her own and her father had left. A promise that she wouldn't tell Kellan a thing.

Charlotte had been very clear to Sabrina how important it was that Kellan know nothing about the cracks in Phillip's smooth facade. Family. That's what it was about, and Sabrina, having lost her own, could only agree. Her own father had once been the Blakes' live-in gardener and when he'd simply left one day and never come home, Charlotte had taken her in and made her part of the Blake family.

Well, maybe not quite part of the family. Charlotte was always very careful to make sure that Sabrina knew she wasn't actually a Blake. Her purpose was to be Charlotte's confidant without all the "messy" stuff around being her actual child, which was how Charlotte herself had put it.

Anyway, Sabrina had always been grateful to the Blakes for their kindness to her and to Charlotte in particular for making her feel less like an abandoned stray and more like a valuable family member.

God, Charlotte would be appalled if she knew what was happening now—and she'd certainly be expecting Sabrina to make sure Kellan had no part of it.

Except . . . Sabrina had no idea how to do that, not if this mission was driven by Jacob Night. None of the team had met him or knew anything about him, only that he had the money and connections to somehow run an ex-military team—well, except for her, as she wasn't ex-military—who took on "special projects" that were just on the right side of legal.

Soon after she'd joined the team herself, she'd looked for traces of him online—and she, if anyone, knew where and how to look—but she'd found nothing. Weird. Because everyone left some digital trace, *everyone*.

But not Jacob Night.

A worry.

She reached out for the glass again, picking it up as the door behind her banged open.

"Bree?" Kellan's voice, deep and with that husky edge that never failed to raise a shiver across her skin, came from behind her. "What's up? Why did you walk out?"

So he'd followed her. Well, that wasn't a surprise. She was going to have to get her game face on though, because although she didn't have to explain her own shock, she couldn't show him her fear. Especially given how protective he was and what a terrible liar she was.

Then again, she'd been successfully hiding things from him for years, so there was no reason to think she'd fail now.

She took another steadying sip of the bourbon, then turned around.

Kellan was standing just outside the door that led from the bar to HQ, filling the doorway with six foot three of long, rangy muscle. He was built like a quarterback and looked like a Hollywood movie star, massive shoulders, high cheekbones, and a perfect jawline. Dirty blond hair and stunning ice-blue eyes. He was in faded blue denim that clung to his lean hips and a fitted T-shirt that outlined his broad chest, powerful biceps, and flat stomach to perfection. Today's T-shirt was a dark navy that made his eyes look even bluer.

He made her heart beat way too fast whenever she looked at him, and no matter how many years passed or how many other guys she dated, it had never gotten the message that he wasn't for her and never had been.

They were best friends and nothing more.

Sabrina leaned back against the bar, cradling her bourbon. "Why do you think I walked out? It's a hell of a shock. And I . . . didn't appreciate being told what to do."

He snorted, thrusting his hands into the pockets of his jeans. "I'm not apologizing for that. Not that it matters anyway since the mission isn't happening." The expression on his face was guarded, but she knew him. She could see the shock still resounding in his eyes.

Her chest felt tight and she put her bourbon down, her first instinct to go give him a hug. It was a measure of her own shock that she almost did, but at the last minute held herself back. He wasn't physically demonstrative—none of the Blakes were—so she tried to keep her own need to give physical comfort to a minimum.

"I'm sorry, Kel." She folded her arms instead. "The whole thing is crazy."

"Damn right it's crazy." He glanced away, his jaw hardening, anger written in the tense line of his shoulders. "I don't know where Night got his information from, but it's wrong. Dad's got nothing to do with this."

For a second Sabrina debated about what to say. She wanted Kellan to know she was on his side, but her lying skills were crap and if he picked up on the fact that she was hiding something from him, he'd soon get it out of her; he could be relentless when there was something he wanted to know.

"Maybe he has," she said carefully. "Perhaps you should speak to Night personally?"

Kellan's sharp blue gaze came to hers. "Are you really shocked about this?"

She froze, feeling like a rabbit in the headlights. "Sure I am. What makes you say that?"

"You just seem . . . unsurprised."

Shit. Had he picked up on something in her voice?

Sabrina shifted against the bar, trying not to give herself away any more than she already had. "I guess you could say I'm a little . . . stunned." And she had been, though not quite in the same way as Kellan.

His gaze narrowed at her for a second, then he let out a breath and came over to where she stood, grabbing a glass for himself and reaching for the bottle of bourbon that stood on the bar. "Yeah, Christ. It's a bit un-fucking-believable."

Okay, perhaps she hadn't given herself away too badly. Thank God.

Hoping her relief wasn't too obvious, Sabrina picked her own glass back up again as he poured himself a drink.

"You're right though." Kellan turned around and leaned back against the bar beside her, mirroring her stance, lifting his glass and taking a hefty swallow. "I should talk to Night. Figure out where the hell he got his intel about this file from."

"Good plan." She kept her voice neutral. "He and Faith seem pretty ready to move on it."

"Yeah, but that's not going to happen." The words were hard, certain, and not a little grim.

Kellan was generally laid-back, his good looks and easy smile masking a nature that was pure, sharp-edged steel. It was that steel that had driven him into two different branches of the military, pushing him to become the best of the best. She could hear that steel now. Whoever Jacob Night was, Kellan would give him a hell of a run for his money.

With any luck, Night might even change his mind about the mission and decide to leave well enough alone.

Except she had a horrible feeling that wasn't going to happen, no matter how stubborn or forceful Kellan was. Night was a law unto himself and he was powerful. Then again, when Kellan wanted something, he tended to go out and get it.

Pity that's not you.

Sabrina took another swallow of her bourbon, the rough alcohol sitting in her gut, trying to ignore the thought. God, she hoped this wasn't building up into another one of her moods.

She had them periodically, where all she could think about was how badly she wanted him and how much it hurt that she didn't have him. They didn't last long, but when they did, she usually got out her dating app to find herself a hookup.

Maybe it was time to find a guy again, one who didn't have blond hair or blue eyes. A nice guy who was up for a couple of dates and a few pleasant hours in bed. Though to be honest, she'd never found sex all that fulfilling, no matter who it was with. She could give herself a better orgasm with her own imagination and her vibrator.

"Bree? Are you even listening?"

Feeling him staring at her, heat crept into her cheeks. He was very close and she was very conscious of the warmth of his long, hard body next to hers. Of the familiarity of his aftershave, a fresh scent that reminded her of the sea, or of rain.

Oh hell. She was *definitely* going into another of her I-want-Kellan moods.

"What? Sorry, no, I wasn't." She drained her second glass of bourbon and put it down on the counter. "I still . . . can't believe it, I guess."

Kellan had three smiles: one for charming people generally,

one for charming women he wanted to sleep with, and one for her. The one he kept for her was warm and protective and tender, and she loved it as much as she hated it. And she hated it because it was very like the one he kept for his mother.

His long, beautiful mouth quirked in that smile now. "Hey, don't worry, okay? I'm sure it's only that Night got some bad intel from somewhere, and it's all a mistake." The smile became a little sharp, though the look in his eyes remained reassuring. "This mission isn't going ahead. I'll make sure of it."

He always thought he was protecting her.

He had no idea it was the other way around.

Sabrina gave him a smile in return, because what else could she do? "Sure," she said, ignoring the cold foreboding that curled its way through the warmth of the alcohol. "Of course you will."

Connect with Us

Visit us online at
KensingtonBooks.com
to read more from your favorite authors, see books
by series, view reading group guides, and more.

Join us on social media

for sneak peeks, chances to win books and prize packs,
and to share your thoughts with other readers.

facebook.com/kensingtonpublishing
twitter.com/kensingtonbooks

Tell us what you think!

To share your thoughts, submit a review,
or sign up for our eNewsletters, please visit:
KensingtonBooks.com/TellUs.

31901064498787